BLUEGRASS

Also by this author and available from New English Library:

BLUEGRASS Book One

BLUEGRASS

BOOK TWO

Borden Deal

NEW ENGLISH LIBRARY/TIMES MIRROR

This is a work of fiction.
Any resemblance to actual persons or situations is purely coincidental.

First published in the USA by
Doubleday & Co, Inc in 1977 in one volume
First published in Great Britain by
New English Library in 1977 in one volume

First NEL paperback edition November 1978

NEL Books are published by
New English Library Limited from
Barnard's Inn, Holborn,
London EC1N 2JR
Made and printed in Great Britain by
William Collins Sons & Co Ltd Glasgow

45004211 1

CHAPTER 1

In the old days, the great yearling sale of the year was held in August at Saratoga Springs, New York. Choice yearlings from Kentucky, Maryland, Virginia, were shipped in to be viewed and discussed and eventually purchased in the high excitement of auction bidding. Saratoga in August meant more than a racing meet, more than a sales auction. The great names in racing were as familiar as next-door neighbours: Harry Payne Whitney and the Lorillard brothers, John E. Madden, James Ben Ali Haggin; Regret, Man O' War, Kelso; the Travers Stakes, Spinaway Stakes, Hopeful Stakes. Under the great elms the horses and the people moved, each with their own grace, their own meaning.

The ancient patterns were broken by World War II, when restrictions on transportation caused the Saratoga race meeting of 1943 to be transferred to a downstate track. Kentucky was forced to offer their best yearlings for sale at home instead of shipping east. Keeneland, closed for racing, offered its facilities; and the fear that the important buyers with important money would not make the long trip to Lexington proved groundless. A real horseman will go where the horses are.

From that first successful auction grew a Select Summer Yearling Sale that came to rival, eventually to surpass, the Saratoga August Sale – along with sales of breeding stock and horses of racing age at other times of the year, including a fall yearling sale that is not 'select' – all conducted by the Keeneland Association, owned and officered by the leading breeders themselves.

The Keeneland Association Select Summer Yearling Sale has become a spectacle as exciting, and nearly as tradition-laden, as Saratoga-in-August. The yearlings are stabled in the backside barns, where, on the Sunday before the auction begins, they are available for inspection. The shedrows, on this momentous day, are populated by the prospective buyers and their cohorts, each with catalogue in hand; the yearlings, sleekly groomed and thoroughly schooled, are led out time after interminable time; there are film celebrities relaxing with a drink in lawn chairs thoughtfully provided by the management, photographers and lovely women and men with serious eyes, trainers and exjockeys and money managers. Most important of all are those known to be buyers of yearlings in the hundreds of thousands of dollars: Americans and Japanese and Latin Americans, Texans in white hats and hand-tooled cowboy boots, bloodstock-agency representatives from Ireland and France and Great Britain. Courted and flattered and cajoled, they keep privy counsel in low-voiced consultations. There are busy men with sharp eyes and short purses who, relying on nerve and their own eye for a winner, are looking to pinhook a yearling before anyone is aware of what's taking place.

Tom Gentry hands out cigarette lighters and yardsticks and frets about whether the gap in the hedge leading to his barn area is wide enough for John Paul Jones, a man bulky in flesh as in pocketbook, to pass through without annoyance. Humphrey Finney, for forty years reputed to be one of the world's great judges of horseflesh, wearing khaki walking shorts and a pith helmet, leans on a shooting stick and appraises a fine yearling through Ben Franklin glasses low on his nose. This is a place where wisdom in horseflesh is respected mightily, whether in a multimillionaire or a yearling groom.

In 1952, a dissident group broke away from the Keeneland Association, only to follow the Keeneland pattern in establishing a third major yearling auction under the aegis of the Daingerfield Association, which also operates the Daingerfield Race Track a few miles from Lexington. So there were, at the time I started my bold venture, three major yearling sales which jointly offered the cream of the annual crop at absolute auction to the highest bidder. The premium yearlings brought an average price, at that time, of something better than thirty thousand dollars – with the very top figures escalating to as much as half a million.

These are yearling colts and fillies, one must remember, nearly a year away from racing; they have never borne a rider, they have yet to be asked the all-important questions of speed and stamina and soundness. Of all the Thoroughbreds foaled in a given year, no more than 2½ per cent will ever win a stakes race. (The sales associations, extraordinarily fond of statistics though they are, never furnish for interested comparison the percentage of stakes winners among the Summer Sales yearlings, as contrasted to the average of the breed.)

My simple ambition? To offer a yearling at the Daingerfield Association sale which would reach the magic figure of one hundred thousand dollars.

Why, one might ask, when the Daingerfield Association turned down my first yearlings, did I not go to the Keeneland Association, or to Saratoga? Indeed, Dancy soon suggested we set our sights on Saratoga in August. Many Kentucky yearlings still go that long route, rather than remaining in Kentucky, for any one of various reasons. Some Kentucky horse farms simply follow the old tradition; others have, perhaps, for reasons good or bad, rebelled against the virtual monopoly of the local associations.

But, damn it, the Daingerfield Association race track and sales pavilion were next door to my acreage; I had set my sights on seeing my yearlings parade through that particular auction ring. I couldn't see the percentage in trying for acceptance at the Keeneland or Saratoga sales. At times, I know, I can become a touch stubborn. But, like General Grant, I was prepared to fight it out on this line if it took a dozen Summer Select Sales. That's sometimes known as butting your head against a stone barn. But that's how I am, and I have to live with myself a lot more than anybody else does.

Though I had set everything in train for the housewarming with as much energy and dispatch as I have ever brought to any project, the big day was so quickly upon us I had a feeling a thousand things must have been left undone.

I couldn't have bought a better day if I had put in a special request . . . which I had been doing for a week, I must admit, in my prayers. July now, the bluegrass in the paddocks lush, the burley of our tobacco allotment tall and broad-leaved. The yearling colts, aware of their masculinity, were companions still but competing with each other a bit more fiercely with each passing week. The foals, first growing high-hipped and leggy, were slowly filling out their bodies to match. Their tails stubby and inadequate, often they stood close enough to their dams to receive the benefit of a more efficient chaser of summer flies.

The mares, those we had succeeded in stopping, again dwelled in the placidity of pregnancy, affectionately tender with their sucklings, though daily the foals were asserting a greater independence – and, contradictorily, more imperious demands upon the milk of their mothers, though they were already sampling hay and grass and oats.

I made evening stables early with Dancy, paying particular attention to the individuals we planned to show tonight. The yearlings were spectacularly handsome; we had been feeding them on a schedule geared to this day, and their hides, variously bay and chestnut and black and grey, were richly toned by twice-daily groomings. Sir Outlaw, on vacation from his labours of the breeding season, had also been groomed for the event, though his protein-rich diet had been cut the day he had covered his last mare. The broodmares with foals at their sides had also received their modicum of attention; Outlaw Prince's foster-mother probably looked more like a Thoroughbred than ever in her life.

I had been particularly concerned that Outlaw Prince should handle well. I needn't have been; Alice had schooled him beautifully. He exhibited the poise of a colt months older. I cautioned Alice again, she mustn't forget his high spirits; he might, excited by the floodlights and the presence of strangers, choose exactly the wrong time to display the temperament of his inheritance.

'Everybody knows about Sir Outlaw,' I told her. 'If he acts up the least bit, the word will go out that the stallion is breeding on his temper.'

'Don't worry, Miss Maude,' Alice said. She was wearing the uniform I had provided for her and Merlin, an orange shirt with Kentucky blue pants – orange for Florida, blue for Kentucky – and she looked trim and lovely. 'He'll be fine. For the last week, I've had Mr Dancy and Merlin shout and laugh and beat on buckets while I was schooling him. He's learned to ignore anything short of a fire under his belly.'

'You might even have to deal with that,' I said, laughing. 'Who knows what might happen, as much Kentucky Bourbon as I've laid in.'

I visited Sir Outlaw last of all. Coming to me at the fence, he gave me his tongue. I grasped it, shaking it back and forth while the great horse looked as idiotically affectionate as a schoolboy in love.

'Well, good buddy, tonight's the night,' I told him. 'We're going to show these people what you're capable of making.'

He pulled back his head, pinned his ears, feinted at me with bared teeth.

I slapped his muzzle. 'Oh, you're incorrigible,' I said. 'Now, be on your good behaviour yourself, you hear?'

As though in response, yawing his magnificent head sideways, he lolled his tongue again, drooling grass-green saliva. I grasped it, careless of the slobbering wetness.

'You may be a great stallion, but you're just a baby. And just you wait until everybody sees your son tonight. Why, they'll applaud when you're led out.'

As I went past the Great Stone Barn, the westering sun slanted a lovely light against the ripe July folds of Kentucky earth. I paused to look back, to see Merlin leading Sir Outlaw from his paddock, stopping to allow Dancy to pick up his feet in turn, cleaning out the frogs.

My heart was full with it all. It had been such a short span of time since the beginning – only a little over a year. But somehow it had been forever ago when I had arrived in this empty place driving the yellow VW with the British racing green stripe. I could scarcely remember, not only the life I had lived before that day, but the person I had been.

This time in which I had become the Maude Sage of now had been replete with small accomplishments and big bruises. But there had been, I realized suddenly, a triumph that until this moment I had been too engrossed to perceive. The farm had come alive under my hand. Empty at my arrival, dead as fallow earth, now it was flourishing, the bluegrass in the paddocks and pastures nourished with fertilizer, stimulated by grazing and mowing; the barns – so shabby and neglected then with disuse – refurbished with fresh paint and repair, the stalls bright and shining, the floors soft with bedding straw, the air newly redolent with the rich warm smell of horseflesh. Even the house was alive with soft lights and a warm welcome. Tonight, for the first time, it would live again in the old tradition of hospitality, with elegant ladies and handsome men moving through the rooms and about the grounds, laughing, talking, drinking, eating . . . looking at horses. *My* horses.

I went up the curving driveway, passing between the yet unlighted *luminaries*, candles in stiff brown paper bags weighted with sand, an idea I had imported from Florida – I think it originated in Mexico – to light softly the guests' pathway from the parking area at the Great Stone Barn to the mansion. When full dark came, they would be lovely and mysterious, flickering in their curved arc outlining the driveway: a proper introduction to the residence.

I paused at the edge of the yard. This, too, would have its appeal when the magic of evening had settled over the scene. Japanese lanterns were strung from oak to great oak, outlining the arrangement of tables with white cloths gleaming. There would be no awkward eating standing up, or crouched on the steps with paper plate in lap. No: all buffet style, but with china and good silver, tables and chairs for dignified dining.

At the other side, a portable bar had been installed, two red-jacketed bartenders now busy setting out their wares. Over all wafted the delectable aroma of Kentucky burgoo. The renowned burgoo chef, a black and jovial gentleman, had arrived before the day was an hour old with his small-boy assistant, surveyed the situation, chose the site to set up his great iron kettle, and requested to be left alone for nine hours, at which time he would produce a burgoo to be remembered for all time.

I walked between the tables, nodding to Jan and Eva standing quietly together, to Tiffany Thomas fussing still with the placement of silverware. The burgoo chef was wearing a tall white hat and his face was shining with perspiration.

'Is it about ready?' I asked.

He grinned. 'When guests arrive, burgoo's done. That's the way I do it, ma'am.'

Ceremoniously he dipped a long-handled spoon into the savoury kettle and handed it to me. I tasted cautiously. It was too hot. I blew on it, tasted again.

'Delicious,' I said. 'What goes into burgoo, anyway?'

He retrieved his spoon, held it at attention, and stated: 'I begin with the old-timey recipe I learned from my pappy. Two hundred and fifty pounds of the best beef, three dozen tender hens, two dozen squirrels young and fat. You boil all that good meat off the bone, then you add four sacks of potatoes, four cases of corn, a hundred pounds of onions and fifty of tender cabbage. Six cases of tomatoes, five gallons of carrots, already halfway cooked, and then I adds my pepper and my salt and my herbs and such, and I don't tell nobody about my herbs. That's the secret I aim to pass on to my son here in all good time.'

'Sounds like a lot of burgoo,' I said dubiously.

He chuckled. 'It'll give you six hundred gallons of the best you've ever tasted. I start with that recipe, then scale it down according, Ain't never done six hundred gallons myself, though my daddy used to claim you couldn't make good burgoo any less.'

'You've been cooking it all day, haven't you?'

'Tell the truth, ma'am, ought to been started yesterday and cooked all night.'He shook his head sadly. 'Don't nobody have that kind of time any more. Wait till tomorrow, it be just about right.' He looked mournfully at me. 'By then, it'll be long gone, down to the last spoonful.'

I laughed at his expression. 'Let me have another taste. Seems fine to me right now.' I let the spoonful cool, savoured it drop by drop. It was hot and spicy, as subtle as well-aged sour-mash Bourbon. I cut an eye at him. 'You won't tell me what herbs you use?'

'That's my trade secret,' he said with dignity. 'What makes my burgoo better than anybody's.' He relaxed into a grin. 'Truth to tell, ma'am, sometimes I use a little more of this and a little less of that . . . depends on how the meat's cooking and the mealiness of the potatoes and how far along the cabbage has got. I just go by what smells right, and that's the whole secret.'

I thought about the two hundred and fifty invitations I had sent out, graced by a head shot of Sir Outlaw and proclaiming: AN OLD-FASHIONED KENTUCKY HOUSEWARMING. BOURBON, BURGOO, AND HORSES.

Putting out my hand, I said, 'Thank you for coming. I'm sure your Kentucky burgoo will make our housewarming a success.'

We shook hands solemnly and I went on. Everything was ready now. Except for Maude Sage.

I sat down for a moment on the side of my bed. Tired already, before the party had even started, for all the long day I had been exhilarated by a tremendous inner excitement. I yearned for the presence of people, receiving my greetings, drinking my liquor, eating the good things. Most of all, viewing my yearlings, my foals, realizing what I had accomplished. When Outlaw Prince should be led out before these horse-wise guests, they could not help but know what he represented.

I remembered almost irrelevantly that I had not chosen a name for the farm. In my mind I had called it simply The Farm, as though it were the only one in the world. (To me, so true!) On the invitations I had used the old name for the convenience of immediate recognition.

I like the names of horse farms: Darby Dan, Greentree Stud, Calumet and The Stallion Station, Mill Ridge and Mereworth, Plum Lane, Hamburg Place. Many honoured great sires, like Domino Stud and Spendthrift. The wonderful old name of Elmendorf – chosen in 1881, by Daniel Swigert, after his wife's grandmother – had remained unchanged through a succession of owners. I really ought to choose a name, I thought, register it properly. But, in naming a piece of the earth, the sound of the name must ring true within your soul. There had not yet occurred within me such an inevitable resonance of sound and meaning.

I went into the bathroom and turned the taps. The old-fashioned tub, squatting on claw feet, was high and long and very deep, coming all the way up to my shoulders. When it was a third full, I squirted liquid Vitabath into the downrushing stream and watched the bubbles, rise instantly. Out of doors in all kinds of weather, I had started using the gelée to keep my skin soft.

I tested the temperature tentatively with a toe, then eased with a sigh of luxury into the hip-deep water. I liked it very hot, so I increased the flow from the left-hand tap, cut down on the right, and leaned back with another sigh, gazing at the old-fashioned blue tiling that, chipped and scarred by the years, circled the walls to shoulder height. I was careful, however, to keep my head erect; for three weeks now I had been going to a beauty shop in Lexington recommended by Tiffany Thomas, and I didn't want to disturb the feather cut that shaped my head as elegantly as a Grecian helmet.

Such a hectic time of preparation. I had called Murray, asking him to come out for a special conference. I told him first about the change in the breeding programme. It made him frown.

'I can't advise you about the rightness or wrongness of your idea,' he said. 'I don't know that much about breeding. But . . .' He paused, went on more slowly. 'One must assume then, that until now you've only been wasting time and money. You're starting all the way back at square one.'

'I don't agree, Murray,' I said. 'Just think about how much I've learned. All right, we'll probably have to sell some mares for less than we paid for them. We can absorb that loss, can't we?'

'Yes. I think so. But . . .'

'On the other hand, we should be able to buy War Admiral mares for much less. For one thing, they'll be twelve years old at the least, since War Admiral died in 1959. Of course, if they have become proven producers, they might still come pretty high. But we don't care any more whether they're stakes winners, or have produced stakes winners. We don't care if they've ever even started, for God's sake. All we're after is the War Admiral blood with the Blue Larkspur cross.'

Murray sighed. 'I don't understand all I know about this business of a breeding nick.'

I laughed. 'It's a simple concept, Murray. All it means is that a certain bloodline appears to have an affinity for another specific bloodline. Crossing the two, you produce individuals superior to both sire and dam. That's all there is to it. Of course, a lot of people don't believe in it.'

He looked dubious. 'And you think you've discovered such a nick? When all these horse people, all these years, have been breeding to the best of their knowledge and observation and experience, and haven't discovered it first?'

'I am proceeding on that assumption. If I'm right, we'll produce something new in the horse world. If I'm wrong . . .' I shrugged. 'If I'm wrong, we ought to get as good runners, following my theory, as any other way. Good bloodlines there, Domino for speed and the Fair Play line for getting a distance of ground. You can't sneer at the Blue Larkspur blood, either. Only thing is, everybody in Kentucky is so enthralled with Princequillo and Nasrullah pedigrees they've forgotten these fine old bloodlines. None of those horses were slow runners, or failures at stud. Hell, Domino was about the fastest horse there's ever been; and even you know about Man O' War.'

Murray smiled. 'It's not me you have to convince, Maude.' He quit smiling. 'I'm thinking about the tax situation. It *is* a setback – *that* you must admit. Remember, if you don't show a profit two years out of seven, you'll have hobby losses, which you can't charge off as legitimate business expenses. Which means: By the sixth year of operation, you'll be in a real bind if your situation requires you to put two years in succession in the black. You might well have to sell off much of your basic breeding stock in order to show a profit.' His smile was bleak. 'I know it's ridiculous to require an owner to liquidate his operation in order to prove that he's a serious man of business. But that's the requirement of the Internal Revenue Service Code. So what I worry about, Is there time left to prove that you're right? You're already into the second year.'

I frowned. 'It can't be rushed. Old Mother Nature takes her own sweet time, the IRS to the contrary notwithstanding. This year we've got two Sir Outlaw foals . . . only one out of a War Admiral mare. So next spring, in our third year of operation, we'll be starting from scratch; yearlings to sell in the fourth year, but not many, I don't suppose – though I intend to buy every War Admiral-Blue Larkspur mare I can lay my hands on. Runners the next year, our fifth year of operation, which will be our first chance – except for Outlaw Prince – to prove my theory.'

I paused. 'Gonna run pretty tight, isn't it?'

He shook his head. 'Too tight, Maude.'

I took a deep breath. 'I can't afford a hobby loss, can I?'

He nodded. 'It would mean that every dollar you've spent, on wages and grain and upkeep – whatever – will come out of your own pocket. No. A hobby loss will put you right out of business.' His voice was rueful. 'You'd think six million dollars would go further, wouldn't you?'

I grinned at him. 'In this day and time? In this business? It's petty cash.'

'Maude, you're a strange woman. I couldn't sleep at night, taking that kind of challenge, knowing how the calendar and the government are narrowing in on you.'

'Win or lose, I'll have made my run, goddamn it, and I'll have known that I made my run,' I said. 'No, Murray, it's quite clear. Everything is staked on Outlaw Prince. Next year he'll be a yearling, the year after, a runner. If he's anything close to what I think he is, people will come flocking, not only to buy the new yearlings but bringing their own mares to breed to Sir Outlaw. Because if there's one thing about these Kentucky hardboots, it's this: They never argue with success.' I grinned at a ludicrous thought. 'If a mule had won this year's Kentucky Derby, they'd all be out right now buying up the finest jacks in the land.'

'It's risky,' Murray said.

'So is living. Now listen, this isn't why I needed to talk to you today. The Daingerfield Association turned down my yearlings. Now I've got the job of selling them at private treaty – and my best shot is during the time everybody who's worth anything in the horse business will be in Kentucky for the Summer Yearling Sale. Which means my housewarming has become more important than ever. Can you get me the right names and addresses? I want everybody prominent in breeding, in buying and selling, and in racing. And their ladies. The ladies are very important.'

Murray looked embarrassed. 'Maude, I don't exactly move in those circles. I don't know anybody who does. What you need is a social secretary.'

'Then get me one,' I said impatiently. 'The breeders, they'll be easy because they can be reached through their farms. But I need to know who comes to the sale from New York and Europe and the West Coast.'

'Give me a few days,' Murray said. 'Surely there are people who . . .' He still looked troubled. 'Maude, you're sure you're not being premature? These horse people, they're clannish . . . it's pretty much a closed world. Wouldn't it be best to wait for them to come to you?'

I brushed it off. 'Oh, I don't expect them *all* to show up, by any means. I'm only hoping to get a representative group, whether out of curiosity or genuine interest or whatever, I don't care. OK, maybe they'll think I'm brash and I'm pushy. But I can't afford to wait. Because, by God, once they see my horses, they'll know I've got a right.' I levelled my gaze at Murray. 'Outlaw Prince will be in that Select Summer Sale next year.'

'All right, Maude,' he said. 'I'll find a social secretary.'

Three days later a very angular individual descended upon us. She arrived in a taxi, all legs and elbows and an air of unassailable superiority. Forewarned by Murray, I awaited her in the living-room, wearing what the well-bred horse breeder should wear (if she happens to be female), and Jan was posted in his white jacket to open the door.

When the doorbell rang, I ajusted my skirt under me and sat back more comfortably on the sofa. Jan escorted her to the open archway of the living-room, and I rose to greet her.

She gave me three fingers of her right hand. 'I haven't been in this house in ten years,' she said, surveying the room with a haughty stare that included me with the furniture.

'I'm Miss Sage,' I said. 'I didn't catch your name.'

'Tiffany Thomas,' she said as though reluctantly casting pearls.

'Miss or Mrs?' I enquired briskly.

'Miss, of course,' she said. She had not yet looked at me.

Wondering about the 'of course' (was 'Miss' ordained of God?), I indicated a chair and took my place again on the sofa.

Even sitting, she was tall, for her waist was long in proportion to the length of her fine legs. She had a bony face, with a thin mouth, a prominent Roman nose in one grand unbroken sweep, with tight flanges at the nostrils. For her age, which I estimated as the middle forties, she had a surprisingly clear and unblemished skin which she knew enough not to conceal with make-up. The eyes were narrow and hard, her worst feature, marked by a deep frown-line etched in her forehead. She was wearing a brown skirt, and a beige sweater rolled high and soft on the neck; her long, thin fingers ringless, her only jewellery an austere silver bracelet on her right wrist. She also wore spectator pumps on her rather large feet, a style I had thought disappeared some time ago.

'Would you care for tea?'

'Thank you,' Tiffany Thomas said. I tapped a bell – Jan was primed for this – and we proceeded to get acquainted.

'This was once a great house for parties,' Tiffany Thomas said, reverting to her prior theme. 'Everyone loved to come here. I see that you purchased the furnishings along with the estate.'

'Yeah, the same old sticks,' I said. I couldn't help it; that frozen voice made me yearn to be slangy.

'I know an excellent upholsterer,' she said. 'If you wish to keep these pieces, that is.'

Which pretty much closed out that line of conversation; I was grateful to Jan for appearing with the tea tray. He placed it on the table between us and I busied myself with pouring, remembering, as I did so, the awful English phrase: 'Will you be mother?' I had an impulse to ask Tiffany Thomas if she wished to be mother, simply because of the haughty stare it would evoke. But I resisted, and poured.

'I really think brocade looks right only when it's old enough for the colours to fade into each other,' I said. 'Are you a native of Kentucky?'

'We,' Tiffany Thomas said, 'are from Charleston.' As though dubious of my geography, she added, 'South Carolina. My grandfather unfortunately moved our branch of the family to Kentucky.'

'Then you *were* born here?'

'We have always thought of ourselves as Charlestonians,' Miss Thomas said with cold dignity. 'For *ages* we returned for a long visit at least once a year. The happiest moments of my childhood were passed in that lovely city.'

She's been putting down mere Kentuckians all her life, I thought. 'Never been there,' I said. 'I'm from Florida myself.'

She drank from her cup. 'I know an excellent English breakfast tea,' she said. 'Shall I bring you a packet the next time I come? There's only one place in Lexington that stocks it.'

I decided abruptly to get down to business; I didn't have the time necessary to discover the human being who might dwell underneath that pose and that nose.

'Mr Steiner, I'm sure, filled you in on my plans. The beginning point is an accurate guest list of the prominent horse people. It is not simply a social affair; it's important that I introduce myself to the people who count. Do you understnad?'

'Quite,' she said. 'Of course, you came prepared, I'm sure, with letters of introduction from Florida?'

'Afraid not,' I said. I added brutally, 'Two years ago I was a Licensed Practical Nurse.'

I watched the shock filter through her.

She placed her teacup precisely in the saucer. 'I'm afraid it will all be rather difficult.'

I could only continue in the vein I had opened. 'If it were *easy*, I wouldn't need you. I was relying on you to build the guest list, then to fulfil it. You *can* do that, can't you? . . . pull the strings that need to be pulled . . .'

She murmured modestly, 'I must say, there is not a house in Kentucky in which I am not welcome. I do command, Miss Sage, a certain . . . allegiance . . . among powerful friends.' Her face, if possible, became colder, more prideful. 'The Thomases, you must understand, have fallen upon evil times since the days of my grandfather; for so many years there have been only daughters born to the family. My grandfather was a breeder of horses on a small but very select scale. Of course, he was interested in hunters, not these commercial flat racers of today. He rode quite well himself, you know. Indeed, he was killed while taking a fence when he was seventy-six years old.'

'Then you can get the people I need.'

More dignity yet. 'Old family loyalties live on forever. They depend not at all upon wealth.' She allowed herself a small frown. 'I shall need to make a few phone calls, explore the situation discreetly . . .'

She let it trail off. But I got her meaning. I felt as though I were applying for a position with her, rather than vice versa.

I stood up. 'Fine, then. Go to work. Choose a convenient room for an office, ask Jan for anything you need in the way of desk, telephone extension . . . anything.'

That was the beginning. Quickly, it got worse. I couldn't stand the woman; and I really believe she was not particularly fond of me. That haughty, cold rigidity automatically made the short hair on the back of my neck bristle. I suppose my rough-tongued directness did the same to her. But damn it, I say what I mean and mean what I say; I never could stand this mealy-mouthed way of putting things.

More importantly, from the first day she suspected I might be a social disaster. Given her attitude – like a sailor signing on with the *Titanic* at the last moment before sailing – I couldn't understand why she stayed on the job. But early every morning she arrived by taxi, remaining sometimes long past sunset.

We scheduled a conference every day immediately after lunch. Every day, it turned into a catfight. Automatically, persistently, Tiffany Thomas rejected all suggestions. She didn't like the invitations I had designed (AN OLD-FASHIONED KENTUCKY HOUSEWARMING. BOURBON, BURGOO, AND HORSES), suggesting, not exactly delicately, that it was rather *nouveau riche* for a newcomer to presume to conduct anything claiming to be a Kentucky tradition. She also bridled at the idea of showing the horses as the highlight of the evening.

'It's really not done,' she informed me. 'You may, of course, be prepared to conduct a discreet tour of the barns with *selected* guests, if they should express such a wish. But one does not push it.'

'Listen, Tiffany Thomas,' I said. (She so obviously disliked being called 'Miss' . . . and I didn't feel friendly enough to use only her first name). 'Listen, Tiffany Thomas, any horseman – or horsewoman, for that matter – worth his salt *likes* to look at horses. Many will come for that reason alone. Besides, showing the yearlings is what it's all about.'

The major battle came over the catering. Tiffany Thomas insisted on one particular firm, proclaiming that it was unwise, in fact impossible, to engage the services of any other. The guests should find familiar faces behind the bars, serving the food, for it would make them comfortable. 'You are not in a position to undertake innovation.'

I wouldn't have opposed hiring her choice if it had not been for Jan Stok. But one day he appeared formally before me to state that he and Eva could handle all food preparation.

'Except for this burgoo,' he said. 'I do not know what it is.'

'It's a Kentucky tradition. I'm sure there's a particular burgoo chef who must be engaged.'

'Other than the burgoo, I would prefer to take full responsibility, Miss Sage. Caterers are horrible people to allow in one's house . . . you have no idea what they leave behind.' He moved his shoulders slightly. 'Besides – in Europe, certainly – it is . . . good style . . . to rely on your own staff.'

Everybody lectures. 'There'll be a lot of people.'

'It is no problem. I will engage temporary help in the matter of washing and cleaning. We will, of course, require bartenders and waiters. But you may leave all in my hands. I promise it shall be done well.'

I looked at him fondly. 'You really want to take it on, don't you?'

He smiled slightly. 'Since Eva and I have been in America, we have not made a truly great party. It is the . . . height of the art of being a houseman.'

'All right,' I said. 'The job's yours. Just let T. Thomas know what you require in the way of a budget.'

Thomas wouldn't have it. 'It is unheard of,' she declared. 'Besides I have already spoken to these people. By the way, we must change the invitations. The Shipwrights have scheduled a party for the night you have chosen. Our caterers have been engaged for it, of course.'

'I have no intention of changing the date,' I said sharply. 'And, since they're not our caterers yet, that solves the problem, doesn't it?'

She drew herself up. 'Not at all.' She hesitated. 'Miss Sage, I don't really see how I can continue in the face of these obstructions.'

I regarded her suspiciously. 'Are you taking a commission?' I said. 'Is that it?'

'Naturally.'

'But you're working for *me*,' I reminded her.

'That is how things are done,' she said. 'No. I must insist on the caterers. Or . . .' She paused ominously, waiting for capitulation.

I had done my best. 'I've already promised Jan that he can take complete charge of the food and the drink.'

When I can't work with a person, I can't work with them. I might well be ruining the entire project. But . . .

Tiffany Thomas beat me to the punch – and, so, made it easy. She sat quite still, looking me almost distastefully. I was sitting on the sofa in soiled blue jeans and work shirt, hardboots crusted with dried stable mud (after the first day I had ceased to dress for her). I'm quite sure I smelled strongly of horses, an odour I find delightful. It seemed to offend her nostrils.

'Miss Sage,' she said. 'If I am to continue, I demand a free hand. May I suggest that you no longer fret yourself with these details, but leave everything to me? You may remain in your . . . stables . . . with a clear mind until the day of the party.'

I stood up. 'No. I don't think so. That's not my way of doing things. In this house, my way is *the* way.'

Tiffany Thomas rose to her angular height. She stared down at me, her lips pale, tight. 'You must understand that I will not leave behind the work I have already done; the guest list, the contacts I have established for you . . . anything at all.'

'Then I'll just have to start from scratch, won't I?'

'You really can't do it without me,' she said, her voice unwavering.

'I'll have to, I guess. Because, Tiffany Thomas, I can't take your presence in my house any longer. It's as simple as that.'

She did not say anything. The paleness showed now in her cheeks; her eyes were bright and hard.

Then, for some reason, I put out my hand, speaking simply, even gently. 'Thank you for trying to work with me. But the truth is, we don't get along.'

I had no desire to dismiss her in anger, or out of an unadmitted jealousy that she enjoyed a security of status and family I would never have. She could even, living in the state all her life, deny Kentucky in favour of Charleston . . . that's in South Carolina.

'You can arrange with Mr Steiner the compensation for the time you have given me to date.' I glanced at my watch. 'Goodbye, Tiffany. I have to get back to the barns.'

Her nostrils flared in the first sign of emotion I had ever read in her. 'You can't do this,' she said.

'It's my decision. And I have made it. You are no longer in my employ.'

'You cannot dismiss me. You simply must not.'

'Why not?'

She showed no sign of softening. Indeed, she became more remote, her neck rigid, her head back, her hands stiff at her sides.

'Because I must earn this money.'

Utterly nonplussed, I sank down on the sofa. Never had I heard such a heartfelt plea couched in such unbendingly arrogant terms.

'Sit down,' I said.

She resumed her chair, perching on the edge, hands clasped in her lap. I looked at Tiffany Thomas all over again. For the first time I saw the threadbare gentility that governed her life. The elegantly tailored shirtwaist had suffered countless ironings, her shoes were worn, obviously the gauntness of her frame came not only from genetic structure but from the plain fact that she had not had a square meal in a very long time.

'Tell me about it.'

She lifted her chin. 'I don't care to discuss my personal life.'

'You're the one who brought it up,' I said. 'If you want a chance to hang on to this job, tell me.'

She looked down at her hands. They moved in her lap. 'Miss Sage, I am a twin,' she said painfully. 'My sister Trenholm, who was born ten minutes after me, is . . . not right.'

'What do you mean, "not right"?' I said sharply.

'She's . . . retarded.' She raised her head. 'She is a lovely person, Miss Sage. She has all the beauty, all the charm, that I have never had. Every hour of waking she laughs and sings, everyone loves her, she is a delight. But . . .' Her voice became reluctant. 'She has never grown beyond ten years of mental age. She is a child. She . . . always will be.'

God, the secrets that people carry around.

Softly I said, 'There are . . . places . . . for people like that. Schools where they can be taught what they are capable of learning, institutions to care for them. Of course, you'd still have the burden. But . . . you could be free to live your own life.'

She tightened. 'I couldn't . . . do that. Send her away, I mean. She loves me, Miss Sage. Once . . . long ago . . . our family doctor persuaded me to try an institution, saying Trenholm would be happier there. That was . . . just after Father died. Mother had passed away some years before.' Her face changed, froze again. 'She cried, Miss Sage. She did not quit crying until I came to take her home.' She shuddered deep inside. 'No. I couldn't do that to Trenholm.'

'But what about yourself?' I gazed in pity at her narrow, angular body, so tightly contained. Never in her life had she been allowed to give. Except to her twin sister.

'It's *my* fault. Don't you see that?' she whispered. 'I . . . I took it all, Miss Sage, while we were in the womb together. The intelligence, the skills of life, leaving Trenholm only the beauty and the charm.'

'That's not how it works,' I said strongly, though I knew right away it was hopeless. She had premised her life on a natal guilt.

'So you've always taken care of her,' I said. 'Day in. Day out. All these years.'

'For a long time, there was money,' she said. 'Not much, not enough, but . . . some. It's been gone quite a long time.' She straightened herself, fingers smoothing the pleats of the skirt over her long thighs. 'So I must have this job, Miss Sage. I must have my fee, and my commission from the caterers. I cannot allow you to dismiss me.'

I was baffled, caught helplessly between feeling and sense. 'Then why did you come in here like Queen Victoria? From the first day, you were asking me to fire you.'

She stared, obviously uncomprehending. 'One must do things in one's own way. You are a rough diamond, to be cut and polished and made to shine socially.'

'Well, you're not going to cut and polish on me,' I said. 'You ought to have realized that from our first meeting.'

I stopped. It was useless. But she was right; it was now impossible to send her away. Yet I knew that she would go right back to her dictatorial ways the moment I granted the reprieve. There was no give in her, none at all.

'Listen,' I said. 'We can't work together on this social thing. I see that. I hope you see it. But . . . have you ever worked in an office? I need an office manager badly. The paperwork on a Thoroughbred breeding farm is complex and tedious, all those Jockey Club forms and so on. But you have the intelligence to learn.'

She was on her high horse again. 'I could never do office work,' she said. 'A lady simply doesn't . . . go out to work every day.'

'Necessity knows no bounds, not even for ladies,' I snapped. 'This social-secretary business is only temporary. The office, if you can learn to handle it, would be permanent. Well paid, too. Do you know how to type?'

'I am an excellent typist. When I realized that the money would soon run out, I taught myself . . . for years, now, I have been typing theses for graduate students at the University. I think it would be safe to say there isn't a better typist in Kentucky.'

'Fine. What about shorthand?'

'I never had occasion to learn.'

'All right, we'll get a dictating machine.'

Her back was stiff again. 'I am sorry, Miss Sage. I'm afraid I couldn't bring myself to do office work. It would be . . . demeaning.'

'No honest work is demeaning! God knows it's honest, and God knows it's work. You wouldn't believe the detail. There's the payroll, and hospital insurance, all the Jockey Club forms, registrations, records to be kept on each mare, each foal. I'm drowning in paperwork, and so is Mr Clutterbuck.' I swallowed hard, swallowed her pride. 'You'd be doing me a great favour, Tiffany Thomas. We really need someone . . . if at first only to be there and answer the phone.'

'I'm sorry. I couldn't consider it.'

Damn it, I thought to myself. 'Look, it's not ordinary office work. You'll work alone, in total command once you've learned the routines. It's a very high-class job. After all, this *is* a Thoroughbred breeding farm.'

'I detest horses,' she said haughtily. 'Great, smelly things. My grandfather wished to teach me to ride when I was ten. I was terrified to feel that great animal under me, the muscles driving and driving, the terrible strength and the smell . . .'

Her cheeks showed a spot of red as the agitation of memory moved through her.

'I adored my grandfather. But I had to disappoint him in his great desire to make of me an accomplished horsewoman.'

'You won't have to see a horse if you don't want to,' I said. 'On paper, they don't smell at all.'

'I'm afraid it's out of the question.'

'Listen to me now,' I said. 'It's that or nothing. I'm offering you a good, steady job. If you can handle it.' I took a chance. 'Maybe you're afraid you can't do it.'

She drew herself up. 'I can do anything I put my mind to.'

'Fine. And you realize that you will be dealing, on the phone at least, with the best people in the horse business. You'll be handling enquiries about stallion bookings, requests to view our yearlings . . . why, you'll be the face that the farm presents to the world.'

She wavered.

'May I . . . continue the work as social secretary also?'

'Sure, and even afterwards, for I intend to make the party an annual affair. But – you will confine yourself to the guest list exclusively. Jan will be in charge of the food and drink, all the material details.' She was getting her back up again, so I hastened to add, 'You'll have to delegate that, because of your responsibilities in the office.'

She sat still. She looked at me, as I looked at her. She remained remote. But I could see the woman in her now, not merely the façade she struggled so bravely to present to the world.

'I shall give it a trial period,' she conceded graciously.

Sitting in the foaming bath water, feeling the liquid warmth comforting against my tired flesh, I laughed affectionately. The damned woman was so efficient it took your breath away. Within a week she was running the office like a fiefdom, as jealous of prerogative as she was competent in administration. Which was a little bit of all right with me – I was free at last to devote my attention to the horses.

I got out of the tub, dried on a fluffy towel, and walked naked into the bedroom. The party was growing in me, floating in my mind like a great multicoloured balloon, so that I shivered, whether from excitement or chill I couldn't tell. The lights were on in the yard – it was barely coming dark – and slipping on a negligee I went to the window. The front of the mansion was washed softly by spotlights concealed in the shrubbery; Jan had cleverly moderated the glare with cheesecloth screens. The Japanese lanterns, lit now, swayed gently in looping lines from tree to tree. Jan had displayed astonishing talents in the preparation; on the white tablecloths were displayed linen napkins arranged into lovely foldings, no two exactly alike, as intricate and subtle as architecture.

Turning away, I put on underwear – pretty classy for an ex-LPN, a lovely silken fabric textured in a pattern of roses – picked up my gown, slipped it over my head, and sat down to make up my face. Only when I was complete down to the gold sandals did I turn to the full-length mirror.

The gown was an ankle-length linen, creamy white, Halston. I had fallen in love with its lines, so subtle in simplicity – so much so, I had not allowed myself to wear it before this great night. I felt a momentary doubt. I suppose every woman as small as I entertains a dream of herself as svelte and long-legged, moving in mysteriously graceful pace on barely seen feet. Surely everyone, man and woman, would be captured by such a garment. What I was not sure of was if Maude Sage, plainly a rough diamond, could carry it off even with Halston's help. But, as I kept looking, doubt was replaced by confidence. That, by God, there in the mirror, was a woman! Standing with just the golden toe of one sandal peeping from beneath the hem of the gown, I was patrician. Only a piece of cloth cut by a genius could drape with such faithfully revealing/concealing folds. It made my breasts look deeper, my hips wide but thin.

'Old girl, you're not over the hill yet,' I said aloud. 'It might take a mature man to appreciate this vision, but . . .'

I laughed at myself. I hadn't thought about a man in that way since . . . I faltered, a tic somewhere deep inside . . . since Tim Conti had cantered out of my life. Oh, there had been another tic or two, a momentary hesitation . . . but always, ultimately, a rejection. Simply not worth it. And certainly *now*, with all the work and concentration of running the farm . . . Still, I would not be at all averse to intercepting an admiring glance or two.

I smiled at myself again. Dwelling on the edge of triumph, I had become the Maude Sage I had desired so greatly to be: useful in the world, every inch the dedicated horsewoman, yet feminine in style and feeling as I had never been. I was, for the first time in my life, using all of myself. A sudden dampness in my eyes, I whispered so deeply it was more a resonance than distinct words: *Thank you, Timothy Breen. Oh God, thank you; for being so wise and so kind.*

I don't know how to tell about the housewarming. Not much to say, really; it happened as it happened.

It was not quite dark when I came downstairs. Jan waited at the entrance, along with Eva and Tiffany Thomas.

'Jan, you and Eva and Tiffany have done a beautiful job,' I said, surveying the scene.

'A pleasure, madam,' Jan replied with grave formality.

'Thank you, Miss Sage,' Tiffany said in her carefully cold voice.

'Now, I want you to stay close so you can tell me who the people are.' I glanced towards one of the bars. 'I think I'll have a small stayer of Jack Daniel's.'

The bartender fixed my drink exactly as instructed. I returned to the steps before I took the first sip.

Then we waited. And we waited. The night came full dark as Tiffany Thomas and I stood on the steps, as the serving girls waited scattered among the tables, the bartenders behind their bars, the burgoo chef on guard at his huge pot of bubbling goodness. I had another drink, a sparing third. I didn't dare have another.

Finally a car came, whirling rapidly up the driveway to the edge of the yard, though Merlin was stationed at the Great Stone Barn to direct the parking. A splash of young people erupted, laughing and shouting, their evening obviously well under way. I moved forward to greet them but they charged past me through the empty white tables towards the burgoo pot and the bars.

Boys and girls together. I watched remotely as they laughed and swirled and talked, focused exclusively among themselves – another carload had arrived before the first had supplied themselves with refreshment – as they ate and drank. Then, like a flock of birds responding to an instinctive signal generated not by an individual but by the group as a whole, they were gone, leaving behind a twisted chair or two, dirty burgoo bowls, half-finished drinks.

'Kids,' I said indulgently. 'Running a rip-off. More fun any time than coming to a party legitimately.'

We waited again. And looming within us all was the growing, stark knowledge: The housewarming was to be a monstrous failure.

Oh, people came. A few. They drifted in, one or two cars at a time, the guests hesitating in realization as, approaching the lighted lawn, they saw how sparsely populated it was. I suppose, all in all, there might have been fifteen or twenty couples. Certainly no more.

Tiffany Thomas and I moved bravely among them, making them welcome. It was a sticky situation for all concerned. My face felt so stiff I thought the skin would crack every time I had to make myself smile. The luckless few guests who had been so foolhardy as to accept my invitation were so awkwardly uncomfortable that I was pleased when I noted a couple, two couples, drifting inconspicuously to the edge of the lighted area, then rapidly disappearing towards their transportation. I wanted them all to leave; the disaster was so interminable in its prolongation that I didn't know, from one minute to the next, how much longer I could endure it.

Fewer than a dozen remained when Dancy appeared, wearing suit and tie. Coming to me on the steps, he said in a subdued voice, 'What about showing the yearlings?'

'Forget it,' I said.

'There are *some* people I shall never speak to again,' Thomas said in her haughtiest, most implacable, tone.

'It's not your fault,' I said wearily. 'You were so right in your original opinion. I'm a social disaster.'

'But *I'm* not,' she said coldly. 'I had *promises*, commitments . . . They didn't even have the nerve to telephone their regrets.' Her taut voice took on a bitter edge. 'I suppose they're all having a great time at the Shipwrights'.'

'I don't think it would have done a bit of good to have chosen another night.' I stared out over the white tables, at the spare scatter of guests who remained in shipwrecked clusters here and there, chatting with sporadic nervous laughter.

'We can still show the yearlings,' Dancy said. 'Merlin and Alice are standing by.'

'Forget it,' I said again. 'I just want them to leave.' I stared almost resentfully at the guests. 'Why did they come, anyway? I suppose somehow they failed to get the word.'

Dancy made a smile. 'Those who didn't come, they'll never know what they missed, seeing you in that dress.'

The dear man. If he had only been there before the party had died in me, to look at me like that . . . it was too late now. In every way.

'Maude,' Dancy said.

'All right, Dancy,' I said wearily. 'But it's such a damn waste.' I gazed at the uneaten food banked on the buffet tables. 'All that to be thrown out . . . enough for two hundred and fifty people.' I turned to him. 'Dancy. Isn't that an orphanage I pass, down the road about ten miles?'

'Yes,' he said. 'Run by one of the churches, I think.'

'Tiffany Thomas, get these people out of their agony,' I said. 'Tell them we are grateful for their coming, and let them know they can now depart gracefully. If you have to, tell them I've already retired.'

Moving briskly, I went into the house, looked up the number, dialed. My mind was focused now. As long as I could keep it moving I wouldn't have to think about what had happened.

'Who am I talking to?' I asked. 'Good, I wanted to speak to the director. Listen, I'm Maude Sage, I run a horse farm a few miles up the road from you and I've just given the least likely party of the century. I've got scads of good food just going to waste, and it occurred to me that perhaps your charges would like a party at my place, eat the food, maybe see some Thoroughbreds . . . what do you think?'

'It's a good thought, Miss . . . Sage, is it? But too late, I'm afraid. They've already had their supper, and we're early to bed around here.'

I hadn't thought about the time. I looked at my watch. Only ten-fifteen. When the evening had seemed so interminable!

'Sorry, I'm just out of my skull, I guess.' I paused, thinking. 'I'm sure most of the goodies can be kept. What about tomorrow afternoon?'

'There's the transportation problem,' he demurred. 'We only have one old bus, not nearly adequate to haul the entire . . .'

'I'll take care of it,' I said. 'Just let me know how many buses you need, I'll charter them. This is not a charitable gesture – you'll be doing me a great favour, actually. Food and drink here for two hundred and fifty people, and it's a sin to let it go to waste.' I laughed. (Thank God, I could laugh now.) 'Of course, I don't suppose you'd want your charges to soak up all the Bourbon I've got on the premises, so we'll lay in plenty of soft drinks.'

'The children don't enjoy many outings, I'm afraid,' he said in a considering voice. 'However, it would be quite a strain on us, I have a very limited staff, you understand, our budget being what it is . . .'

'They'll have a wonderful time,' I urged. 'I'll bet most have never seen a horse farm. They can eat and drink and be merry, then we'll take them on a tour of the barns. They'll *love* the new foals.'

'I shall have to discuss it with my staff,' he said finally. 'May I call you in the morning?'

'Of course,' I said. 'But I'm going to count on it.'

I went outside. To Jan I said, 'Close up the bars, store the liquor. Save what food you can, though, we're feeding an entire orphanage tomorrow afternoon.' I walked on to the burgoo chef. 'Can you keep that pot going until tomorrow?'

The tragic look that had settled over his face early in the evening lifted. 'Ought to be just right by then.'

'Fine,' I said. 'Because there's going to be a bunch of kids here who'll empty that pot for you before you know it.'

I turned and looked at my people standing in a forlorn huddle on the steps of the mansion, watching me in perplexity and wonder. Alice and Merlin, wearing their Florida-orange-and-Kentucky-blue uniforms had come up from the barn to join the others.

I faced them, no longer prideful, Halston's gown hanging on my bones as though I had dragged it through a Florida swamp. They're hurt by all this as deeply as I am, I thought. More, maybe, because I've made no secret of how much it meant to me.

'Let's all get to bed,' I said quietly. 'Tomorrow will be a busy day, those orphanage kids will run us ragged, I bet.' I laughed. 'So get all the sleep you can, while you can.'

It was not enough. They were still looking at me. So I went to Alice, seeing the unshed tears in her eyes, and put my arms around her shoulders. 'It's all right, Alice. We'll show your grand foal to some people yet.' I went on to Eva, embracing her in turn, feeling her heavy arms come strongly around me. I stepped back, looking at Tiffany Thomas. What the hell, I thought, and put my arms around her, too; though I had a feeling her flesh would be like ice.

'Miss Sage . . .' she said brokenly.

Damn her. 'All right, let's break it up,' I said loudly. 'I just want everybody to see to it those kids have a great time.'

Really nothing more to be said. They turned away, reluctant

to leave me without expressing what they felt, yet not knowing how to say it.

'Merlin, will you and Alice drive Tiffany home?' I said. 'She probably can't get a taxi at this hour.'

'Yes ma'am,' Merlin said.

'And wait a minute. You've got to be pretty handy about lettering signs, haven't you?'

'Yes'm,' he said. 'Fair.'

'Fine. I want you to find a beautiful piece of wood and make a sign for the entrance gate. Very large letters.'

'Yes'm,' he said. 'Be proud to do it. But . . . what do you want on it?'

'The name of the farm,' I said.

'What is it?'

I looked at Dancy. He was watching me with a frown. He's worried about my state, I thought, feeling warm with the realization. A little scared of it, too.

I grinned at him 'OUTLAW FARM,' I said. 'Not just because of the stallion, either, though that's a part of it.' I stopped, the grin fading, and let them hear the deeper vibrations in my voice. 'Because that's what we are here, all of us, you and me *and* the stallion. Outlaws. So let's be proud of it. OUTLAW FARM.'

I went past them, up the steps and into the house. Only when I was safely inside, by myself, did I let the trembling surface.

Let me tell you, the party for the orphanage kids was something else. They came spilling out of the two chartered buses so full of excitement it was like drowning in a human thunderstorm. Shouting a great hurrah at sight of the food, their skinny legs twinkled like a distraught flock of chickens as they raced to claim places in the buffet line. Though seemingly as incapable of control as that same flock of pullets and fryers, their attendants miraculously quieted them as the line formed. Smiling involuntarily, we – Jan and Eva, along with Merlin and Alice, waiting to serve their plates, the burgoo chef with his great ladle, Dancy and I standing on the broad steps to watch – were quite moved by their appearance.

These boys and girls, ranging from six or seven to nearly grown, in an astonishing variety of hair colourings and sizes and types of physique, in spite of being reasonably well-fed and decently clothed, had lived deprived lives. Their eyes, especially, made me vulnerable to them; they gazed out upon a world from which they expected nothing – least of all love, affection.

The director, a tall man with benevolent face and extraordinarily severe eyes, took his place at the head of the tables to speak grace. The instant the 'Amen' was uttered, they fell to.

They had brought appetites. There were exotic foods, including caviar and pâté de foie gras and smoked salmon, that I am sure they had never seen. It didn't faze them, no more than the linen or the patterned silver. Some, of course, only sampled the more exotic items, but a surprising number devoured them along with the ham and turkey. The burgoo was such a favourite that the first seekers of seconds were drawn to the great pot rather than the buffet table.

The director, Reverend Tompkins, came to me on the steps. 'It's a good thing you are doing today, Miss Sage.'

'Not exactly a charitable gesture,' I said, dryly rejecting the accolade. 'I simply had all this food I didn't know what to do with,' I smiled. 'I have a distinct impression that the problem is solved.'

He turned to gaze upon the scene. 'It's so difficult for us to give them outings. We're terribly overcrowded and understaffed; it's all we can manage to feed and clothe them. We would wish to do more, you understand, but . . .' He shrugged. 'First things first.'

'Some of them seem mature to be living in an orphanage.'

'The longer a child remains institutionalized, the more difficult it becomes to place him for adoption,' Reverend Tompkins explained. 'When babies come to us, most are quickly placed . . . there's always a waiting list. Few couples, however, wish to assume the responsibility for a child of eight or nine or ten, after his character is substantially formed.' He glanced at me. 'Once they've been with us for several years, we expect to have them until they're eighteen, able to make their way in the world.'

'It's a big job.'

'What bothers me most of all, they grow up without love,' he said seriously. 'Care, concern, yes . . . but human love, no matter how hard we try, cannot be institutionalized. A human being learns to know affection by learning how to receive it.'

'Reverend, you must remember that human nature is irrepressible.'

He sighed, and laughed. 'I see that fact of life demonstrated daily. But they're having themselves a red-letter day today, aren't they?'

'Come on,' I said. 'Let's join them. I'm hungry, too.'

Before the adults had finished eating, the gargantuan adolescent appetites were beginning to be sated and some of the children were drifting about in hesitant clusters. I looked for Alice; she was already on the way.

'All right, kids,' she said loudly. 'Game time. Who's ready to choose up sides?'

'Cake 'n' ice-cream!' someone yelled.

'Later,' Alice said firmly. 'You don't want dessert right on top of a big meal like that, do you? No, sir. Give it a chance to shake down. Come on, everybody.'

She led them to the lawn, accompanied by Merlin, and soon had games going, Tag and Drop the Handkerchief, all the old standbys. Merlin, bringing a soft ball and a bat, started a fungo competition among the older boys.

'I swear to God, those two can do anything,' I said to Dancy.

'Still just handling yearlings,' Dancy said, laughing. 'Same principle of firmness and gentleness exactly.'

Hearing the phone ring inside the house, I hastened to answer. Tiffany Thomas, from the office ,said, 'Miss Maude, some Japanese gentlemen are here to see you.'

'What do they want?' I said impatiently. 'I'm busy right now.'

'They have *asked* to view the yearlings,' Tiffany said stiffly.

'Oh,' I said. 'That's different. Dancy and I will be right there.'

There were three, dressed alike in careful black suits with white shirts and narrow ties. Neat men of implacable politeness, each bowing slightly as we shook hands.

'I understand you wish to view our yearlings.'

The one in the middle bowed again. 'We have come to America to purchase Thoroughbreds,' he said. 'It is our desire to see the summer-sale yearlings that are not in the Summer Sale.'

I laughed. 'You've been reading my advertising. This way, please.'

Dancy led them out while I supplied the commentary. The visitors listened as intently as they looked, politely making their comments to each other in English rather than their native tongue. I watched their faces as I talked but, given their uniform blandness, couldn't read a thing.

When we had finished, the spokesman turned to me. 'You have told us all but the purchase price.'

'I haven't set a price,' I said. 'If you decide you'd like to buy, name your figure and we'll go from there.' I paused. 'Fair enough?'

He bowed again. 'Fair enough. Of course, we shall wish to view the sales offerings before coming to a decision.'

'Fine by me,' I said. 'But let me tell you this, gentlemen. With the exception of the Saidam colt, you won't find any yearling over there at Daingerfield which will outclass what you've just seen – in breeding *or* in conformation and condition.'

'I am sure that you are correct. Thank you again. We shall go now.'

'What do you think?' I asked Dancy as we watched the chauffeured car disappear.

'God, I don't know,' Dancy said. 'Never dealt with the Japanese . . . in my time, they weren't coming over to buy bloodstock. They tell me it's a big thing now in Japan.'

'All over the world,' I said. 'Well, we've had our first lookers. Let's get back to the party.'

It was not to be; another set of visitors arrived before we had time to leave the Great Stone Barn. They were Chileans: a spare, excellent old man with a face like an eagle – extraordinarily handsome with his narrow head framed by grey wings of hair, his strongly shaped nose and, most of all, the ancient grace of thin-boned hands – accompanied by a very young man, obviously his son, and an extraordinarily beautiful girl with platinum-blonde hair, spectacular against her olive skin.

The old gentleman tendered his card, the long Spanish name engraved in flowing script. 'I have promised my son and my new daughter an American Thoroughbred for their wedding present,' he explained. 'Preferably a filly that will in time be a worthy broodmare for my own premiere sire.'

'Señor Paredo, I shall be delighted to show our yearlings,' I said. 'Have you seen our advertisements?'

'That is why we are here,' he said. 'We are interested particularly in the Intentionally filly. Of course we should be pleased to see the colts also.' He smiled. 'With horses, one never knows, does one?'

I was fascinated by his voice: precise English carrying an undertone of authority. Obviously a man born to the power of wealth, who wore it as lightly as a cape about his shoulders. I wondered how many years he could count; the ascetic face was ageless.

The old man stood leaning on his cane as the colts were led

out, the boy and the girl arm in arm, the girl talking breathlessly, low-toned, in Spanish. Then we moved to the Filly Barn, where Dancy showed first the Intentionally filly. The old man walked around her slowly three times, stepped back without comment, and Dancy brought out the grey filly by Nearctic.

Doing my commentary, I detected, I thought, a spark of interest in Señor Paredo's eyes; I noticed that his son looked at him, too. Dancy walked the filly away, turned, came back.

'The other one again, please.'

The Intentionally filly was brought back. 'Now, again, the grey.'

Patiently, Dancy responded. This time Señor Paredo walked around the filly only once, then stood leaning on his cane. The girl, obviously not knowing horses, clung to her bridegroom's arm and looked so damn beautiful it could break your heart. She was no more than fifteen. This time last year I thought, she was wearing a plain convent uniform not this very expensive very revealing, dress.

'Buy it,' the old man said in Spanish.

The son turned to me. 'Your price?'

I explained about not having set a fixed price. He nodded, eyes thoughtful. He glanced at his father; obviously, there would be no help from that quarter.

He studied the Nearctic filly all over again. When he spoke, his English was not as assured and precise as his father's. 'I will offer thirty thousand dollars.'

I looked at the young man again. So young, the child of an old man's loins, obviously so in love. But he had done his homework. I glanced at Dancy; his face was carefully bland almost Japanese.

Gazing at the grey filly, I thought irrelevantly: She will go to South America, all her racing, her breeding lost to this continent. All chance gone for fame in the great American filly stakes, the Mother Goose, the Coaching Club American Oaks, the Alabama. But perhaps a son, a daughter, will return to glory . . . and I knew, wryly that Dancy would think I was being terribly sentimental and impractical.

I allowed my thoughts to curl cautiously around the bid. Thirty thousand. Just about right. Something more than I had expected, less than hoped for. Damned little room for bargaining either way. I looked at the handsome old man. Something about him reminded me of Timothy Breen. I love marvellous old men of great breeding and presence.

Don't insult the man by haggling, I decided abruptly. It would be dead wrong. Take it or leave it.

'Son,' I said, 'you've bought yourself a fine filly.'

He blushed, whether at the acceptance or my way of stating it I couldn't tell. I glanced at the old man. A secret grin at his son's discomfiture showed on his thin lips.

'I have deposited a letter of credit with the Second National Bank and Trust Company in Lexington,' he said to me. 'In the morning payment will be arranged, and transportation. Will that be satisfactory?'

'Absolutely,' I said. I held out my hand. 'Señor Paredo, you have given your son and his bride the first yearling we have sold from Outlaw Farm. I hope her racing and breeding career will be as happy as their marriage obviously will be.'

'Thank you, Miss Sage,' he said. 'May it be so.'

'Keep us posted on her progress and accomplishments,' I said. 'We'll always be interested.'

I returned to the party so elated I was walking on air. My advertising genius was paying off . . . one filly sold – in my opinion the best of the two – before the Summer Sale had actually started.

I walked right into a brawl. Two boys were fighting, those nearest surging away, the director charging from the house steps, Merlin futilely trying to separate them. As I arrived, the little one – he was fighting a boy twice his size and considerably older – was knocked down. He got up, his nose bloody, and piled in again without hesitation, only to get knocked flat again . . . but only after he had succeeded in bloodying the boy's mouth.

'Stop it!' I shouted.

Dancy grabbed the small one as he came up again. By this time Merlin had pinned the other fellow's arms. They stood panting and dishevelled, the small boy, anxious to continue, writhing in Dancy's grip. I couldn't blame him; he'd been getting the worst of it.

'You ought to be ashamed of yourself, fighting someone half your size,' I said chidingly to the bigger boy.

'Ashamed!' he said hotly. 'He'd of killed me if I hadn't . . .'

'I'll still kill you if this big bastard will turn me loose,' the little one declared.

I looked at him. Thin, bony, no more than thirteen, maybe fourteen. His eyes were malevolent, a flat, hard blue. The shocking thing was, they remained unaffected by the rage, but dwelled calm and very seeing in the tight, furious face. He was whiteheaded, the hair flat and lank, and his young mouth was too thin-lipped, too mean.

'What's your name?' I asked suddenly.

'None of your damn business!' he said. He twisted his neck to look up at Dancy. 'Will you let me go or not?'

'Will you promise to quit fighting?' Dancy said.

'Hell no,' he said. 'I'm gonna kill him.' Writhing suddenly, he kicked Dancy cold-bloodedly in the shin. Dancy let out a sound, doubling over with the excruciating pain. Immediately the boy catapulted himself, fists flailing, at the larger boy, still helplessly pinned by Merling. He got in a dozen good licks before Dancy, with the aid of the director, could again secure him.

'You will both go sit in the bus . . . separate buses . . . until we're ready to leave,' Reverend Tompkins said sternly. 'I will deal with you later.'

The older boy was abashed by guilt; not the white-headed kid. He stood braced, his arms still firmly grasped, and gazed a flat blue hatred at his mentor.

'I want to see the horses,' he declared. 'I wouldn't have come if I couldn't have seen the horses.'

'Then you should have behaved yourself,' the Reverend said unrelentingly. 'To the bus. Now.'

The boy shrugged himself free of restraint. If he had suffered disappointment, I couldn't read it in him, as though he had never expected to get his heart's desire on this day . . . or any day. Calmly, without a glance towards his erstwhile enemy, he pushed through the circle and walked to the nearest bus. Without a backward glance he climbed up and disappeared from view.

'What's that kid's name?' I asked Reverend Tompkins.

'Dahl,' he told me. 'The kids call him Whitey.' He chuckled. 'In fact, that's all the first name we've got for him . . . all he knew when he came to us.' He shook his head. 'A tough one. A real problem.'

'I can imagine,' I said. 'His eyes . . . I don't suppose he ever knew who his mother was, his father . . .'

'On the contrary,' Tompkins said. 'He comes from a big family, he told us, travelled around the country working in crops. They dropped him off with us one morning, leaving a note saying they didn't know how to handle him any more. He was about seven, eight, at the time.'

'That's a terrible thing to do to a kid.'

'Yes . . . Miss Sage, he is a bad one. I've always felt that, with any child, there's always a way if you can only find it. But Whitey . . .' He shook his head. 'In all the time I've known him, he's never given an inch.'

The excitement over, the children returned to ice-cream and cake. Feeling tired, I went to the steps and remained sitting until Dancy and Merlin began organizing the barn tour. On an impulse, as they marched off I rose and went to the director.

'Reverend Tompkins. Will you allow Whitey to see the horses?'

He frowned. 'I never rescind a punishment, Miss Sage.'

'Suppose he promises to stay strictly at my side?' I persisted. 'He did want to see them, you know. Very much. I'll be responsible for his conduct.'

Adamantly he shook his head. 'Sorry.'

'For me,' I said. 'I'm asking it as a favour, Reverend.' Seeing his continuing denial, I added, 'I'll make a bargain with you. Let me show Whitey Dahl the barns and I'll . . . I'll do the party again next spring.' I laughed. 'The greatest good of the greatest number, Reverend.'

He eyed me. 'You really think it's that important?'

'I'd like, just once, for the kid to get something he didn't expect,' I said. 'All right?'

He inclined his head. 'All right. With you, separated from the others. But . . .' He paused. 'I would advise you not to get too . . . involved with Whitey.'

'I just want to show him my horses,' I said.

I went to the bus. Whitey Dahl, sitting on the front seat, looked straight ahead, apparently oblivious to the passing parade of happy children. I climbed up on the step.

'Want to see the horses?' I asked. 'With me?'

His eyes came to my face. 'I've had it with the horses, lady. Don't you know that?'

'Don't you *want* to see them?'

He shrugged. 'Want or don't want, don't make no difference. *He* wouldn't let me.'

'I have his permission. If you'll stay with me.'

He didn't move. 'I decided I don't care if I never see a horse,' he said in his colourless voice. 'So just go away and leave me alone. If you don't mind.'

'Listen, good buddy,' I said. 'I had to lay another party on the line for next year to get the Reverend's permission. So haul your ass out of that bus and come on.'

He looked at me again. Those flat blue eyes. That calm malevolence. How could such cold hate build inside a thirteen-year-old? It was enough to scare you.

'Is that any way to talk to a kid?' he said.

He wasn't being funny, only ruthless. But he got down, moving as surely as when he had walked to exile, and came with me. We followed behind the group while I told him Sir Outlaw's history, how I had come to buy him, what his breeding was, the races he had won, keeping up a steady line of chatter as we progressed. Whitey Dahl remained as opaque to me as the Japanese buyers had been; I could read in him no surge of curiosity or interest; indeed, any response at all.

Returning to the house, I said, 'Whitey, why did you want to see the horses, anyway? You didn't . . . seem to like them very much.'

He gave me his stare. 'I don't know. Just did, that's all.'

'Well? What did you think?'

'They're big. Strong.'

I had to dare him. 'The fact is, you're afraid of them. You wouldn't even touch that little foal, friendly as he wanted to be.'

'Me? I ain't afraid of nothing,' Whitey Dahl said. Marching from my side, he climbed into the bus and sat down. Baffled, I turned away. I hadn't got to him. Nobody, I had the idea, ever had. A hell of a world for anybody to live in, the way he saw it . . . especially a child.

The party over, the buses departed with the subdued children. I sat with Dancy and Merlin and Alice on the steps, gazing out over the trampled lawn, littered with crumpled party hats and napkins.

'Sure went through the groceries, didn't they?' I said in weary pleasure. 'I think they had a great time. Don't you?'

'They loved it,' Alice said. 'Nice kids, Miss Sage. So . . . responsive when anyone pays the least bit of attention.'

'Yeah,' I said. Mentally, I shrugged. Likely I'd never see the kid again. I didn't *want* to see him again. There must be a small answer, at least, when one asks the human question.

'Listen, Merlin,' I said, remembering the great event with renewed excitement. 'We sold the Nearctic filly this afternoon. To a gentleman from Chile. Thirty thousand dollars.'

'That's great!' Alice said, while Merlin looked quietly pleased.

'I hate to see her shipped out of the country,' I said. 'But . . .'

'But,' Dancy said quietly, 'next year there'll be another filly, then another and another. Like children, they get born and they grow up and they go away.'

'I guess so,' I said rather sadly. 'Some are winners, some are losers.' I thought of Whitey again. 'And some never get a chance to prove it one way or the other.' I stood up. 'Good party, wasn't it?' I looked into their good faces. 'We'll sell the other yearlings, too, just you wait and see. So . . . Outlaw Farm is alive and flourishing.'

Within a week after the Summer Sale, the yearling stalls were empty. Without exception, they went to foreign buyers. Though the Japanese trio didn't return, the Dancer's Image colt was purchased for twenty-four thousand by a red-faced Irishman with a silver brogue, representative of an Irish bloodstock agency. We felt we were lucky to get seven thousand five hundred for the Saidam colt, after considerable haggling, because the price represented double the stud fee that was in him. He was bought by an Italian who stared at me as much as he looked at the colt. The Intentioned filly went to Australia for twenty-three thousand, which surprised me because I had not realized that his fillies were more prized, on average, than his colts. The Australian really wanted that sprinting blood.

So, without the benefit of the Daingerfield Select Summer Yearling Sale, we didn't do badly; four yearlings bringing a total of eighty-four thousand five hundred for an excellent average of more than twenty-one thousand dollars. Not bad for the first year of sale.

It left me no less determined, however, to see Outlaw Prince pass through the auction sales ring next year.

CHAPTER 2

It wasn't easy.

To begin with, the Daingerfield Association turned down, as automatically as a knee jerk, the pedigrees of the yearlings we had submitted for consideration. It burned. Rigorously selective, Dancy and I had spent hours poring over the statistics of sire and dam, of maternal grandsires and granddams, trying to visualize exactly how the black type – or lack of it – would look in the sales catalogue. Of our eleven yearlings, we chose three colts – among them, of course, Outlaw Prince – and two fillies. All, of course, blandly rejected.

I didn't tell anyone – least of all, Dancy – what I meant to do, because I knew he would try to talk me out of it. Perhaps I kept the plan secret for fear that I was making the wrong move. But if there was another way to go, I couldn't see it.

After breakfast the next morning, I went upstairs and took a long bath. With ample time for preparation because the offices wouldn't open until nine o'clock, I went through my entire wardrobe. The impression I intended to make? Elegant but understated, feminine but ready for business. I finally settled on a very pale green silk dress by Norell with a matching linen jacket, lined with the same fabric as the dress, the jacket made with exquisite detail and perfect fit. A matching hat recalled in subtle shaping the riding helmets jockeys wear, and those Italian shoes, never worn, were an intricate combination of fine leathers.

Jewellery – after all, one doesn't want to appear poverty-stricken. First of all the emerald ring; a big diamond ring for the other hands, so gaudy it looked like junk jewellery (but it wasn't!); and on the left arm a solid-gold bracelet, simple and massive.

In confidence and anger I paraded downstairs, climbed into the VW, and departed to make a call on Mr Walter Trenton.

Still too early; I drove on beyond the office parking lot into the backside where, during the auction sales, the yearlings were stabled and exhibited. There was activity, because training goes on even when there is no racing. Many of the nearby farms bring their young horses in season. So early in the year, the new two-year-olds, scarcely more than yearlings, were still slight-bodied, flighty in mind. Parked near the training track, I watched a set just arriving, led by a sedate old horse bearing a small-statured but thick-set man. Young boys, light of weight, were up (some of the 'boys' were girls), and the juveniles made dainty, quick steps, their ears pricked with interest, observant of all that went on. They were not here for exercise, not yet, but were being schooled to bear calmly the hectic activity of a race track. One colt, a chestnut, pranced sideways, his body curved, his neck bowed. The leader spoke to the boy, his voice quiet, and when the lad couldn't bring the colt under control, swung the old horse alongside to calm him.

A runner came pounding around the curve of the track, the boy's seat high in the air, hands taking a firm hold to keep the exercise to a slow, steady pace. With each thud of hoof, the colt's lungs made a soft explosion of energy and effort. The gust of his breath misted as lung-warm air met the outside chill. He was sweating lightly in the flanks. The set of colts exhibited a stir of restless excitement, the boys gentling them with hand and soft-spoken voice.

Next came a colt close on the rail in a hard run, his breathing more explosive, his hoofbeats a rapid, rhythmic thud. His head was thrust out, his nostrils flaring; the boy pumped with him, hands and body moving with the stride, lifting him into the stretch run. As he passed the marker, a man wearing a plaid coat clicked his stopwatch, then gazed at it in satisfaction.

Behind the wheel of the car, I sat thinking. Like sex, the matter of horses is essentially simple and direct and honest. This, here, now, was what horse breeding and horse racing is all about: gentle, careful people schooling young horses to an art they were bred to perform. But the raising and racing of Thoroughbreds – again, like sex – are fouled up with peripheral considerations, money and prestige and social rank, who's who, who's on top, all the needless complications – until the basic facts of life are trampled upon. What was that quotation from Frederico Tesio I had liked so much the first time I had read it? *To breed a horse that runs the longest distance, carrying the heaviest weight in the fastest time*. Those words encompassed the pure and simple essence of the matter.

I sighed, consulting my wristwatch – peripheral complications like this one. But soon I was grateful for the waiting interval; I knew, now, it would have been wrong to have descended upon the Daingerfield Association in anger. No matter how righteous your cause, anger only hardens the opposition.

In the parking lot, I put on my white gloves, took leather bag firmly in hand – wholly inside myself and feeling good. Feeling ready.

A very pretty girl with extraordinary breasts graced the reception desk. Card ready to hand, I laid it before her. 'I'm here to see Mr Trenton.'

She glanced at the card, one hand going to the telephone. I turned away as she spoke, gazing at the framed prints of photo finishes in celebrated Daingerfield Track races. When she replaced the phone, her expression had changed; not as automatically friendly now, accompanied by a certain remoteness in the tone of her words.

'Mr Trenton is in conference, I'm afraid.'

'I can wait.'

Leaving her uncertain, I made strategic withdrawal to a leather sofa against the wall, picking up a copy of the *Blood-Horse* to leaf through, though I had read it last week.

The pretty girl went prettily about her business; her voice trilled as she efficiently punched buttons, she had a smile and a welcome for each person who entered. Only I remained in the reception room; the others, Kentucky hardboots to the last man, disappeared immediately into the deeper reaches, often with a curious glance towards me. Each time the girl reminded herself of my presence, she frowned tentatively, as though her training had not included enough practice in disapproval. I ignored her discomfort. After a final troubled glance in my direction, she rose abruptly to disappear into the corridor. She was gone quite a long time, the telephone lines left unattended. Returning, she came reluctantly, burdened by the message. After all, she *liked* being pleasant to people.

'Miss Sage. Mr Trenton will be tied up for quite a long time. All morning, in fact.'

'That's all right,' I assured her. 'I've got all the time in the world.'

Her pretty face showed deeper trouble. 'But . . .' she said. Then, tentatively, 'Perhaps another day . . .'

It was like shooting fish in a barrel. 'Not sure when I can get back,' I said. 'Since I'm here . . . Mr Trenton should be able to give me a few minutes if I can only be patient enough.'

I smiled with the words, leaving her with no answer. She returned to her desk and, as though it were a haven of security, plunged into the board of impateint lights.

She must have kept him informed. I was, admittedly with a

touch of malice, taking advantage of the basic courtesy of the Kentucky horseman. I knew well that my refusal to depart gracefully would trouble his soul by the acute knowledge that he was keeping a lady – at least, a woman – waiting.

It made the pretty girl almost happy when, after an hour, the siege broke through his resistance. 'Miss Sage, Mr Trenton can see you now.'

I stood up, pulling at my gloves. 'Thank you,' I said, grinning at her conspiratorially. 'I knew that between us we'd break him down.'

She blushed, pleased but disconcerted. 'It's the last office on the right.'

Mr Trenton stood up, coming around the desk to shake my hand and usher me gallantly to a deep leather chair.

'Miss Sage, delighted to meet you,' he declared.

'I am pleased, also,' I said, looking around. A large corner office, dark panelling, bookshelves ranked with produce records and stallion registers, several shelves filled with the catalogues of past sales.

I studied him thoughtfully as he resumed his seat behind the uncluttered desk. A sturdy, red-faced man, voice smooth and hearty. His bland face was shaved and powdered into smoothness, showing high on the cheekbones the tiny rosettes of a Bourbon drinker. About my age, I decided. Perhaps a bit younger.

Having done my homework, I knew something of his history. Of an old Kentucky family, owners of Trenton Run Farm for longer than most could remember, he had first taken, however, the way of business, coming to the Daingerfield Association with a Harvard degree at the age of thirty, rising rapidly, through skill and connections, to treasurer and, after an internal power struggle against the old guard, to president.

'Sorry to have kept you waiting,' he said, smiling. 'Hate to keep a lady waiting.'

I had caught a glance of admiration in his eyes. The dress had paid off.

'That's all right, It's a terrible imposition to arrive without notice.' Now I smiled in return. 'If I requested a formal appointment, I'd never get it.'

He leaned into his tall-backed chair and said calmly, 'Now that you're here, what can I do for you?'

'Mr Trenton, last year while your Summer Sale was going on I sold my small crop of four yearlings for a gross of eighty-four thousand five hundred dollars. Three of those yearlings should have passed through your auction ring.'

'I'd . . . heard that you had done well,' Trenton said noncommittally. He smiled. 'Always nice to know people are realizing good prices for their bloodstock.'

'That's all water over the dam. Now I'm talking about this year.'

His eyes shifted. 'I suppose you've sent in the pedigrees of your candidates . . .'

'And they've been turned down. Without exception.'

His eyes didn't shift. 'Most of our consignors are members of the Association, Miss Sage. Supporters ever since we broke away from the Keeneland Association, they are people we can rely on to have at heart the best interests of the organization. As you may know, the Daingerfield Association is nonprofit, operated in the long-range interest of all breeders of Thoroughbred horses. Each year, a varying percentage of commissions earned are returned to the member-consignors.'

'But you accept consignments from nonmembers,' I said. 'Not that I wouldn't consider joining if you issued an invitation.' I leaned back. 'Mr Trenton, I came to Kentucky to stay. I expect to be offering fine yearlings for sale for a long time to come.' I smiled at him. 'It's my dearest desire to sell them through the best organization I know.'

His eyelids flickered. 'We appreciate the compliment, Miss Sage. We . . . do try to perform the best possible job for our memb . . . our consignors.'

'But you won't accept Outlaw Farm yearlings. Why?'

His voice gathered strength. 'Miss Sage, you must realize – you are not only very new in this business, you've elected to stand an unproved stallion. You really can't expect . . .'

'Let me tell you about my yearlings,' I said.

He moved his hands in warning. 'I'm not the man to convince,' he said hastily. 'I'm a businessman. Harris Harris, our chief auctioneer, is the authority in the selection process. He's one of the most knowledgeable judges of horseflesh in the world, both in terms of pedigree and in terms of conformation and conditions.'

'Then I should be talking to Harris, shouldn't I?'

Smooth, inexorable, impenetrable. 'I'm afraid he's a very busy man this time of year. I'm not even sure he's in the building . . .'

I settled myself comfortably. 'I can wait. Believe me, I have nothing more important to do.'

For the first time, remembering how I had calmly outwaited him, he looked flustered. He didn't know how to deal with a determined lady; not deal and remain the gentleman he knew himself to be.

'I'll . . . see if he can give us a few minutes,' he said reluctantly, reaching to punch a button on the telephone, turning away to speak softly.

A few minutes later, Harris Harris swung through the doorway on his crutches. Thirty years ago the hottest young jockey on the New York circuit, the first day he rode without his bug (a special weight allowance for apprentices), his mount reared over backwards in the starting gate, crushing his legs. It left him paralysed for life. But, his spirit still fiercely alive, he had started all over again at menial backside tasks, becoming in time an official clocker, one of those men with sharp eyes and accurate watches who register the official works of horses in training.

Which is the best apprenticeship in the world for a man to know a good horse when he sees one. In the off season, he did tobacco and livestock auctions, beginning as a bid spotter and eventually becoming assistant auctioneer. He had moved into Standard-bred horse sales, becoming a leading auctioneer by the time he was thirty-five. When the Daingerfield Association was organized he was named chief auctioneer.

White-haired, an enormous fan of eyebrows over deep-set brown eyes, lines carved into his hatchet-thin face. A small man, of course, but shoulders and forearms were muscled from years of negotiating his progress on crutches. The charm he exuded was as palpable as after-shave lotion. When he spoke, his voice was surprisingly deep, a controlled and flexible instrument.

'Miss Sage, I understand you're here to talk about your yearlings.'

'Yes. You're not doing right by me, turning them down with only a glance at their pedigree.'

He loaned me a charming smile. 'I'd be the last man to claim to be an infallible judge of horseflesh, Miss Sage. But – it is my responsibility to make these decisions, and I stand by them.' He lifted one thin, strong-fingered hand from a crutch to gesture. 'Understanding, of course, that next year one of your colts may make me out a liar.'

Charm, I'm afraid, often makes me bristle.

'Will you sit down and let me talk about them?' I said.

'Of course,' he said graciously, sinking into the other leather chair and deftly arranging his crutches at his side. 'Say on, Miss Sage.'

I sat silent for a moment. He was being so tolerant of my imposition. It was obvious that he considered it a waste of his valuable time to listen to this know-nothing amateur, with more money than horse sense.

'Of my eleven yearlings, my manager, Dancy Clutterbuck . . . I'm sure you know him . . . and I nominated five for the Summer Sale.'

'Yes,' Harris Harris murmured. 'A good man.'

'Then you should have some respect for his judgement. Of those we selected for your consideration, let me mention first a bay filly by Tudor Minstrel out of Twilight Glimmer, a Herbager mare. Now, that breeding is black type as far back as you want to go. Twilight Glimmer, from the female family of A Gleam and Twilight Tear, and full sister to major stakes winner Gleaming, is a stakes winner of nearly two hundred thousand. You know the sire, Tudor Minstrel. He's had out more than thirty-five stakes winners, including Kentucky Derby-winner Tomy Lee, and the best three-year-old filly of 1965, What A Treat.'

I took a deep breath. 'Last year you offered a colt and a filly by Tudor Minstrel, neither of which showed half as much black type because the dam wasn't as good. I'd like to hear an explanation of your grounds for turning down my filly.'

'I'm sorry,' Mr Harris said gently. 'The Daingerfield Association does not explain its decisions.'

A stone wall. I plunged on.

'All right. I've got a Nearctic colt. Out of Polymah by Native Dancer, which makes him brother-in-blood to Northern Dancer. Polymah is full sister to Natalma, half-sister to Cosmah, the dam of Tosmah and the sires Maribeau and Father's Image. She traces in tail-female to Mah Mahal; her dam is Almahmoud, stakes winner and a producer of stakes winners. I don't think I need to tell you about Nearctic.'

His eyes flickered. 'I'm acquainted with these pedigrees,' he murmured . . . clearly surprised that *I* was.

'Last year you sold a Nearctic filly for sixteen thousand,' I said. 'My Nearctic colt should bring more. I sent his full sister to South America last year for thirty thousand.'

'Maybe you don't need the Daingerfield Select Summer Sale,' Harris Harris said.

This was a very tough man.

'You know I do. Just like I need to understand how, without even looking at the individual, you can turn down a pedigree like that.'

Harris didn't respond. I gazed at his bladed, kindly-seeming face. It showed me nothing but attention, courtesy: stone wall.

'Talking about Maribeau, I've got a grand-looking colt by him out of Moneymusk,' I said stubbornly. 'She's a full sister to Rare Perfume, a stakes winner and producer. Moneymusk is a stakes winner, has already produced a major stakes winner in Near The Money.' I stopped. 'This isn't doing a bit of good, is it?'

Harris didn't respond. The answer was plain in his face.

'You must understand, Miss Sage, that many considerations must enter into these apparently simple decisions,' Walter Trenton said. 'I'm quite sure that one of these years you'll have the pleasure of seeing a yearling pass through our sales ring . . . if you remain in Thoroughbred breeding.'

Neither I nor Harris Harris paid attention to his glib intervention. At least I had Harris's attention now, though guarded still.

'You've studied your bloodlines, haven't you?' he said.

'For years,' I said. 'Before I even knew I'd have the opportunity to breed horses. Let me mention just one more. He's by Sir Outlaw, my own stallion, out of a War Admiral mare named Blackspur, which died the night the colt was foaled. A truly exceptional individual. Sir Outlaw, of course, hasn't proved himself yet as a sire . . . in fact, this yearling is his first get.' My eyes locked on the man's eyes. 'I defy you to look at this colt and tell me he doesn't have the quality you demand.'

Harris smiled without speaking. But I thought I detected in his thoughtful expression the faint edge of a new respect.

I kept on staring at him. 'That's all I ask. Not that you accept him. Simply that you visit Outlaw Farm, one hour of your time, to look at my Sir Outlaw colt. If you can then turn him down, I will accept your decision.'

I waited. Then I stood up, gathering my purse and gloves. I felt good. I had made my mark on Harris Harris. Maybe not Walter Trenton; but Harris knew me now. He was too honest a man to conceal it. Entirely.

Trenton was already standing. Mr Harris, gathering his crutches, came up in an agile swing of his body. Balancing, he thrust forth a hand.

'Enjoyed meeting you, Miss Sage,' he said in the warm, full voice so surprising in such a slight man. 'I can't tell you how much.'

The total charm again. But no promises.

'You must understand, Miss Sage, Mr Harris has a full schedule of visits to inspect all the yearlings proposed for the sale,' Trenton was saying. 'He's really booked solid.'

'Thank you for explaining Mr Harris's position, Mr Trenton,' I said. 'But I'd hate to think that if he can't find an hour to inspect the Sir Outlaw yearling, Mr Harris will go down in horse history as the man who passed on this colt. Because he is a champion.'

I walked to the doorway and turned, my eyes seeking Mr Harris. His eyes, under the expressive brows, accepted the challenge; a thin smile showed on his face. He inclined his head slightly, almost a bow. I smiled. I understood him. He understood me. But I didn't know, yet, whether or not he would place a crutch-mark on Outlaw Farm before the Summer Sale.

Yes, I was satisfied, in a curiously unresolved manner, with my visit to the Daingerfield Association. I had failed to penetrate the bland imperviousness of Walter Trenton, had awakened nothing in him. Perhaps there *was* nothing beneath that whisky-veined façade except another façade and then another, like a hall of mirrors, surfaces reflecting surfaces.

But Harris Harris, the crippled ex-jockey who had made himself one of the two or three renowned auctioneers of Thoroughbreds, was something else again. There had been an event of recognition between us, secret signals of challenge and response. He might, for all I knew, continue to block my charted path. But even as enemies, a bond, not of love or liking or even sexual attraction – simply mutual respect – would remain.

It was the season for breeding again, for bringing new foals into the world, and I immersed myself in the great annual rhythm. And, I must say, this time I took as much comfort in the people as in my horses and my land. Daily I knew myself fortunate.

There was a cohesion that made us a family . . . even Tiffany Thomas and Murray Steiner.

Murray came to see us at least once a week. I was glad to see him as he was anxious to see Sir Outlaw. I had long since come to recognize that he always told me the exact and utter truth, had given me precisely reasoned advice based on an intelligent study of the horse business. Relying on his integrity, on the steel-hard mind behind a liquid, courteous voice, I had come to trust him implicitly.

Besides, his intense relationship with Sir Outlaw was always good for a laugh. He loved the stallion, and he feared him; he refused to touch him, and if the horse stamped a foot or tossed his head, Murray would startle away. But he could stand for half an hour, gazing upon Sir Outlaw as though he were a work of art.

Tiffany Thomas administered the office with fanatic devotion to detail and rigid rules about the stable help wiping their feet as they came to collect their paycheque or ask an advance against next week's work. With a cheery wave of a hand, she arrived and departed each day in the yellow Volkswagen (having decided a Lincoln Continental better suited for such expeditions as my recent visit to the Association offices, I had sold it to her, and Dancy had taught her to drive). Tiffany revealed herself, with increasing confidence, as a warmer, more accessible person. She even seemed to lose something of her physical angularity, though perhaps that was only because she was eating better.

The flourishing romance between Merlin and Alice continued to progress, if minutely, at the stately pace established by Merlin. Every day of the week but one they worked side by side tending the horses, cleaning the stalls, so easy and natural with each other, laughing, finding pleasure and fulfilment in the work. At day's end, however, Merlin changed his clothes while Alice bathed and changed at the mansion and solemnly, formally, they would stroll hand-in-hand down the lane.

'It's lovely for a girl to be courted,' I remarked one night to Dancy as, from the tack-room window, we watched their departure. 'But I'm afraid Alice will be past the age of breeding by the time Merlin gets around to proposing.'

'Do you think they'll get married?'

'Is Merlin a serious man?' I retorted. 'Of course he means to marry her. But in his own good time. I've already got their wedding present settled in my mind: a title for Merlin as your assistant, along with a nice raise in salary, and one of the houses rent-free to live in.'

'You ought to name him assistant now,' Dancy said. 'He's earned it.'

'No, he's got to pop the question first,' I said, laughing.

'He ought to pop her buttons. Maybe a promotion would peed him up. If she won't, something should,' Dancy said, smiling broadly. 'You know Merlin . . . maybe he doesn't intend to propose to the girl until he's secure. Alice must be getting a little impatient.'

'She doesn't show it,' I said. 'If ever I've seen a contented girl, that's Alice.'

The new spring wrought a major step forward in courtship. Two days in advance, Merlin diffidently applied to Dancy for permission to use a pick-up truck on personal business. On Saturday night he escorted Alice to a movie in town, returning at eleven o'clock to park in the office lot and, again, walk her towards home down the lane. From then on, the Saturday-night date was incorporated into the pattern.

I took enormous satisfaction in watching their love flourish so truly. Any woman, however modern her persuasion, would secretly wish to be courted so gallantly, with such courtesy and tenderness. I wondered, sometimes, how many girls of her age were missing out on the tender memories Alice would have, once she became ensconced in Merlin's home as in his heart.

Dancy and I, personally fast friends, were also on an even keel in the owner-manager relationship. Once having accepted my commitment to the breeding nick, he proceeded to implement it with disaptch . . . though when the new purchases arrived one by one, he looked them over with a rueful countenance.

Of course, with so many horses to tend – and the help problem as chancy as ever – neither Dancy nor I had the time to hunt for War Admiral mares. After consultation with Murray Steiner, we commissioned a bloodstock agency, impressing upon them the necessity for discretion, to conduct the search nationwide, in California and Florida, Virginia and Maryland, as well as Kentucky, and even in minor breeding states such as Washington and Arkansas and Texas.

They found the mares. In December of the old year, Belle of Troienne and Gala Blue had arrived. (Even Dancy was satisfied with Belle of Troienne, for, though she had won only three out of twenty-five starts, she traced in tail-female to the great foundation mare La Troienne.) Gala Blue, undistinguished as a runner and as a breeder, had black type in her dam and granddam.

'Of course you realize, Maude,' Dancy said after inspection of the latest arrival, 'we won't be able to maintain our excellent conception rate with these mares. They're older – you have to call them problem mares – and we're going to lose some foals.'

'You can't say they aren't coming cheap, at least,' I said. 'A hell of a lot cheaper than the mares we've been buying.'

'Maude,' Dancy said ruthlessly, 'your're getting just what you paid for.' And then added, 'Unless you're dead right about the nick . . . in which case, you're stealing them.'

In January, four more arrived. Busy Blue, out of Bluelarks – a full sister to the great race mare Murtlewood, but with a stark history of barrenness – arrived in foal to Tim Tam . . . and aborted two days later. April brought three more, and in May a good stakes winner named Warspur.

So we rounded out the season with Ten War Admiral-Blue Larkspur mares available for next year's breeding. No doubt about it, they did not meet the standards we had set of owning only young mares which had, at the least, placed in stakes themselves, and preferably out of a stakes-winning dam and granddam. The average age, for another thing, was much higher, for War Admiral had died in 1959; from years of bearing foals, they were matronly and swaybacked. Only two or three, I must admit, possessed a distinguished breeding record. I comforted myself with the thought that they had been bred to the wrong stallions and revelled, with a secret excitement, in the knowledge that in only a few more years my inspiration would have come too late. I was, I told myself, rescuing the storied line from oblivion.

As I watched Outlaw Prince grow, however, I felt confirmed in the great gamble. He was a living jewel, such an outstanding individual in conformation and condition and temperament that he was already having his effect on Sir Outlaw's book. I showed him to every horseman who came to look at the stallion, as a sample of his get, and I am sure that, more often than not, the subsequent booking, when made, was influenced in large part by the colt. This year, for the first time, combining our enlarged band of broodmares and the greater number of outside engagements, it began to look as though Sir Outlaw might finish his season with a full book. I had already prepared a full-page ad. to announce the fact.

The successful acquisitions made acute the problem of selling some of the broodmares we had bought before; Murray insisted that, as I bought, I must also sell. Dancy resisted; he had himself chosen these splendid young mares of impeccable pedigree and he wanted to keep them.

'After all,' he told me over and over again, 'they'll be a second string to your bow if the breeding nick fails to materialize. You've got some great bloodlines there.' He paused shrewdly. 'Remember, they'll be foaling Sir Outlaw's second crop this year, at least ten or twelve foals if we're lucky. If we cull them now we'll have to sell the foals *in utero* . . . before we even know what they look like.'

I remained ambivalent. Uncommitted to these mares, selected with great care and purchased at large investment though they were, as I was to the, relatively speaking, undistinguished War Admiral mares, I found that the decision was like trying to decide which books to discard from your personal library – every one you considered seemed suddenly the most precious of all. Conscientiously I pondered over them, but at last fell back gratefully on Dancy's argument, convincing the dubious Mr Steiner, concerned about my financial liquidity, that it would be shortsighted to sell even one Sir Outlaw foal *in utero*.

'We can wait until fall, surely,' I said. 'The foals will be weanlings by then, so we'll have a basis on which to decide. Besides, the best way to sell mares is through the fall sales of breeding stock.'

With few mares and, consequently, intense individual attention, we had been exceptionally fortunate, so far, in getting them in foal and carrying them to successful term. This year, the larger band brought more problems. Our first experience of the new season was Busy Blue aborting her Tim Tam foal on January twenty-ninth. But in February, Turn The Cards gave birth easily to a chestnut colt by Sir Outlaw, his first foal of the new year; a good-looking youngster, though, as he developed, he toed out a bit. St Patrick's day, Outlaw Prince's real birthday – though of course he had been counted a year old since January first – was not such a happy occasion this year; Flight Medal, a Citation mare, slipped twins. We had got her cheap, though a stakes winner, because of her history of barrenness – only three reported foals out of ten years at stud – and now we were paying for it. I mentally marked her down as the first choice for dispersal . . . if we could find someone to take her off our hands.

The next week brought Sir Outlaw's first filly, out of Moneymusk. Another chestnut . . . Dancy remarked that Sir Outlaw looked to be prepotent as far as transmitting his colour was concerned, anyway. I happily agreed; chestnut is my favourite colour for a horse. Then early, on Easter Sunday, Marry The Man dropped a Sir Outlaw filly which, for the first time, did not carry on the chestnut coat . . . just to make a liar out of Dancy,

I suppose. A lovely bay filly with dark points.

This deep into spring, the War Admiral mares, unless barren, were arriving with foals at their sides. So the Big Barn was filling up, the New Barn was slowly emptying, and April was a busy month. In the last week, we lost another foal, Gala Blue dropping a dead colt by Ahoy.

These errors of nature hurt deeply, each time, as though it had never happened before. It didn't help to realize that such losses were inevitable. One is fortunate to get eighty per cent of the mares in foal; throughout the year there is the ever-constant threat of spontaneous abortion, of slipping twins; at foaling a certain attrition occurs also, foals being born dead, or twins, or so obviously incapable of viability they must be humanely put down. Nature corrects her mistakes with a cruel hand.

Even worse were the accidents. With my heart in my throat I would watch the yearlings at play, rising on their hind legs to strike at each other with lightning feints too swift for the eye to follow, whirling to kick out with strong hind legs. As they grew older they became more aggressive, and Outlaw Prince led them all. Inevitably they scarred each other; one or another would come up at evening with a filled ankle, to be treated and worried over; a flank or a shoulder would show a superficial cut that, in healing, would leave a hairless black scar.

The most heartbreaking – and fear-provoking – event occurred in April, when Dinner Music's black colt by Crewman came down with a fever. Merlin, one morning, found him listless in the stall, coat rough, head hanging. He called Dancy, who immediately summoned the vet. The colt was isolated because Doc Powers, in spite of all effort, could not diagnose the illness.

Dancy told me that a colt, like a growing boy, will often run an inexplicable high fever, only to recover within a few hours. It didn't happen this time. Merlin, drinking coffee from a thermos to stay awake, napping in the straw beside the colt when he had to close his eyes, stayed with the yearling for more than seventy-two hours straight. On the third day, when I came to see if the fever had broken, Merlin said dully, 'He died. About an hour ago. He just died.'

I looked at the boy compassionately. One would have thought, from his woebegone expression, it was his fault.

'Go home and flake out,' I said. 'We won't need you today.'

'There's so much to do,' he replied, so listlessly I ached for his hurt as well as my own.

'Flake out,' I said sternly. 'That's an order. I don't want to see you before sundown.'

We sent the carcass to the University of Kentucky Pathology Lab; the autopsy revealed an abscess as large as a soft ball in the abdominal wall, draining into the intestines. Dancy heaved a sigh of relief that it had not been a contagious disease.

To compound our loss, we failed to get Dinner Music – and she was a grand handicap mare, earner of nearly two hundred and thirty-five thousand dollars – in foal, leaving her barren for the following year. Such is the texture of hope and loss and frustration and fulfilment in the raising of Thoroughbred horses.

Because we expected to be busy at the time of the yearling sale, I held the second annual party for the orphans early in May. A great day for all; the children, with last year's memory to whet their anticipation, brought a zest to the occasion that put smiles on the face of every watching adult. After searching for him in the throng, I enquired about the boy named Whitey Dahl, thinking he might have run away, or returned to his family. No, the director told me, Whitey had flatly refused the occasion, professing absolute disinterest in Kentucky burgoo, ice-cream and cake, and Thoroughbred horses.

'Actually, I was relieved,' Reverend Tompkins admitted. 'Remember the trouble he caused last time?'

'I rather hoped he'd be here,' I said. 'He was afraid of the horses, you know. He should overcome the fear.'

'If he showed fear, it was the first time I know about . . . of anything.' He looked at me. 'Miss Sage . . . can we tell them they'll be invited back next year? It's becoming as big as Christmas for them.'

'I have no designs on replacing Santa Claus,' I said sternly – then I grinned. 'Wouldn't miss it for anything.'

May, now, and still I dwelled in the unfounded confidence that I would sell Outlaw Prince through the Daingerfield Select Summer Sale. He was ready. With careful feeding he had developed the massive hindquarters and good shoulders of his sire, and his chestnut coat, under daily grooming, glowed with its own light. He was not only a superb animal; he *knew* he was something exceptional. How many nights, before falling asleep, did I allow myself to entertain the fantasy?

His spectacular entrance into the sales ring, hip number taped to his hide, the spotlights bringing out the rich chestnut highlights; standing with alert ears, his head so much the hatcheted fineness of his sire's magnificent head, his liquid eyes gazing tranquilly upon the throng.

A stillness would come to dwell within this horse-wise gathering as each onlooker realized that he was seeing a champion. Harris Harris's voice would break the silence with a crack: 'All right, ladies and gentlemen, who's going to start him? Let me hear fifty, I won't take less than fifty thousand for the opening. Let's hear it now!'

And so the hypnotic chant would begin, the bid spotters ramping in the aisles, pulling bids with their frantic arms, their sharp yells a counterpoint to the rapid beat of the auctioneer's call. The price would climb, sixty, seventy-five, eighty, it would falter momentarily, Harris exhorting in the golden persuasion of his deep voice, the price would rise again and then again, bringing a collective gasp of astonishment as it broke over the magic mark of one hundred thousand.

Yes. I knew. I don't know how. But I did, and I was not at all surprised, one morning only two months before the sale, when Harris Harris, accompanied by two men, arrived at Outlaw Farm.

Getting out of the front seat on to his crutches, he shook my hand. 'Miss Sage, I finished earlier than expected this afternoon over at Claiborne. So I decided to stop by on the way home to take a look at the yearling you keep shoving down my craw.'

His hand was small but strong, calloused in the palm from the crutch. 'You'll have to see them all,' I said, smiling. 'I won't show you only one.'

He nodded. 'A man can't look at too many yearlings in a lifetime. If I don't see them all, I won't be able to tell what you're doing here.'

Hurrying into the office, I asked Tiffany Thomas to call Dancy from the New Barns. As I returned, an excitement quivered in me that I hoped didn't show on the surface. Make or break now; within the hour we would know.

But what if break, if the decision were negative? I understood well that if Harris Harris, on viewing Outlaw Prince, should mentally shake his head, there would be no further appeal. It was his responsibility to select the yearlings for the vendue. No one in the organization would think of questioning his call. Would I, should I, in that event, surrender? . . . sell off the mares, abandon the lease, retreat into the ease of a Florida retirement purchased with the money remaining from the aborted venture?

I wavered. The prospect was unexpectedly tempting. No more worries, no more commitment . . . to horses, to people, to the struggle against odds. I would, in any event, carry warm memories of these short years – of the allies who had rallied to my cause; of the chill Kentucky dawn in which for the first time I had gazed upon a foal to be named Outlaw Prince, had realized, so fully, what he would become.

Then, in a sudden rise of spirit, I knew myself again. No matter. I would carry on. Let Harris Harris look at my yearlings and walk away if he could. Just let him! I'd challenge the Association then, by God. A full-page conformation photograph of Outlaw Prince in every issue of the *Blood-Horse* and the *Thoroughbred Record* between now and the Summer Sale. The cutline, in staring red letters: WHY ISN'T THIS YEARLING IN THE DAINGERFIELD ASSOCIATION SELECT SUMMER SALE?

They would not be able to ignore it. Because I had learned one valuable lesson about the horse people. They needed their image of themselves so deeply that they could not bear to have their wisdom challenged. Perhaps such open warfare would ensure that never would they consent to accept an Outlaw Farm yearling. But, if Harris Harris should deny me now, I had nothing to lose.

On the other hand, the scheme might succeed. Prestige is so important in the world of the horse people. Once all the world knew, through the agency of a great Tony Leonard photograph, they would have to live with the knowledge that this grand yearling might well prove them wrong when he came to the races. That was how I had got Harris to Outlaw Farm, wasn't it?

When Dancy arrived, Harris and I were chatting amiably. Getting out the battered station wagon, he came forward to shake hands. 'Well, hello,' he said, his expression betraying a certain surprise that quirked Harris's potent eyebrows.

'Hello, Clutterbuck. Haven't seen you in a long time.' Harris nodded towards me. 'Your boss dared me to come look at her yearlings. So here I am.'

Dancy glanced towards me. I had not told him about my traffic with the Daingerfield Association.

'Be an honour to show them to you,' he said.

'Let's start with the Filly Barn,' I said. 'Dancy, drive me down. They can follow.'

In the station wagon, Dancy said, 'What's going on?'

I grinned. 'Got him here, didn't I? That's all you need to know.'

Perversely, I began the showing with the yearling fillies Dancy and I had ourselves rejected for the Summer Sale, beginning with the Khaled and going on to the Candy Spots, the Olden Times, the Crozier, reserving for the last our nominations by Vertex and Tudor Minstrel. Knowing quite well that Harris Harris had prepared himself beforehand, I did not spiel off the ritual information about bloodlines and female family, the racing and breeding records of dam and granddam, the great accomplishments of the sires. Instead, I stood silent while Dancy led them out one by one, posed them, walked them away and back again. Harris Harris, absorbed in his specialty, was equally silent.

When the Tudor Minstrel filly, the last and best of the lot, appeared, Harris, whistling softly between his teeth, contemplated her for a long moment before turning his head to nod at an assistant. The man – must have been a veterinarian – opened the filly's mouth to look at her teeth, ran a hand down each leg to the ankle, examined minutely a superficial scar on her right shoulder. Nodding to Harris, he stepped back.

'Nice one, isn't she?' I said.

'They're all in splendid condition, Miss Sage. I must congratulate you.'

'Mr Clutterbuck's doing,' I said. 'Let's see the colts now.'

We trekked to the Great Stone Barn. Merlin was waiting to see if we needed his help; Tiffany Thomas must have told him what was going on. In the same ritual of silent contemplation, he brought out the colts, beginning with Marry The Man's offspring.

'This is our other Sir Outlaw yearling,' I told Harris. 'We didn't nominate him for the sale only because we didn't think we'd be ready in time.'

He nodded in understanding. 'Bit backward, isn't he? His dam is a Prince John mare, right?'

'Yes,' Dancy said. 'Good handicap mare. Staying blood, there. But you have to be patient . . . they're slow in coming to form.'

'Sometimes the best ones are,' Harris commented. 'She'll get you some nice foals yet.'

'All right,' I said to Merlin. 'Bring out the champion.'

Outlaw Prince emerged from the barn, stepping delicately in his characteristic way. My eyes were fixed on Harris. Standing quite still, balanced forward on his crutches, he took in the totality of the magnificent colt. One of his assistants drew in his breath sharply, causing Harris to frown, beetling his eyebrows. Slowly he stumped around him on his crutches. He returned to my side, leaned forward, gazed fully again. Outlaw Prince, as Alice had so patiently taught him, had taken a perfect conformation pose, head up, ears alertly forward.

Harris nodded to his vet, who went through his close inspection of teeth and legs and feet, finishing with a quick glance to verify that the colt was an entire horse. He nodded, satisfied.

Harris turned his head. As he looked at me, his face was solemnly appreciative. 'You said the mare died.'

'Apparently a perfectly normal foaling, but before she could pass the afterbirth she began haemorrhaging.'

'Pity,' Harris said. 'War Admiral mare, wasn't she? By Blue Larkspur.'

My heart thumped. Had he discovered, so quickly?

'Yes,' Dancy said when I didn't speak. 'Blackspur was twenty, so I guess you have to figure on the risks of her age. Still, we hated to lose her, she might have given us another foal or two. She was the first broodmare we brought to Outlaw Farm.'

'Let me view the stallion, if you don't mind,' Harris Harris said. 'I saw him race once or twice . . . a real runner. But that penchant for savaging the competition . . .'

'It must have been the handling, not his temperament,' I said. 'You know how little of the wrong kind of handling it takes to ruin a Thoroughbred. At least, we've seen no signs of such temper in this yearling . . . of course, like any good one, he's got his ways.'

Harris looked at me. 'Don't we all?'

Merlin stabled the yearling and went to bring Sir Outlaw from his paddock. The stallion was heavier now, the crest of his neck thickening into an imperious curve. His belly was still tight; every morning, on being turned out, he exercised, galloping about the paddock in an excess of energy that kept him reasonably trim.

Harris Harris, after a brief but all-encompassing gaze, nodded in satisfaction. 'You can tell that's his daddy, all right. Shall we go into the office?'

'Of course,' I said, my heart suddenly painful in my chest.

'You fellows can wait in the car,' he said, turning to his assistants. 'Won't be but a few minutes.'

I led the way past Tiffany Thomas's desk into the inner sanctum. Harris Harris sat down, began slowly kneading the muscles of his right leg. For the moment the silence was oppressive.

'Bad thing for me, this time of year, all the standing around.' he complained mildly. 'I've been on these sticks since I was twenty-two years old and I still can't get used to them.'

The first time I had seen the man, I had recognized in his face the marks of long-dwelling pain. 'It can be a burden,' I said sympathetically. I smiled. 'I notice you don't let it slow you down.'

'Yes. In many ways, I've been a fortunate man.' He frowned, coming to the business at hand. 'Miss Sage, you must understand that many considerations come into our selection of yearlings for the Summer Sale. First of all, I have to think about the world-wide reputation of the sale. The selection process is all-important; the buyers must be confident, when they make the trip, that they will have the opportunity to see the finest Thoroughbred yearlings money can buy. We have established that reputation. It's my job to maintain it.'

I nodded. 'I understand that.'

'Next, I have to think about our old-time consignors, the people who created the organization in the first place, have supported it ever since.' His good voice, deep and velvet, levelled out. 'After all, this is a competitive business. *Very* competitive. We co-operate with each other; but the competition is there all the same.'

'I'm competing the best I know how,' I said evenly.

'All right. Now, let's talk about the colt. You undoubtedly know that Domino blood is not the most fashionable bloodline in Kentucky at the present time. For some years now the stirp has been fading from prominence.' He paused. 'Our buyers come to us for the best of the most desirable sires.'

'Maybe it's time the Domino line was brought back to Kentucky breeding,' I said. 'We're pretty deep in Princequillo and Nasrullah blood.'

'They've been winning the races.' For the first time today he flashed the charm at me. 'I suppose you thought all this out when you stood in the box at Daingerfield Race Track and bought Sir Outlaw from John Paul Jones.'

'No. I was saving him from being gelded.'

Harris glanced at the silent Dancy, returned his attention to me. 'I notice that your colt is inbred to Man O' War, four by three.'

'Looks like a good cross to me,' I said. 'Domino was probably the fastest horse ever to take the track; he was called the Great Miler. Man O' War could, I suppose, get any distance of ground he was asked for. Stamina on speed . . . and much soundness. That's the best you can hope for.'

'I'm not overly fond of inbreeding,' Harris said. 'Just in the nature of things, there's a lot of it in the breed. I don't feel there's any need to compound it deliberately.'

'Then you ought to encourage the establishment of a good Domino sire in Kentucky, Mr Harris,' I said quickly. 'Just to have an outcross for the Princequillos and Nasrullahs.'

I had scored a point. But was it wise? I still didn't know where we stood. The man was tough. No doubt about it. I suppose, with his responsibilities, he had to be. Well, I could be tough, too.

'You know, of course, the Blue Larkspur blood in your mare carries a cross of Domino blood through Peter Pan and Commando. Pretty far back, but it's there. So you have Domino top and bottom, crossed with Man O' War top and bottom.' He paused thoughtfully. 'By rights, there shouldn't *be* any Domino blood . . . he was at stud only two seasons before he died. The odds against a stallion getting a son capable of carrying on the line in such a short time are so astronomical I don't even want to think about it. Domino got two – Lord Domino, which established the stirp to which your stallion belongs, and Commando, which had only three seasons at stud but got three prepotent sons, Colin, Peter Pan and Ultimus . . . names appearing in the pedigrees of at least half the stakes winners of the nineteen-thirties. That's what makes your yearling's pedigree so interesting . . . old-fashioned, but interesting.'

'I can see you've gone to school on my stallion,' I said. 'And now you've seen the result. A champion yearling if there ever was one.'

'I have to think about how the buyers will view him.' His eyes sharp on my face, his tone was more forceful. 'I also have to think about my established consignors. In one sense, as members, sometimes officers, of the Association, they are my bosses. There'll be questions asked, Miss Sage. You must understand that. Not only why I accepted a yearling by a young, untried stallion which hasn't even been getting a good book of mares . . . but why I let you in. I don't like the idea of having to meet such criticism.' He paused, but only for a second. 'But, though you may be wrong about breeding, Miss Sage, you were right about one thing. I can't afford to pass on this colt.'

For an instant I felt that my voice would strangle and die in my throat. Dancy was leaning forward tensely, his eyes alight, as though he feared to believe what he had heard.

'Mr Harris, you're an honest man,' I said.

He drew his head back as sharply as the movement of a snake. Then, laughing, he relaxed. 'I'll be as honest as you think I am. I've given some thought to that challenge you issued. That's why I came to Outlaw Farm. Now that I've seen him, I don't intend to wait through his track career to find out just how wrong I was to pass on him. You see, there is one other interest – after the buyers and the consignors – I have to think about Me. I have my reputation to consider, also.'

I was joyful, a tension so utterly vanished I was only now aware of having lived with it for so long.

'I must warn you, however, you may well be disappointed,' Harris cautioned. 'A new consignor, an umproved stallion of unsought pedigree . . . Oh, he'll bring a price on looks alone. But chances are it won't be anywhere near what you're hoping for. You might do better selling at private treaty.'

'I'll take that chance. Thank you, Mr Harris. I do thank you.'

Abruptly Harris shifted his attention to Dancy. 'Clutterbuck, you're to be congratulated on your management. Well-run outfit.'

'Miss Sage makes the decisions. I just carry them out the best I know how,' Dancy said.

'How many mares you got now?'

'Twenty-four, counting the one which came in yesterday. We're thinking of getting rid of a few of the earlier purchases, so we might want to talk to you later on about the Fall Sale of breeding stock.'

'Made a few mistakes, did you?' He chuckled. 'We all do, from time to time.'

'We found our ideas changing as we went along,' Dancy said. 'I think it's important to cull your breeding stock right from the beginning.'

Harris glanced at his wristwatch and began gathering his crutches. 'I still have some time; could we see a few of the brood-mares?' He glanced at me with sudden merry eyes. 'I have a feeling I'm going to have the same fight with Miss Sage next year. So I might as well prepare.'

'I just hope you'll take my word the next time I tell you I've got a Summer Sale yearling,' I said.

He rose, swinging forward to a balance. 'By the way, the Tudor Minstrel filly . . . let me think about her tonight, I'll talk to you in the morning. I like that female family.'

I had forgotten the other candidates.

'It would be marvellous to have a filly in the sale, too,' I said happily. 'All that black type would sure look good in the catalogue.'

'You might get your feelings hurt by seeing her bring more than the colt,' Harris Harris said.

'Then why didn't you make her an "A" yearling?' I asked.

'I told you. Many considerations. But . . . if I'm going to get hung for the colt, I might as well . . .' He shrugged. 'Come on. Let's see some mares.'

We were halfway through the Big Barn before I began to suspect what was going on. Harris Harris didn't ask to have them led out individually, viewing the mares and their foals in the stalls as he stumped steadily along on the crutches.

Dancy, of course, was reciting the pedigrees. It was only after the name of War Admiral had rung in my ear half a dozen times that I glanced sharply at Harris's absorbed countenance. It showed only a calm interest, except that, the next time, he asked, 'The maternal grandsire?'

'Blue Larkspur,' Dancy said.

I wished fervently we had somehow avoided showing the mares. I had a shrewd suspicion that the man was absorbed in confirming a shrewd suspicion of his own.

At the next stall, again he asked for the maternal grandsire; from then on Dancy supplied the information automatically. So I kept hearing 'War Admiral!' and 'Blue Larkspur' over and over again.

Finished, we stood beside the cars in farewell. 'Some nice mares there,' Harris said complimentarily. He glanced towards me. 'Like that War Admiral blood, don't you?'

'They come cheaper because, in general, they're older,' I said. 'We set our sights originally on young, stakes-placed mares, at the least . . . but that's seventy thousand and up, as you well know.' I shrugged and laughed. 'Had to pull in our horns a bit, I'm afraid.'

The man was too knowledgeable for my misdirection (hell, my lie!) to have its desired effect; I remembered again how casually he had managed a tour of the broodmare barn.

'Dancy,' I said as we stood watching them leave, 'Harris is on to us.'

'Think so? I thought he just wanted to see what we'll be producing next year.'

'That's what he wanted us to think.' I brooded after the automobile. 'I just hope he keeps his mouth shut.'

'There's nothing you can do about it if he doesn't.'

'The only way we'll know the word's out is if we find the prices of War Admiral-Blue Larkspur mares suddenly going up.' I shrugged philosophically. 'We'll just have to redouble our efforts to buy our basic stock before it happens.'

'Good God, Maude, you ought to be jumping with joy about your Outlaw Prince,' Dancy said almost exasperatedly. 'Here you've already located a new worry.'

'I *am* jumping with joy,' I said soberly. 'It's all inside.' I quickened. 'What if he brings a hundred thousand, Dancy? Think of it. And it could happen!'

I felt an irresistible impulse, which I didn't try to resist; I slapped Dancy between the shoulderblades with the flat of my hand. The joyful assault startled the hell out of him. But I didn't care.

We 'shipped' to the Daingerfield Association grounds by the simple expedient of walking the two yearlings through the intervening gate. So early on a Sunday morning, the sun had scarcely shown itself above the horizon line of trees; but there was a bustle of arrival and preparation as the consignors got ready for the afternoon showing. Yesterday Dancy and Merlin had driven a pick-up truck loaded with supplies – hay and feed and straw for bedding, not to mention a bit of sour mash for prospective customers – and cleaned out the two stalls. Now they strung an orange banner with blue lettering – OUTLAW FARM – across the overhang of the shedrow.

We already knew from the catalogue that we were selling on the big night, Monday. It bothered Dancy that we were the next two hip numbers after a Raise A Native filly which was touted to bring the highest price of the sale . . . perhaps a record. Saying, 'At least the large money will be there,' I refused to be disheartened.

It was not a time for doubt. A warm, sunny morning, not too hot; the scene was lively and exciting, the handsome yearlings arriving to fill up the stalls, consignors moving and talking, looking at each other's consignments, everyone tuned to the undercurrent of anticipation. Now was the time when a breeding farm would realize its precise degree of success or failure; the labour of an entire year was on the line. The grooms were hard at work, bringing fresh buckets of water, putting out hay, tidying up their stable area with rake and shovel, steadying the yearlings in these unaccustomed surroundings with soothing hands and quiet voices. These were the reliable 'boys' (many were girls) and I watched them with envy, wishing I could hire some of them away.

'Guess we're all set,' Dancy said at last. 'I'll take Merlin home, and send Alice. Be back myself around noon unless something comes up.'

Alice arrived and, as though dissatisfied with Merlin's work, groomed Outlaw Prince and the filly all over again. The colt, I was glad to see, took the turmoil with majestic calmness. Alice experimented with walking him up and down the gravel path between the barns. He stepped out beautifully. Stabling the colt, she joined me in the lawn chairs we had fetched along for comfort.

'Tomorrow night,' I told her. 'The big night.'

'Do I lead him into the sales ring?'

I shook my head. 'They've got their own man. You'll bring the yearlings to the horse entrance in the back, hold them there until their hip numbers are called, then turn them over to the fellow. Dancy, of course, will be there to help.'

'I wish I could stay with him all the way.'

The girl was pretty today, her eyes lively, her blonde hair, tied neatly in a ponytail, clean and bright. She was dressed casually in new blue jeans and a work shirt, open on her tanned throat, and the same old scuffed hardboots. I had, myself, dressed for the occasion: a plain, gored, nubby linen skirt, pale tan, and a lovely silk beige blouse with a gallantly winged collar. Fearful it would become draggled and limp in the afternoon heat, I had prudently brought along two fresh blouses in a weekend bag.

'He knows how to handle fractious Thoroughbreds,' I said, reassuringly. 'He's led thousands of yearling into the sales ring.' I paused. 'Now, the instant the hammer falls, the yearling becomes the responsibility of the buyer. But take them in charge when they come out of the ring, lead them to their stalls, and stand watch until the buyer sends someone.'

'I hate to see Outlaw Prince sold,' Alice said wistfully. 'Who knows how they'll handle him? He's so used to . . .'

'Nobody with any sense would abuse a great colt like him,' I said. I laughed. 'Especially after laying out as much money as I expect.'

Alice went to get a Coke while I sat relaxed in the lawn chair. The stalls nearest us remained empty, so I was somewhat isolated from the burgeoning scene. No matter: I was full with achievement. Here, now, was Maude Sage, just as I had dreamed with two grand yearlings to be offered at the world's greatest sale of horseflesh. Big-money time.

Instead of pride, however, I experienced a degree of humility rare to Maude Sage. What dwelled most deeply in my mind were not my struggles to achieve this goal, but the people who had so wholeheartedly assisted me along the way. Timothy Breen first and most of all, of course; I wished he could be here today, to know the woman I had become. Maybe he was. I had a feeling he would be pleased.

Then I thought of Dancy Clutterbuck and Merlin Honeycutt and Alice Mayfield, dwelling in turn on each their excellences; they would know also the triumph of tomorrow night, for their commitment was as wholehearted as mine.

I put away the thoughts. Today was not for brooding, but for savouring.

Immediately after noon, the lookers began to arrive in force. I was ready, for Dancy had brought a picnic lunch prepared by Jan. After eating, I emerged from the tack room to find a young couple gazing at Outlaw Prince, his head thrust through the open upper half of the door, idly munching a morsel of hay.

'Hello,' I said. 'Care to view him?'

The woman smiled. A plain face but a lovely body, lean and taut. She was wearing a delicately flowered print dress that flowed on her elegant figure. Even with the tasteful effect, she was too flamboyant to be Kentucky.

'Oh, we're not buying this year,' she said. 'Made up our minds to that before we flew in. Just wanted to see the new yearlings, that's all. I love yearlings.'

Outlaw Prince hadn't been out of his stall since the last grooming. 'Let me fetch him out, anyway,' I said. 'This is one colt you won't want to miss seeing.'

'John, she's tempting me,' the young woman said, turning to glance coyly at her escort.

The young man – wearing a very traditional navy-blue blazer and expensive slacks – smiled indulgently. 'Be tempted. He's got a good head. I'd like to see the rest of him.'

I nodded to Alice. She led the colt out of the shedrow into the sunshine. His coat gleamed in the full light. I was delighted with the awed expression on the woman's face.

'Oh, he is beautiful!' she breathed.

'Walk him, Alice,' I said.

Outlaw Prince stepped out straight and true, as self-possessed as in his own paddock. Alice turned him, walked him back. The couple watched with obvious appreciation.

'Yearlings are the most beautiful things there are,' the woman said.

'I think so, too.' Recollecting myself from the sheer pleasure of first showing, I added, 'He's Sir Outlaw's first foal, out of a stakes-winning mare . . . at three, she beat colts and older horses in the Humphrey S. Finney Stakes . . . and her sire is War Admiral.' I glanced shrewdly at the woman. 'The mare died the night this colt was foaled. So this is her last. Her fillies have earned almost a million dollars.'

'That's terrible, dying like that,' she said.

'It happens. But you never get used to it.'

I nodded to Alice. She walked the colt again. Even with my concentration on the present viewers, I was acutely aware that, from a large crowd clustered some distance down the shedrow, several had turned to gaze speculatively at Outlaw Prince.

'John . . .' the woman said in a lingering tone.

'Glory, we *said* we wouldn't buy this year,' the husband said. 'We were only coming to look.'

'Then why did you give your trainer a plane ticket?' she said, laughing but with her voice showing a touch of whimful imperiousness.

He looked at her, a bit exasperated but with fond indulgence still. 'All right,' he sighed. 'I'll ask Albert to take a look. All right?'

She snuggled against his arm. 'That's all I wanted,' she said happily. 'Just let Albert know about him, that's all. It doesn't *mean* we have to buy him.' Graciously she turned to me. 'Thank you.'

'Any time,' I said. 'Tell your trainer to introduce himself when he comes around.'

They went away, and Alice returned Outlaw Prince to his stall – only for a few minutes. A sharp-featured man with one cast eye came along, shaking hands and saying he hadn't had a chance to get a good look the last time he was out, and so would I mind . . .?

Outlaw Prince was walked again and, for good measure, we also showed the filly. He studied them with absorbed attention, made cryptic notes in the blank pages of his catalogue and, politely thanking me, left without another word.

I sat down to wait. Up and down the shedrow, the yearlings were being shown continuously as the swirl of people thickened. Most, of course, had come only to enjoy the spectacle; the real prospective buyers were submerged like raisins in a cake. The crowd persisted, people departing but others arriving to keep the area constantly crowded. Across the way, an ageing movie star – I recognized her immediately – arrived in a flurry of attention to be photographed with a yearling colt. She had to be cajoled into standing close enough to the animal, to place one hand on the halter; because of her enormous picture hat, designed to shade the sun away from her famous skin, the colt had to be coaxed, too. It was, I thought, ridiculous.

Dancy arrived. 'Any lookers?'

'One couple, and another man,' I said. 'The couple might be bidders.'

'Really?'

'Kept insisting they hadn't come to buy, but the woman fell in love with Outlaw Prince, and the guy's in love with her . . . and I have an idea she's pretty used to getting her way. He's sending his trainer around. He said.'

'Great,' Dancy said. 'Want to go home, take a break?'

'Not on your life. What's going on up there?'

'That's the Raise A Native filly being offered by Fleet Run Farm. They're predicting she'll set a record price; she's sister-in-blood to Majestic Prince and Crowned Prince.'

'Crowned Prince?'

'In 1970, in the Keeneland sale, he set the record for a yearling: five hundred and ten thousand dollars. They expect her to bring over half a million, too. Why don't you go down? She's something else.'

'Think I will.'

Strolling to the edge of the crowd, I stood on tiptoe as the filly was again led out. A murmur of delight washed through the spectators. She was special, all right, a black filly with one white stocking, made delicately, yet strong in the shoulder and hip. A particularly lovely eye, I saw as she was turned and posed, tossing her head a bit nervously. Poor thing, I thought, she'll be walked a thousand times before she enters the auction ring. But that's the name of the game.

I returned to our territory. 'She'll probably fetch the money,' I said. 'If they don't wear her to a frazzle first.' I paused thoughtfully. 'Alice. Every time you walk Outlaw Prince, take him as close to that crowd as you dare. Maybe we can toll some of them up here.'

It worked. Throughout the afternoon we dealt with a steady drift of lookers – not nearly so many as the star attraction, of course. Some arrived with obvious forethought, having consulted their catalogues to seek us out – though more often to view the Tudor Minstrel filly than Outlaw Prince. But, to my gratification, nearly every time Alice walked the colt close to the throng around the Raise A Native filly, heads turned in sudden interest. Occasionally a man, a couple, would stroll down to ask, seemingly casual, to view the colt.

In the middle of the afternoon I took a tour of inspection. The crowd was enormous now, a steady murmur of excited pleasure wafting through the warm afternoon. Here and there, among the clusters of benches, were spotted Coca-Cola and Pepsi-Cola coolers. Some of the farms had set up their own entertainment centres in a convenient tack room, dispensing Bourbon, scotch, sometimes champagne, to favoured clients.

A great co-mingling of types. I recognized faces from photographs in the horse magazines, or more public prints: a well-known and very rich comedian who was much into racing; Vanderbilt and Whitney and Phipps faces from the society pages; shrewd, tight-eyed men who were the advisers to wealthy interests, or out to pinhook on their own. A scattering of foreigners in the crowd, hearty Irishmen with brogues that had apparently been greatly thickened by the transatlantic crossing, Englishmen with remote faces, Japanese always in dark-suited groups, Continental types, Latin-Americans . . .

To my delight, I ran into Paredo, accompanied this time by a dark, squat, silent man. 'Señor Paredo!' I said in surprise. 'Maude Sage, remember, Outlaw Farm? How's the Nearctic filly doing?'

'Miss Sage, I am pleased to see you,' he said warmly in his beautifully modulated English. 'She has not started yet, but we have great hopes. She had to be fired soon after we began with the serious training, so it was necessary to stop on her.'

'Too bad,' I said sympathetically.

'We think she will be ready in the fall. We still have hope she will be a good one.'

'What did you name her?'

'Arctic Anna.' Señor Paredo shrugged. 'It is not very . . . Latino . . . but it was the wish of my new daughter.'

'A good choice, it shows the Nearctic connection. Well, I wish you good luck with her. Are you buying this year?'

He smiled again. 'For my own account this time.'

'We're showing Sir Outlaw's first colt,' I said. 'Barn Number Three. You really ought to see him. There's also a nice filly by Tudor Minstrel.'

'I am again more interested in fillies,' he said. 'We have our own *haras*, you understand.'

'She's great breeding . . . female family of A Gleam and Twilight Tear. So come around when you have a moment. We'll show you two grand yearlings, give you a drink of Jack Daniel's to boot.'

'I shall be most pleased to accept your invitation,' he said, bowing precisely.

I passed on, pleased to have encountered again the imperiously handsome old man.

Here, secure in their own world, I noted, there was no observance of a social pecking order. What counted was knowledge of horseflesh; one could see a man of obviously impeccable standing in serious conversation with a blue-jeaned yearling groom; trainers in absolute ascendance over their moneyed clients, rejecting or accepting their enthusiasms with equal assurance. The ladies were out in force, dressed casually and with great care for the occasion. The real horsewomen – as opposed to those wives simply accompanying their husbands – could be spotted at a glance; they were such a special breed in their expensive but conservative clothes, their light tans, their intense and informed interest.

On the way back, I saw John Paul Jones sitting on a bench, the ubiquitous bottle of grape soda in one hand, legs braced to support his enormous belly. He was flanked by the wife, two younger and more beautiful women, and three dark-suited men, all standing and waiting while Jones rested. He was wearing a violently flowered Hawaiian shirt, gaping between buttons to show his hairy belly.

I hesitated to approach. But *what the hell*, I stopped. 'How are you, Mr Jones? Good to see you again.'

He looked up without apparent recognition. His white-rimmed eyes bulged glacially with too much pressure. A sick man, I thought involuntarily out of old experience in such matters. And, with all his wealth, all his power, he knows it.

'Maude Sage,' I continued. 'I have Sir Outlaw's first colt in the sale.'

He knew me then. I watched an inexplicable expression flow muddily across his face. Did he hate me for having engineered the purchase of the stallion? Or was he as indifferent to memory of public humiliation as he was to me?

He drank from the pop bottle, wiped his mouth with one thick hand. 'Is he a good one?' he said hoarsely.

'I think he'll be a champion.'

A subterranean movement in his system emerged as a chuckle. 'So is every other yearling here. To hear the sellers talk.'

'All I can say is, you'd be doing yourself a favour to take a look. After all, Sir Outlaw did run under your silks.'

Without moving his head, he said to one of the men – I couldn't tell which he was addressing . . . 'Let me know whether the yearling is worthwhile for me to see.'

The middle man said, 'Where are you located, Miss Sage?'

'Barn Number Three,' I said. 'You'll see our banner . . . Outlaw Farm.'

When I got back, Dancy was showing Outlaw Prince. Instead of participating, I sat down, for all of a sudden I was beginning to tire. It was more exhausting than I had realized it would be, the constant impingement of people, the ever-present need to sell the yearlings verbally as well as visually. Somewhere in this vast crowd there might be the two buyers who would race my yearlings, eventually breed them, to end either greatly gratified or abysmally disappointed in their investment. But, determined to stay to the end, it was after dark before I went wearily home. I enjoyed a healthy shot of sour mash and a long soaking in the claw-footed tub. Terribly tired. But contented, too, though I knew that this night, throughout the Bluegrass, there would be cocktail parties, large dinners, and much talk of horses, occasions in which the real selling would be done . . . and I was invited to none. I didn't care. I was in the sale, wasn't I? Nothing to worry about. Nothing at all.

That night I dreamed of Timothy Breen. Such a pleasant dream; I was still snugly ensconced in his Casey Key house. Then Mr Breen changed abruptly into Harris Harris and the dream became so terrifying I shocked awake to escape from it. Afterwards, I merged into a dreamless sleeping that held me safely until the day had arrived.

Monday morning on the grounds – there were still lookers,

though not the throngs of yesterday. My first showing was for John Paul Jones's man, who, with never a word, gazed at the colt, felt his legs and ankles, picked up his feet. He went away. Well, that's that. All you can do is try. An hour later, the great man himself made a progress down the shedrow to see Outlaw Prince.

I must admit, I felt myself singed inside with a burning excitement. A single nod of that massive head could make my fortune. The price paid would be of no real consequence; simply the feat of selling a yearling to John Paul Jones would be the real accolade.

He stood for a long time looking at the yearling before he asked, 'Temperament?'

'A kind colt,' I said. 'He's been handled with love since the day he was dropped.'

He turned ponderously, looking with patent distrust at the flimsy lawn chairs. 'Where can we sit down?'

I led the way to the tack room. His attendant satellites attempted to follow into the confined space, but with a firm hand Jones closed the door against them. Sighing, he sank into the old leather couch and regarded me.

'Got a drink of sour mash?'

'Of course. With branch water, or . . .'

'Straight shot.'

He took the jigger, contemplated it for a fraught moment. 'I'm not supposed to touch this stuff,' he observed, and tossed it back, making a gusty sound as it washed over his taste buds.

He looked at me for another long minute. 'I'd buy this yearling,' he declared. 'But . . .' He stopped to study me again. 'How good are you at keeping your mouth shut?'

'Never had any problem that way,' I told him.

He waited for another cautious minute. I was patient with the slow movement towards decision. He was not clumsy or stupid, simply careful with the power he wore like a cloak.

'I've got three doctors, and they all tell me to get out of racing,' he said finally. 'So I have to think about dispersing my stable instead of adding to it.'

'That's a shame,' I said sincerely. 'You've got one of the truly great international racing stables.'

He nodded. 'Never won the Prix de l'Arc de Triomphe. Wanted to win *that* one.' He said it without self-pity, without palpable regret. He was stating a fact of his life.

He began heaving his enormous, diseased body to a standing position. When he had succeeded, he said, 'That's the only reason I'm not buying the colt. Understand?'

Buying, said, not *bidding*. That would be his way; whenever he made a bid he bought the horse. Regardless of cost. I remembered that someone had told me once he got many runners relatively cheaply that way, because few men would venture to contest his bid.

'All right,' I said quietly. 'I understand.'

He moved towards departure. I couldn't hold back the final words. 'Mr Jones,' I said, 'I can't help but believe, though, that you're pleased I bought Sir Outlaw.'

He wheeled ponderously for the last time. I couldn't read his feeling. He merely said, 'Thank you for telling me I ought to look at the yearling,' and opened the door. With mixed emotions I watched his regally slow progress down the shedrow. I noticed two things: He walked as though his feet hurt; and he passed the Raise A Native filly without a glance.

The word that John Paul Jones had looked at Outlaw Prince must have filtered through the grounds like water through porous limestone. Suddenly we enjoyed a definite momentum of interest; not a large and lingering crowd, but a steady demand and for another hour I was engrossed in the showing.

The Raise A Native filly down the shedrow, the reigning royalty of the sale, wasn't all that busy this morning, I noticed. Everybody and his dog, having seen her yesterday, waited now for the high moment of her entrance into the sales ring. Still buoyed by the excitement of Jones's visit, I took advantage of a slack period to treat myself to another look . . . I like a grand yearling as well as the next person, whether she belongs to me or not.

Standing next to an atrociously dressed woman, I remarked, 'I don't think I've ever seen a more outstanding filly.'

'Thank you,' she said. 'Sister-in-blood to Majestic Prince, you know.' Her eyes sharpened on my face. 'Are you a buyer? . . . I'm Mrs Payson Shipwright. I'm the breeder of record.'

'Maude Sage,' I said. 'I have a couple of yearlings down the shedrow.'

'Oh,' she said. 'Yes.'

I looked at her. This was the lady whose dinner party had so thoroughly pre-empted my housewarming. It wasn't her style of dress that did it, either, I thought . . . she was much too large for the flowered print, too old for such frilliness. The blood must be terribly blue for one to wear such a thing with assurance.

'Tiffany Thomas works for me now,' I said. 'Our office manager.'

'Oh,' she said again. And again, 'Yes.' Then she added, 'The poor thing has come down terribly these last years, hasn't she?'

'She's on her way back up now,' I said. 'Really a nice woman, once you get down through all that haughtiness. Don't you think?'

'Oh, I've known Tiffany Thomas for donkey's years,' Mrs Shipwright said vaguely. 'Old Charleston family, you know.'

She was obviously becoming nervous with the prolonged conversation. 'Nice meeting you,' I said. 'If you get a chance, come down and take a look at my yearlings. I have a pretty grand colt myself.'

I retreated into my own territory before she could refuse. I had the comfortable/uncomfortable feeling that she would know me the next time she saw me; here eyes had not missed a detail.

When Dancy and Merlin arrived, shortly before the afternoon auction, I went home to rest, taking Alice along to assume charge of the barns. I wanted to sleep well, be at my best tonight. But the excitement, dormant in waiting, was strong still, and though I dutifully closed my eyes I remained alert. At two-thirty, Alice called from the Big Barn to tell me Bird War's foal by TV Lark had the colic, so I got up to check on the trouble. With Dancy absent, I took the prudent course of calling the vet. I waited until Doc Powers came, made his examination, and dosed the colt, assuring me he would undoubtedly come right by morning. After four now, too late for the nap I had counted on, so I helped Alice and the other hands bring in the mares and foals. Dancy, arriving for evening inspection, examined the sick colt while I told him that Doc Powers was coming tomorrow to examine all foals for intestinal parasites again, since he figured the colic was parasitic in origin.

'I'd better stay close tonight,' Dancy said.

'You can't miss seeing Outlaw Prince sold,' I said. 'Merlin will know to call Doc if there's need.'

'I'll have to watch from the back anyway,' Dancy said. 'Have to be there to help Alice.'

'I want you in the pavilion,' I said firmly. 'The minute Alice relinquishes the halter, come on around and sit with me.'

'All right.' He grinned out of his own suppressed excitement. 'Hate to miss it. Back there, you can only see it on closed-circuit television.'

I ate a quiet dinner and went upstairs. As I bathed and dressed, a deep feeling moved in me, as though I were a bride on her wedding night. It counted as much: Tonight I was making my debut, my formal entry into the closed world of the horse people.

Recollecting the unfashionable Mrs Payson Shipwright, I decided on a bit of daring, a really smart outfit made in Spain of an incredibly soft leather that had been treated to give it the blue of old denim. The skirt was plain, the matching jacket also, but with a high collar and broadly cuffed sleeves. To dress it up a bit I tied a silk scarf, multicoloured in delicate shades of red and blue and green, around my neck, letting the broad ends flow down the left side. With it went blue suede shoes and a bag, frankly cowhide, large enough to hold binoculars.

Dancy, wearing a blue suit and a red tie, waited beside the Lincoln Continental. His eyes bright with admiration, he said, 'Maude, every time you dress up you surprise me. Where have you been hiding *that* outfit?'

True, around the farm, I often dressed like a hobo. I laughed with pleasure, feeling in my throat the vibrato of a thrilling excitement. 'Let's go sell a yearling.'

The auction had started by the time we arrived. Since seventy-five yearlings would be offered tonight, with our two coming late in the proceedings, it didn't matter. Indeed, others were tardy in attendance; after Dancy had relinquished the car to a parking attendant, we stood aside to watch. Many in this belated throng were coming from social occasions, the women in long gowns, the men resplendent in dinner jackets. It was not, I noted, a hard-drinking crowd . . . at least not tonight. The excitement of the Select Sale was more than enough stimulation. Besides, in the tenseness of a public auction at high stakes, a cool, sober head was essential.

Dancy accompanied me inside to find our two seats; we were far in from the aisle on a middle row. 'I'll go take a look at the yearlings,' he said.

'Get back in time, now,' I warned and, as he departed, apologized my way to my seat.

Because I had made a resolution not to attend an auction until I could bring a consignment, I had never been inside the pavilion. My attention was drawn first to the platform where

Harris Harris, perched on a high swivel chair to relieve himself of the crutches, reigned in a formal black dinner jacket with unfashionably wide lapels, flanked on one side by an assistant auctioneer and a bid spotter, on the other by an announcer to read out the pertinent information on each yearling as it entered the sales ring. In the aisles were bid spotters, each wearing the poweder-blue jacket of the Daingerfield Association. The semicircular sweep of cushioned theatre seats was filling rapidly now with buyers and sellers, advisers and hangers-on, and, though there was much chatter of greetings, much turmoil of social movement, the tension hung in the air as thick as cigarette smoke. I was pleased that my yearlings were not scheduled early in the evening. Harris Harris, leaning back in his swivel chair, gazed benignly on the crowd, seemingly unperturbed by the continuing commotion of late arrivals.

As I settled myself, a handsome colt was led into the bright lights focused on the arena. The announcer intoned, 'Hip number sixty-six, dark bay or brown colt, property of Spendthrift Farm, by Never Bend out of New Lęde by Tudor Minstrel . . . half-brother to winner Arturito, out of a winning half-sister to . . .'

As he provided orally the information everyone had at their fingertips in the catalogue, I found the appropriate page and studied the black-type lines. The colt was turned and posed, turned and posed again. Suddenly he let go a cluster of droppings, piling steaming on the outdoor carpeting of the sales ring. An old Negro came arthritically forward to sweep it up into a long-handled scoop.

Harris Harris's smooth voice cut into the announcer's flow of information. 'All right, Marshall, we all know this is a good one. Now, who's gonna give me fifteen to start? Fifteen, fifteen, all right, Earl, you've got seven, I've got seb'n, seb'n, seb'n, I wanna eight, wanna eight, got eight, wanna nine, nine, nine . . .'

As he chanted the words and half-words, undulating in a hypnotizing rhythm, then suddenly picking up tempo, I could see how Harris was creating a drama, lifting the buyers into a mood conducive to offering their dead money for this splendid living animal.

In the aisles, the bid spotters were launched into their ritual, as frenzied and choreographic as a dance, the powder-blue coats strained by shoulder muscles as they pranced and gesticulated, charging halfway up the aisle, crouching with both hands beseeching a raise, triumphantly leaping like a cheerleader when they got it, their upper bodies and arms whirling rapidly as they emitted a penetrating yelp.

'Lebn, lebn, lebn, wanna wanna wanna twel, wanna twel. Little John! Are you in or out? Twel, twel, twel, wanna twel. Big Al, Whistler's got it in the back. Twel, twel, wanna twel ...'

Harris stopped. The unexpected cessation of his chant brought a hush of silence.

His voice crackled. 'Now listen, boys, you're not paying attention! I know a lot of you folks haven't seen each other since yesterday, but let's get down to business here. This is a fine colt, and all he can do is finish in the money. Now, let's get with it!'

He shifted himself in the chair, waited a moment, then said, 'Whistler has got eleven in the back. Now, if you want that fellow out there to pinhook this colt, just sit on your hands and let him get away with it. Let's go . . . lebn, lebn, gotta twelve, you've got it, Earl, not Little John, thirteen, thirteen . . .'

The tempo of the bidding picked up under Harris's exhortation, sweeping rapidly until it hung at twenty thousand. The bid spotters worked themselves into greater frenzies as Harris's voice coaxed it to twenty-one, then twenty-two. There it, stopped.

'Twenny-two, twenny-two, wanna three, wanna three . . . are you all done back there, Whistler? Wanna three, wanna three, what about your man, Earl, is he finished? I'm gonna close the gate now, twenny-two, twenny-two . . .' His hand swept down the gavel as he cried, 'All done at twenty-two, Andy's got it.'

An assistant hurried up the far aisle with the sales ticket for the successful bidder to sign as the audience relaxed into momentary ease. I sat stunned; incredible how quickly it had happened. Less than five minutes after the colt had been led into the ring, he was now being taken out to his new owner as another yearling entered on the other side.

I found myself wishing that Dancy was already with me. The successive escalations concealed by the secretiveness of their bidding, the casual lifting of a catalogue or an eyebrow, the tap of a pencil against the teeth, I had failed to spot the active bidders, had been enabled to follow the price only on the electronic bid board. Good God, I thought, we could sell Outlaw Prince in about two minutes without even knowing who bought him.

As the yearlings paraded so briefly through the ring – a Bold Bidder filly bringing twenty-seven thousand, the following colt soaring all the way to fifty thousand, then a Fleet Nasrullah filly going for only nineteen – I absorbed myself in watching Harris Harris manipulate the crowd with the supple instrument of his voice. Charming, cajoling, occasionally admonishing in lofty phrases, he held them, worked on them, chided them to a ripple of relieving laughter . . . and extracted their money. He sold over three million dollars' worth of yearlings that night, I discovered later from perusal of the sales statistics. Seventy yearlings – there were several withdrawals and I wondered, with an ache for the disappointed owners, what had happened, an injury in the stalls, a sudden fever? – were sold for an average of forty-three thousand dollars. Even without including the record-breaking filly, the average was nearly thirty-seven thousand. The lowest price for any yearling was six thousand, the only one in less than five figures.

During the middle part of the evening, attention slackened; the drawn-out tension was too much to sustain. People went in and out, fetching drinks or taking a breather in the outside corridor where they could still keep track of the action through plate-glass windows. In the press box high up in the left-hand corner, reporters rose to stretch and chat, willing now to accept the sales information belatedly after it had been typed out on long sheets.

But as the hour marched onwards towards the moment when the Raise A Native filly would take the spotlight, the anticipation became so tense it brought a hush of stillness. In an aisle seat down front I could see Mrs Payson Shipwright; during the brief pauses between yearlings she was being courted assiduously, men bending beside her to exchange discreet words, a photographer crouching to snap her picture in a sudden flare of light. Her big night. Well, one of these days it would be my turn. And I'd know how to dress for it.

The moment – and the filly – arrived. She stepped delicately into the spotlight, head nervous on a curving neck, to the accolade of utter silence. Flashbulbs flickered throughout the pavilion as the hip number flashed on the bid board.

Harris Harris underplayed it. Listening to the announcer reading the catalogue information, he gazed down upon the filly with an inscrutable expression. When the announcer was done, he thrust himself forward in the swivel chair, elbows on the high desk before him, and said quietly, 'All right, ladies and gentlemen, there she is. Who'll start her at two hundred thousand?'

All the talk, all the publicity, all the anticipation . . . She's presold, I thought, as someone bid one hundred and fifty and Harris took up the chant. But she *was* a grand filly, perfect in conformation, and that pedigree . . . Then I remembered that the previous record filly had never passed a starting gate.

The bidding rose in increments of fifty thousand, Harris intoning hypnotically, 'Two hunnerd, two hunnerd, wanta fifty, wanta fifty, two hunnerd and fifty, wanna three, gotta three, wanta fifty, got a fifty, three hunnerd and fifty . . .'

The bidding was quick, almost ecstatic. I wondered how many, caught up in the euphoria of participation in an historic moment, had already passed their previously determined limit. The bid spotters, spurred by the auctioneer's voice, gradually worked the scene to a fever, their yelps crackling, their bodies spinning. Harris was operating at the peak of his craft, and I understood now why he had started so low-key. He meant to take this one to the heights. Everyone kept twisting in their seats, seeking to know who remained in the contest. I couldn't spot a single active bidder.

Dancy slipped into the seat beside me. 'Wanted to see this one, too,' he said breathlessly.

'Who's bidding?' I whispered tensely. 'I can't tell . . .'

'One guy, I know, is operating from the press box,' Dancy said. 'Saw him as I came in. He's acting as agent for somebody, though, because I know he doesn't have this kind of money.'

'Hush,' I said intensely. 'I want to hear.'

I was as caught up in the fever as if the filly belonged to me. And, with a twang of nerves, I suddenly realized again that Outlaw Prince would be the next offering.

The bidding slowed as the figure achieved the lofty plateau of four hundred thousand. Bidders began dropping out as the incremental jumps shrank to twenty-five thousand, then to ten. At four hundred and seventy, only two bidders remained, the one in the press box, another somewhere over on the far side of the pavilion. The spotters stood quietly, for Harris Harris was now taking the bids directly.

'Four eighty, eighty, eighty, wanna ninety, ninety, you're not going to stop now are you, gi' me a ninety, got a ninety, wanna five hundred thousand!'

Incredibly sustained tension again, the chant droning, dropping in tone with the urgency, then soaring as the magic mark of half a million was reached for. Sweat gleamed on Harris's face as, refusing to drop the hammer, he coaxed and wheedled and cajoled. Finally, again, he stopped dead still.

'I'm not going to sell this champion filly for less than half a million,' he announced in clear, deliberate tones. 'Now, you've got it there on the left for ninety, so I'll ask the fellow hiding in the press box, what's ten thousand dollars at this stage of the game? Now let me hear it! It's time to put your money where your mouth is!'

Without a pause he swung into the chant: 'Ninety, ninety, wanna five, gotta have a five, fi', fi', fi', fi'.' The auction hung fire for what seemed an immeasurable time as Harris's hypnotic voice sought the breakthrough. At last, even as the chant continued, he slowly lifted the hammer in his right hand; and then, sorrowfully, he spoke.

'I hate to do it, ladies and gentlemen, but I'm closing the gate. We can't take all night to sell one filly, no matter how good she is. Four hundred and ninety thousand once. Four hundred and ninety thousand twice. Four hundred and . . .' Even as the hammer started its descent, his voice soared triumphantly. 'I got five, I got five, now let's go, boys, no time to lose your nerve now, gi' me five ten, fi' ten, wanna fi' ten.'

Another rise of triumph. 'I got five five, now gimme the ten, gimme the ten, ten, ten, ten . . .'

But that was it. Harris Harris knew it, though he continued the chant for another thirty seconds before saying, 'All done, boys? All done at five five? It's your last chance, up there in the press box. Fi', fi', fi' . . .' Almost casually he brought the hammer down, announcing with the solid crack of wood on wood, 'Sold for five hundred and five thousand dollars to Mr MacLaren Phillips.'

The tension collapsed, people began to stir in satisfied relief. Flashbulbs fired again, documenting the filly with the record price showing behind her on the bid board. There was a rush to congratulate the buyer, another rush to congratulate Mrs Shipwright, leaning broadly back in her aisle seat now, smiling graciously as she accepted the homage of her peers.

Harris wiped his face with a large white handkerchief, spoke in low tones to his assistant while he lit a cigarette, taking three quick puffs before tapping the desk with his hammer, saying, 'Now, ladies and gentlemen, pay attention. We've still got yearlings to sell tonight.'

So suddenly that it was a shock to my eyes, Outlaw Prince was in the sales ring. My heart clutching, I put my glasses on him. God, he was a grand colt! . . . and, intelligently, he knew it was his moment. Head high, feet planted firmly foursquare, he stood gleaming in the strong light, the hip number plastered to his chestnut hide. I was gripping Dancy's hand with both of mine as I listened avidly to the announcer reading out his credentials to be sold in this place.

'Hip number one hundred and twenty-eight, chestnut colt by Sir Outlaw out of Blackspur, property of Outlaw Farm. The dam is Blackspur, by War Admiral, she a stakes winner of more than one hundred and thirty-five thousand dollars, a producer of three stakes winners out of six reported foals. The granddam is Bluelarks, a Blue Larkspur mare that's a full sister to that great race mare Myrtlewood . . .'

I turned my gaze towards Harris Harris, knowing that my fate rested in his hands, his voice. In my secret heart I yearned for a hundred thousand dollars. That would be enough. More than enough. His face remained impassive as he gazed down on the chestnut colt, the cigarette between his fingers sending up a spiral of blue smoke.

'All right now, boys, this chestnut is the first get of a grand young sire, Sir Outlaw, and he's the first offering of a new consignor to the Daingerfield Association Select Summer Sale, Miss Maude Sage, owner of Outlaw Farm where Sir Outlaw is standing. A grand colt, whichever side of him you look at.'

I was thrilled to hear the words, a personal recommendation by the prestigious Mr Harris, but at the same moment I realized, with a leaden heart, that he was only stalling, trying to give the audience time to settle down. They remained in a moil, their attention wandering after the climax of a record sale, buzzing among themselves, going in and out the doors at the back, standing to talk in clusters. It was tough to follow that last act.

Harris lifted his voice in warning. 'Here we go now! I want twenty-five to start, twenny-five, twenny-five, twenny-five, who'll start him at twenny-five, all right, Little John, I'll take your fifteen, fi'teen, fi'teen . . .'

Caught into my personal drama, I sat forward, both hands clenched white-knuckled in my lap. the audience, settling down somewhat, was beginning to listen. But not hard enough. The figure, creeping agonizingly by the thousands, went to seventeen one, seventeen two, inching into the eighteen hundreds, climbing laboriously towards nineteen.

I looked at Dancy. His lips showed white. Harris Harris began asking for twenty: 'Nineteen, nineteen, gimme twenny, twenny, needa twenny . . .'

I was twisting around trying to discover where the reluctant bids were coming from. I spotted an open signal among the cluster of white hats in the last row that marked a group of Texans as Harris's voice lifted, 'Got a twenny, got a twenny . . . gi' me a one, a one, a one . . . You're out, Whistler, gi' me a twenny-one . . .'

He stopped in that startling way of his, his voice dramatic with indignation: 'Boys, you haven't been studying your lessons. Now, take another look at this grand colt and let's put the show on the road. I'm ashamed of you! Now, who'll gi' me a twenny-one, twenny-one, all right, Whistler, I've got your twenny-one, Little John, your white hat is out now, wanna two, wanna two, gotta have a two . . .'

There were only two bidders, the white hat, and someone out back.

'Oh God, he won't even reach twenty-five thousand,' I groaned to Dancy.

He stared at me. 'What reserve did you put on him?'

I was wild-eyed. 'Reserve? Not any. It didn't cross my mind we'd need . . .'

Dancy was galvanized. 'Good God, Maude, they're trying to pinhook him!'

'What's pinhooking?'

'It's stealing him, that's what it is.' His voice steadied. 'It's a tobacco-auction term. It used to mean to bid in a lot at a low figure, resell immediately for more. Now it just means to catch everyone unaware and get the horse at a bargain price. That fellow out back, he spotted this good colt coming up right after the big filly and decided it was worth a try.' He looked around. 'Just might get away with it, too.'

'What'll I do?' I whispered in an agonized voice, squeezing it through the constriction of my throat. My hands were suddenly clammy. Even as we conferred in such agitation, the hammer might fall and . . .

'Bid!' Dancy said harshly. 'Don't let them get away with it. Bid!'

The chant continued inexorably. 'Gotta two, gotta two, wanna three, three, all right, gotta five hundred from Whistler in the back, still wanna three . . .'

I signalled to the bid spotter working the nearest aisle. Little John, eyes fixed on the Texan, didn't see me. Careless of decorum, I stood up, signalling frantically. Still he ignored me.

'Wanna three, wanna three, three, are you all done up there in Texas? Three, three, can you g' me a three?'

I looked helplessly at Dancy. 'He won't take my bid,' I whispered. 'What'll I do? He won't . . .'

Dancy, rearing to his full height, plunged towards the aisle over the intervening spectators. He ran to Little John, whispered urgently into his ear. Little John's eyes suddenly switched towards me, his face doubtful. Turning, he signalled to Harris, obviously making an enquiry. Without pausing in his chant, Harris nodded. Little John spun around, leaping with sudden energy as he yelped the news of a new bidder.

Harris's voice lifted. 'Got a twenny-three, twenny-three, wanna four, four, you're out, Whistler, you're out, Texas, what you gonna do, gi' me a four, a four . . . All right, Whistler, got your four.'

I waited an instant to see if the white hat would bid. He did, taking it to twenty-four five, the unseen man in back responding with a twenty-five . . . and there it hung until I went to twenty-six. I was battling automatiaclly, unsure in my own mind where I would be willing to stop and let Outlaw Prince be sold. Dancy was again at my side, a hand clutched my arm, beseeching courage and endurance. The drama of bid and counterbid was attracting the wayward attention of the audience now that Harris had made it plain new money had entered the struggle.

I signed the sales ticket on Outlaw Prince for twenty-nine thousand dollars – of course, I'd only have to pay the commission. Texas dropped out at the twenty-six thousand level, apparently his limit, but Whistler's pinhooker proved more stubborn. At the last he descended to raises of one hundred dollars at a time, though Harris protested in vain that he couldn't take all night to auction this yearling.

When the hammer fell, I sank weakly into my seat. Wrung out, so anguished I could have wept had I been a crying woman. Again the horse people had defeated me, shown me up for an interloper, put me solidly in my place. They had nearly stolen my champion colt.

'Withdraw the filly,' I said numbly to Dancy. 'They can't have her, either.'

'Too late,' he said. 'She's already in the ring.'

'To hell with it,' I said. 'Let her go.'

Exhausted emotionally and physically, I could take little interest in the fortunes of the Tudor Minstrel filly. Without any feeling of accomplishment, though it was a decent price, I watched as the hammer fell on her at thirty-five thousand. Only later did I learn that Señor Paredo had bought her.

'Come on. Let's get out of here,' I said to Dancy.

We squeezed through to the aisle and walked around the circular corridor to the horse entrance. There I gazed almost with hatred at the faces in the crowd, wondering which man among them had worked so stubbornly in an effort to pinhook my yearling. A real Kentucky hardboot, I knew as well as if I knew his name, shrewd in the ways of horses and of horse traders, for this was where they tended to congregate.

Alice having already departed for the shedrow with the two yearlings, we followed. She waited beside Outlaw Prince's stall, her face troubled. 'I was . . . hoping he'd bring more. The filly's price was all right, but . . . Who bought him, anyway?'

'I did,' I said harshly. 'We're taking him home.'

'But . . .' She was bewildered. 'But what will you do with him?'

'Race him,' I said, my voice strong with an undiscovered reserve of strength. 'I'm going to show these damned people what kind of champion runner they wouldn't pay any kind of money for.'

'OK, Maude,' Dancy said.

'Alice, you'll have to stay until Merlin can get here. They probably won't pick up the filly until sometime in the morning. I'm taking Outlaw Prince home now.' I looked at Dancy. 'We can leave the car, let Merlin bring it when he comes.'

Opening the stall door, I snapped on a shank and led out the colt. Together, Dancy and I walked him through the parking lot towards the gate that opened on to our property. The yearling occasionally nuzzled my shoulder affectionately.

It was a long, slow journey home, Dancy and I and Outlaw Prince. We did not talk at all.

CHAPTER 3

Since we had not planned to get into racing, I knew nothing, not even theoretically, about the breaking and training of yearlings. As a result, when we began the task, I was more spectator than participant. Indeed, Dancy, who had often in his early career done his own breaking, decided it would be best to contract out the job, a decision that brought a new personality to Outlaw Farm.

Brock Walter was a forty-five-year-old ex-jockey with the lean hips of a horseman. With indulgent eating, however, his stomach had grown large on his small frame, his shoulders were stooping, heavy. Though he had had to fight a weight problem, Brock had been a successful jockey. He had a rugged, lumpy face and a wry neck – broken twice in his riding career, he told us – so that he habitually carried his head to one side, peering up so crookedly that he seemed sly and devious when, instead, he had the jarringly blunt aggressiveness of the small man.

Once having made the decision to race Outlaw Prince, we didn't sell any of the second crop, reserving the option to offer one or more next spring as two-year-olds-in-training. So we sent in a list of names to The Jockey Club – something I enjoyed working out, though it's not as easy as it sounds to choose names that haven't been used – and Dancy busied himself with conditioning our long-neglected training track.

The basic instinct of a horse, developed during the millenia of living in the wild, subject to the attacks of predators, tells him that if something gets on his back, it's there to kill him. So the idea of bearing the weight of a man – in spite of the latter thousands of years in which that weight has been his principal reason for existence – goes against the grain of a naturally spirited animal.

This beginning is a critical point of training; a yearling handled badly will never recover from it. Our Thoroughbreds, of course, were accustomed by daily handling to a basic trust in the human beings around them. Even so, it is imperative to proceed with great care and gentleness.

The day Brock Walter arrived to take up his duties, he studied each yearling painstakingly. I watched his face when he came to Outlaw Prince; all my hopes were riding on his back. Brock only nodded, however, keeping his own counsel.

So I was forced to ask, 'What do you think of this one, Mr Walter?'

He peered at me in his seemingly sly manner. Through the constricted vocal cords, his voice was harsh. 'At this stage of the game, Miss Sage, I don't allow myself to think anything. Ten thousand things can happen to a yearling, once you start to work him . . . and, in my experience, most of them will.'

'You're not much of an optimist.'

Leaning to probe at Outlaw Prince's knee with a sensitive finger, he didn't bother to turn around. 'They can buck their shins, they can bow a tendon, they can get osselets you wouldn't believe. Or . . . they don't run fast enough to be worth a dime. There's no knowing until we can get them into good enough condition to ask the question.' He turned to Dancy. 'Glad to see that you've got some of the summer-sale fat off already.'

'We've been feeding them down, turning them out a lot more,' Dancy said.

'OK. We'll start with a Chifney bit in the morning.'

That evening during sour-mash time, I said to Dancy, 'I don't like the fellow very much.'

'He's a hell of a horseman,' Dancy said. 'Good utility rider in his day. When he couldn't fight the weight any more, he did everything, walked hots, exercise boy, even held a trainer's licence for a while.'

'He's a bitter man. He just doesn't expect anything good.'

'I guess it can make a fellow that way to see his career over at thirty just because he likes to eat.' He repeated, 'A good horseman. I've known Brock a long time. He won't polish your ego, but he'll condition your yearlings as well as any man.'

Alice appeared suddenly in the doorway, surprising us because I had thought she was taking her walk with Merlin. She had changed into a white dress, though.

'Miss Maude. Can I talk to you?'

'Of course,' I said comfortably.

An awkwardness of constraint showed in her body as she came further into the room. 'Miss Maude. I've handled Outlaw Prince since he was a foal.'

'Done a good job, too,' I said. 'Wasn't your fault he didn't fetch a price at the sale.'

'Yes'm. I know. But . . .' She lifted her chin. 'I want to keep on with him.'

'How do you mean, keep on? You don't know any more than

I do about breaking and training.'

'I can ride him.' In the intensity of desire, she had lost the awkwardness of voice and posture. 'He's always been handled with good love. I'm afraid a strange boy . . . he could be ruined, Miss Maude, just ruined.'

I stared. 'Do you know how to ride?'

'I've ridden . . . quite a bit. Not in the last year, but it wouldn't be any trouble to get back into the swing. I rode in pony shows when I was a kid, then jumpers . . . I've even taken part in a few hunts.'

'Well I'll be damned,' I said. 'You knew more about horses when you came to us than you let on.'

'Yes'm, I guess so,' she said, abashed at having revealed herself. Her tone became pleading. 'So . . . can I ride him?'

'Sooner or later he'll have to carry a stranger.' I laughed. 'Unless you plan to become a lady jock, just so you can stay with him until he's retired to stud.'

'The breaking is so important,' she said, still pleading. 'I can at least get him started right.'

I looked to Dancy. 'It'll have to be up to Mr Walter, won't it?' Dancy nodded. 'Alice, it's fine with me if it's all right with him. We'll talk to Mr Walter in the morning.'

No problem. Brock heard me out, then asked casually, 'She's handled the yearlings all along? Good with them?'

'The best,' I said. 'She loves those yearlings. Especially Outlaw Prince.'

'Means we won't have to hire a boy yet,' he said. 'When we get to the riding part, we'll find out if she can handle it.' He turned to the girl. 'What do you weigh? About ninety-five?'

She blushed. 'Maybe a hundred. I can take some off . . .'

'Plenty light enough. Don't want to put too much weight too soon on these young horses.' He gazed down at his protruding stomach. 'Like me, a hundred and forty-five, wouldn't dare get on anything younger than a well-grown two-year-old. Quickest way in the world to ruin a colt. Often have to put inexperienced boys on yearlings just to keep from giving them too much weight to carry.'

First, for a couple of days, the yearlings were accustomed to the feel of a bit in their mouths by means of a Chifney bit snapped into the halter. Then Alice, carring a bridle, went one morning into Outlaw Prince's stall, Dancy and Brock alongside her. The colt pricked his ears as if to ask, Why the big crowd today? Brock spoke quietly, gentling with one hand while he snapped a shank on to the halter. Dancy had stationed himself at the other shoulder, touching the yearling with a spread-fingered hand.

'All right, Alice. Slip the bridle over the halter,' Brock said. 'Gently, now . . . don't pinch his ears. Don't want to make him head shy.'

Alice followed instructions, chatting to Outlaw Prince as she let him see the bridle, smell it with an inquisitive nose, before she slipped the bit smoothly into his mouth, the headpiece over his ears. Trusting her so greatly, the colt didn't take exception.

'Tighten up the cheek straps. Don't want the bit so loose he can get his tongue under it.'

She did so, caressing his head after she was finished. The yearling curved his neck to gaze at her. After a moment, in which the colt continued to stand quietly, Brock unsnapped the shank, freeing him from restraint. The yearling suddenly shook his head vigorously, as though hoping to make the bridle go away. He was drooling saliva from the strange taste of metal in his mouth.

Brock moved quietly out of the stall, followed by Dancy. Alice remained a few more minutes before she came out. Outlaw Prince shook his head again, ears slapping. Then, accepting the inexplicable new desire of his handlers that he wear such a thing, he took a mouthful of hay.

'He's all right,' Brock said with satisfaction. 'Now the next one.'

With Polyarctic, the task became more difficult. He fought the bridle, so Brock told Alice to take it apart. She did so, laying the headpiece carefully behind his ears, then bitting the yearling and buckling on the cheekpieces to hold it in place. The colt stood with spread legs, trembling, for fifteen minutes before Alice, with voice and hand, could calm him into relaxation.

The first day, we left the bridles on for only an hour; it wouldn't do to push them faster than their individual rate of learning. All the time they were wearing the bridles we remained in the barn, alert for signs of trouble. Then they were turned out, in their accustomed halters, and the same procedure was repeated in the Filly Barn.

I was pleased to see Brock Walter's patience. When Candy Box, our Candy Spots filly, fought desperately to avoid the bridle, he persisted until she began to sweat, then ceased the effort for the day. Later he returned to spend time with the nervous filly, talking to her, playing with her ears, accustoming her to his presence. The next morning she let Alice put on the bridle without much trouble, though she stood drenched in the sweat of fear until it was removed.

So it went, day after patient day. Once schooled to the bridle, we put a surcingle and pommel pad on their backs – a greater struggle because, for the first time in their short lives, they felt weight. It was almost comical to see how the young horses would stand trembling, so absolutely certain that the least move would cause the thing to attack them in that most vulnerable area, the crest of their necks.

After they had accepted the surcingle, Brock began teaching them, in the stall, to move under the slight weight and respond to the pressure of the bit on their tender mouths; turning the yearling first to the left, then to the right, later taking him outside to walk – the shank still fastened to the halter for more secure control – in figure eights, each alone at first, then in sets of three.

The next step, once again in the stall, was placing on their backs a saddle without stirrups. Then the final – and most critical – event in their young lives was upon them. The first yearling to bear a human being was Outlaw Prince. With Dancy and Brock at his shoulders, each with a shank in hand, Alice, chatting casually, eased herself belly down across the saddle. The colt squatted, trembling, then suddenly bucked forward. Alice patted his shoulder, still talking, while Dancy and Brock held him steady. Next, he attempted to back out from under, crowding his hips against the wall. He was sweating in the flanks, on the neck. Alice slipped down, walked around to his head, cradled it, soothing him, murmuring, telling him everything was all right, it was only old Alice.

Conditioned by countless corral scenes in western movies, I had expected violent action. But our yearlings, like most Thoroughbreds, had been hand-raised so, though they sweated and trembled, they didn't give us a hard time. In a few days Alice was sitting astride, feet in stirrups, riding easily as Dancy or Brock led the yearling in figure eights. At this time, Doc Powers X-rayed their knees, to make certain they had closed up.

'Tomorrow I can bring a couple of boys,' Brock said after studying the X-rays with Doc. 'They must get used to working in company from the very beginning.' He nodded with satisfaction. 'Now we can begin to lean them down, put some strength into them. That much closer to asking the question.'

Exactly at that time – the second day the yearlings had been taken to the training track to walk slowly around and around – Whitey Dahl, apparently by sheer instinct, chose to show up at Outlaw Farm.

I don't know exactly how I realized he was there. Leaning on the rail beside Dancy, watching the fillies come slowly around the curve – Brock stopped the set, instructing Alice on Discotex to take the inside now, and keep her mount close to the rail – when I looked around to see him standing not ten feet away.

'What are you doing here?' I asked.

Ignoring my astonishment, Whitey moved against the rail, watching the fillies.

'All right, now, pick them up a bit,' Brock called. 'Don't let them trot yet. Just faster walking, that's all.'

The set took up the quicker pace. The outside filly, Royal Ditany, began going wide, but the boy brought her deftly to hand. I looked at Whitey Dahl. Not missing a detail of the action, something bright and focused showed in his eyes.

It gave me the chance to study the boy as he stood in profile. He was wearing a pair of overalls and a shabby work shirt, collar and cuffs frayed by much washing. He had a sharp, hungry look, the mouth so thin, so angry, it made his whole face ugly. Hell of a world he's had to live in, I thought suddenly. Even with the meanness, he looked so incredibly young.

Since he had chosen not to reply, I didn't speak again. He stayed with us while the fillies, finished with the day's work, were unsaddled and washed down, Brock, with the delicate instrument of his educated fingers, checking their ankles for heat or swelling. The contract riders, still wearing their helmets, chin straps dangling, got into a battered car and departed for their next assignment.

Whitey, all this time, had remained totally absorbed in the details of the work. Now he turned to gaze after the departing automobile.

Going to Dancy's side, I nodded towards Whitey. 'Look who's with us.'

'Yeah, I saw him.'

'Apparently only interested in looking,' I said. 'Not in talking.'

'I'll find out what he wants.' Dancy, going close, stood gazing until the boy, with a defiant lift of the head, stared into his face.

'Aren't you supposed to be at the orphanage?' Dancy asked.

'I've done left that place,' Whitey Dahl said, making a scornfully obscene gesture with one hand.

Dancy glanced towards me. 'Soon as we get to the office, better call, tell them he's here.'

'Call all you want, I ain't going back there,' Whitey said. 'They can't make me go back no more.'

'But why did you come here?' I said. 'The director told me you absolutely refused to attend my lawn party last spring.'

His pale eyes moved finally to me. 'I come to ride them horses of yours.'

It surprised me. 'I thought you hated horses.'

'I don't reckon you have to fall in love with a horse to get on his back and make him run.'

'No,' Dancy said dryly. 'But it helps.'

Brock and Alice, aware of the conversation, drifted towards us. Whitey stood braced against the array of regard. Alone, I thought. Always alone. His eyes were hating us in our solidarity of attention.

'But you're afraid of them, too,' I said gently.

'I ain't afraid of nothing.'

'What do you know about riding?' Alice asked.

Whitey Dahl stared at the girl. At first he went on hating her, as he seemed to hate everyone just because, existing in his world however momentarily, they were by nature his enemies. Then his eyes changed and he was looking at her in a way no boy of his green age should know how to look at a woman.

It had its effect. Alice blushed slightly, her eyes shifting in instinctive self-defence.

'Don't know nothing,' Whitey said. 'But that pussle-gutted old fellow there could teach me, I reckon.' He grinned. 'Or maybe *you'd* like the job.'

Brock Walter, not exactly the kindliest person to come lately down Paris Pike, said, 'This pussle-gutted old fellow can teach you to keep a civil tongue in your head.'

Whitey's pale eyes found him. 'You want to try it?'

Brock moved towards him. 'Now wait a minute,' I said hastily. Whitey, instead of backing away, had taken a step forward. Both stopped, caught in the stasis of my command.

'Now listen, Whitey,' I said. 'I want you to tell me what this is all about. Apparently you've run away, with the idea of getting a job riding for Outlaw Farm. It's not all that easy. We're breaking yearlings, and they must be handled gently. You don't like horses anyway and, if you ask me, they scare you to death. So why do you want to ride?'

He turned on me the full battery of his eyes. A sudden glow there, an internal fire. 'Because,' he said, 'I aim to make a jockey.' Now I stared at him. 'Ever since that time I come here, I been following them jockeys. I've made up my mind to be one.'

'Why?'

'Because they make lots of money!' He looked again at Alice. 'They get the money and they get the clothes and they get the women.'

Now I was angry. 'Come on,' I said. 'Right now, to the office, so I can call Reverend Tompkins.'

'Wait a minute,' Brock said. I turned to him in surprise. Ever since the challenge, he had been studying the boy. 'Miss Sage, the boy has got the right build and, more important, what looks like a good pair of hands. Not to mention being mean enough to cut it. What do you think, Dancy?'

'He's young,' Dancy said doubtfully. 'Awful young. Can't tell about a kid . . . next year, for all you know, he might shoot up to six feet.' He paused. 'Does have small hands and feet. Which generally means they were naturally meant to make a small man.'

'I been little all my life,' Whitey Dahl said. 'Everybody called my daddy "Peanut". Reckon I can stay small if I want to.'

Brock shook his head sadly. 'Not as easy as you think, fellow. Been down that road myself.'

'Yeah,' Whitey said. 'I see that gut on you. You'd bring a fast horse down to a crawl, and a slow one to a standstill.'

When Brock Walter had been the only one to give him the time of day. Whitey knew how to win friends and influence people, all right. He stiffened as Brock, face suddenly red, took a jerky step nearer. Time to intervene again.

'Whitey, it's a fine thing to have an ambition, even if a fellow doesn't know how to go about following it up. But it's against the law to hire anybody under age . . . especially a boy who's run away from an orphanage. Maybe in a few more years . . .'

'What about my age?' Whitey said.

I regarded him dubiously. 'How old are you, anyway?'

'Eighteen.'

We stared at the bald-faced liar. A slender, unformed body,

taut and muscled though it was, not even peach fuzz on his upper lip. I wondered at the intensity of purpose that had induced such blatant untruth.

Brock laughed. 'Dancy, if he's already eighteen, think he might still grow to be six foot?'

Dancy laughed with him. 'Not likely. Unless he's lying.'

'Ain't lying,' Whitey Dahl said.

'Easy enough to find out,' I said, challenging him. 'You won't object to me calling the director? He told me, once, the orphanage can't keep anyone past eighteen.'

His mouth was thin as he considered the trap. Then, with a defiant lift of the head: 'All right with me. But even if he tells a lie on me, I ain't going back there. No more.'

'Come on, Dancy,' I said. 'Brock and Alice can look after the fillies.'

As we walked down the field road towards the office, I saw that, the nearer we came to the moment of truth, the more Whitey's step lagged. With all his bravado, bad manners, and belligerence, I was still sorry for him. I had, from the beginning, been vulnerable to Whitey, drawn, I suppose, by his tatterdemalion, desperately courageous, pugnacious stance. Though God knew, my sympathy, instinctive, unthought, illogical in the extreme, was probably as wasted as sympathy can be. Trying to be Whitey Dahl's friend was like trying to make a house pet out of a rattlesnake. It can be done, but only at risk.

All compassion aside, I didn't want the kid on the place. Plainly I had seen how he had looked at Alice, the mere weight of his eyes on her breasts making her blush; listened to his ruthless appraisal of Brock Walter; and knew full well he entertained as little respect for me.

Yet it was my fault he had chosen Outlaw Farm as the place to launch his career. I didn't fool myself, either, with any idea that he had been attracted by the sympathy I had shown. He had perceived it as a sentimental weakness he was fully prepared to exploit. Having created here a small Eden, I had unknowingly introduced a serpent. Making a pet of a rattlesnake . . .

Whitey let me hold the office door as he marched in, coming out of his sulk long enough to smirk at Tiffany Thomas as he passed her desk. Tiffany stared down her nose, sniffed, raised an eyebrow at me.

'A runaway from the orphanage,' I said, pausing. 'Get the director on the line, please?'

Whitey was sitting in my chair behind the desk. When he didn't rise, I said, 'Pardon me, Mr Dahl.'

Flat blue eyes, an immediate challenge. My anger blazed. 'Get the hell out of that chair!'

Satisfied with the provocation, Whitey, ostentatiously meek, said, 'Yes ma'am, Miss Sage,' but with a triumphant grin that made me angrier still.

'You sure work at it, don't you?' I said.

'Work at what?' he said innocently.

The buzzer sounded and gratefully I picked up the phone. 'Reverend Tompkins? Maude Sage here. I've got one of your boys.'

'So that's where he went,' he said. 'Just hold him until I can get there. I hope he isn't giving you too much trouble.'

'Trouble? No. A bundle of love. He's being as pleasant as he knows how, which is not very. He came to ask for a job. Says he wants to ride horses.'

'Really?' The director was interested. 'Never heard him express such an ambition.'

'How old is he? We can't consider hiring anybody under age . . .'

'Well now, let's see. He came to us when he was eight, more or less. That would put him in the vicinity of seventeen now, maybe eighteen. Never knew his birthday, you understand, so I'm only guessing.'

'He doesn't look to be a day over fifteen,' I said, astonished.

Whitey's face wore a second smirking triumph. 'I told you,' he said. He shrugged. 'Of course, you'd rather believe I was lying.'

'He claims to be eighteen,' I said into the phone.

'I don't think he's quite that. But pretty close.'

My voice came slowly. 'At any rate, you won't be able to care for him much longer.'

'Another year, maybe. We do try to find them jobs, you understand, place them in a situation where . . .'

I gazed at the evil face. It was up to me, then. Up to me. 'Listen,' I said. 'Let me call you back. All right?'

'Miss Sage,' Reverend Tompkins said earnestly, 'I couldn't advise . . .'

'I'll call back,' I said, and hung up.

Soberly, I looked at Dancy, then at Whitey. 'Well, son, he says you're about old enough.'

'Counting on catching me in a lie, wasn't you?'

I nodded soberly. 'Yes. Because I don't want to have to deal with the likes of you.'

He didn't answer.

'What makes you think you could be a successful jockey? It's a highly skilled trade.'

'I've got the build. I'm little and I'm strong, and I'm as mean as a yard dog . . . ain't a boy in that place I ain't whupped at one time or another. So all I got to do is learn how to stay on one of them animals, and make it do like I want it to do.'

Sighing, I looked at Dancy. He was impassive. I examined my feelings again. Could I, in spite of all misgivings, find it in me to deny the boy the only chance he might ever have to make something of himself? I yearned for the strength, the will, to send him away. He was nothing but trouble. And I knew full well that all I would get for my pains was an absence of gratitude. It was not in him. Never would be.

My mind so troubled, I said, 'I suppose, really, it's up to Brock Walter,' knowing even as I spoke that, in the hope the irascible Mr Walter would do the dirty work, I was evading the issue.

'He's the one who'll have to deal with him,' Dancy said.

I turned to Whitey. 'I'll leave it up to your pussle-gutted friend. Since he's in charge of breaking and training, you'd be working for him.'

Whitey stood up. 'Well, that lets *you* out, don't it? When I thought you was the boss.' With apparent indifference he added, 'I might have known.'

'You can try to persuade him,' I said sharply.

'Ain't persuading nobody,' he said. 'If you all don't know a champion jockey when you see one, I'll find somebody who does.'

'You can talk to him, can't you?' I said in exasperation. 'My God, boy, do you have to work so hard at being impossible?'

He didn't know what I was talking about. I shoved myself back from the desk. 'Come on.'

We found Brock and Alice in the Great Stone Barn, Brock watching while Alice walked Outlaw Prince up and down the aisle.

'Thought I saw him put a foot wrong this morning,' Brock said to Dancy in an absorbed voice. 'But I can't feel any heat in his ankles, and he steps out all right now.'

'That there's the one I aim to ride,' Whitey said, gazing at the handsome colt. 'I remember him.'

Alice turned sharply. 'No one rides Outlaw Prince but me.'

He grinned, the evil thought in his mind as plain as if he had spoken the words. She tried to stare him down, but her eyes faltered against the bulwark of his gaze.

'Brock, the orphanage says he's old enough, all right,' I said. 'What do you think?'

'I'd rather not have to deal with the little bastard,' Brock said calmly. But his eyes were speculative.

Without stopping to think why I was doing it, I said to Alice, 'What do *you* think? Can we make a rider out of him?'

She glanced at me, startled. Her eyes moved towards Whitey, and as quickly fled away. He was waiting with an evil confidence.

'Miss Maude, I . . . I don't think I . . .'

It occurred to me, again, that I knew nothing of her life away from Outlaw Farm. When she went down the lane at the end of a day's work, she might as well have disappeared, for all we knew, from human ken. And, I thought suddenly, I doubt that Merlin knows any more than I do.

'It's not your decision to make,' I said. 'I'd just like to hear your opinion, that's all.

She busied herself turning Outlaw Prince into his stall, unsnapping the shank, hanging it beside the door. Her troubled face concentrated on the simple movements she had performed a thousand times before.

When she answered she didn't look at me. 'I think he might become a jockey – a good one, too – if he can learn to have some respect for the horses.' She did stare at Whitey Dahl then, her firm chin lifting. 'Hating a horse, that means you're really afraid of him. A Thoroughbred can tell it . . . and as long as he can smell the fear, you won't be able to do anything with him.'

'How come you know so much?' Whitey said.

'I don't,' Alice said. 'But I know horses.'

On firm ground now, sure of herself. Whitey, unabashed, shifted deliberately into the other arena, a lewd grin warping his thin lips as his eyes explored her body in the worn blue jeans and boy's shirt.

'Figured you'd like for me to stick around,' he said. 'Me and you, we got something to talk about, ain't we?'

The sexual assault drove her into prompt retreat. 'You . . .' she said. 'I don't . . .'

'Now listen,' I said sharply. 'None of that. If you can't keep a clean mouth, you can leave now.'

Forgetting the girl, he turned. 'She thinks I can do it,' he said. 'The old jock here, he knows a real jockey when he sees one. So I guess you aim to run me off without a chance to show what I can do.' He sneered. 'I might have known. You ain't got the guts to deal with a real man, not unless'n he'll kowtow to you, saying, *Please*, *Miss Maude* and *Thank you kindly*, *Miss Maude*.' Suddenly he was looking at me as he had looked at Alice. 'Seems to me like you women could use a real man around here for a change.'

It was a shock; I knew suddenly, and intimately, the mixed emotions Alice had felt.

I didn't have time to assimilate my reaction. Because Dancy came into it, saying with controlled fury, 'Now listen, *boy* . . .'

Whitey's eyes went from me to Dancy, back again. 'So that's how it is. Well, well.'

I was seeing something in Dancy I had not seen before. But there was no time to assimilate that reaction, either. Because Dancy, in this moment, scared me.

I could only say quietly, before he moved, 'Dancy. You'd have to destroy him only if it were true.'

The words stopped Dancy, turned him. His eyes were smouldering. His mouth shaped itself in a way I had not seen before. 'Yes. I guess so. But, by God, it . . .'

I couldn't let that be spoken, either. 'Everybody hold on for one damned minute,' I said.

A blessed stillness. They looked at Whitey Dahl. I looked at Whitey Dahl. He looked at us, arrayed against him.

Did I have, I wondered, the princess complex he had accused me of? Did I require complaisant fealty, loyalty . . . gratitude? Was I seeking simply self-gratification, not at all an honest attempt to feed the hungers of this bitter, callous human being? If he had asked politely, full of sincerity and humble ambition, I wouldn't have thought of rejecting him.

I had to think about it. In nursing, had I not sought out the helpless old, had I not made myself indispensable to their fading days? Had my career of geriatric care been entirely unselfish . . . ? or had it fulfilled some unacknowledged need of my own? And these days, with my inherited millions, gathering about me a loyal band, had I not felt myself safely secure?

No! Violently I rejected the evil concept he had so perceptively presented. After all, I had a decent appreciation of good people, competent people, and I had made them my friends as well as my employees.

It would be an evil deed, I told myself, to bring this . . . this *thing* . . . into the equable orbit of my first and best man, Merlin Honeycutt. I had to look at that, too, didn't I? . . . recognize that Alice was as much attracted as repelled by the malevolent sexuality so concentrated in Whitey Dahl that it allowed him to look upon her as though he had already seen her naked. But . . . maybe Merlin needs a shaking up, I thought. He needs to know Alice better than she's let herself be known. Just as Alice needs to know herself. If there's a lust in her that seeks a Whitey Dahl . . . What good is Merlin's love, anyway, if he can't withstand competition?

I realized, as suddenly as the whole train of thought and feeling had started, that again I was evading the real issue. Did I, Maude Sage, demand kowtowing? Was it not enough to recognize the quality that Brock saw, that Alice saw: the single-minded concentration that, properly directed, could lift him into a kinder world in which he might – perhaps – become a better person?

The boy had not had a chance. Abandoned by his family, reared competently but without love, so much smaller than his peers that he had been forced to fight without giving quarter, or expecting any . . .

He had, after all, sought me out. *Me*, Maude Sage, even if only with the deliberately cynical idea of exploiting my rash sympathy.

Whitey Dahl was waiting. Then he gave up. Without a word he turned to walk away, his back rigid with contempt.

'Wait a minute.'

He stopped. He turned. But there was in him no hope that I would speak the words that would allow him to stay. What the hell, it was Outlaw Farm, wasn't it?

To Brock: 'Will you take him on?'

'I'll give it a try,' Brock said. 'If that's what you want.'

'It's up to you,' I said. 'As far as I'm concerned, he's got a job. If you'd rather not apprentice him to the saddle, he can muck out stalls, learn to be a groom.'

I looked at Whitey. No change, no softening. I hadn't expected it, had I? I looked at Alice, wondering what she felt at this moment. I couldn't tell.

Brock walked to the boy, put a hand on his upper arm, squeezed the muscle. He moved the hand to the shoulders, probing hard; turned him, looked at his thin behind.

'Are you willing to work, work hard?' he asked.

Whitey sneered at him. 'Harder than you know about work.'
Brock's voice came quietly. 'Tell me your name again, kid.'
'Dahl,' Whitey said. 'D . . . A . . . H . . . L.' The memorized rote he must have learned before he had learned to read.
'I don't want just your last name.'
'Ain't nobody never called me nothing but Whitey. What's it to you?'
Brock turned his head. 'You say he's eighteen, right?'
'Close to it, at least.'
'Whitey,' Brock said, 'when you speak to me, hang a "sir" on it. When you win your first race, you can drop the "sir" and just call me Mister Brock.'
'Shit on that crap,' Whitey said casually.
Before the words were out, Brock had pushed him hard against the wall with one thrust of an arm. Jarred, foaming with immediate rage, Whitey flew at Brock, his head butting for the vulnerable belly. Brock, quick as a cat despite his bulk, stepped aside and turned warily.
'Dancy,' I said.
Dancy didn't move. Whitey was coming again. Brock put both hands on his shoulders, holding off the raging boy. He looked at me almost pleadingly. 'You're sure he's that old?'
'I'm sure,' I said calmly. How would Brock, now that he had started it, manage to end this?
He shoved Whitey against the wall again, harder than before, and dropped his hands to signal that it was over. A mistake; Whitey's bullet head slammed into his belly, making him gasp, almost going down under the onslaught. He caught at Whitey, whirled him, following so close Whitey had no room for attack.
'Come at me one more time, I'll have to use my fists.'
Whitey, lips pale and tight, furious eyes as calm and blue as a paddock pond, paid no heed. As he started the rush, Brock slapped him solidly with an open, hard palm, the sound of the blow cracking explosively. The force of it rocked Whitey, dazing his senses. Whitey stood still, face sullen. He was not whipped. He simply recognized that Brock was too big, too strong.
Brock was panting. 'All right. That's your first lesson. Tell me that you liked it. And say "sir".'
Whitey contemplated him. 'That preacher tried for five years and couldn't make me name him "sir".'
A grudging smile. 'All right. We'll compromise, sonny. Just tell me that you liked the lesson.'
Whitey lifted his head. 'I liked the lesson, pussle-gut. And

when you're dying in an old-age home, you'll be bragging how you knew me.'

Brock, with a grimace and a small laugh, turned to me. 'When I get all that meanness out of his head and into his hands, he'll be one hell of a jock,' he said. 'Mark my words.' He contemplated the boy again. 'If he can learn something about horses. Can't tell yet whether he'll ever understand a horse any better than he understands people.'

It was something marvellous to watch the yearlings shape towards their life's task. Their minutely planned and executed training programme, tailored to fit each yearling's personality and stage of growth, was subtly strengthened day by day. As playful as ever, they were yet aware of their meaning as their minds, along with their bodies, grew into the potentiality of their destiny. Bellies became tight, the hindquarters larger, stronger, with each day of exercise; even walking, their strides were longer, more graceful, their gaits a flow of strength and grace.

Each yearling was an individual. John Domino, very upright on the fetlock joints and with straighter ankles than one would like to see, showed the earliest ability, though he had always been the smallest of the colts. Brock had him marked as an early starter in sprint races . . . of course, with the Prince John blood on his dam's side, he ought to be useful up to a mile.

Our Maribeau colt, Mari Money, was neat, well-made, with exceptionally good balance. We had good hopes, but as soon as he was asked to trot he got a puffiness in both front ankles that, left untreated, could lead to unsightly and damaging osselets – bony growth caused by a leakeage of fluid from the ankle joint. Brock immediately stopped on him and, after rubbing the ankles with a mixture of alcohol and glycerine, wrapped them in cotton and bandages. After the swelling had gone down, and the ankles were cold, he pin-fired the colt – the application of scorching heat by means of a hot iron directly to the affected area in an effort to stimulate the circulation of blood and allow the subsequent medication to penetrate – and turned him out. We'd have to wait on him for a while.

Polyarctic was well-mannered and amiable, but with a strong tendency towards laziness. He puzzled Brock; he would look at the colt each morning with a thoughtful frown. No reason why he shouldn't be a runner, except that he didn't seem much interested. Worked fairly well in company, though the boy had to keep pumping on him, but, alone, he took an acute interest in everything but the idea of moving fast around a race track.

Of the fillies, Candy Box was so flighty that, though she showed good ability, she was so often washy and sweating, there was doubt she could endure the turmoil of the race track. Impossible to make any sort of preliminary determination of what she might turn out to be, for she handled differently every day. Brock used his steadiest, most experienced boy on her.

Discotex, the chestnut Vertex filly, was much like Polyarctic in being kind to handle. But Brock had a feeling, unproved as yet because she hadn't been asked the question, that she simply didn't carry much speed. From the beginning, Royal Dittany had trouble with her legs, first getting bucked shins . . . nothing serious, for many yearlings buck shins at first training. But her left front remained particularly troublesome, so tender she would flinch if one merely pointed a finger at the area. Brock painted her legs with Antiphlogistine, laying on a thick coat, to take out the fever and soreness, then wrapped the legs in brown wrapping paper, applying over it cotton and bandages. As soon as he was sure all the heat was gone, he applied blisters to toughen her shins. But when she came back into training, she did the same thing again, only worse. Every time we got started with her, it would become necessary to stop. 'Tender Legs,' Brock called her.

So Fine was a rangy, masculine filly – making rather a misnomer of the name I had chosen – and Brock didn't put her to serious work, telling me that she probably wouldn't handle hard training until spring.

To my surprise, Olden Song, the dark-grey filly by Olden Times out of Royal Music, showed us the most. I had never particularly liked her blocky build, though she did have very good legs, exceptionally strong in forearm and gaskin, with well-laid cannon bones. She also had a temper. However, she seemed to have been born with the concept of racing engrained into her being. Strongly competitive, when her mind became set on beating the other fillies – which was every time the tack was placed on her back – she was easy to handle, except that she had to be ridden with a strong hold. She never bucked a shin, was always eager to work, and once, when the boy lost control, she made a beautiful move down the backstretch and into the turn. It gladdened Brock's heart, though he chastised the boy. He couldn't feel too bad, though, because she really wanted to run; and she never forgot what that one intransigent minute of freedom had felt like, so that Brock started galloping her long before the others simply to absorb her energy and desire.

Outlaw Prince, naturally, was of particular concern. At this stage, only Alice rode him, and the relationship between girl and colt was beautiful to see. He was besotted with love; nickering softly when she entered his stall in the mornings, curving his neck to rub his head affectionately against her shoulder, whuffing soft breaths of contentment while she groomed him. They carried on a constant conversation, Alice telling him over and over again what a great champion he would be, Outlaw Prince placidly agreeing. She would even tell him, while putting on the tack, exactly how she wanted him to work today . . . and I don't know but what the intelligent colt didn't understand every word.

Alice, far more than Brock Walter, planned and executed his training schedule. Every day, while he was being hot-walked on the mechanical walker, she would confer with Brock, detailing in minute recapitulation how the colt had felt under her during each minute of the session. Then, totally absorbed, she would go on to work out what tomorrow's training should accomplish. Listening more than he talked, Brock would nod approval.

Since Outlaw Prince was still growing, they were in agreement that he should be brought along slowly. One couldn't tell yet just how many hands he would stand once he had reached his natural size. He was a good doer, always cleaning up his oats, so Brock was content to be patient, telling me, whenever I protested that he was lagging behind Olden Song in his development, that often the best ones are slow to come to form.

'Now take Olden Song, I don't think she'll ever work around more than one turn, because she'll never learn to be rated,' he told me. 'So we might as well use her early and hard. Outlaw Prince, he's more a European horse than anything I've seen in a long time. A shame it's not practical to ship him to Ireland, where he could be pointed for the great English and French races that require bottom and durability as well as speed. He may turn out not to be well-adapted to our American style of racing, the fast breaks out of the gate and lots of early speed. You might well not know what he can do until he's four, and ready for the handicaps.'

'That's a long time to wait,' I said, thinking about the crop of

Sir Outlaw–War Admiral-mare foals coming along next year.

Brock shrugged. 'You have to let the colt tell you,' he said. 'Hurry him too much, you're likely to ruin him. Though God knows, he's as sound as a dollar used to be.'

Brock took as much care with Whitey Dahl as with Outlaw Prince. It was fascinating to watch the interplay of personality between the boy and the man. Brock, cynical and irascible, with much of the bitter hate in his soul that Whitey had lived with all his life, took the boy under his wing, to the point of sharing his mobile-home quarters. After outfitting him with boots and riding helmet and breeches out of his own pocket, he spent hours every day teaching Whitey how to ride.

Whitey concentrated on learning his trade. Actually, training yearlings is an excellent opportunity for beginning a green boy, because so much of the work is tedious walking and trotting. It gives him the chance to develop confidence as well as the skills of hand and body and mind.

Whitey Dahl could be faulted in many ways, but one could not call him stupid. Learning so quickly – he had great co-ordination and a strong, lithe body to begin with – he became impatient with Brock's restraint. Within two weeks he was talking about going over to Daingerfield Race Track to see if he could pick up a few mounts for morning works.

Brock didn't neglect a single aspect of Whitey's apprenticeship. He established a regimen of body-building, counting over Whitey as he sweated through push-ups and running-in-place and lifting light barbells. Outfitting a tack room in the Filly Barn as a training gym, including a long table he found somewhere, he gave Whitey thorough massages, his jockey-strong hands digging into the muscles of back and arms and legs, finding the sore places, instilling strength and suppleness. He even ran with the boy in sweatshirt and sneakers to encourage him in the tedious roadwork and, as a result, began to lose the 'pussle-gut' Whitey mocked him with.

A strangely symbiotic relationship; I think the man needed the boy as badly as the boy needed him. Snapping and snarling at each other like hostile dogs, their voices harsh and unforgiving, goading each other constantly to the brink of physical retaliation . . . though never again did Brock allow it to go so far. Whitey was ruthless in gibing at Brock's age and overweight and his failed ambitions, probing so accurately at the vulnerable places that he could make Brock turn white with anger. Brock was equally ruthless in his daily analysis of the boy's faults. He never allowed Whitey an inch he had not earned to the fullest degree.

But Whitey had come to learn, and learn he did, absorbing all that the older man could tell him of horse and track. Brock could not demand a performance so great that he would not strive with every atom of body and of will to accomplish. And, so often, I would see Brock watching him, when he thought Whitey was too intent to be aware, with a strange light of unwilling respect in his eyes . . . maybe even of love.

The unsatisfactory aspect of Whitey's training remained his attitude towards the horses. They were objects, not individuals, conducive to no display of affection or concern, simply vehicles for his driving ambition. It was astonishing, nevertheless, how well he came to know the yearlings. Something told him Outlaw Prince was a runner which could carry him to riches and glory and he pestered Brock continually for the opportunity to work him. Brock Walter wouldn't let him get on Outlaw Prince's back – only partly because of Alice.

'You won't get the best mounts until you can learn to appreciate them,' Brock told him. 'There's a lot more to riding than simply climbing on a horse and whipping him into his best effort. You have to know and trust and understand your mount . . . your mount must trust and understand you.'

But every time Brock Walter reverted to this mystical relationship between man and mount – a relationship that extends all the way back into prehistory, glorified in ten thousand songs and legends – I could tell that the boy's love-starved soul simply could not encompass the emotion.

It frustrated Brock. Privately he told me, 'He'll never be anything but an exercise boy unless he can learn to love his horses. The drive of hate that's in him, the ambition, can carry him only so far. Sure, he has control of these yearlings because he's strong. But once in a race, when he needs a horse to run simply because Whitey Dahl is asking him for all he's got in his heart . . . it won't be there, that's all. I can't seem to tell him that.'

Perhaps, I thought, it's an incommunicable knowledge that can emerge only from one's own depths of being . . . and many shallows were revealed in Whitey Dahl. Increasing competence bred a greater arrogance. When Brock made a rare compliment, it evoked only a smirking sneer of self-congratulation.

Whitey was using Brock Walter as he used the horses, as a vehicle for the launching of his career. It was so obvious, I began to feel sorry for Brock, regretful I had got him involved. Brock, a man burdened by his own failures, had long since become resigned to his small niche as a breaker and trainer of yearlings. No glory there, beyond the reflected illumination of knowing, occasionally, that a yearling he has trained has gone on to the winning of a stakes race.

In loving the boy, he was making himself vulnerable to almost certain betrayal. Surely he knew it; but, to give the man credit, he didn't hold back an iota of himself. Already he talked of taking out a trainer's licence so he could hold Whitey's apprentice contract.

'You see, Miss Maude, it works like this,' he explained. 'Whitey can't get his bug until a trainer will sign him to a three- or five-year contract. Without an apprentice weight allowance, a trainer has no incentive to give an inexperienced boy a mount . . . it's the only way he's got to gain experience. Of course, I'd rather place him with an established man operating a good stable; I could act as his agent in getting outside mounts. An apprentice can make money only by riding outside horses, you understand, because the contract trainer pays only a small salary with no cut of winning purses. The boy's so hungry for money he can taste it.'

'If you should decide to take out a trainer's licence, you can handle the Outlaw Farm runners,' I told Brock.

A glow of gratitude. 'That's nice to know, Miss Maude, but . . . I'd rather find you an experienced man. I know a lot of trainers, I've thought them over, but . . .' He shrugged. 'There's time yet. For the boy. And for the yearlings.'

I watched his face. 'You're going with Whitey Dahl all the way.'

He was apologetic. 'I don't know about all the way. But he's got to have somebody to look after him. God knows, mean as he is, and the way he works at it, he's gonna get his ears knocked down plenty once he goes to the track. And when he starts making money – he's never had more than a dollar in his pocket, and an apprentice with a hot hand can clean up once he starts getting good outside mounts – well, you can't expect a fellow like that to handle money sensibly. It'd be a shame to see him fritter it away as fast as he earns it.' He sighed. 'It's gone that way with a lot of jocks . . . including me.'

'You mean it can happen *that* quick?'

Brock nodded. 'Yes indeed. A boy like Whitey can suddenly

find himself earning a thousand a week if he gets the right outside mounts . . . which is the jockey agent's job. Of course, the real breakover point comes when he loses his bug. Many successful apprentices never make it as a journeyman jockey simply because, without the weight allowance, a fellow never gets another chance at winning mounts. That's when he'll need me the most, when . . .' He paused. Then, softly, he said, 'It would be a good thing to do. Because he's *got* it, Miss Maude. He's got it.'

I didn't understand how this weary, cynical, tough-mouthed man could tie himself so irrevocably to a creature like Whitey Dahl. There is so much about the human heart it is impossible to understand; one can only sense it, marvel at it, accept it.

As I did not understand Alice Mayfield. For long, now, she had seemed content with the courtship of Merlin Honeycutt. Every evening they walked hand in hand down the lane, moving slowly, absorbed in each other. Perhaps something in her yearned for a man aggressive enough to sweep her willy-nilly into full-fledged womanhood. For whatever reason, though she did not consciously encourage Whitey, she was femininely tolerant of his attentions.

He made a dead set at her. He was forever swaggering about, talking with insistent insinuation about how she couldn't fail to take notice of a man who would soon be making his first million.

'Think about it, baby,' he'd say to her. 'We'll be riding in a Cadillac, diamond rings on our fingers, and hitting all them night spots in big cities. I'll show you a *time*, baby, I'll show you a time.'

He developed a complete and explicit scenario. She would smile, turning him off by saying that she did not care for noisy nightclubs, and fancy cars never had done anything for her. But Whitey had one satisfaction: She was listening, after all, to his randy talk.

Another aspect of their relationship betrayed her fascination with the hard-minded boy. Whitey, whenever the yearlings were not being worked, was expected to put in a full day of labour. Alice taught him how to do it, for Merlin tacitly ignored his presence. As a consequence, it was Alice and Whitey working side by side these days, not Alice and Merlin . . . only partly because they were both so much more involved than Merlin in the training of the yearlings.

Whitey, of course, aware of Merlin's long-abiding love for the girl, exhibited an open contempt for what he perceived as faint-hearted competition. One evening, I noticed that he had perched himself on the rail of Sir Outlaw's paddock to watch the couple depart on their evening stroll.

'Take a look, Dancy,' I said.

Dancy got up and looked out the window. The boy, sitting the top rail as though it were a horse, his booted feet tucked under him, was wearing the riding breeches and the open-fronted white shirt, designed to show off the chest muscles, he had bought with his first wages. He even had on the riding helmet – he liked to wear it, a badge of status, even at menial tasks – and with one hand he tapped a whip against the railing, practising switching it from left to right and back again. All, of course, egotistically designed to demonstrate the large distance in attractiveness between a boy who would soon become a top jockey and a man forever engaged in the plebian tasks of raising the horses that jock would ride to glory.

'Trouble coming,' I said soberly.

Dancy nodded. 'Afraid so. Certainly made no secret of his intentions, has he?'

'What's the girl up to, anyway?' I said in exasperation. 'Surely she isn't so dumb she can't see . . .'

But that's it, I thought without trying to tell Dancy. The mysterious depths of a woman. What does she see, what does she *allow* herself to see, of her own desires? Always, at the best of times, so quiet, so secretive . . .

I observed a rigidity in Merlin's back as they passed Whitey. He returned too quickly, walking with head down, his hands stiff at his sides.

Dancy said later, 'There's nothing we can do about it, Maude. Any interference would only make matters worse.'

'I could fire Whitey Dahl, forbid him to set foot on this place again,' I said with a sudden flare of anger.

'You'd lose Brock Walter too . . . right in the middle of training. He'd go with the boy. You know that.'

'I guess you're right,' I said, sighing. 'But damn it . . . somebody ought to give that girl a talking-to.'

'If Merlin can't handle her, it's about time he found it out, isn't it?' Dancy said gently.

'Oh God, yes, you're right as rain, as usual,' I said, yet angry with my helplessness. 'If she's falling for a nasty little bastard like Whitey Dahl, what the hell would Merlin want with her, anyway?'

Trouble was brewing. Whitey Dahl was working at it. Next evening, he waited on the rail, a sneer on his face as he watched Merlin, washed and combed, wearing a clean white shirt and dress pants and black shoes, walk up the driveway towards the mansion. He waited until they returned, hand-in-hand as always, and when the pair passed him he beat the riding whip against the rail in a vicious rhythm as he carolled insolently, 'Oh, a froggy he would a-courting go, um-hum . . .'

Merlin, moving steadily beside his beloved Alice, ignored the provocation. I thought I saw Alice glance surreptitiously up into his face.

The next day, Whitey waited until they were twenty yards down the lane before he jumped down, calling after them. 'Hey, hold up a minute. I'll walk with you.'

Alice half-turned, whether in refusal or invitation one couldn't tell. Whitey ranged alongside her, his head tilted alertly for Merlin's reaction. So suddenly, it had become a threesome, the blonde girl between the small man and the large man. I waited. It was a long time before I saw the two returning without the girl. Whitey walked silently in one grassless rut, stretching his legs to keep up with Merlin's longer stride. Merlin ploughed stubbornly along, as silent as his rival. When he turned to go towards his living quarters, Whitey Dahl stood with hands on hips, watching after Merlin with a triumphant lift of the head.

Next morning, after the stock had been turned out, Merlin came into the office to ask Tiffany Thomas if I could see him. He made it very formal as he entered and took a seat; the moment I saw his face, I knew it was an important occasion.

'What is it, Merlin?' I asked.

'If it's all right with you and Mr Dancy, I'd like to take off for a while.'

'What do you mean, *take off*?' I said sharply.

His hands were uneasy. 'Well, I ain't had no time off since I come here. We've just been so busy,' he explained painfully. 'But everything's pretty well in hand, seems to me like, and so I thought I'd pay my folks a visit.'

Knowing Merlin as I did, I gazed at him for a quiet minute, pitying the boy's helpless love. But damn it, if he didn't have the gumption . . .

'Getting homesick for the mountains, I suppose.'

He was grateful for the suggestion. 'Reckon so,' he said. 'Been thinking about home a lot. It's fall, coon-hunting time.' He gazed at me with a pathetic eagerness. 'Might even get me a deer.'

Oh God, I thought. Does he really expect me to believe it?

'I thought Outlaw Farm was home to you now.'

His eyes betrayed his misery. Momentarily. Then his face took on a stubborn expression. 'Well, yes'm, it has been. But my folks, they're not much on writing letters, and so . . .'

I leaned back. 'The fact is, Merlin, you're quitting me,' I said. 'Isn't that right?'

He sat still. Reluctantly, 'Yes'm. I reckon so.'

'What the hell will you do up there in the mountains? Go back to hardscrabble farming?'

He hadn't thought about it. His hands twisted together in his lap. 'Well . . .'

I laid one hand flat on the desk. 'Merlin. You can give that little bastard a better run for the money than maybe you think you can.'

His face reddened. 'I don't know what you're talking about.'

'Come on now. Don't play dumb.'

His face got redder. But his eyes came up, unwillingly enough but brave on my face. 'She . . . likes him, Miss Maude. I can't blame her for that. He's pretty gaudy, while I . . .'

Gaudy? Whitey Dahl? I stared at the broad, honest face. Merlin was worth a gross of Whitey Dahls, even if Whitey did become the world's greatest jockey. But he didn't know it.

'He's always telling her about the money he's going to make, the places he'll take her, the good times . . .'

'You think Alice cares?'

'She listens. While I . . .' He was looking at me again. 'I won't never be anything but a horse groom.'

'No reason why you shouldn't become a farm manager eventually,' I said, my voice sharp again. 'Mr Dancy and I, we've already talked about naming you assistant manager, in case you'd like to know.'

He brightened. 'That would be nice, all right.' Immediately his spirits slumped. 'But I don't have the education. Mr Dancy has taught me a lot since I've been here. Still . . .'

'There are courses in farm management at the university.'

'It would be nice,' he said earnestly. 'So much I don't know about proper feeding, pasture management, the diseases of the horse . . .' Then, remembering his troubled resolution, 'But I don't know. Not much use to it, far as I can see.'

'Listen, how long have you know Alice Mayfield now? Pretty long time, right? And pretty well.'

Merlin nodded. 'Yes'm. But I can't understand why she'd want to . . .'

'Pay attention to Whitey Dahl?'

He didn't reply.

'There's all sorts of likings,' I said. 'Maybe she feels sorry for him, raised in an orphanage like he was. But, Merlin . . . there's a nice thing between you and Alice that Whitey can't hope to touch. Don't you believe that?'

'I *did* believe it,' he said reluctantly. 'But . . .'

'Can't you trust Alice?'

His baffled eyes told me I had found the sore place. He wanted to trust the girl as much as he loved her. But, aware of Whitey's open intentions – Whitey was not fighting love with love, but with raw sex – he wasn't sure which was most desired by Alice. So Merlin was going home.

'Well, you can quit, if that's what you want,' I said. 'But I'd be damned before I'd let the little bastard run me off without a fight. I counted you a better man than that.'

He straightened. 'I could fist-fight him, Miss Maude. But what good would that do, as long as Alice . . .'

I didn't know what to say. Merlin was a man so gentle, so courteous and kind . . . so deeply into a good love for the girl. But, being a woman, I knew also that, often, a good man isn't enough. There's something in the female heart that yearns after a callous son of a bitch who'll use her ruthlessly, treat her like dirt, toss her contemptuously away once he's finished with her. Hadn't I also, in my time, taken such a man to my heart? Would I have given a good and gentle man what I had given Tim Conti? I never had, had I? . . . before or since.

Damn women, I thought.

'Merlin, I can only tell you this. The girl's worth it. I don't know what she'll do, any more than you. No more, I think, than she knows herself. But there's one thing for sure. If you leave Outlaw Farm, you'll take away her choice. I'll tell you true, Merlin, Whitey Dahl will break her heart. If she's got a heart to break.'

I waited for an answer. There wasn't an answer, except that he stood up and walked out of the office. A minute later, he re-appeared in the doorway.

'Thank you, Miss Maude.'

I looked up at him. 'What will you do?'

He took a deep breath. 'I don't know. Just . . . be here, I guess.'

When he went away, I didn't know whether I had done the wrong thing.

Given Merlin's slow nature, things came to a head quicker than I had expected. Even when Whitey grossly intruded upon their next Saturday-night date, Merlin tolerated it. But Whitey, being Whitey Dahl, had to push too far.

The brash boy had always been physical with Alice, pressing a palm into her back between the shoulder blades, making her laugh breathlessly and twist away; flicking water while they were rubbing down the yearlings; even, at times, wrestling her playfully in a pile of straw. All in fun, of course, but so sexually provocative. Alice, though protesting, laughing, flinching from too-great familiarity, didn't seem to mind.

Late one afternoon, as the last task of the day, they were shaking a stall in the Great Stone Barn. Waiting in the tack room for Dancy to arrive for our sundowner, I heard Alice squeal and, detecting a new note of seriousness, I came out to see what was going on.

It had obviously started as another half-playful, half-sexual game. But it had turned, with the swiftness of such things, into an intent far more serious. Whitey meant to kiss her; Alice was trying to keep it on a cheerful, uncommitted level. Pinning her arms against the wall, Whitey pressed his small, strong body against her, and suddenly she was fighting him with silent determination.

Holding her imprisoned wrists high over her head, Whitey stood silent, his weight leaning into the warm curves of her body as close as if they were naked. His voice carried a low, savage note. 'Damn it, you're going to know once in your life what it's like to be kissed by a man.'

She ceased the physical struggle. Her eyes glazed, directly rebuffing, into his eyes, her only shield against violation – and I couldn't tell, as their gazes locked, whether they remained a shield.

A movement catching the corner of my eye, I turned my head. Merlin stood in the doorway. He had just entered. His face was white.

Not wanting to know, he started to turn away. Whitey pushed himself up on tiptoe – he was shorter than Alice – and laid his mouth against her mouth. She accepted the kiss. Even, for an instant, she responded, causing him to crowd his hungry flesh against her flesh. In the stillness, I could hear the harsh rhythms of their mingled breaths.

Releasing one wrist, he put the hand brutally against her breast. She gasped. Then, with the sudden release of violation, she slapped his face.

The blow echoed. For a split second Whitey stood frozen. I think, even then, nothing would have happened – Merlin was still turning away – had it not been for Whitey's instinctive response. All his life he had known the world, everyone in it, as an enemy. He wanted this girl. Maybe, in his loveless way, he even loved her. But when she struck him he couldn't help himself; with an uncontrollable instinct he doubled up his fist and hit her in the face.

The blow knocked her back against the wall. The pain, as much from surprise as from the force of the blow, drained the strength from her body. Putting an unbelieving hand against her cheek, she stared in horror. Whitey stood with legs braced, breathing hard. He had shocked, I think, even himself.

The sound that Merlin made stirred the hackles on my neck. Whitey, hearing it too, recognized the peril and turned to meet it. There was no time to defend himself before Merlin was upon him, throwing a sweeping fist that, for all the clumsiness of the blow, slammed Whitey into a corner of the stall.

Whitey was up immediately, hitting out at Merlin, finding his mark once and then again. Merlin, in spite of the counter-attack, came on, arms spread wide, seeking to corner Whitey's darting figure as he retreated desperately.

I glanced towards the girl, thinking almost spitefully, Now that you've started it, let's see how you like it. Her face showed white and strained, the bruise on her cheekbone purpling, puffing one eye.

Whitey, manoeuvring for the doorway, escaped from the stall. Merlin, rushing after, knocked him down again and flung his body down, trying to pin the smaller man. Whitey, escaping nimbly, getting to his feet, fought coolly, getting in his licks even as he gave ground.

Dancy suddenly loomed beside me. 'Want me to stop it?'

'Let it go,' I said. 'Might as well be settled now.'

Alice crept out of the stall, one hand touching her face. There was – I must admit I could understand it, for how often, these days, does a girl see two men go to battle over her? – an excitement glowing in her eyes.

It was, academically, a helluva good fight. Once Whitey had gained the clay apron outside the barn doors, he stopped retreating and mounted a clever attack of his own. Quick on his feet, he shifted in and out, his small fists peppering against Merlin's head, every flicking blow leaving its mark.

But Merlin, clumsily unschooled – I doubt, given his nature, he had ever been in a fist-fight – was unstoppable. No matter how deftly Whitey's quick fists marked him, cutting him with the sharp knuckles, spraying blood, he kept moving in. Every time he connected, in spite of his clumsiness, he hurt Whitey.

But, with Whitey's darting and swooping, Merlin was losing; sooner or later the cuts, the bleeding, would take its toll. Mountain boys are, perhaps, more accustomed to rough-and-tumble wrestling. Whether for that reason, or simply out of the frustration of attempting to combat the quicksilver slipperiness of his opponent, Merlin gave up trying to trade punches. Instead, taking the blows when he had to, covering up when he could, he waded stubbornly after the darting figure, arms spread wide to cut off another escape. Whitey was grinning now, preening, showing off for the benefit of Alice. He began feinting with his head, shifting Merlin off guard, pecking away with his left and then hitting hard with the right. He even did an Ali shuffle once or twice.

His contempt proved his undoing. Careless in the clowning, he turned his head to grin lecherously at Alice even as his left tattooed insolently into Merlin's face. Merlin suddenly grabbed his wrist, held on against Whitey's wild surge, and stumbled in to throw both arms around Whitey's waist, tumbling him to the ground.

A different story now. No matter how Whitey squirmed, Merlin kept his weight heavy on the smaller man. Every time he got the chance, one arm lifted high to pound a blow into Whitey's anguished body. They were both breathing hard, a cloud of dust rising, and Merlin grunted every time he hit Whitey. Whitey suddenly submitted, lying defenceless under the heavier Merlin, head cradled in his arms.

He was counting on Merlin's innate gentleness to yield to the implicit surrender. Perhaps he was truly signalling defeat; perhaps he was only faking it. It had no effect on Merlin. Shifting astride Whitey, pinning both elbows with his finees, he gazed almost sorrowfully into Whitey's frightened face.

He began to hit him. Slowly, ponderously, he pounded at the

enemy held helpless under his weight. Immediately it had become a terrible thing to behold, the unstoppable violence retching suddenly in my stomach, for it was awful that this great desire to kill could dwell in a man as gentle as Merlin Honeycutt.

In desperation, I turned to Dancy. In response to my plea, Dancy moved forward. He did not try to restrain Merlin physically. He merely touched him on the shoulder, saying, 'You've got him whipped Merlin. Now all you can do is kill him . . . or let him up.'

Merlin stared up at Dancy as though he had never seen him before. But the words had filtered through. Slowly almost regretfully, he got to his feet. Whitey began to scramble up, but stopped, for Merlin stood over him spraddle-legged.

Merlin gazed down on the beaten man, Whitey instinctively curling against renewed assault as he stooped. But it was only to lift Whitey to his feet.

'Listen to me, now,' Merlin said.

He stopped, because he didn't have enough wind.

'Listen to me,' he said again. 'You touch Alice again with one little finger, I will kill you.'

Whitey knew he meant it. Sullen, beaten, knowing he was beaten, he made no protest. Merlin, his face bleeding profusely from the many cuts, watched Whitey's eyes until he was sure Whitey understood. Then, shoving him away with both hands, he said, 'Get out of my sight.'

A flurry of movement from the girl. For a breathless instant I thought she was running to comfort the beaten man – as it happens in romantic movies, lose the fight and win the girl. It doesn't work that way in Kentucky, at least, where everybody likes a winner!

As Merlin stood with trembling legs braced against exhaustion, brushing one hand against his face and then staring bewildered at the blood on his fingertips, Alice came full-tilt into him, almost knocking him off balance. Instinctively his arms closed around her, as much to save himself as to support her. She put both hands to his face, crooning in love and anguish. She was trembling, too.

Gently, Merlin put her away from his bloodiness. Gently he touched her bruised face. She flinched as he probed the soreness.

'You're getting a black eye,' he said.

She laughed and cried and embraced him passionately again.

He held her, gazing over her shoulder at me and Dancy. I swear it, the boy was embarrassed to know that we were watching.

'Get yourself ready to go home,' he told Alice.

'I'm ready,' she said. 'I don't need to change. But let me wash your face first, put some stuff on it.'

His wounds attended to, they walked together down the lane . . . alone. I don't know exactly what happened afterwards; but I have a good idea, for a subdued and thoughtful Alice came to work the next morning, with a shy glance for her man, and a blush when she realized I had intercepted its meaning.

After the morning work was finished, Merlin came to the office to let me know he wanted to arrange his time to take courses at the university.

'What we talked about, farm management,' he said.

'I suppose, then, you and Alice have got everything arranged.'

'Yes'm,' he said in his grave manner. 'I reckon we have.'

'There's a house I can let you have. My wedding present.'

'Thank you, Miss Maude. But we won't want it for a while. We've decided I need some education and a better job before we can think about getting married.'

'Wouldn't it be better to get married right away?' I said, irritated all over again by his deliberate approach to the important things of life.

'I believe in first things first, Miss Maude. Alice is willing to wait.'

'Well, that's nice,' I said. 'Though I never knew it took a college education to qualify for wedlock.'

'That's how I feel like we ought to go about it. Alice agrees.'

What if another Whitey Dahl comes along? I thought. But I didn't say it. Merlin did seem to be able to deal with the Whitey Dahls.

As for Whitey, the defeat did no permanent damage. He consoled his ego, for God's sake, by having a go at Tiffany Thomas. The first time I saw him perched – booted and wearing the white shirt that showed off his small muscular chest, riding whip in hand – on the corner of her desk, I nearly blew my stack. But then, by God, seeing the dawn's early light in Tiffany's eyes, I didn't say anything.

And the first time they departed Outlaw Farm together in the VW, when I saw next morning a Tiffany Thomas translated ten years younger, with a happiness in her face and eyes softly dreaming, I congratulated myself on my rare restraint. Whitey

Dahl would have her and hurt her, but he could not steal from her anything half so precious as the experience she would gain from knowing a man.

What about Maude Sage? Through these weeks of an activity in which I had never expected to find myself engaged, the training of young horses for their racing career wearing my colours – while we conditioned them to walk and trot and gallop singly and in company, accustomed them to the startling experience of a starting gate, even made arrangements, before stopping until the new year, to take them over to Daingerfield Race Track in the early mornings to inure them to the presence of strange horses and unknown people – how was Herself doing?

I had come down to the rock bottom of something very solid. I knew, now, that I wasn't going to take the Kentucky Bluegrass by storm. I wasn't going to be accepted gradually. In fact, Kentucky didn't give a damn about me. But I could, you bet your ass, outlast them.

This was the one thought which dwelled in my being: Duration. Lasting. Putting one little thing with another little thing. Not lashing myself with the failure of the large ambition, but simply running the farm from one day to the next the very best I knew how.

We had some good horses. I had some good people. It was, I felt in a serenity of purpose somewhat alien to a restless soul, only necessary to stand firm. This I was determined to do, not in brave resolution but with a calm recognition of assets and liabilities, my failures and successes, the risks it was necessary to undertake.

So, in my way, I was as directed, as ruthless, as Whitey Dahl . . . I had little of the gentleness of Merlin, the solid quietude of Dancy. And, Jesus knows, not the shining beauty of Sir Outlaw and his great son, Outlaw Prince. But it was up to me to hold it all together, make Outlaw Farm amount to more than the sum of its parts.

It was just at this point of serenity and inward confidence that I began to make a fool of myself.

CHAPTER 4

November when the man came: the slack season. Last spring's foals are now weanlings, having suffered in October through the traumatic experience of being separated from mother and mother's milk. Wearing their winter coats, shaggy and warm, they romp in the paddocks on ungainly legs, or turn tail to an icy north wind until brought into the warmth of the barns.

The pregnant mares, rough-coated too, are beginning to round out their bellies. Only routine care is required. More attention is paid to the barren mares; they are cultured to determine if the vaginal tracts are clean, for, while waiting for the pregnant mares to foal, the first effort of next spring will be devoted to stopping successfully these failures of last year. All over again, Dancy and I ponder aloud the question of putting the barren mares under lights in January in order to start their ovulation cycle earlier than nature provides. Dancy, as ever, is opposed to such artificial stimulation; it is his conviction that the use of fluorescent lights does not lengthen the breeding season, only moves it up in time.

The yearlings, after preliminary breaking and training, have been turned out to grow through the next stage of maturation. Brock Walter has departed, taking Whitey Dahl to Hialeah in Florida so that he can continue his apprenticeship, at least to the extent of a heavy schedule of morning works if he cannot find a trainer willing to sign his apprentice contract. They will return after the first of the year, when the yearlings will have become two-year-olds, ready, for better or worse, to enter serious training.

It is also a time for maintenance and repair. Dancy and Merlin work daily with the maintenance man, painting when the weather allows, replacing weak or broken railings in the paddock fences. The weather so often bad, we go about in heavy coats and gloves, and Tiffany Thomas insists that the mud on our boots must be scraped off before entering her clean office . . . no exceptions, not even Miss Maude. We suffer through days of dreary rain, wishing it would snow instead; the Kentucky Bluegrass is enchanting when the paddocks glow with the luminous white presence. The weanlings and yearlings are as excited by first snow as schoolboys, they snuff at it, paw at it, throw their heads high to race in curveting circuits, their deep-cut nostrils blowing puffs of white vapour.

We had long since become accustomed to visitors, greeting them always with patient courtesy even if only tourists. So it was no surprise to note a Mercedez-Benz roadster tooling up the driveway late one cold and sunny afternoon, nor to see a foreign gentleman alight from it. Just emerging from the office, I paused to greet the stranger.

'Miss Maude Sage?' he enquired, a subtle lilt in his voice betraying his astonished delight to encounter such a lovely lady on such a lovely day.

'Yeah,' I said. 'Welcome to Outlaw Farm.'

He bowed over my hand. 'Allow me to introduce myself. I am Count Gracchi.' He tendered me a brilliant smile. 'But my friends call me Tony.' He was still holding my hand, his fingers warm and strong. 'I shall insist that you will call me Tony.'

Well, I thought, Count Tony comes on pretty strong, don't he? That's the Italian way.

The subtly warm intonation of his tone insisted that I was a desirable woman. My smile was warmer, my voice more responsive, as I withdrew my hand to thrust it safely into a coat pocket. I was acutely conscious that, today of all days, I was wearing shapeless blue jeans.

'OK, Tony,' I said. 'Did you come to look at my stallion?'

He made an expansive gesture with both hands. 'I have come to look at *everything*,' he exclaimed. 'Since I arrived from Palm Beach with Mr and Mrs Shipwright last week, I have heard nothing but what a showplace you are creating here. So . . . Count Gracchi must see for himself.'

'I rather doubt you've heard all that much good about this farm,' I said dryly. 'Not in Kentucky, at any rate. But I'll show you around.'

I studied the gallant liar a bit more critically. He was tall and very lean, his thin, handsome face of that indeterminate age between thirty-five and fifty-five. His nose was absolutely Roman, an arrogant, classic line, and the ascetic spareness of his cheekbones was belied by a small, full-lipped, sensuous mouth. His head, bare to the cold, was high and narrow, wings of grey hair brushed carefully over the ears. His black eyes were gay, almost sparkling with aliveness.

He was wearing a canvas-coloured coat with a fur collar that lapped broadly over his shoulders. It came only to his knees, showing the legs of trousers in a subdued plaid, obviously a bit thin for a Kentucky winter . . . a bit too colourful, as well. Florida, no doubt. Palm Beach. His narrow feet were shod in sharp-toed shoes that were glossily black. He limped slightly, undoubtedly the reason for the Malacca cane. It looked too fragile to be of much practical use.

He had continued talking. 'But of course, Miss Sage. Mrs Shipwright, she has spoken many words of you. You saw, of course, her great filly at the Summer Sale.'

'Yes,' I said curtly. 'Come along, if you want to see the place.'

He walked eagerly at my side, gazing down with a glow of excitement and approval in his black eyes. 'I have heard *all* about you, you know,' he proclaimed. 'Were you not the heiress of the great Timothy Breen? I have been a guest in his house on Casey Key in Florida, not once but three times. A wonderful man, Mr Timothy, I must tell you, we talked for hours, there was nothing he did not know.' He glowed at me. 'It is a pity we did not meet at that time.'

'You knew Timothy?' I said, warming to him. 'Yes, he was a marvellous man.'

He shrugged, grimaced. 'But a boat person. I would fault him only in that. Yachts have always made me seasick, I am telling you now a dark secret of my life, and he cared nothing for horses. I have always cared for horses. On my grandfather's estate in Italy, we had always horses.'

We were now inside the Great Stone Barn to view Sir Outlaw, brought in early from the paddock because of the cold. His nose in the feed trough, he raised his head, dribbling oats.

'A magnificent animal,' Count Gracchi announced. He laughed. 'I have heard how you purchased him from the great Mr Jones.' He glanced slyly at me. 'Mr John Paul Jones has a yacht so large that even I am not sick to the stomach while aboard. I was with him last season on the Riviera. I can deeply admire a woman with the courage to buy a stallion from John Paul Jones in the manner that you accomplished.'

'He meant to geld him!' I said. 'The very idea made me so mad I couldn't see straight. So . . . I bought him.'

'A million dollars is ever a gallant gesture,' Count Gracchi said. 'Your patron Mr Breen would have been proud.'

A warm glow again. I had always believed it, too.

'Let me show you his first son.'

We walked down to Outlaw Prince's stall. Alice was with the colt, through for the day but chatting in farewell while she waited for Merlin. I asked her to lead him out.

The Count became intently silent. I watched his face, wondering just how well he knew horses. Until now he had paid more attention to me than anything else.

He watched Alice walk the colt away, back again. 'You will race him?'

'Yes,' I said. 'I didn't mean to, but that's the plan now.'

'Let me know,' he said. 'I shall have a large bet when he goes to break his maiden.'

I looked at Count Gracchi. So he knew his horseflesh. 'He's out of a War Admiral mare by Blue Larkspur,' I said. 'She died. But I have other mares with the same bloodlines.'

A quiet moment. 'Yes. It is certainly worth trying again.' He turned to the colt. 'It is perhaps a good thing that you did not lose him at the sale.'

I wondered why Count Gracchi had done so much homework; though probably he had only acquired the current gossip. A social man, apparently a perennial house guest, he would be avidly interested in gossip.

'Come on, let me show you the mares.'

I expected to encounter Dancy, but we seemed to be progressing just behind his regular round of evening inspection. Count Gracchi was particularly interested in the War Admiral mares, and stated that he meant to return in the spring, unless he happened to be in Europe, in order to see their Sir Outlaw foals.

As we were returning down the hill to the Great Stone Barn, his foot slipped in mud and instinctively I grabbed his arm to aid his balance. He floundered for a moment, stabbing at the ground with the Malacca cane, one hand clutching at my shoulder. It was unexpectedly fierce in its grasping need.

Again secure, he smiled apologetically. 'I am sorry. It is my poor leg. So often, at the best of times, it betrays me.'

'Did you hurt it riding?'

'No . . . though I was a great rider, the most difficult jumps held no terrors for my youthful foolhardiness.' He grimaced. 'It is a wound from the war.'

'Oh,' I said. 'I'm sorry.'

He laughed lightly. 'Not a very gallant war wound, I fear.' We were going on, the Count picking his way gingerly. I noticed he had got mud on his elegant shoes . . . he should have been wearing boots.

'How did it happen? Or would you rather not . . .'

'Oh, it is an old shame,' he said, a chuckle accompanying the words. 'I am long accustomed. We were in abject retreat from the British in the desert – my family, those who made a career of the military, had been always cavalry, you understand, but in World War II I was in tanks – I had the misfortune to retreat into a Bedouin scout . . .' (I was fascinated by his intricate pronunciation of 'Bedouin') . . . 'and he winged me with a rifle so ancient that surely the bullet was rusty also.' He glanced at me merrily. 'Gravely wounded though I was, I contrived to surrender to the Americans instead of the British.' He shrugged. 'The British mess is so horrible for an educated palate, you understand, while the American Army was rich in ice-cream and thick steaks. Not to mention the excellent American cigarettes.'

I laughed. 'You sound as though you had your eye on the main chance.'

'In a time of war, one must look out for oneself,' he said gravely, then chuckled conspiratorially. 'Also in times of peace. That is how I first came to America. Of course the great American Army, courteous though they were even to an officer of the cowardly Italian Army, in its wisdom decided that I must be imprisoned in Texas.' He shuddered delicately. 'So much sand in Texas, I expected any moment to encounter another Bedouin . . .' (that lovely pronunciation again). 'And the Texas women . . .' He shuddered again.

'Your wound?'

He tapped his left leg with the cane. 'But it was fine by then . . . your wonderful American doctors in your wonderful American hospitals. However, even with the best of care lavished upon my poor body, I emerged . . . as you see me.' He tapped the leg again, smiling sadly. 'I have never again ridden. It is the great loss of my life.'

'A pity to go home to your grandfather's estate and . . .'

'My dear lady, I did not go home. My grandfather was Fascist, you understand, so the estates were gone. No.' He shook his head. 'A great benefactress rescued me from Texas, this was after America and Italy became allies against the Nazis, you understand, and took me home to her ranch in California.'

'Landing on your one sound foot again, I see,' I said, laughing at the involved story of his wartime adventures.

He laughed as freely as I. 'Even with my poor leg. This huge ranch, of course, was alive with horses . . . but mustangs, broncos, cowboy horses, not a Thoroughbred in the lot.' He looked at me solemnly. 'I put her into Thoroughbred breeding and racing. Now my benefactress owns one of the great California stables. It was my doing.'

'So you *do* know race horses,' I said. 'I thought so.'

'Yes. For ten years I remained with that lady, I advised her, I bought and sold on her account. I did everything, and in all this time I did not return to my country.'

'But why . . . ?' I hesitated, then pushed on. I really wanted to know. 'Why aren't you still with her? Sounds just the life for a man like you.'

'I must tell you why. For a very long time, we were two lovely people together, you understand.' He paused delicately. 'But I discovered, after a time, that she . . . regarded me as an employee. She delighted to introduce me as her . . . Thoroughbred stable manager.'

'Well. Weren't you?'

'Of course. But . . . I cannot feel that I am *working* for a woman. It is not in my nature. So . . . regretfully . . . I said farewell.'

A strange shiver moved through me. It's his eyes, I told myself. So merry and gallant, yet so . . .

'I guess so,' I said nervously. 'Though I'm working for a woman, and like it fine. Come on, let's get in out of the cold.'

'But I have taken enough of your time,' he exclaimed. 'You must have social demands . . .'

'The only social demand I've got is for a taste of sour mash along about this time,' I said. I didn't want him to leave. Not yet. 'Will you join me?'

'Sour mash?' he enquired sceptically.

'It's a Bourbon,' I said. I laughed. 'Surely you've encountered Bourbon in the Bluegrass. Though this particular one is distilled in Tennessee, so I'm still an outsider and a traitor to Kentucky.'

'I seldom drink anything but a small white wine,' Count Gracchi said. He bowed slightly. 'But of course, for a lovely lady, I would try anything.'

Dancy, his face showing a faint surprise, rose when I ushered the Count into the tack room. It was the first time anyone had shared our sundown session.

'Count Gracchi, my farm manager, Mr Dancy Clutterbuck,' I said in introduction. 'Dancy, Count Gracchi.'

'Tony,' he said. 'I must insist on Tony.'

The two men shook hands, Dancy, I noticed, with some constraint.

'Tony came to tour Outlaw Farm,' I said inanely, busying myself with ice and glasses . . . Dancy already had his drink. 'He was for many years the . . .' I hesitated over the word, but there was really nothing else to call it, was there? '. . . the manager of a California breeding ranch.'

'Far more a friendly adviser, I'm afraid. Your Miss Sage has performed a remarkable work here, and in such a short time.' He added, 'With your invaluable assistance, I am sure.'

'Here, now, try a taste of this,' I said, thrusting a glass into his hand. 'It'll put you off white wine for ever.' We sat down. 'I couldn't have done a thing without Dancy. It's all to his credit far more than mine.'

'But, my dear lady, yours was the mind that first created the farm, yours the guiding hand that shaped the creation,' Count Gracchi countered warmly.

I tried to laugh. 'If so, it was the blind leading the way. Right, Dancy?'

This little tête-à-tête wasn't working out as I had hoped; Dancy remained too reserved, Count Gracchi far too expansively attentive. Dancy participated in the conversation, but barely, and except for my efforts the talk went haltingly as the Count sipped gingerly and Dancy, for moral support, gulped at his glass.

After a few minutes Dancy arose, saying, 'Better take another look at that weanling's ankle. It filled pretty badly, I'm afraid.'

Count Gracchi rose also, placing his nearly untouched drink on the table. 'And I must go,' he said. 'I have taken quite enough of your time for one day, Miss Sage.'

Fairly disgruntled with Dancy, I said, 'If you're going to insist that I call you Tony, you call me Maude.'

He glowed. 'But of course. Maude, it is a lovely name, so *American*.'

Dancy, shaking hands quickly, was gone. I regarded the Italian visitor, then drank quickly. 'He's worried about his weanling,' I said defensively. 'That man, he works night and day.'

'But of course. He is undoubtedly a . . . manager . . . you can rely on.' Count Gracchi's eyes were speculative upon me for a moment.

I walked him to his car, stood beside it as he opened the door. Stowing the Malacca stick between the bucket seats, he turned to me, left hand braced on the car door. Taking my hand, he raised it delicately to his lips. The gesture sent a flutter through me.

'Thank you, dear Maude,' he said. 'Thank you so much for a kind afternoon.'

'Any time,' I said.

Relinquishing my hand, he slid with a lithe twist of his long body behind the wheel and closed the door between us. With the wave of a hand he rushed the car down the hill in a sudden roar of power.

Looking after him, I felt strangely alone in the chill of approaching nightfall. A great story he had told about his war wound, the American experience. Italians, I thought fondly. They're something else.

I began walking slowly towards my solitary dinner. Afterwards I would sit before the fire and study the book on Varola dosages . . . I found it abstruse, but was determined to understand the theory if I had to read that book, study those charts, a dozen times.

Hearing a roar of motor, I turned to see the roadster sweeping up the hill. Whirling to a gravel-scattering stop, Count Gracchi got out, smiling down at me.

'Dear Maude, I cannot leave a lovely lady so suddenly. The Shipwrights are giving a small cocktail party tonight. Do come with me.'

I drew back. 'I couldn't do that. I don't really know them . . .'

He came closer, taking both my hands. 'But of course. Irene will be delighted, she has talked much of you.'

I was tempted. A door was open I had not expected to open in the next hundred years.

'You sure it'll be all right?'

He laughed. 'For the Shipwrights, I can do no wrong. I assure you. They expect of Tony crazy things.' His eyes glowed on my face. 'It is a craziness that I do not wish to leave you. But it is true.'

Excitement burned within me, to match the enticement of his daring. What could the lady do, anyway, except welcome me, arriving in the company of her house guest?'

I looked down. 'I'm not even dressed.'

'You are beautiful in jeans,' he exclaimed. He whirled to open the door on the passenger side. 'Be brave, my love. Be impetuous. Hop in and let's go.' The colloquialism was aggressively American, but enchanting in his accent.

I had already surrendered. Yet I retained a modicum of sense. 'You'll have to give me fifteen minutes,' I said firmly. 'Come on up to the house, where you can be warm while you're waiting.'

He yielded the point, naturally – I know it would have shocked him if I *had* got into the car dressed as I was – and we walked together to the house. Jan came to meet us, wearing his white jacket.

'Jan, can you give Count Gracchi a glass of white wine while I dress?' I hurried upstairs.

In fifteen minutes, as promised, I had a hurried bath, chose a cashmere dress, soft and warm and the colour of cocoa, hesitated a moment, then decided I'd wear the sable jacket and to hell with it.

I was at the bedroom door, one hand on the knob, before I realized that it would only confuse a man like Tony Gracchi for a lady to dress within the stated time. So I went back to sit on the bed for another fifteen minutes.

Which gave me time to think about what I was doing. Until now, swept along by an intense reaction to his delightful presence, there had been no time for thought.

I had to admit it: I was both thrilled and terrified by the prospect of appearing at the Shipwrights'. All this time in the Bluegrass, I had never received an invitation.

I understood the risk I was taking – because I didn't know whether Gracchi had the social clout with his hosts to carry it off. We could walk into a very chilly atmosphere. It could be embarrassing. Or it could be the sesame I had desired for so long.

Sitting on the side of the bed, stroking the sable with both hands, my senses marvellously alive to the texture of the fur, I thought: It doesn't matter. I'll count on nothing. I'll enjoy the company of Tony Gracchi. That will be enough.

I had to admit it: He emanated, not totally unconsciously, an aura of masculine strength and charm, made more exciting by the exquisite manners, an impeccable politeness warmed by his sensitivity to me as a woman.

I looked at my watch. Three more minutes. Of course, I don't intend anything *serious*, I told myself . . . carefully not defining 'serious'. Unnecessary to consider that unlikely aspect. But it was pleasant to know that a man – and such a man, of obvious experience and taste – could find an hour with me rewarding.

I looked at my watch again and went downstairs. When Count Gracchi heard my footsteps, he appeared in the living-room archway, glass of wine in one hand. I stopped while he advanced to the foot of the stairs. The fingers of his right hand brushed lightly against my sabled shoulder.

'You were right; you shouldn't have worn blue jeans,' he said. The throatiness in his tone was warmer than that fur.

I laughed. 'Blue jeans would serve the Shipwrights right. But not me. Are you sure you want to go through with this?'

'Where Irene is concerned, I can do no wrong. And Payson . . .' He shrugged. 'With Payson, no one can do a wrong. Payson is a very nice man.'

He tucked my hand under his elbow and escorted me to the door, Jan materializing to open it for our passage.

'Good night, Jan,' I said. 'Thank you.'

'Good night, Miss Maude,' he said gravely. 'Have a good time.'

He knew, and I knew, that without fair warning I had abandoned a well-prepared meal. As I knew that, when I came home, he would have a snack ready in case I desired refreshment, reviving, or reconstruction.

The Shipwright home was a traditional southern mansion, movie-style, graceful white columns lit softly by spotlights concealed in the shrubbery. Count Gracchi had called it a 'small' party, but a rather large number of cars were parked in the gravelled area. The Count slid the Mercedes roadster into the last empty spot inside the long shed of garage and came around to open my door, taking my hand to assist me.

'Well, too late to turn back now,' I said. 'So . . . let's have at it.' I laughed. 'If she throws me out, will you catch me? Or be thrown out with me?'

'But of course. We shall retire to the nearest Holiday Inn in good order.'

'I don't know about that. I'm not exactly homeless, you know.'

'Then I shall be your house guest, and we will invite the Shipwrights to *your* next party.'

I felt suddenly as light as air. With my hand on his sleeve, I said, 'Come on, then. Let's have a look at the lioness in her den.'

With all flags flying, we marched up the broad steps and through the front door, to be met by a maid in crisp white, who gave Count Gracchi her broadest smile as she took his coat.

'Hello, Helen,' he said. He was wearing a lapel-less jacket, almost a cardigan, and a turtleneck sweater, the rolled collar lapped white against his brown neck. The style went well with his aquiline features. 'This is Miss Maude Sage. Many people here?'

'They're *all* here,' she said extravagantly. 'And then some.'

He helped me off with the sable jacket, tendered it into the care of the maid with an approving pass of his palm over the dark fur. He delighted in everything beautiful, sensual, and expensive.

We had not reached the living-room before Irene Shipwright showed herself, saying, 'Oh, Tony, I heard the door, and I was hoping it was you at last . . .'

She stopped talking, stopped her movement, as her eyes took me in. The Count went to her, bussed her firmly on the cheek, and said, 'Look who I've brought along.'

'Oh,' she said. 'Yes. Miss . . . Sage, isn't it?'

'Maude,' I said. 'We were stabled in the same shedrow at the sale, remember?'

'Oh,' she said. 'Yes. You . . . bought back your colt, didn't you? That nice chestnut.'

'Yeah,' I said. 'I decided I'd race him rather than sell him cheap.'

The Count moved gracefully into the following silence. 'I was out all afternoon looking at horse farms. After Maude had showed me about her place, I realized I would be late for the party. So, to make amends, I brought her along.' He gave Irene a dazzling smile. 'Women with so much beauty in common really must be friends, don't you think?'

It didn't help much. It only gave her an opportunity to ignore me. Putting both hands on Tony's arm, she said fondly – and exclusively, 'You're a real card, Tony.'

'I didn't know there was a Count in the deck,' I said. 'Only jacks.'

That didn't help either; it went over her head. She laughed dutifully, however, when the Count laughed, and then said, with an obvious effort, 'Well, welcome to Fleet Run Farm, Miss Sage.' She hesitated. 'I should introduce you around, shouldn't I? I'm sure you won't know anyone.'

'It will be nice to meet your guests.'

At least the first barrier had been breached. Irene Shipwright conscientiously escorted me down one side of the living-room and up the other, pausing at each cluster. Given her reluctant bow to the social amenties, I was prepared against the impact of their inquisitive eyes, the faint hesitation before acknowledgement of my unheralded presence in the Shipwright living-room. Tony had left my side; I wondered, seeing how the chill winds were blowing, if he had deserted the cause. But he returned quickly with a drink, earning a grateful smile from me.

These were names I knew familiarly, by now, from the horse magazines; owners of farms and breeders of race horses. The horse people. I couldn't help noting how the men's eyes approved; the women looked at me critically, though with grudging admiration for my dress and manner.

But I did not encounter real warmth until we came to Harris Harris, braced on his crutches at one side of the huge fireplace, chatting with another man. He greeted me with genuine delight – and some surprise, signalled by his expressive eyebrows – and leaned forward, crutches clamped under his armpits, to take my hand with both of his.

'Oh, you know each other,' Irene said blankly.

Harris's eyes twinkled. 'Yes indeed,' he said. 'Wouldn't you say that we do, Maude?'

I laughed. 'Yes. We're old antagonists.'

'And friends,' he added gravely. 'Don't forget that, Maude. Friends, too.' He turned to the other man. 'Payson, allow me to introduce you to a great lady . . . and a formidable woman.'

Irene's husband, a small man with a peaceful face and a shock of white hair, was the only man in the room wearing a dinner jacket. (Tony said later that he dressed every night.)

'I have heard a great deal about you,' he said quietly. 'Harris has told us we ought to see your stallion's get.'

'Maude gave me the grand tour this afternoon,' Tony interposed. He had placed his hand possessively under my elbow – I was acutely conscious of his strong fingers – and I felt he was prouder of me now that Harris Harris had given me a genuine welcome. Irene, I noticed, had become easier with my presence, also.

'How's that colt doing, anyway?' Harris asked. 'Did he stand training?'

'So far,' I said. 'No problems with bucked shins, anything. He's rather growthy, though. Maybe in the spring we can ask more of him. Though I don't think he'll be an early starter.'

'He was in beautiful condition for the sale,' Harris said. 'Should have brought fifty thousand at least.' He laughed and shrugged. 'That's the way it goes at any auction. An hour later or an hour earlier, he might have topped fifty. A grand colt.'

'Everyone was so worn out with the drama of Irene's filly,' I said. I turned to her. 'By the way, I never did get a chance to congratulate you. It must have been a great moment.'

A surprised, delighted warmth struggled to glow through the ice. After all, Irene was a horse perons, as I was, and on this level we could understand and accept each other.

'I can think of only one that could be better,' she said. 'To enter the winner's circle at Churchill Downs on Derby Day as the breeder of record.'

'Maybe you'll have that, too,' I said. 'Even if a filly hasn't won the Derby since 1915.'

'Irene, didn't you show me a War Admiral mare in your barn?' Count Gracchi said confidentially. 'You really should send her to Maude's stallion. I saw some foals this afternoon from that breeding cross worth looking at.'

'The yearling colt I accepted from Outlaw Farm for the sale was by Sir Outlaw out of a War Admiral mare, Irene, if you remember,' Harris said quickly. 'The maternal grandsire was Blue Larkspur.'

Irene's eyes were bright with interest. 'She's not Blue Larkspur,' she said. 'But . . .' She turned to her husband. 'Didn't I decide to use our Prince John season this year for her?'

'I believe you did, dear.'

She glanced at Tony, then at Harris Harris. 'You'd *both* recommend Sir Outlaw?'

Harris nodded, his face serious. 'I think there might be something there.' He glanced at me. 'Maude thinks so, too. How many War Admiral mares in your barn now, Maude?'

Irene looked to Tony. He shrugged, saying lightly, 'I can only tell you, Irene, to view her foals. I'm sure Maude would be delighted to receive your visit.'

'Any time,' I said, grateful that the conversation had veered away from Harris's sly question without the necessity of direct reply.

Irene turned to me again. This was no longer social chitchat, but business. 'Is Sir Outlaw's book full?'

'Not yet,' I said. 'But I'm sure he *will* have a full book this season. For the first time.' I smiled at Harris. 'I credit Outlaw Prince being paraded through the sales ring for that, Mr Harris. Even if no one was interested in spending real money on him, it has brought many enquiries.'

Irene said shrewdly, 'You do intend to continue the stakes jackpot?'

'Yes,' I said. 'For the last time, though. When Outlaw Prince starts running, I'll be in a position to pick and choose.'

'You're *that* sure of him,' Payson said.

'Yes.'

'I'll check my calendar, see when I have a free afternoon,' Irene said with decision. 'But . . . do hold a season open until I can make up my mind.'

I could have said, First come, first service. And she knew it. But she had, at least, been decent with me. 'Of course. You can count on it.'

And that's how business gets done in the Bluegrass, I thought as Tony took my glass for a refill and Irene bustled away to attend her other guests, leaving me with Harris and Payson. Casual conversation. Quiet, ingrown decisions of consequence. Within the week, every hardboot in Kentucky would know that a Fleet Run mare was going to Sir Outlaw. That simple fact, far more than any number of full-page advertisements in the *Blood-Horse* and the *Thoroughbred Record*, would help to establish Sir Outlaw as a fashionable stallion.

The Count returned with a fresh drink, departed to pay his respects to other guests. I shifted position to watch his progress down the room, noting how the women brightened at his approach, how they responded to his gallant compliments.

'How did you happen to meet the Count?' Harris asked.

I turned from the scene to meet the inquisitive brightness of his eyes. '*He* happened to meet *me*. Tony just turned up at Outlaw Farm this afternoon, like *you* did once. We get nice callers. Both of you. Anyhow, I can't say I know him at all well.'

'Harris, I want to show Miss Sage my horse prints,' Payson Shipwright said firmly. 'You surely resist invitations to look at a man's etchings. But I know you love horses, Maude. Do you like ancient horse prints?'

'I don't know,' I said.

'Come, then. Allow me to show you my collection.'

Through a discreet door at the back of the room, he led me into the library, a lovely room, books with old bindings, leather chairs, a small fire burning steadily. A man's room.

Payson Shipwright read minds as well as books. 'Yes. The rest of the house belongs to Irene. This is mine.'

'So lovely and quiet,' I said. 'It's just right for you.'

'Sit down,' he said. 'So I can gallop my hobbyhorse at you.'

Placing me before a long, narrow table under a good light, he went to the shelves lining one wall, returning to put down a Solander box, designed to keep out insects, vermin, dampness, and other dangers to valuable prints.

'I began collecting horse prints as a boy in this house,' Payson said. 'I really do believe I have the finest collection in America. I hope to will it to a Museum of the Thoroughbred.'

'Oh. I didn't know there was one.'

'There isn't. That's one of the things I hope to accomplish. I've been urging such a museum be established in Kentucky for years. A little gift might also be a little prod.'

'Well,' I said, 'at least they can't look a gift horse-print collection in the mouth.'

He chuckled and began removing the 100 per cent rag protective mats one by one, explaining each print in detail, where he had found it, at what period in his life. I was fascinated by these ancient depictions of the Thoroughbred in its various manifestations of race and steeplechase and fox hunt, all the graphic details of the kinds of life centred around the horse. And I liked this soft-spoken, obviously kindly man. He had seemed, at first meeting, to be overshadowed by his wife; as we talked in the stillness of the library, I realized that he had preserved an oasis of personality in the midst of her more flamboyant presence.

Absorbed, I was not aware that so much time had passed until the door opened and Irene said, 'I thought I'd find you two in here.'

Payson straightened. 'Boring Maude with my horse prints, I'm afraid.'

Irene, smiling, came on into the room. 'That means he likes you, Maude.'

'They're fascinating,' I said. 'So much detail.'

'Some of our guests are leaving, Payson.'

'Let me put these up,' he said.

Irene was easy with me now – because of, I knew, Harris Harris and her own husband far more than Count Gracchi.

'A few people are staying for a light supper,' she said. 'Payson would never forgive me if I didn't ask you.' She laughed lightly. 'Not to mention Tony. And Harris.'

It was the final yielding. But I knew how to quit while I was ahead. 'Thank you, Irene, but I really can't. You know how early we horse people have to get up in the mornings. So, if Tony will take me home, I'll beg off this time.'

'Yes. Of course. I'll call tomorrow about viewing the foals.' She went to the door. 'Don't be long, Payson.'

'Just tidying up.'

Irene disappeared. I took a step towards the door, stopped to see if the host was ready. He put up the last Solander box, dusted his hands briskly with a handkerchief, stood beaming.

'I shall browse among my prints, choose one as a gift for you,' he said. 'Would you like that?'

'I'd love it,' I said. 'But . . .'

'I have occasional duplicates, I shan't give you an irreplaceable treasure.' He paused. 'Tony Gracchi . . . charming man, isn't he?'

'Yes,' I said. 'He seems to be.'

'Irene found him in Palm Beach last winter,' Payson Shipwright said. 'An expert on horses, surprisingly enough, managed a California breeding ranch for a number of years.' His gentle smile became rather sly. 'He knows horses, and he understands the ladies. Charming man, easy to talk to.' He shrugged. 'Of course, he doesn't have a dime. Only his title and his charm to carry him through life.'

I had the dinstinct feeling a careful warning had been delivered. Something in me wanted to resent it; but, looking into Payson's peaceful face, I knew that one could never resent the kindliness of this man.

'Payson,' I said, 'when Irene visits Outlaw Farm, I hope you'll come along.'

His shy smile showed delight. 'I'll make a point of it,' he promised. 'Now I'll deliver you to your Count Gracchi, and do my duty by my departing guests.'

Fast friends, we emerged from the library. The Count, all the way down the length of the room, turned alertly and came to my side.

'I must go,' I said to him. 'Can you take me home now?'

'Of course,' he said. He glanced at his host. 'Payson show you his prints?'

'Yes,' I said. 'Promised to give me one, isn't that marvellous?' I turned to Payson, held out my hand. 'Thank you, Payson. Don't forget, now, you're coming to Outlaw Farm, too.'

He took my hand, held it a moment, went away. 'A nice man,' I said to the Count.

'Isn't he? It's *his* money, you know, not Irene's.' There was an abruptly sombre note in his voice. 'Shall we go?'

We spoke farewell to Irene, standing at the door amid departing guests, and suddenly we were out into the chill night air, then into the quick warmth of the little car. All the way home we chattered gaily about the party. Count Gracchi had stories to tell, malicious and faintly mocking, about people I had met tonight; he was amusingly critical of Kentucky society in general, and we laughed a great deal. He was not only euphoric with his success in introducing me into Irene Shipwright's hallowed circle, but congratulated himself on having remembered that she had in her barns a War Admiral mare.

'That mare will be covered by your stallion,' he said. 'I'd bet my last *sou* on it.'

'I hope so,' I said. 'Be a great stroke for the home team.'

He began teasing me about the size of the commission he expected from Sir Outlaw's stud fee, and, so diverted, I was surprised when the Count wheeled the Mercedes-Benz to a stop in my driveway. The trip had seemed too short, bringing the evening to an end before I was ready for an ending.

We sat silently side by side in the bucket seats. Count Gracchi's hands were on the steering wheel. The porch light Jan had left on cast a sheen on their backs, so I could see the spokes of fine black hair on the knuckles.

I stirred. 'Thank you for taking me to the party,' I said. 'I didn't expect to enjoy it, to tell the truth. But I did.'

'Shall I . . . see you again?'

I turned to look at his profile. 'If you like.'

He suddenly aimed his brilliant smile across the darkness of the compartment. 'Of course I like.' He slid lithely out of his seat, bracing his bad leg with the cane, and came to open the door on my side. I stepped out, taking his hand momentarily to do so, and we walked slowly to the porch. I hesitated, not exactly sure how to say good night, not exactly sure how I wanted him to speak good night to me.

I held out my hand. 'Thank you, Tony. Good night.'

Instead of shaking it, he raised it to his lips. 'Sleep well, lovely lady.' Relinquishing my hand, his fingertips just brushed my cheek, a delicate gesture so unexpected I almost startled. Then he was gone, leaving me to fumble in my evening bag for the key, and as Jan opened the door before I could find it the headlights flashed again, the roadster sped rapidly away.

I came into the house, told Jan I didn't want anything, and went directly upstairs. I was astonishingly weary as I undressed thoughtfully and got into bed. The evening had taken a lot out of me. But it had given something, too. A promise . . . and a danger.

It was a long time before I slid over the wall of thought into sleep. Because, for the first time in years, I found myself thinking about Tim Conti, who had been my husband.

I was twenty-six years old, working at Tampa General, when Tim Conti entered the hospital with a broken pelvis and other troubles. He was a jockey, riding at Hialeah at the time of his injury. A broken pelvis is bad enough at the best of times; but Tim, as I learned when I came to know him better, was also suspended for a year. I never knew the details, only the little that he deigned to tell me; but it seemed to me that the injury alone should have been punishment enough for whatever racing infraction he had committed.

His family had brought him home to Tampa – he had been brought up here, across town from the section where I had been reared – because he faced a long and expensive convalescence. I was on his floor when, after the first two weeks, he was shifted from the private room he had demanded upon arrival to a semi-private. By this time, with the resilience of an athlete, he was already quite chipper, even though his hips were still in a cast.

Tim Conti was a little fellow – naturally – but so neatly put together, physically speaking, and so cheerful and charming that he seemed more like a boy than a grown man. I'd never known a jock, and I liked that all-conquering air of his; he was a cocky little devil, let me tell you.

A small man, with short, strong legs and large hands. A tight-fleshed, thin-lipped face, overshadowed by a great blade of a nose. Italian, of course, with black, black hair and eyes and a smooth olive skin. And talk . . . that fellow could talk a one-eyed man out of his good eye.

He talked me out of considerably more than an eye, when all was said and done. He always had a smile ready when I came into the room, as he did for everyone. But his greeting for me seemed just that much warmer, more personal, than for others. It made my day go better just to have him in it for a few minutes; so I slipped into the habit of paying Tim a personal visit at the end of my shift.

My greatest pleasure was to get him talking about the track. Tim Conti had been riding for five years – he had started at eighteen – and he was fiercely certain that in good time he would be recognized as one of the great jockeys.

'Miss Maude' (from first to last, he called me that), 'I was just beginning to get good mounts in the important stakes. Had me an agent at last who knew his business. You just watch . . . I'll make them forget about Shoemaker and Arcaro, all those fellows.'

At the time, it was still uncertain whether he'd ride again. But he refused to believe that possibility.

One day I came on duty to find his bed empty. He couldn't have been discharged. I enquired casually, in an attempt to conceal my panic – only to discover that he had been moved again . . . to the charity ward.

Knowing how this would devastate a spirit like Tim Conti's, I fretted through my shift until, off duty at last, I could go to him. For the first time he had no smile for me, no lighting of his eyes. He sat glumly, looking straight ahead; and he seemed much smaller than before.

'So OK, Tim, what happened?'

He wouldn't look at me. 'Ran out of money,' he said bitterly. 'And the family swore up and down to the hospital people they didn't have the first dime to spend on my welfare. So I wind up here.' His eyes, those hard black olive pits, flicked contemptuously at the ward.

Tim Conti had got used to the high living that goes with success. I couldn't blame him for feeling so hurt and angry. And yet . . .

'You told me they were poor,' I said. 'Maybe they really can't afford . . .'

'If they had a million, they wouldn't spend two dollars on me,' he interrupted. 'I told you, I ran away from home when I was sixteen, didn't I, just to get a chance to ride?'

'It'll only be for a few more weeks, Tim. You can bear anything for a few weeks.'

'Listen.' He grabbed at my hand, held on to it. 'If anybody comes over from Hialeah to see me, don't you let them in here. Hear me, Miss Maude? Especially my agent, Johnny Schwartz.'

'Why?' I said. 'Surely if they came this far just for a visit . . .'

'I *can't* let 'em see me like this,' he said. 'For God's sake, Miss Maude, a top jock like me in a *charity* ward?' He shook his head. 'Not on your life. To be a winner you got to look like a winner.' His scornful glance again. 'There ain't no winners in a charity ward.'

Tim Conti needn't have worried. Nobody came. Even his family had abandoned him, though he swore if they did come he would refuse to see them. It was as though, on entering the ward, he had dropped out of the ken of all mankind.

Except for me. I visited twice a day: before the beginning of my shift, and after work. It hurt deeply to see how, day after day, his belief in himself, his fighting spirit, ebbed away. He was like a bantam rooster whipped in a fight; it's not the physical pain, but the mental anguish, that makes those bright tail feathers droop. Nothing I could say seemed to help.

One day , in the pettish voice he used more and more, he said, 'For God's sake, Miss Maude, I wish you'd *change* before you come. All I ever see are women in starchy dresses.'

I never again went to his bedside in uniform. I bought some new clothes, choosing each dress carefully. I had to believe that it helped. Yet no longer did he talk about becoming the greatest jockey the world had ever seen. Tim Conti, like so many men of high accomplishment in a narrow field, rode the thin edge of self-esteem.

I knew I would be a fool. But, unable to help myself, I went in with wide-open eyes. One day, before my better sense could stop me, I blurted out the idea.

'Tim,' I said, 'I've been working for a long time, so I've got a good bit saved. Suppose I . . . suppose I *lend* you some money, enough for' (I meant to suggest 'semiprivate' but, at the crux, I said mentally, *What the hell*! and went all the way) 'a private room?'

Warmly, his whole face lighting up, he took my hand in both of his. 'Miss Maude, I knew, the minute I saw you, you had a heart.' He braced himself visibly against temptation. 'But I can't take money from a woman. Not on your life. Tim Conti takes care of his woman, his woman don't take care of him!'

I hadn't let myself think of it exactly that way . . . *his woman*. My heart thumped painfully at the sexual assumption.

'But you won't be taking money from me,' I protested. 'You're going to be a great jockey, aren't you? Once you're riding again, you can pay me back. Every penny. It's a loan. I'll insist. All right?'

In short, I talked him into it – I thought – and that night, over his own little dead body, Tim Conti slept luxuriously in a private room . . . after having made a flurry of fresh phone calls to everybody he knew at Hialeah. I had to laugh smugly in secret self-congratulation to see how he was sitting up in bed as he told his listeners how soon he'd be returning to the races.

'And, Johnny, you go to work on that Commission,' he told

his agent. 'You *hear*? Pull their heartstrings about poor, brave Tim Conti – or, hell, slip 'em some money if you have to. Anything to get that suspension lifted. It'll be worth your while, Johnny, I swear to it.'

When Tim came out of the hospital he was dead broke – beyond owing me a couple of thousand – and with no place to go. So . . . I took him home.

There was no room, really. But I made room. In consideration of his still-fragile body, I gave him the bedroom and prepared, that first night, to bunk out on the living-room sofa.

In the middle of the night, I woke suddenly to find him kneeling beside the sofa, his lips on mine, and then on me. I responded with a heat I did not recognize.

But then, forcing the words, I said, 'No, Tim. No. That's not part of the deal.'

He remained kneeling, gazing into my face though he could not have seen me well in the darkness . . . for which I was grateful.

'Miss Maude,' he said, placing the palm of one hand warm against the side of my face. 'Marry me. Tomorrow.'

The words hung between us. I had no answer. No man had ever made that speech to me – not that I had given any man much of a chance. Then . . . I put my arms around his neck.

'Yes,' I said. 'Yes. Yes. *Yes.*' And in a minute or so, after his silent moves, 'You'll have to be careful, Tim. Remember, you're just out of the hospital. Remember . . .!'

I forgot. Forgot all I ever knew. A fool. Yes. But any woman, I suppose, has the right to make an idiot of herself over a man just once in her life. God knows, I made the most of my opportunity.

I lived with Tim Conti, man and wife, for all of six months. He was a narrow, ignorant person except for his track savvy; his idea of reading matter was a comic book, and he knew nothing beyond horses and women. He could be sweet and charming and masculine all at once – oh God, how masculine that man was! – and sometimes when I walked through the doorway, home from work, he made me feel like a little glowing princess. I let myself devour it all, because, as I said, I went into it with eyes and heart and legs wide open. But once in a while, in a weak moment, I let myself begin to hope, to believe . . .

At the beginning of his outpatient rehabilitation, Tim spoke of leaving the track, making another career for himself. 'After all,' he assured me more than once, 'there's a thousand different ways of getting rich. I don't have to ride an animal with fast legs and no brains to do it, do I? Not Conti!' He paused to look at me with warm black eyes. 'Besides, it's no life for a woman, gypsying from track to track. No life for a woman at all.'

I let him talk his silly talk. In my own smug heart, I knew that if he was able to ride again, he would ride. And I knew that I was perfectly willing to become a race-track gypsy if that's what it took to remain in his bed.

He never gave me the chance to let him know I was prepared to give up the Maude Sage I had made in order to become the woman he needed. On a day barely six months into our marriage, I came home from work to find a note propped on the kitchen table.

Johnny Schwartz called . . .
suspension lifted. Thanks
for everything.
Tim.

No love. No talk of money. Or time or the future. I sat down at the kitchen table, holding the scrap of paper in both hands, and wept on it for five minutes. For, a fool no longer, I knew he was gone for good – or gone for bad – and he would not come back.

The next morning, I filed for divorce.

I was an hour behind schedule – a rare occurrence – when I found Dancy at the Coach Barn supervising the blacksmith as he trimmed the dinner-plate feet of the barren mares. He turned to my greeting with a curiously hesitant expression.

'Good morning, Maude. Tom, see if you can do something about the crack in this hoof.'

'I'll work on it,' the farrier said. 'Won't promise anything, though. This mare has always had shelly feet.'

'Just do the best you can.'

'Dancy,' I said, 'You'll never believe where I was last night.'

'Saw you leaving with that Italian fellow,' Dancy said noncommittally.

I put a rush of enthusiasm into my voice. 'At the Payson Shipwrights. And I think Fleet Run Farm will be sending a mare to Sir Outlaw.'

'That's real nice.' Dancy turned to Tom again. 'I'll be in the

Big Barn. If you need me, just get on the squawk box and holler.'

'Yessir, Mr Dancy.'

As we walked together, I tried to rouse an enthusiasm to match my own.

'*Nice?*' I said. 'It could be the making of Sir Outlaw, Dancy.'

'He's doing very well without the patronage of the Shipwrights,' Dancy said. 'I'd bet my last dollar his book will be full by the end of January.'

'But . . .' I was nonplussed. He actually seemed to resent the idea. 'They're going to call and come over. They want to see Sir Outlaw's foals. Payson Shipwright is a very nice man, don't you think?'

'Don't know,' Dancy grunted. 'Never had any dealings with him.'

At the Big Barn, I watched resentfully as Dancy went about his morning duties, paying a call on each mare and then, in the New Barn, on the weanlings, checking to see how each animal had cleaned up the feedbox.

'Looks like a nice day for November,' he told Merlin. 'Let's turn out as soon as the sun gets a little higher.'

Stubbornly I stayed with Dancy until the inspection was finished. We talked about the horses as usual, his voice pleasantly normal; but with his remoteness, my resentment of it, there was a difference. At last I said abruptly, 'Well, there's paperwork to be got through,' and left for the office. I think he was relieved by my departure.

Tiffany Thomas was at her desk. I told her, 'Mrs Payson Shipwright may call. She's interested in sending a mare to Sir Outlaw.'

It was a small triumph to see the surprise, then the blaze of curiosity, in Tiffany's eyes. I was tempted not to satisfy her, but it would have been cruel; she was, if nothing else, a social creature.

'The Italian, Count Gracchi, who was here yesterday, took me to their cocktail party. He's their house guest.'

'I never heard Irene mention a Count Gracchi,' Tiffany said thoughtfully.

'I think they met him in Palm Beach last winter,' I said. 'Isn't Payson a good person, though?'

'He leaves things too much in Irene's hands,' Tiffany said. 'All he's interested in is peace and quiet, and time to fiddle with his everlasting horse prints. I suppose he bored you to tears with them.'

'He's promised to give me one. A duplicate, of course. I found them damned interesting.'

'Well.' She regarded me. 'You seem to have been quite the social success. But you'd better watch your Italian. You know how *they* are.'

'Oh, I think I can handle Tony,' I said lightly, and went on.

Too pleasant a day to be working inside; I felt restless. Every time the phone rang, I paused to listen while Tiffany answered. It was long after lunch before Tony called, and then only with a disappointment.

'Maude, I'm afraid it'll be a few days before I can see you again. A friend called from New York, there's an important party, and she wants me. I'm catching the three o'clock plane.'

'That's too bad, Tony,' I said slowly. 'But . . . have a good time.'

He chuckled. 'Oh, Madeleine is one of the great party-givers. I wouldn't miss it for anything.'

I grasped for a straw. 'Call me when you get back. We . . . we shall have dinner. Jan and Eva are marvellous cooks.'

'Delighted, dear lady. I may even ring you up from the airport.'

I laughed. 'Do that.'

The empty feeling I experienced after hanging up persisted through the next days, no matter how I busied myself. Irene Shipwright did not call and I decided the entire proposition had been only social chitchat. She had probably thought better, too, of the social entrée tendered me in her house, I decided gloomily. After I had abandoned hope, however, her office manager spoke to Tiffany Thomas, and the next afternoon Irene, with Payson in tow, descended on Outlaw Farm.

I gave them the grand tour, of course, looking at Sir Outlaw and the yearlings and the weanlings, even the mares. I could tell from her concentrated interest that the visit was a success long before, leaving Dancy at the Great Barn, we had gone up to the mansion for tea.

Cosily settled before the fireplace, Jan hovering in attendance, Irene said straightforwardly, 'Maude, I'm sold on your stallion. I'll take the season.'

'Wonderful,' I said. 'I hope he gets you a Derby winner.'

'Well,' she said sensibly, smiling, 'it's a long way from the covering of a mare to the winner's circle at Churchill Downs.

But we can always hope, can't we?' She glanced at her husband. 'We've never bred a Derby winner, you know. Six of ours have started in the race, over the years, but not one finished in the money.'

'That's too bad.'

'You have to learn to endure disappointment in the horse business.'

'Yes,' I said dryly.

Business concluded, we sat relaxed, sipping tea and chatting. Payson told an amusing story about a party held once in my house, but otherwise confined himself to listening. Only on leaving did Irene deliver her other message.

'We're off next week for Palm Beach, we always spend Christmas in Florida,' she said. 'But I'm giving a very small sit-down dinner the night before our departure. I hope you can come.'

'I'd love it,' I said. 'Of course, as a single woman, I'll throw your table out, won't I?'

'Oh, Tony will be back by then. I'll send him for you.'

I noted the imperious assumption in the final phrase, but said only, 'Good. It'll be nice to see Tony again.' But I had received an impression, along with the invitation, that Mrs Payson Shipwright was telling me, not too subtly, that she expected me to see Count Gracchi only once more – under her tutelage – before she whisked him off to Florida. The instinctive competitiveness of women.

At the car, Payson, with a shy smile, took a frame, sheathed in brown paper, from the back seat and gave it into my hands.

'Hope you'll like it.'

'I know I will,' I said. 'Thank you, Payson. I shall cherish it.'

In the house, I stripped away the wrapping paper and gazed on the lovely old print, my appreciation as much for the giver as for the gift. A legendary stallion alone on a hill, one tree in the background, his elegant head narrowly elongated in the fashion of those old prints, his barrel so long and slim it was almost out of proportion.

As I consulted with Jan about exactly where it should be hung, I chided myself for feeling such a sense of loss in knowing that Tony would surely return to Florida with the Shipwrights and, probably, I'd never see him again. What the hell, Maude? I told myself. He's done you a good turn in introducing you to the Shipwrights. Not to mention getting the service for Sir Outlaw. So . . . take the cash and let the credit go. Right, Maude?

But there's no dealing with the heart. I had to face the self-knowledge that, because I had found the man enormously attractive, he had opened areas in my mind that had been neatly shuttered these many years. My body had not gone unstirred, either. I understood quite cynically that the charm he had lavished upon me, the glow in his eyes, the entire implicit relationship he had so quickly and expertly established, was only his social stock-in-trade, to be expended upon every suitable woman within his ambience.

But I had liked it, found it satisfying, even exciting. It would dwell within me for a long time.

So I'm afraid I betrayed an obvious pleasure, that afternoon the telephone brought his voice to me again.

'My dear, I've kept my promise . . . I'm calling directly from the airport.' An unmistakable caress in the very tones and inflections. 'Now you must make me also a promise.'

'A lady never promises sight unseen.'

'But it is so innocent,' he protested. 'I desire only that you hop into your car and run over to Bluegrass Field so we can have a drink together before I have to check in with my hostess.'

She's let him know, too, that she claims first priority on his time and attention.

I didn't let the thought bother me. 'Be right there.'

Being-right-there involved a complete change of clothing, after careful consideration of the effect I wanted to create. Certainly I should make the impression of remaining the hard-working owner of a horse farm, caught in the midst of a busy day. But not in a slum. So I settled on a tweed skirt and jacket in a soft blush of rose, without even pearls to set it off, and a fingertip-length coat with a fleece collar.

Driving to the Lexington airport, snug in the heater-warmth of the Lincoln Continental, I found myself humming in contentment. Of course the man had his obligations; as long, as he remained a house guest, he must cater to the Shipwrights' interests and demands, always available as an extra man, ever charming, with a ready wit and a gallant air.

Such a man, come to think about it, was a remarkable product of both nature and artifice. He toiled not, neither did he spin; but in society he fulfilled a definite role, spinning in another fashion. He had obviously emerged from the disaster of World War II impoverished of ancestral lands and ready money. He had parlayed his charm and handsomeness and a leftover title into years of comfortable living at the highest levels of food and drink and good company.

And he had, bravely against Irene Shipwright's expressed wish, dared to show that he wanted to see me first of all.

His greeting was up to par; taking both my hands in his, he held me at arms' length so his eyes could devour my appearance.

'Maude,' he said, 'I forgot what a lovely woman you are.'

I felt myself blushing even as I said, 'Naturally, in the midst of all those New York beauties.'

'No,' he said seriously, 'you are a difficult person to keep fixed in mind. You fade on me, so that I can't remember your remarkable chin, nor the exact shade of your eyes.' His demeanour changed with the swiftness of laughter. 'Now come on, let's have a drink. The Campbell House has a very snug bar. Shall we go?'

In the parking lot, Tony tossed his bag into the back seat and, as a natural male prerogative, slid behind the wheel. The massive machine responded to his touch far better than to mine as he manoeuvred with deft speed through the streets towards our destination. Women, horses, *and* cars, I thought. Hate to count myself in that line-up. But he handles us all well.

In the bar, I had my usual Jack Daniel's and water, while he ordered white wine. 'Now,' he said, 'tell me all that you have been doing while I was away.'

'Running the farm and thinking about you. What else?'

'You *have* thought of me?' His eyes were sincere.

A casual turn of his wrist trapped my eye; he had not, I was sure, been wearing that watch before. It was a wafer-thin timepiece with a plain band of white metal. The glitter that had attracted my attention came from a discreet array of diamonds outlining the dial.

In a bold move, the first time I had deliberately touched him, I grasped his wrist and turned it to look at the watch more closely.

'Some souvenirs they sell in New York,' I said.

'Oh, that,' he said carelessly. 'Madeleine gave it me.'

'Should a man accept gifts from a lady?' I said, keeping the tone light, entirely without implication.

'But of course. It is a very nice thing when a lady wishes to make a small gift.'

'It doesn't . . . make you feel . . .'

'A terrible American attitude,' he said, his scorn curling about the word *American*. 'Don't you think?'

'I guess so. I never gave a man a present in my life.' Involuntarily my mind conjured Tim Conti. I had made him a present of everything *but* a watch.

'Pity,' he said. Then, as deftly as he had steered the automobile, he turned the subject away from the gradient of potential seriousness. 'I shall, one of these days, make you a gift, Maude. Absolutely delightful, absolutely unexpected. I shall wait until you have forgotten entirely this conversation and then . . . *voilà*!'

'You're just the man to do it, too.' To my own surprise, across the narrow table I touched the back of his hand with my fingers. Turning the palm upwards, he clasped warmly, and for a narrow instant we were looking so deeply into each other's eyes I could feel my senses diving into a deep drowning. Maude, Maude, I chided myself. What are you getting into?

Taking my hand away, I said, 'Irene has asked me to her going-away dinner. You are to be my escort.'

He smiled. 'By command of Queen Irene. She will so inform me. Not, you understand, that I mind . . . on the contrary.'

'Doesn't Payson . . . object to your presence in his house?'

'Object?' He was genuinely puzzled. 'But there is nothing . . .' His countenance clearing, he made an indescribable gesture with one hand. 'Did you think I was Irene's lover?'

The directly stated question made an embarrassment. 'Well, not really . . .' I floundered. 'I didn't really think about it at all. It just seemed . . .'

'Maude, I will stay in anyone's house who provides proper food and drink, and good amusement,' he said gaily. 'I am virtually a professional house guest. Didn't you know that?'

'Yes. But . . .' I shrugged. 'Oh, all right, I'm sorry. It's none of my business.'

His tone came warmly again. 'It *is* your business if you wish it to be your business.' His voice lingered. 'Do you . . . understand?'

I made a gesture of dismissal. 'Maybe more than I *want* to understand.' I changed the subject. 'You'll be returning to Florida.' I found myself wistful with the thought of sunshine and palm trees, the nearest to homesickness I had felt since I had come to Kentucky. 'On these cold days, so dreary with rain, I think about all that sun.'

He signalled with one finger for a fresh round of drinks. 'I had far rather spend the Christmas holidays in Kentucky.'

My heart lifted. 'Then why don't you?'

He shrugged. 'No one has invited me.'

It came to the tip of my tongue, but something warned me

against saying it. Instead, I looked at the time. 'I must get back. Isn't . . .' I hesitated. 'Aren't the Shipwrights expecting you?'

He glanced at his brilliant new watch. 'Yes, I'm afraid so.'

Leaving the second drink almost untouched, I gathered up my gloves and my purse. 'I can . . . deliver you to Fleet Run Farm. Or had you rather . . .?'

'It would be more discreet if you dropped me at the airport where I can telephone for a car.' As we rose, he put his arm around my waist, holding me close. 'Isn't it delicious to be so clandestine and wicked?'

For once, the perfect Italian gentleman had made the wrong move; I felt myself arching away from his hard-muscled body as I said soberly, 'I'm not at all sure, Tony, exactly how wicked I want to be.'

It made a chill between us, but only briefly, for he thawed me again with the air and cheer of his leavetaking, assuring me that he would not eat or sleep until we met again. Since the dinner was only tomorrow night, I told him, he would survive.

A silly thing. I knew it, even as I enjoyed it. Such a very long time since a man had dwelled in my thoughts, vividly present when I awoke and again at night as I went to sleep. I could recall the strangest details: the quirk at the corner of his mouth when he was secretly amused, his unconsciously revealed vanities, a small wart on the knuckle of his left thumb. It made the winter days brighter, there was a singing in me as I went about my work. I was suddenly more alive to everything, the harsh caress of a winter wind, the taste of sour mash, the smells of horses in warm barns. Even my rare cigarette tasted better.

There is no accounting for the heart. I knew well enough that he was something of a professional ladies' man, that he used his charming masculinity like a machete to hew his way through life. I understood why he had obeyed the summons of his Madeleine in New York; wherever he might be, there would always follow long-distance calls, scented letters, and insistently personal gifts. The words he used to me might well have been spoken in exactly the same phrases last night or last week to another woman.

It didn't matter. That's what other men, and some women, don't understand about the appeal of such males. Sure, they've said it before. Sure, they mean it only for the moment. But the best of them do not waste themselves on the worst of women – and certainly not the worst-looking. So, oddly, there is a sincere compliment built in when a first-class, high-level, skilled, and still-successful gigolo makes his pass.

Indeed, in a strange way, his style made the adventure so much more possible; it meant I wouldn't have to sit down with myself and think seriously through the problem of exactly where I expected the . . . well, *affair* wasn't the right word, it had not come near to reaching that status . . . to go. No. I could simply enjoy the one day, the next day, and the next, without having to concern myself with a happy ending. Sometimes a lady needs that kind of secret reassurance.

Primarily for this reason, I could ignore the palpable disapproval of my people. Not even Tiffany, with her instinct for the sources of social power, could bring herself to express approval of Count Gracchi. In her old Charlestonian book, he was a fly-by-night scoundrel of no permanent account, bank or otherwise.

And Dancy. He had retreated into an impenetrable shell of rigid correctness. No longer was there between us the easy camaraderie of those nights in the foaling barn working together with crisp words of direction and encouragement to bring safely to birth a new foal. Even our sundowner time was different. He didn't cancel out entirely; he preformed his duty as manager to owner with one quick drink, a fast and formal rundown of the day's problems, the activities planned for tomorrow; then he was off to his solitary quarters.

Competition, I assured myself. He knows Tony once managed a farm; he's afraid the Count might be after his job. After all, Tony Gracchi was not only competent with horses, he also disposed of a social entrée that could be useful to the future of Outlaw Farm . . . the sort of acceptance that Dancy Clutterbuck, no matter how good a manager, could never hope to have.

By carefully maintaining the old air of friendly confidentiality, I tried to reassure Dancy that nothing had changed. But, after all, I couldn't say to him, 'Look, good buddy, Tony Gracchi might become my lover, but he'll never replace you in the management of the farm. No way!'

I will frankly admit that I was scheming to find a way to keep Tony in Kentucky. I had no wish to lose him so quickly to the sunny social blandishments of Palm Beach. I even spoke to Tiffany Thomas, enquiring, if Count Gracchi should come to Outlaw Farm, would she consent to move into the mansion for the duration of his visit?

'There's Trenholm to think about,' she replied coldly. 'I

couldn't possibly leave her alone at night. She looks forward all day to my homecoming.'

'You could have a nurse. I'd pay the bill, of course. Your sister is such an emotional burden . . . it would be a vacation for you, actually.'

'I'm sorry,' Tiffany Thomas said. 'I couldn't possibly.'

I kept my eyes steady on her face. 'The real reason is, you don't approve of me inviting Tony, do you?'

'It's really none of my business,' Tiffany said in her most aloof tone . . . then, drawing a deep breath, she proceeded to make it her business. 'Maude, if ever I've seen a fortune hunter . . .'

The phrase, dwindling into unspoken implications, aroused an astonishing resentment.

'You can't believe that Count Gracchi could possibly find something attractive in me, can you?' I said bluntly.

Her eyes wavered. 'I didn't say that. But . . .'

I could not tolerate the opinion I had so rashly solicited. 'The truth is, Tiffany Thomas, if anybody's being used, I'm using *him*. After all, he *has* introduced me into the Shipwright orbit. Don't think I haven't considered that aspect of the matter, not for myself personally, you understand, but for the future of Outlaw Farm.' I paused, struck by a thought.

'Listen,' I said, 'if Tony did stay with us, it would be the perfect opportunity, wouldn't it? Nothing grand, you understand, but a small cocktail party or two, maybe a dinner . . .'

The idea excited me. If he could introduce me to others, he could also draw those people to my house.

'Listen,' I said in rising excitement. 'I really ought to persuade him to stay. By the time the Shipwrights return, we could be well established.'

'Surely you wouldn't think of making him a *permanent* house guest.'

'Doubt he'd stay very long, even if I wanted him to,' I said frankly. 'He probably has visits planned for a year ahead, an English country house, a yacht for the summer in the Mediterranean, California . . .' I laughed, feeling the wry twist of truth. 'We'd only be a way station on his itinerary, I'm afraid. But . . .' I paused, thinking again.

'Certainly we should . . . exploit . . . this social opportunity. Would you . . . Tiffany, would you consider moving into the mansion permanently? With your sister, I mean. I just rattle around in the place, you know, and there's that whole wing with two bedrooms and a bath where you'd be quite private.'

Instant temptation. It had been a long time since she had lived in the manner to which she fondly believed herself accustomed.

'It would be wonderful for Trenholm,' I assured her. 'These grounds to play in – of course we'd have to keep her away from the barns – Eva could look after her while you're working. You wouldn't have a thing to worry about. And think of the money you'd save. If I should decide to give one or two small parties, I'd need your help anyway, you'd know who to ask, all that . . .'

Surely she was contemplating lovely breakfasts prepared and served by Jan instead of hurried toast and coffee before dashing to work. She might not reign as hostess, but certainly she would become an important element. Working at a steady office job helped her to live but had impaired her self-image; living in the mansion could go a long way towards restoring it.

'You mean to ask him, whether I agree or not.'

'Maybe Tony and I should live together in the mansion,' I said, wryly aware that she had struck near to the truth.

She was wavering towards acceptance. But, in her own way, Tiffany Thomas was rigidly honest. 'I still can't tell you I think it would be wise to invite him at all.'

'You're probably right,' I said. Then, cruelly reminding her that she was a woman, too: 'No wiser than your . . . friendship . . . with Whitey Dahl before he left for Hialeah.'

I wouldn't have believed she was capable of blushing. It was a mean thing to say, I know; but, damn it, she had laid her opinion freely on me, hadn't she? And she was getting in my way.

'All right,' she said. 'I guess I . . . asked for that.'

'I'm sorry, Tiffany. But you did.'

She took a deep breath. 'I'll do it.' Defensively, she added, 'It will be so marvellous for Trenholm. I have only a tiny house, you know, practically no yard at all. She spends her days watching television.'

Good. So it was arranged, and at least two lives were to be improved . . . and maybe two more. I went to the dinner party with my mind made up to talk Count Gracchi into coming to Outlaw Farm.

A good dinner party; Irene greeted me as an accustomed guest, Payson as a friend, his shy smile and quiet welcome making me feel valued. Around the table the talk was of horses, of course, mostly next year's yearlings – weanlings now – and what kind of prices, given the state of the economy, could be expected.

Harris Harris was confident last year's record price wouldn't stand for long. Slyly he said to me, 'Maybe even one of your Sir Outlaw–War Admiral-mare yearlings. How many will you have in the sale?'

I was thrilled by the assumption of acceptance. 'That's more up to you than me. Unless you people are changing the rules of the game.'

'I'll come around, take a look at your weanlings. Maybe I can give you some advice on which ones to nominate.'

'That would be a very nice thing.'

'Wouldn't it be something to have the record-price yearling?'

'That's not likely to happen unless Outlaw Prince wins his first six stakes races,' I said, laughing. 'Actually, I'm afraid he won't even start before the Summer Sale. He can't seem to quit growing.'

'He made a great impression, though,' Harris Harris said.

'Yeah. In everything but money.'

He shrugged. 'That's the name of the game. Nothing ever surprises me in the horse business except the constant surprise. Every year something happens that's never happened before.'

'Isn't that the truth!' I said, thinking in a sudden revel of luxurious self-congratulation how I was sitting now at the Shipwright table, talking to one of the most powerful men in Kentucky. I smiled at Tony across the table. So who's hustling who around here, Tony my boy?

'I'm not even thinking about records,' I continued. 'It's my modest ambition to sell a yearling at your vendue for one hundred thousand dollars.'

Harris pursed his lips. 'Not exactly modest, Maude. Only something like two hundred yearlings, out of all the Thoroughbreds which have passed through an auction ring, have ever brought that kind of money.' He chuckled. 'I'm proud to say I've sold more yearlings of that class than any auctioneer except George Swinebroad, head auctioneer of the Keeneland Association . . . and he's been at it years longer than I.'

'I'll give you one more,' I said gaily. 'At least.'

A good dinner party, comfortable, friendly, inner-circle. Everyone, before, during, or after dinner, made a point of talking to me. And when Irene and Payson said good night at the door, Irene kissed my cheek when I wished her a good Christmas in Palm Beach. I told her they must come to my house on their return.

'Of course,' she said. 'Payson will insist.' And then, with a secret glance, 'Maybe we can persuade Tony to return with us. Would you like that?'

'Naturally,' I said with a laugh that would seem to betray her insight. But it did not betray the fact that I had no intention of allowing Count Gracchi to leave Kentucky in the first place.

Driving home, Tony first of all addressed himself to a discussion of the dinner guests. He always knew what could be known about the individual personalities of his social sponsors; often, with a certain gay malice, choice morsels of information he shouldn't have known. So we laughed a lot, and only when he had pulled the Mercedes to a stop beside the mansion did I say, 'Come in for a moment, Tony. Please.'

Hesitating almost imperceptibly, he consented. Jan, of course, was in evidence in his white jacket and I asked him for two glasses of white wine.

Settled on the sofa in the living-room, I went right to the point. 'Tony, you hinted that you really didn't want to go to Florida with the Shipwrights.'

Tony chuckled. 'There are so many terribly *old* people this time of year. Rather slows the pace, don't you know?'

'Wonderful, then. Because I'd love for you to come to Outlaw Farm for a visit.'

The idea rather shocked him. He looked directly into my face – it made me realize that his eyes were as subtly indirect as the touch of his hand – and said, 'Maude, do you . . . think it would be discreet?' He hastened on. 'Oh, I know you American women live your own lives. But this is Kentucky, after all . . .'

Into the breach. 'It's all right, Tony. I'm gutsy, but not *quite* as brazen as you're making me out.' I laughed at his quenched embarrassment. 'My . . . social secretary and office manager, Tiffany Thomas, lives with me. She is the epitome of proper chaperonage. She's from an old Charleston family. Everyone in Kentucky knows her. So . . .' I smiled mischievously. 'You'll be safe.'

I was quivering inside.

Tony regarded me still. He's wondering exactly what I mean.

'It *would* be lovely,' I said. 'I'm busy all day, so you'd be to yourself. And . . . we'll have a small party or two for the Christmas season.' I plunged all the way. 'You can invite whomever you like. Even Madeleine in New York if she'd care to come. Quite Liberty Hall.'

'Maude,' he said softly, 'I had already arranged – practically arranged, I might say – to remain with you for a time.' He smiled. 'I can be . . . gutsy, too. You should have seen me angling for an invitation from the Grannis beldame. I think I've got it. If I want it.'

'Well, if you'd rather stay there . . .'

A moment of hesitation. Then his most brilliant smile. 'What do *you* think?' With utmost delicacy, 'Unless you'd rather not risk a breath of . . . after all, Maude, there is a . . . *thing* . . . between us. Isn't there?'

The man had not kissed me. But he had made me know, through a thousand socially impeccable signs, that he considered me an attractive and desirable woman, that in our relationship lay infinitely rich possibilities.

But something – a hard edge to his tone perhaps, a difference in the glow of his eyes – told me that I was in imminent danger of sliding, in his mind's classification of female breeds, out of one category into another. And, I realized, I liked the category where he had first place me. For one thing, it was nice. For another, safer. Not against him; against myself.

'Don't get me wrong, Tony,' I said evenly. 'I like you. I enjoy your company. But . . . I'm inviting you into my home, not my bed.'

He drew back. 'Maude, you couldn't believe I meant to imply such a thing.' His voice hastened. 'Not that I . . . But of course . . .' It was nice to see him fumble.

I stood up. 'It's your decision. If you think it would be better to stay with your other friends, do so by all means.' I gave him my hand. I gave him my eyes. 'Either way, I'm glad you're going to be around a while longer.'

For a long moment he covered my hand with both of his. It turned me into jelly inside. Then, almost reverently, he rose and pressed his lips into my palm. The difference made this gesture so much more intimate than the many times, in greeting and in farewell, he had kissed the back of my hand.

'My dear Maude,' he said, a tremor in his voice. Calculated? I didn't know. But I did know that I was dwelling in a delicious danger. For I understood quite well that an option had been opened tonight.

'My dear Maude,' he repeated. 'Of course I will come to you. Whenever you wish.'

'Tomorrow, then,' I said. 'Or, whenever the Shipwrights ship out.' I grinned. 'I'll leave it up to you to break the news to Irene. You'll know how to handle it.'

'Oh, she'll be relieved to be rid of me for a time,' he said. 'There is one thing a house guest must know more surely than anything . . . when to pack his bags.'

'We'll see. Good night, Tony,' I said, turning to walk him to the door.

In the hallway, Jan was hovering. At least I won't lack for chaperons, I thought. Then: maybe more than I could wish.

The era of Count Gracchi's sojourn at Outlaw Farm began well. It was good to have people in the big old house; even with Jan and Eva in attendance, there had always been too many rooms full of silence. A house needs people quite as much as people need houses.

Tiffany and Trenholm were installed in one wing. Trenholm, showing the body of a mature woman surmounted by a child-like beauty of face and mind, was an uncomfortable shock. But she was a happy person; the years had not aged her, because thought had never marred her brow. Delighted with the new situation, she flitted about the house and grounds like a bright butterfly. Eva Stok, maternal instincts immediately aroused, showed herself capable of enduring hours of Trenholm's mindless chatter; she actually seemed to enjoy the children's television programmes Trenholm watched daily. She always took particular care with Trenholm's tray – she ate her meals upstairs – and kept tons of her favourite dessert, raspberry Jelly, in the refrigerator.

Tony had a bath and a bedroom to himself, discreetly on the far side of the Thomas suite, and, of course, Eva surrendered immediately to his charm. When not busy with Trenholm she devoted herself to tasks for Tony, washing and starching and ironing his shirts instead of sending them out, blacking his shoes with tender loving care. Jan, also, was pleased to have a Continental gentleman on the premises, one who could appreciate properly his culinary efforts and his table settings. He and Tony and Eva conversed in fluent French, the only language they shared other than English. It made me feel positively illiterate to sit at table, for of course Tiffany spoke passable French also.

Our dinners *en famille* were jolly affairs, Tony, at the head of the table, orchestrating the wine and food with laughter and conversation, as though it were a piece of music to be created all over again every night. Once a week we entertained, if not a small dinner at least a cocktail party. December in the Bluegrass is a social time anyway, the slack period of the year, with much entertaining and visiting back and forth.

Count Gracchi and Tiffany Thomas were wary of each other. But each recognized the other's kindred qualities and they put their heads together in plotting each entry for our social calendar. They used an irresistible social ploy: Tony, one after another, persuaded friends – from New York, from Florida or California, from London or Paris or Rome – to visit him in Kentucky; Tiffany, in turn, telephoned her connections to tell them they really must meet the lion of the week.

She had breathtaking names to conjure with; Tony seemed to know everyone worth knowing. For years he had battened on their invitations and now, for the first time, he was in a position to reciprocate. He was, of course, also building a savings account of social IOUs against future need, but I didn't care. Tony, as well as Tiffany – and, I must admit, Maude Sage also – took a snobbish delight in seeing the Kentucky people, hitherto so aloof, flock to Outlaw Farm to meet these irresistible names.

It made me so proud to stand beside Count Gracchi, he tall and slim in his dinner jacket, I in one of my Halston originals or, more daringly, an Oscar de la Renta, to greet the guests. Later, moving about the living-room or presiding at table, I was living the dream I had dreamed of in the Kentucky Bluegrass. When the last guest had departed, when the social lion of the occasion had retired, Tiffany Thomas left us discreetly alone to share a glass of wine as we, in the satisfaction of mutual accomplishment, chatted in sated tones about the evening. Tony, at parting, would escort me up the stairs and, on the landing before my bedroom door, kiss my hand and say good night.

I neglected the working farm. It was simply too much, after a late night, to rise up in the chill of an hour before sunrise to make the rounds with Dancy. Instead, we established new routines: After a leisurely breakfast alone – Count Gracchi never rose before eleven, and Tiffany Thomas was at her desk by eight-thirty – I would stroll down to the office, at nine-thirty or ten, to take Dancy's report.

Only if there were something special I should see, a colt with colic or a mare which had lost her foal during the night, a shoulder bruise to look at, did I visit the barns. After all, I told myself, Dancy, with the aid of Merlin and Alice to direct the stable help, is fully capable of carrying on the routine work; I was not in any sense relinquishing control.

Still, I must admit, I missed making the rounds, hearing Dancy's cheery voice saying, 'How's Merlin this morning?' on first meeting, or 'How's Big John?' to a new stable hand. He always spoke their names, his greeting a personal thing and it had always delighted me to see their appreciative response. I also missed our sunset hour, but so often, at that time of day, I was greeting cocktail guests.

Dancy was especially silent in Tony's presence. Tony made a point, after a late breakfast served in bed by Jan, of coming down to the office at noon to join me in a tour of the stables, often bringing along our current house guest. He took an acute and informed interest in the bloodstock, quickly learning their individualities, remarking that this weanling or that weanling was coming along well, another seemed to have gone right off its feed the last couple of days, and had the vet had a look?

At first he made an effort to include Dancy, but Dancy would reply to his questions or suggestions only in monosyllables which, once or twice, brought a quick reminder to my lips that, after all, Count Gracchi was a guest. Fortunately, I never spoke the words.

Tony, as acute about people as only a social man can be, quickly decided he could not enlist Dancy's friendship. His manner changed; he addressed Dancy in the subtly condescending assumption that Mr Clutterbuck was a hired minion whose tenure was entirely subject to my whim. Which, of course, was the truth, strictly speaking. But there was no point in making it so manifest.

On one occasion, in the presence of a visiting English lord who raced his own stable, Tony asked Dancy to lead out a weanling so he could take a closer look at how badly the filly toed in; he directed to me, exclusively, his dissertation on exactly how the problem could be corrected, when she was older, with proper shoeing. Dancy, silent and remote, stood holding the shank until Tony indicated that he was finished.

From then on, I noticed, Dancy made a point of absenting himself from any barn Tony and I were visiting. Quietly, without a word, he avoided my Italian friend and a clash over authority.

I absorbed myself in the company of Tony. A wonderful man to have in one's daily life. If he suffered bad moods, moments of self-doubt or private angers, he never revealed them. Every morning his eyes warmed with the first sight of me, at night his firm lips lingered in a good night kiss on the back of my hand. Something in me had been fearful that just perhaps – after all, he *was* Italian – he might, assuming an implicit invitation, knock quietly one night at my bedroom door. There was no hint, no knock.

Tony was utterly appreciative: of me, of food and drink and companionship, of the excellent service rendered by Jan and Eva, of the farm itself. Almost daily, after we had completed our round of inspection at the Coach Barn, he would pause on the crest of the hill, where the layout could be surveyed in a glance, and gaze upon Outlaw Farm with something like the satisfaction of ownership.

'It can become the most beautiful horse farm in Kentucky,' he would say, turning to me with a quiet smile. 'And the most successful. Maude, you have the foundation of something great here. Absolutely great.'

Thrilling with the pleasure of affirmation, I would reply, 'Yes, Tony. That's how I feel, too.'

Once, taking my hand in his, he opened his mouth to speak in abrupt impulsiveness. My heart tightened in my chest. But, after a lingering glance, he laughed lightly and said, 'I only wish I could still take some of these fences. But of course, on a Kentucky breeding farm, no one rides.' He chuckled. 'Wouldn't it scandalize your hired help if you should give me a horse to train as a jumper? I'd insist on it, were it not for my poor leg.'

I knew he was talking about Dancy. 'I'm afraid it would,' I replied. But, as we walked on down the hill, I wondered what words he had been on the verge of speaking.

All right. I was blind in love with the man. I was intoxicated by his male presence, by the scent he used, the sculptured line of his lips, the warmth of his gaze that promised blissful moments. Utterly captured, like a schoolgirl is captured, as much by the idea of maleness as by the fact. I was deaf and dumb and blind to everything and everybody but Count Antonio Gracchi.

I wanted him to kiss me, to touch me; without quite letting myself know it, I wished him to make love to me. There were times when, feeling impatient with his too-great discretion, I wanted to blurt out, 'All right, good buddy, we've established the fact that you're a man and I'm a woman. Now let's do something about it.' This, even as I was captivated by his punctilious adherence to the protocol of a male guest with his hostess.

It would not do, I understood full well, to make the aggressive move myself. He would be repelled by the least hint. I was certain that many women had thrown themselves at him. Maybe he had caught a few, too; but it would forever change his idea of Maude Sage. I could only wait for that one minute out of all time when he would step over the boundaries of our agreement.

Besotted with love. Skillfully he wove a warm web that insulated Maude Sage from everyone but him. I felt wholly alive only when he was present, so that I listened only to his voice, opened myself only to him. I even confided my secret belief in the breeding nick I had discovered, accepted his solemn concurrence as absolute confirmation. He ran my household, he arranged my social life, he told me who to invite and whom not to invite; more and more he made critical suggestions about the operating of the farm. And each night he kissed my hand on the stair landing.

The situation could not endure for long. But I did not know how or when it was to change and it was near to Christmas – I had already sent away to Tiffany's in New York for Tony's gift, a set of diamond studs for his dress shirts, had hidden them in my underwear drawer – before Dancy communicated his decision.

Sitting across the desk in my office, speaking in an even tone, he had finished his morning report. I asked a question or two, made a note to look up the pedigree of the new mare which he had booked early this morning for Sir Outlaw. She was the last one we could take.

'A full book,' I said, smiling with the pleasure of achievement. 'I'll run the full-page ad announcing it as soon as I can get it scheduled. I've had it ready for a while.'

Dancy nodded, saying soberly, 'Yep, Sir Outlaw will earn his oats this season.'

It should have been a moment of celebration.

'Is that all, Dancy?' I said.

He stirred without rising. 'I ought to tell you, Maude. I'm looking about for a new situation. I've already spoken to a couple of people.'

The finality of the statement jarred me. I looked down at my hands on the desk. 'Why, Dancy?'

He wasn't looking at me either. 'I don't feel I can be of service to Outlaw Farm much longer. I have to look ahead, think about myself . . .'

I avoided the implications. 'But . . . where will you go?'

He was silent for a moment. 'Don't think it'll be another farm. The race track's what's on my mind. This quiet life, it gets to a fellow after a while. If I could catch on as an assistant trainer, be just the thing. Good work, but no ultimate responsibility . . .'

He let the words run down. But already the trend of his thinking had stirred alarms in my soul.

'Dancy . . . what about the gambling?'

His hands became restless. 'I think I'm cured.'

'But what if you're not? 'Here was an area where, regardless of all other considerations, I could show my concern for the man. 'If you ask me, Dancy, this sudden restless desire for the track life, living like a gypsy, just goes to show . . .'

'It's time I found it out, isn't it?' He snapped it out.

'You nearly destroyed yourself once,' I said. 'Do you have to run the risk again?'

'People do grow out of things,' Dancy said. 'Don't they? We ought to be able to see things more clearly, even ourselves, as we get older.' He brooded. 'If we can't, there's not much hope for humankind.'

'But the risk!'

He shrugged. 'However it goes, I can't stay here.'

I made him meet my eyes. 'Dancy. You've got the job as long as you want the job. I don't think I've ever done anything, said anything, to make you feel differently.'

'Maude, you know as well as I do that the day the Count takes over Outlaw Farm, he'll fire my ass off the place.'

A crude way of putting it. I had never heard Dancy speak so roughly. I had to read it as an index to the depth of his feeling.

'What makes you think Tony will ever "take over" Outlaw Farm?'

He shrugged again. 'You're going to marry him, aren't you?'

'*You* may know that,' I said slowly. 'Everybody seems to know that. But *I* don't know it.'

'If you don't, you ought to. Because he's exactly what you want . . .' He stopped himself abruptly, stood up. 'That's none of my business. My business is to look after my personal interest, Maude, and that's why I'm looking around. I just thought you ought to know, because I wouldn't do anything behind you back.'

'Dancy,' I said 'I don't want to lose you.'

He looked at me. 'It's not all that hard to find a good farm manager,' he said. 'You probably won't even need one, if your

Count can learn to get up at a decent hour.'

'That's unfair!' I said hotly.

'Yes, and I'd better get out of here. I'll let you know, Maude, as soon as I know anything.'

He marched his unassailable self out, leaving me trembling with loss and betrayal . . . and anger. If it had not been for the last, uncalled-for attack on Tony, I would have gone after him, sought for and found a road back to the safe ground of our old friendship. But his contemptuously revealed opinion of my . . . house guest . . . had as effectively closed the gate as the rap of Harris Harris's gavel closed a sale.

I know my own stubbornness. The more I realized how opposed were my erstwhile friends to the very idea of Count Gracchi, the more I clung to the man. I would not be informed by all and sundry that I was making a fool of myself. How could they know the warmth of my feelings, how deeply the man affected me?

It's just that, to them, I'm not a woman, I told myself. Including Mr Clutterbuck. I'm Maude Sage the Sexless Wonder, owner and operator, source of good salaries and jobs; a conglomerate of meanings and purposes that does not include the meanings and purposes of being a woman. Which means also that they have never seen me as a person. Not really. I have been only the *image* of a person, without warm blood or thoughts, devoid of feelings, of desires and hungers.

I am a woman, I told myself. And they're not going to take it away from me. Tony knows that I am woman. That's good enough for me.

Three days later, I was shaken even more severely. I was puzzled by Murray Steiner's quiet insistence that we must talk – not in the office, but at the house, because, he said, it was a personal matter.

My agitation arose, as much as from the insistence, from the knowledge that lately I had seen little of Murray Steiner. He had not ceased his visits; but, since he nearly always came early in the morning, I was not around to talk things over with him.

I had invited him, along with his wife, to the first dinners, thinking not only of his pleasure but that it might be useful for him to meet the horse people I was meeting. He had accepted twice, coming alone each time – I had never met his wife. I introduced him, of course, to Count Gracchi, and on the second occasion I had observed the two men, for quite a long time, talking together in a quiet corner. Murray had, however, refused further attendance, pleading press of business or preoccupation with family, until I had instructed Tiffany not to embarrass him with the need to turn down our invitations.

I received Murray in the living-room, the house empty about us, for Tony had gone to Lexington for a luncheon, and Jan and Eva, at my instructions to be absent, had taken Trenholm for a walk.

After Murray was seated on the sofa, attaché case at his feet, I asked, smiling anxiously, if he would care for coffee.

He refused, saying, 'Let's make it short, Maude. I'm uncomfortably aware that I am exceeding my brief, and before I'm done you will have every right to be angry with me – and you *will* be.'

I was sitting in an armchair facing him. Folding my hands defensively in my lap, I said, 'What is it, Murray?'

'Gracchi,' he said. 'Are you planning on marrying him?'

I raised my eyes. 'That is a question which doesn't come within your legal purview, Murray.'

'I know,' he said with lethal quietness. 'That's what I said. But I think of myself also as your friend.'

'Yeah,' I said bitterly. 'So does everybody else. And all capable of telling me how to run my life . . . especially how to be Head Nun.'

His gaze did not falter. 'You are right to be angry, Maude. But I can't stand to one side and . . .'

I stood up. 'You couldn't see me make a fool of myself over a man,' I said. 'Is that it, Murray? Well, damn it, my heart is my own. So is my body, for that matter, and my right to be a fool. You people don't own me, you know, you and Dancy and Merlin and Alice. I'm . . .'

When I had to pause for breath, Murray said, 'Sit down, Maude.'

I sat down.

Pain was evident in the brown liquidness of his eyes. He was performing what he saw as a duty against his own will, his instincts, his sense of himself as an attorney. *My* attorney. Since he was forcing himself to the distasteful task, against my will I had to listen.

'Maude,' Murray said, 'I am thinking of what you have built here, how you're running the risk of letting it slip out of your grasp. When I know . . .'

'I don't know what you're talking about.'

'Has the Count proposed marriage?'

'No,' I said unwillingly. 'I don't think he knows the lines.'

'Will you marry him if he asks you?'

I wavered. 'I don't know,' I said. 'I haven't thought about it.'

It was a lie. I knew it. Murray Steiner knew it.

Quietly he said, 'OK. I must tell you, Maude: Count Gracchi is not after you so much as he's after Outlaw Farm.'

He had no right to suggest such a thing. How could he know how Tony looked at me, how . . .

'Well, thanks,' I said in cold anger. 'Would you please tell me how you can be so sure of what's between us?'

Murray was so uncomfortable one would have thought the sofa was on fire. 'I told you, Maude. I have exceeded my brief.' He drew a deep breath; when he spoke again his voice was dry and thin. 'But I've done my homework, too. I have spent a good deal of your money to find out what I could about the Count.' Taking out a white handkerchief, he wiped his face. 'If, in the long run, you decide it was wrong to do so, I will reimburse you out of personal funds. But I felt – even at the risk of losing your friendship – it was in your best interest.'

I couldn't stand up this time. My stomach had curled into a knot of anger so cold I didn't dare move for fear of exploding into an insensate rage.

'Murray, I hope you understand how deeply you have offended me. You have abused the trust I placed in you as my attorney. As my friend.'

'I know,' he said unhappily. 'Only too well.' He paused, staring at the handkerchief crumpled in his left hand. He patted his forehead with it, looked at it again as though expecting to see blood.

'I hired a respectable firm of detectives, giving them *carte blanche* on expenses and effort.' Grateful for the physical activity, he leaned forward to unsnap his attaché case and take out a thick blue folder. He placed it on the coffee table between us.

'That is what the French police call a dossier,' he said. 'I only wanted to give you some factual information to go on. That's all I meant, Maude. Will you believe me?'

'No,' I said. 'You think you have the right to tell me how to live. I'm not a person to you, a woman, any more than I am to Dancy Clutterbuck or anybody else around here. I'm an institution called Outlaw Farm.' Cruelly – after all, I had suffered cruelly this morning, hadn't I, even though it had been meant as the saving cruelty of surgery – I added, 'You and Dancy, and the rest, are only protecting *your* interests. You're afraid Tony might influence me against you, take me out of your hands. Isn't that it?'

Murray took a letter from the attaché case. 'I have also brought along a letter informing you that as of yesterday I am resigning as your legal adviser,' he said, 'and stating that I will render a full accounting to any legal firm of your choice. I have also recommended two attorneys, either of whom, I am sure, would handle your affairs to your satisfaction. All you have to do is sign the letter and return it to my office.'

The faithful integrity of that gesture stopped me.

'But you're still telling me I'd be a fool to marry the man.'

'I have no desire to trade in opinions,' he said. 'I won't do so. I only wish you to know the man, as well as he can be known, as a basis on which to make up your mind.'

I picked up the blue folder, dropped it. 'How much did this . . . thing . . . cost me?'

'About twelve thousand dollars,' he said steadily. 'The final bills are not all in yet, but it won't run much more.' He stopped. He began again. 'It is as complete an investigation as it was possible to make.'

'I don't need your twelve thousand dollars' worth of dirt to make up my mind whether I love a man or not.'

His face was suffering. 'I'm sorry, Maude. I'll . . . go now.'

'Yes. I think you should.' I made the effort to hold out a hand. 'I want to thank you, Murray, for all that you've done for me in the past.'

He bent to close his attaché case, rose with it in his hand. 'It's been good knowing you, Maude. Maybe, one of these days . . .' Stopping the useless words, he turned to go.

I didn't accompany him to the door. Frozen, I stood looking down at the blue folder. So thick. So real. I picked it up, clutching it with both hands, as I heard the unmistakable sound of Tony's footsteps outside, then the opening of the door.

'Hello, dear,' he said cheerfully. 'Passed your solicitor on the way in. Large conference?'

'Yes,' I said.

'Lovely luncheon,' he said. 'You should have come along.'

'Yes,' I said sombrely. 'I should have.'

He began an animated conversation about the people who had asked him to lunch. I saw him remotely as he spoke. Such a handsome man, brown and aquiline, the nose, the mouth; there were wrinkles in his neck, I noticed, and his hands were older than his face. Even from where I stood, I could smell the cologne. Or was it only the memory of a smell?

Count Gracchi was a sensitive man; abruptly stopping the talk, he came closer. Not touching me, but very near. 'What's wrong, Maude?'

His voice was so tender, so concerned, I could only turn away. 'Nothing.'

He put a finger on the blue folder. 'What's this? There's something troubling you.' He half-smiled. 'I know you too well, Maude, for you to deny it.'

I snatched away the folder, holding it safe under folded arms. 'It's nothing, Tony. Just business.'

He was relieved. 'Every day so involved with business. You need to let go a little, Maude, have fun instead, enjoy your splendid little parties . . .'

'Tony,' I said, 'shut up.'

It shocked him. Giving him a smile of rueful understanding, I said, 'Sorry, Tony. I'm just not in the mood for . . . I'm going to lie down.'

He was relieved all over again. 'Yes. You should. I will go for a walk.' His eyes remained warm. 'Come to me when you are ready for my company.'

I gave him my hand, but briefly. He made a move to kiss it. I pulled away. 'Yes,' I said. 'I will.' I went up the stairs to my bedroom and sat on the side of the bed. I still had the blue folder, carrying it in both arms as tenderly as a baby. Taking it into my hands, I gazed at the blank cover. I had not opened it. I would not open it.

But . . . why not? If every word were true, every scabrous deed, was not Tony still Tony?

After all, I told myself, America has always been a land for new beginnings. How many hundreds of thousands have crossed over into the land of the free and the home of the brave, courageously shedding the burden of old European history to stand forth as a new man?

Opening the blue cover with trembling fingers, I looked at the first page. So neatly typed, with headings and subheadings. In a sudden blaze of fearful anger, I hurled the dossier across the room. It flew with fluttering pages, skidding across the top of a cedar chest to fall behind it, hidden from sight.

In the stillness, I could hear the harsh sound of my breathing.

My body was suffused with an emotion I dared not name. In it, there was too much fear.

For . . . I couldn't trust myself. Knowledge of the contents of the dossier would inevitably taint the pureness of my love. That, I could not endure. I would not read it. Not now. Not ever.

I went in search of my lover.

I found Tony standing on the knoll between the Coach Barn and the Great Stone Barn, the vantage point from which nearly all of Outlaw Farm could be encompassed in a glance. I looked up at him from a distance, tall against the sky, his profile sharp and clean, so absorbed that he remained unaware of my approach. He stood with the Malacca cane braced against his left thigh and, though it was cold today, he was wearing only a turtleneck sweater and the too-thin Florida trousers. Below him was a pasture where weanlings romped, moving with the insistent energy of the very young. He is not young any more, I thought. No more than I. My heart turned over at the tainted elegance, the scarred beauty, of the man. By putting out my hand, I knew as surely as I have ever known anything, I could possess him in all his maleness.

I began to breathe hard as I climbed; I had to tell myself it was from the exertion, not from the impact of his nearness.

Tony turned his head at the sound of footsteps. He smiled. I came to his side and took his free hand, feeling his strong fingers close strongly about mine.

'This is my favourite place on the entire farm,' he said quietly.

'It has become mine, too,' I said. I laughed breathlessly. 'Before you came, I was always too busy to know how beautiful Outlaw Farm looks from here.'

Tony gazed deeply into my face; perhaps he sensed something of the crisis I had passed through, knew that a trouble lingered still within my soul. He did not try to speak to it; we simply stood together, my hand held tightly in his, and gazed in twinned bliss upon this place I had created out of all the earth.

I saw Dancy Clutterbuck emerge from the Great Stone Barn, starting up the road towards the Coach Barn. He stopped, looking at us together on the knoll, then turned his direction the other way.

Tony and I dined alone that night; when there were no guests, Tiffany Thomas sometimes took her evening meal upstairs with

Trenholm. We shared candlelight and wine, with Jan in his white jacket hovering in the background, and talked easily together.

Tony made me laugh even as I inwardly sighed with the comfort of his presence. Perhaps there lingered in him, as in me, the essence of our good minutes together on the knoll. I have never known a man so acutely sensitive to the moods of a woman; though the talk was quick and light, there was an underflow of meaning in the tone of our voices, the flicker of our eyes as they met and parted in quick glances.

When we went upstairs, when he paused before my bedroom door, when he raised my hand to his lips, I said, 'Tony. Isn't it time for you to kiss me?'

Holding my hand half-lifted, he paused. 'Do you wish it?'

'Yes.'

He moved his arms, a gesture of invitation, and I went in close, feeling the hard strength of his long muscles, my arms reaching around his waist, both hands going up under his jacket to know with splayed fingers the warmth and texture of his back. His splendid profile brooded over me for so long it was unendurable; I was straining upwards as he bent his head to touch his mouth to mine.

His lips were cool, curiously hard in line. But I had warmth enough for both; I burrowed my mouth against his mouth, feeling the delicious trembling shake my body like a leaf. He held himself strongly against me, his hands on my shoulders now, pulling me into him, and his lips moved, tasting my lips, savouring the passion I was suddenly yielding.

When we broke away – he initiated the movement, not I – he was breathing hard.

'Tony,' I said, my voice breaking.

He put fingertips against my words. 'Shhh . . .' he said.

We stood silent. His black eyes were so brilliant they were unreadable.

He took his hand away. 'Good night, Maude,' he said coldly and, with a decisive movement, destroyed the nearness. A wordless cry broke in my throat. It did not bring him back to me; with quickened step, he went on, as though fearful he would respond.

He will come to me, I thought calmly. In the darkness he will suddenly be there, and we will be lovers. It is the manner in which it should be accomplished, in the night, with great tenderness. I opened the door to my bedroom. Deliberately I searched out my prettiest nightgown, a filmy Dior gossamer blushed faintly of red, and got into bed. Only as I lay under the covers did I realize how deeply I was trembling.

He did not come.

I don't know how long I waited before I understood that Count Gracchi would not come to me. By the time I had realized it, I had also accepted it, so that, before I knew it, I had gone asleep. Waking to the strength of a morning sun through eastward windows, I got out of bed, took off the shameless gossamer of gown, and put it away into a drawer.

So all right. I let him know. So, now, let *him* choose the time.

That was it, of course. He felt himself too much a man to accept such passionate female behest. How many women must have thrown themselves at him in just that manner? You're a fool, Maude. You must learn to let him do the leading.

Not wishing to remain in the house, without waiting for breakfast I hurried to the office. Even so, there was a singing in me as I plunged into work. In spite of – perhaps because of – the abortive lovemaking, I had come to terms with myself. I had accepted love and desire. And the blue-covered dossier lying secret in the corner of my bedroom did not exist.

At eleven o'clock exactly, the call came down from the house. Tiffany Thomas stood suddenly in my doorway. 'Count Gracchi wishes to know if you can come up to the mansion.'

'I'm done here,' I said, rising. 'Tell him I'll be right there.' I could taste the calmness in my voice.

Tony waited in the living-room, wearing lean black slacks and one of his endless supply of turtleneck sweaters. I looked at the roll of white wool against the brownness of his throat, remembering with frightening vividness how, last night, he had kissed me.

Tony, smiling, took both my hands and led me to the sofa. 'We must talk,' he said.

I sat down. He sat beside me, leaning forward, still holding my hands.

'What is it, Tony?'

'Maude,' he said tenderly, 'I won't consent to become your lover.'

The words were spoken in the tone of love. But the meaning made me take my hands away.

'Was I *that* greedy?'

He captured my hands again. 'Don't be angry before you have heard me out.' He looked into my eyes. 'I have been a lover of women,' he said. 'But you . . . you are different. I don't want to make you only one among the many.' He smiled slightly. 'You know, of course, that going from you last night was a most difficult thing.'

'Dear Tony,' I said, pressing his fingers.

His voice took on a tinge of excitement. 'There must be more than love,' he said. 'More than a night of love. Great as that love can be. Do you . . . understand?'

'No.'

He stood up, his long legs, the cane, moving him away, back again. He loomed over me as I gazed up into his face.

'Think, Maude!' he cried. 'What a great thing we can make together!'

He read the puzzlement in my face. He spread his arms wide.

'Outlaw Farm,' he cried. 'For God's sake, don't you see what can be done here? A partnership, Maude. Count Gracchi and Maude Sage, side by side through the years, making great horses, selling at the highest prices to the best of international racing stables.'

A coldness curled itself, a tiny thread, inside me. 'I don't understand.'

He steadied himself. 'It was a great dream you dreamed, Maude, but you, a woman, cannot hope to accomplish it alone. You must have a man at your side. The right man. Me.' His face was ablaze with passionate conviction. 'You need my knowledge of horses, my acceptance into international society. You see, the kind of Thoroughbred you're trying to breed is better adapted to the European style than your American sprint races. Outlaw Farm can open France, England, to American winners . . . and it is time for American bloodlines to return to Europe.' He leaned intensely, close above me. 'I can bring the international racing men to Outlaw Farm, I will escort them personally through the barns, while you make this mansion a showplace of hospitality and breeding – of all sorts. An invitation to Outlaw Farm will become sought after, cherished by everyone who counts. Can't you see it, Maude?'

I sat chilly as a jockey riding out a ten-length lead. 'Tell me more, Tony.'

He came down out of the excitement into an emotion even more intense. 'You have the money, the land, the horses. I not only have the social connections, I have the great experience of managing such a farm. You will devote yourself entirely to the social side, you will be a great lady, you will never again wear a pair of blue jeans. Imagine how wonderful it will be, Maude. Just imagine!'

I said nothing.

His voice took on a hard edge of practicality. 'You know already what Gracchi can accomplish. I sold the stallion season to Irene Shipwright the very first time I took you there, yes? And the great people who have been guests in this house, in these few days I have been with you . . . they wouldn't have known Outlaw Farm existed otherwise. If I go away, they will not come again.'

I still didn't say anything.

He was standing straight now, almost statuesque. 'You need Count Gracchi, Maude. You know yourself how very necessary I am. As I need Maude Sage, as I need Outlaw Farm, more than I have ever needed anything in my life.'

I could not look at him. 'What about love?' I said. 'What happened to love?'

'But of course there will be love!' He came down on his right knee beside me. Instead of taking my hands, he gripped my thighs strongly as he gazed passionately into my eyes. 'Maude, I would like to propose marriage. It is the only way we can come together. Love cannot be for Count Gracchi and Maude Sage simply a time, or a few times, and then the time is no longer. I will not have it so.' He took a deep breath. 'I am proposing honourable marriage, Maude. You must accept.'

His face was close to me. Too close. Yet I gazed unflinchingly into his eyes.

'Let me see if I understand. You will take charge of Outlaw Farm, while I reign as lady of the manor. Is that about right?'

He smiled. 'You will worry your lovely head only about making the mansion a sparkling jewel for all our friends. You will know intimately dukes and princesses, you will address the royalty of international racing by their very nicknames, the jet set will jet to you.'

'I . . . have always thought of marriage as . . . love.'

He smiled indulgently. 'You Americans, always you dwell on love, always you make such horrible marriages. But of course there will be love, you know from last night how very much, my darling Maude. But . . .'

'But there are other considerations,' I said steadily.

'Europeans have always understood the important considerations in arranging a marriage,' he said, still patient in explication. 'Marriage is a structure of many things beyond mere love:

money, property, a style of living.' He was passionate again, but not with passion. 'Between us we have immense assets, Maude. Making our alliance, one with the other, we can live a richer life than we ever could alone.'

He was gripping my thighs so hard they were growing numb. 'So, before we arrive at love, it is necessary to have a clear understanding of everything else.'

He nodded in satisfaction. 'Naturally. The European way. Your attorney shall draw up a document setting forth exactly the marriage contract, we will both sign it. It is the only way in which to establish a marriage truly.'

'Without an agreement, Tony . . . are you still proposing?'

'But of course we will agree.'

He moved his hands, putting them on each side of my waist, kneeling into me now so that I could feel the warmth of his body.

'*Then* there shall be love. Instead of making myself walk away, I will come into your bedroom, I will embrace you, you will know how greatly I do love.'

'I . . . thought you'd come to me last night,' I said. 'I waited, Tony. A very long time.'

His eyes were warm and black and sincere. 'I desired to come, believe me, you cannot know how deeply I desired. But . . . I will not be your lover, Maude. You shall not be one with the women I have known. You shall be the *one* woman, of all the women in the world, with the right to title herself Countess Gracchi. I am offering to you, Maude, myself and my ancient and honourable title. I am laying them at your feet.'

I put my hand on the side of his head. The silky texture of the long hair, brushed whitely along his temple, beneath it the hard bone, was pleasant. I brushed my fingertips through the wing of hair once, then again.

'Last night, Tony, I decided I was being too greedy,' I said. 'But I was wrong. The larger greed was yours.'

He was very still.

'Quit touching me,' I said.

He moved away. I looked across the small distance. Such a great distance. 'Mr Gracchi, I am sensible of the honour you have tendered me,' I said. 'I must, however, regretfully decline your proposal of marriage.'

Had I not said it in such formality, he might have found a way to override me, enlist my true desire. But those words, spoken without anger, erected a barrier that the daring horseman could not jump. Over it I could read the drawn whiteness of his face as, baffled, wordless, he stared at me.

I rose. 'I would have been content with love,' I said. 'But no man can take this farm from me. Or sell me what you are selling.'

I walked to the archway and turned. 'You might enjoy Christmas in Palm Beach after all,' I said. 'It's warm there. Why don't you give Irene Shipwright a call?'

Leaving him standing in the middle of the room, I went upstairs – but only to retrieve the blue folder from behind the cedar chest and carry it with me to the office. I wanted to read it in the impersonality of that setting. Closing the door against intrusion and taking the phone off the hook, I settled myself and opened the folder. I read the first page, then all the other pages. Carefully. Slowly. Twelve thousand dollars' worth of information about the man who, last night, would have been welcomed ardently into my arms.

The man didn't even have a title; there was good reason to believe that he was actually a private in the Italian Army, that he took the uniform and the papers from the body of the real Count Gracchi and used them to surrender to the American Army in order to receive the treatment of an officer prisoner-of-war. Once safely in the States, after Italy became an ally, he was the kept lover of the wealthy woman he had later persuaded to enter Thoroughbred racing and breeding. He *had*, at least, known something about horses . . . probably, I thought as I closed the folder, in his youth he had worked on a great Italian estate, caring for the horses. A stable groom.

There was, really, nothing in the dossier I didn't already know in my heart. Oh, the details were interesting, the jerry-built structure of a scuffling existence. I would never have believed him criminal, but he had skated close to the edge at least once, when he had reputedly embezzled a large sum of money from his original American benefactress. She could surely have put him behind bars if she had wished to press charges. He must have been, I thought, extraordinarily desperate at the time.

I sighed, closing the folder. What a life. Wouldn't it have been better to have returned to his village after the war, married a village girl and got on her a horde of children, eking out his masculine life drinking wine and talking man-talk in the village cafe? He had chosen the other road. And now . . . he was growing older. The charm begins to wear a bit thin when youth is gone.

What hurt most deeply was the knowledge that from the first meeting his plan had been in operation. He had heard talk of me, had sought me out, and it would not have mattered if I had been a bald, cross-eyed Viet Cong, for I was perhaps his last chance.

He might have made it, too, I admitted ruefully, if he had only stayed with me last night. Once having made love, how could I have denied him? But then something steely in my soul told me otherwise; it could not have happened; the time would surely have come when I would have sent him away.

So, at the end, I arrived at a simple gratitude that my foolishness had not lasted so long as to require a messy ending. I had been vulnerable because, I told myself, you're not getting any younger either, kid, and Count Gracchi was certainly your last chance, too.

I sighed, putting it away. The rest of the day was accomplished with a certain peace in my soul. I made the last round of inspection with Dancy Clutterbuck, as I had not done for so long, and remained serenly undisturbed by his curt responses to enquiry and suggestion. Finished, I went into the tack room and let a little sour mash bring me closer to the Maude Sage of yore.

When I went up to the house, the lights were softly blazing, dinner was ready. Before bathing and dressing, I phoned Tiffany Thomas in her bedroom, saying, 'You'll eat dinner downstairs tonight, won't you?'

Recognizing the unspoken need, she said, 'Yes, of course.'

So we were three at table, Tony, silent, making no effort towards his usual charm as Tiffany and I chatted. As we lingered over coffee, Tony asked, 'Jan can run me into the airport early in the morning?'

'Of course,' I said. 'Just tell him tonight what time your flight leaves.'

Folding his napkin meticulously, he excused himself. I looked at Tiffany – her face was alive with curiosity – and said, ''Night, Tiffany. See you in the morning,' and went upstairs.

The imperious knock, deep into the night, brought me instantly upright. I sat chilled, hearing it repeated, then again. *Please* Tony, I thought silently. Please don't.

For a long minute, silence ensued. I lay down again. At that instant his weight crashed against the door and, old and loosely fitted, it sprang open. He was in the room.

I sat up again. 'Tony,' I said. 'Don't be a beast.'

He was panting as he came close to the bed. I lay under the

covers, looking up at his shadowy outline, wondering if he were nude. Something in me, I am ashamed to say, wanted to think of him as naked in my bedroom.

'I will take you once before I go,' he said, his voice a harsh growl, not at all the voice of the charming Tony Gracchi I had so cherished.

'Don't be a sore loser,' I said, sitting up. 'I don't want to remember you that way.'

He hovered. I knew that, if he touched me, his hand would ignite the pilot light that burned yet brightly in my flesh. But the words were the good words that struck hard at his masculinity and, after a long moment of abeyance, he went away, moving with a rapid, savage limp, slamming the door so hard the sound reverberated throughout the house.

I lay down again. The details of the dossier were not in my mind, but something entirely unexpected and irrelevant. I should have realized the truth of the man long ago, I told myself, from the simple fact that he had always treated Trenholm Thomas, poor mature child, as though she did not exist. It had ticked at me all along, unheeded, a warning of his basic nature.

When he left in the morning, I had long been in the barns, and all he took with him from Outlaw Farm – I didn't realize it until a week later, wondering then how he had known they were hidden in my underwear drawer against Christmas giving – were the diamond shirt studs I had ordered from Tiffany's in New York.

CHAPTER 5

When you've made a grand fool of yourself, the only move is to put it behind you and go on to what you hope will be better times – times in which you will use the better part of yourself, not the worst. There remained a rankling in my soul that would, I knew, become a permanent part of Maude Sage, twinging on the bad days like an old wound in rainy weather. We all acquire scars, emotional and otherwise; one could call them the badges of wisdom, though when you're ready to make a fool of yourself all over again, those well-earned medals don't seem to help, do they?

Beyond Christmas, thank goodness, was the new breeding season: mares to foal and matings to manage, the yearlings to be conditioned towards July and the Select Summer Sale. Not a routine so much as a cycle, ever renewed and ever different, a vital process into which I threw myself with all the old zest and enthusiasm. It is one of the losses of our over-civilization that so much of mankind has put itself out of joint with the cycles of nature. An immense loss; for, like the earth itself, a human being needs the ever new sense of renewal, of new beginnings in an ancient pattern, so that the heart leaps with the happiness of a day-old foal as with quivering tension and enormous curiosity it explores its splendid new world.

My recent conduct had cast a pall, far more than I had realized, over Outlaw Farm. I cannot say that, in returning to my proper place, I dispelled immediately the constraints.

I did my best. I'm not saying I went to Dancy Clutterbuck, to Merlin, to Alice, to confess my abysmal guilt and beg forgiveness for being a fool. No matter how acute the realization of how near I had come to surrendering Outlaw Farm into greedy and unworthy hands, I could only submerge my egocentric in- viduality into the collective life, rising early and staying late to demonstrate mutely that Outlaw Farm once again encompassed all of Maude Sage, as Maude Sage encompassed all of Outlaw Farm.

Once the original basis for trust and friendship has been destroyed, it is impossible of restoration entirely; there remains a residual poison from the bad times. The scars are not only in your soul.

Especially with Dancy. Though we were friendly and co-operative, though we spent as many good hours together every day as in the beginning, there remained a measurable rift . . . though he spoke no more of becoming a race-track gypsy.

Maybe it's all to the good, I comforted myself. So much more tenable for the long haul, instead of the too-great closeness that dares allow emotional factors to unbalance the professional symbiosis of owner and manager.

The first order of business was putting Outlaw Prince and the other two-year-olds back into training, which brought Brock Walter from Florida to finish out his contract.

Brock and Whitey arrived on an unseasonably warm day in a white convertible, somewhat battered about the fenders and showing a touch of age; nevertheless, a veritable Cadillac, a true convertible. Brock was at the wheel, Whitey Dahl lounging in the back seat with an unveritable Florida blonde nestled into the crook of his arm. He did not deign to alight, but remained seated, prepared to receive our greetings like visiting royalty.

I waited until Brock entered the office. I shook his hand, astonishingly pleased to see his sour face. 'Our hero seems to have done well at Hialeah,' I said. Through the window, I indicated the automobile. 'You don't seem to have done too badly yourself.'

Brock laughed. 'That's his, too. Everything you see belongs to Whitey Dahl.'

'Yeah, so I noticed,' I said. 'He must have done pretty good at riding to be able to afford both a white Cadillac convertible and an off-white Miami Beach bimbo.'

'He won the car in a crap game in the jockey dressing room. Our hero is a high-roller as well as, potentially, one hell of a jock. I won't guess where and how he got the woman.'

We went outside. 'Welcome home, Whitey,' I said.

'Didn't aim to be here,' he said. 'Aimed to be riding the New York circuit along about now. But Brock wouldn't have it any other way.' His complaint registered, he allowed himself a grin. 'Let me introduce my friend Gloria. Gloria, this is Miss Maude Sage. She's the owner of that colt I was telling you about.'

'Pleased,' Gloria said.

Gloria, like the Cadillac, was somewhat battered about the fenders, and of indeterminate age. She was wearing an orange blouse and green slacks, filling both beyond the point of simple ampleness. I gave her a week before Kentucky began to bore her out of her gourd.

'Brock says you did well at Hialeah,' I said to Whitey.

'Hottest hand on the track,' he said. 'Give me the good mounts, I would of showed 'em.' Disengaging from the oppressive clinging of his consort, he condescended to touch the earth of Outlaw Farm.

'Come on, baby, let me show you around this old place.'

She pouted. 'You just want to look at more horses. That's all you ever do. Come on, love-boy, take me to the Holiday Inn. I need a bath, I feel so *sticky* . . .'

Love-boy?

I stood gazing in amazement at Whitey Dahl as he walked the woman into the Great Stone Barn. He was dressed in powder-blue slacks that draped his lean hips as only an expensive fabric can, his jacket a darker blue, cut with good shoulders and chastely flaunting a foulard lining. Beneath it he wore a white shirt with a broad, tieless collar that was embroidered in an intricate band of blue thread exactly the shade of the slacks. His small, neat shoes were ultraconservative, looking, at the least, to be a London last.

Brock Walter noted my astonishment. 'Got all his winnings on his back,' he said. He shrugged. 'Can't blame a jock for spending good money on clothes. Most of 'em, until money gets sudden in their pockets, have to dress themselves out of the boys' department, and those clothes just aren't cut right for a grown man.'

'What astonishes me is that the little bastard has almost got good taste,' I said.

Brock chuckled. 'Whitey went to some tough schools in Florida, Maude. And you can't say he isn't a quick study.' He turned to Dancy. 'How do the two-year-olds look? Can we start getting them ready to ask the big question?'

Brock and Dancy withdrew into a concentrated discussion. Whitey Dahl, returning with his Florida piece, looked towards the office. 'Why, hello, Tiffany,' he said.

Tiffany Thomas stood poised in the doorway, the gladness of her anticipation at Whitey's return horribly swept away.

Whitey strutted forward. 'Tiff, old girl, want you to meet my friend Gloria. Gloria, this is Miss Tiffany Thomas.' He leered. 'She was mighty kind to an orphan boy, Gloria, so I want you two to be friends.'

'Pleased,' Gloria said.

Tiffany's face was ghastly. Unable to rise to the heartbreaking occasion, she fled into the sanctuary of the office. Whitey shrugged, saying to Gloria, 'Guess she ain't so glad to see me after all. There's somebody else I want you to meet, too.' Turning to me: 'Where's Alice working at?'

'The Big Barn, along with Merlin,' I said. 'I'm sure she'll be delighted to see what you won – or bought – in Florida.'

'Come on, love,' Whitey said. 'Big Barn it is.'

She pouted. 'Just more horses. I wish you didn't have to *ride* the smelly things.'

Later, Brock filled me in on Whitey Dahl's Florida apprenticeship. He had his ups and downs, all right.

'No trouble getting him works enough to keep us in coffee'n'cakes,' Brock said. 'Had all the morning mounts a hard-working fellow can handle. But the meeting was half over before I managed an apprentice contract . . . I thought he would die, every afternoon when the races were going off and he wasn't riding. He'd hang on the rail to watch the jocks come out in post parade, dressed in the bright silks he hadn't worn till yet – and if Whitey Dahl is capable of suffering, which I still doubt sometimes, he was suffering then. Afterwards, he'd spend the whole evening taking the races apart, telling me how he'd of won it with this runner or that one. He saw all the mistakes the jockeys made, besides inventing a few. Then he'd light into cussing me out for not keeping my promise about lining up an apprentice contract. Impatient, I tell you, and so hard to live with I threw him out about once a week, told him to go see how he'd make out on his own.' He paused. 'Always came back, though, because he knew I was all he had going for him.'

'You can't say he isn't ambitious,' I said. 'And, of course, the money he could have been making . . .'

Brock shrugged. 'Already had more money than he knew what to do with. Knew every horse on the shedrow right down to the night eyes, spent hours watching them work, talking to the men who rubbed them. With that solid background, he became a shrewd handicapper. Didn't make but one bet a day – maybe two – but he won more often than he lost.' Brock laughed. 'He was toting a bigger roll on his hip than most of the boys riding four and five horses a day.

'About the middle of the meeting, an old friend of mine with a public stable, Bob Shirley by name, shipped in from New York. Wouldn't have come at all except his best runner, a six-year-old gelding that's a pretty good stakes horse when he's right, decided he didn't like the cold weather up North and quit running. I talked Bob into signing Whitey.'

Brock fell silent, to regard me dubiously. 'I have to tell you, Maude, Bob Shirley will be shipping into Daingerfield Race Track when the spring meeting opens and I sort of halfway promised that you'd give him serious consideration.' Apologetically he added, 'Wouldn't have done it if I didn't know he's as good a trainer as you're likely to find. But I needed the extra leverage . . . you know the fine impression Whitey can make on somebody he expects to do him a favour.'

'I know,' I said dryly. Then, seriously, 'Of course I'll follow your recommendation, Brock . . . though I was hoping you'd take out a trainer's licence yourself.'

'Thought about it,' he said. 'But a licence doesn't necessarily guarantee a stable of runners, you know. And I've got Whitey to think about, got to get him the good mounts.' He nodded vigorously. 'Because that boy can go the route, Maude. He's a hell of a rider. Absolutely without fear. He won on first asking, on a two-thousand-dollar claimer which went off at twenty-to-one.' He threw back his head, laughing. 'Needless to say, Whitey made me put fifty dollars on the nose, and he pulled out the best race that poor old bangtail had run in his life. Nursed him like an invalid along the backstretch, got up in the last stride to win by a nose.'

Brock shrugged again. 'It set him up, let me tell you. You know how he is. So he had to learn some lessons. The other jocks were just the fellows to teach him, too. For one thing, he walked into the dressing room, the first time, like a general taking over an army. I don't know exactly what went on, because, you know, no one is allowed in the jocks' dressing room except the riders and their valets – and Whitey won't talk about it. His next race, seemed like every time he was ready to make a move, about three horses happened to be in his way. They didn't foul him, but he never could get running room. Those boys can lay it on a fellow, all right, when they want to. Then, the second week he was riding, he came out of the dressing room after the last race with his face so bruised I could hardly recognize my wayward boy. I heard on the grapevine it took three to wear him down, one after the other. That experience settled him, I think . . . at least, he didn't start any more fights.

'Beginning late like that, I couldn't get him much in the way of outside mounts, so most of his riding was done for Bob

Shirley. Which meant there was only bread money, not a cut of the purse. Bob had a string of useful runners, but the gelding was the only one which could be called a stake horse, and he wasn't exactly a world-beater. So Whitey never got to ride in a big race, but hung on the rail with that hungry look on his face, to take the race apart later on and tell me how he would of won it if I had got him something with four legs and a chance.'

Brock laughed. 'He started with a hot hand, all right, though riding the poorest claimers. Earned a reputation for getting at least one five-thousand-dollar run out of a two-thousand-dollar claimer. Since he was a whip rider, once he'd nursed his cripple into contention, the horse might not run again for two months, maybe never; but the backside money was on Whitey Dahl's silks more often than not.'

'Sounds like he was learning his trade.'

Brock nodded. 'Best way in the world. Makes the boy know it's only half himself, at least half the horse. Which teaches him to know his mount. He may not love him, but at least he understands him.' He looked serious. 'They're still only vehicles to him, you understand. If he could only learn . . .' He sighed, went on. 'Got a triple once, his best day, then went into a slump. Rode a week without a winner, and he started cussing the other jocks, saying they were ganging up on him again. Maybe they were . . . that was right after he'd won the Cadillac. Then he got another winner, the next day two, then another triple. He was coming back, riding smarter than before, concentrating on every race like it was the Kentucky Derby.'

Brock looked at me. 'The boy works hard. Any day he's slated to ride, he'll walk the track to study every inch of its surface, so he'll know whether to go for the rail or stay outside. Out at daylight every day to pick up morning works; he'll tell the trainer, afterwards, exactly how he can win if the trainer will let him have the mount. A real hustler. Carried a condition book in his pocket, just like a trainer, knew it so well he could tell me before the entries were posted which horses would likely be entered, and what their chances were.' He nodded again, even more vigorously. 'He's a two-bit human being, Maude. I know that better than you do. But he is entirely serious about becoming the world's great jockey.'

A reminiscent smile. 'The last week, I finally got him a stakes horse . . . a hundred-to-one shot in the Bahamas. Ran dead last from wire to wire, and when he threw the reins over the horse's head and slid down from the saddle, he said to me, "If you ever put me up on a piece of dead meat like that again, Brock, I'll kill you".'

'So Whitey Dahl has come home,' I said. 'Neither a conqueror nor a hero. Except in his own mind.'

Brock Walter grinned. 'Over his own dead body. Wouldn't have it any way but that he was on his way to the Big Apple to make a name for himself. No matter that you and I have a contract; no matter that Bob Shirley, who holds *his* contract, is shipping to Daingerfield. No matter that I am now officially his agent.'

'Why didn't you leave him in Florida, let him ride out the season?'

Brock looked troubled. 'I . . . can't trust the boy to be on his own yet. No telling what he'd get into. And . . .' He paused to look at me. 'Maude, when Outlaw Prince is ready to run, I want to put Whitey up. I've already talked it over with Bob.'

'The way you tell it, he's a horse killer,' I said sharply. 'Outlaw Prince has had nothing but the kindest treatment, as you well know. I don't want anyone to have anything to do with him who . . .'

Brock nodded unhappily. 'Maude, I feel the same way. If the boy can't learn to have some feeling for his horses . . .' He gazed at me earnestly. 'He'll never put an ounce of weight on Outlaw Prince's back until I *know* he's right. I promise you that. But . . . those two, they can go to glory together. If I can only . . .' He stopped himself, stood brooding for a moment, then made a brisk move of his body. 'Come on, I want to take a look at the two-year-olds, see how they're shaping up.'

Daingerfield Race Track opens its spring meeting early in March; it was our hope to have runners ready. Olden Song and John Domino, marked from the beginning as early starters, were our best chances. Outlaw Prince was too growthy still to be asked to run yet; my mind on the Summer Yearling Sale, I fretted about it. A stakes win by him would have a definite impact on the prices realized for our Sir Outlaw–War Admiralmarc progeny.

Mari Money, which had been put aside last fall after firing, came up with leg trouble all over again the first day he was asked to move faster than a trot. Brock Walter shook his head gloomily, saying, 'He'll never stand training, Maude. Such a nicely balanced colt, too. But a horse can't run with heat in his ankles.'

'What can we do with him?'

Brock shook his head again. 'Nice bloodlines, maybe you can get a few dollars for him as a prospective sire. Unraced, it won't amount to much. You'd have done better to sell him as a yearling.'

(Mari Money eventually went to Texas, where he stood for a five-hundred dollar stud fee, getting one minor stakes winner before dying at five of a twisted intestine.)

Discotex, our Vertex filly, was nice, well-mannered, and looked every inch the runner. When we asked the question, she didn't show enough speed to beat a slow turtle. The genius of her bloodlines had passed her by.

(In the fall of the year, we sold her to a Florida breeder at private treaty as a broodmare prospect for six thousand dollars. To date, her five named foals have been winners, including a stakes-placed runner and a stakes winner. You can't win 'em all.)

Polyarctic remained a question mark. With the best breeding – after all, he was brother-in-blood to Northern Dancer – when he started again in training he showed again his lazy streak. Wouldn't work at all except in company; then he had to be constantly urged to keep his mind on his business. He looked to be a good one, large and well-balanced, with a long stride and the credentials to be a top-class runner. But we hadn't found the key to him yet, maybe never would.

(Polyarctic remained in training throughout his two-year-old year without showing us enough to risk an entry fee. In desperation – and some shrewdness, since even David Harum couldn't have talked up that colt with a straight face – Bob Shirley, early in his third year, started him in a claiming race with a twenty-five-thousand-dollar tag. Though he ambled dead last, studying the interesting crowd as he went, he was claimed out of our hands. Didn't break his maiden at three, passing through several claims in the process because he was such a good-looking colt, with an impeccable pedigree – after all, how many owners of claiming horses can boast of a brother-in-blood to that great race horse Northern Dancer? – but at four, running at Ak-Sar-Ben in Nebraska, in a sudden burst of ambition he moved into the stakes company and won three in a row. Shipped to Hawthorne, on his conquering way East, his first start there was an overnight allowance, which he won laughing. A few days later, after being installed as the morning-line favourite for the Chicago Handicap, in his last blowout before the race he took a bad step, fracturing both sesamoids and the cannon bone in his right foreleg, and had to be destroyed.)

Candy Box, though showing flashes of speed, continued so washy she was impossible to train. Her nerves lay right on the surface; living in a world of evanescent fears, she would spook at everything and nothing; no counting the times she dumped her boy and had to be chased down. The first time we walked her through a starting gate, she went into a panic, rearing and thrashing until she caught a front leg in the gate and nearly tore her hoof off before she could be extricated. In the process she managed also to break the exercise boy's arm; he was lucky not to be killed. She was saved for stud duty by a hair's-breadth, though her front foot was only a limping club ever after.

Royal Dittany came back from her lay-up, promptly bowed both tendons in her front legs, so we gave up on her also, keeping her for breeding purposes. So Fine, the rangy Crozier filly, was, like Outlaw Prince, still too growthy to start early in the year.

(To finish out the roster, John Domino and Olden Song were early winners, Olden Song at first asking, and, though never a stakes winner, turned out to be a useful allowance mare at distances up to seven furlongs. She raced through her fifth year, earning some eighty thousand dollars the hard way, before being retired to stud. John Domino placed in several minor stakes through his third year before being sold to South America. So Fine came brilliantly to hand in the fall of the year, after demonstrating a distaste for dirt tracks that Bob Shirley first misread as lack of competitive spirit. Once tried on the turf, she established herself as an excellent grass runner over any distance of ground, and, racing through her sixth year, earned nearly two hundred thousand dollars.)

And Outlaw Prince . . . but that's another story.

One day, with due ceremony, I summoned Merlin to the office to inform him he was now, in title and in salary, the Assistant Farm Manager he had long since become in fact.

Merlin thanked me most gratefully . . . and turned it down.

Which, needless to say, left me with nothing to say. I looked at the ceiling. I looked at the young man. I looked at the floor. Finally I got it out.

'Why?'

'I don't want the responsibility,' he said.

A short laugh. 'Good God, man, you've been *carrying* the responsibility. Afraid it'll take too much time away from your studies at the University? You'll be able to keep your class schedule. I promise.'

'No ma'am, it's not that,' Merlin said stolidly. 'I've already decided not to keep on with the farm management courses, either.'

Sitting quite placidly in the chair across the desk, polite, remote, he was seemingly unmoved by these drastic decisions. Not the Merlin Honeycutt I had come to know so well; a profound change, unobserved by me, had taken place in him.

Getting up, I walked around the desk to stand over him. 'Trouble again between you and Alice?'

A finger on the sore spot. He almost flinched. 'Why . . . no, Miss Maude. I . . . haven't been seeing Alice for some time now.'

I stared, trying to recall the last time I had seen them together. Their daily stroll at the end of work, the occasional outing to a movie, had become such fixtures in the pattern of life on Outlaw Farm, no one paid attention any more. Me, least of all.

'What you mean is, you haven't been seeing Alice for a whole week.'

'Yes'm. I reckon that's right.'

My voice rose sharply. 'Whitey Dahl isn't messing around again, is he?'

Whitey spent his days at Daingerfield Track, now that the spring meeting had started, showing up at the farm only occasionally. However, Alice, still Outlaw Prince's regular exercise rider, went every morning to the track. The Florida blonde had abandoned Whitey to the frozen North of Kentucky four and a half days after their arrival, so the devil only knew what Whitey was up to. The devil was the one to keep track, because it was nothing good, for sure.

Merlin's hands flexed in his lap. 'No. He wouldn't dare.'

'Then what the hell's the matter?' I calmed myself. 'If you want to know the truth, Merlin, I think it's time you got off the dime and married the girl. With a raise in salary, a house to live in rent-free, you two can make out . . .'

'Nothing's the matter,' Merlin said with that gentle mountain stubbornness. 'It's just that I'm not the right man for Alice.'

'Has *she* told you that?'

'No.' He hesitated. 'We haven't . . . discussed it.'

I leaned against the desk, folding my arms. 'What you're telling me, Merlin, is that about a week ago, without any warning, you decided to quit the girl. Isn't that the scam? No quarrel, not even a discussion. Does *Alice* know that you don't count yourself engaged any more?'

'She ought to. By now.'

'But you haven't *told* her.'

For the first time, he was agitated. 'I . . . couldn't tell her. I just figured, after a while, she'd know . . .'

'Merlin, you haven't found another girl, have you?'

He was surprised. 'Me? What would I want with another girl?'

'Is she . . . dating someone else?'

'I don't know. I don't think so, not yet. She always leaves work early as she can, though.'

'Because of you, you idiot. You're shaming the girl, Merlin, letting everybody see that you don't want to walk with her.'

He became stubborn again. 'Might as well be that way. It ain't my place to marry a girl like Alice.'

'Isn't she the one to decide that?'

'No,' he said surprisingly. 'Alice would marry me all right, tomorrow, I guess, if I asked her.'

'Well, then, what's the problem? And what do you mean, *a girl like Alice*?'

'I reckon everybody else knew. Everybody but me. I guess you were all snickering behind my back, laughing about me fighting Whitey Dahl for her favour . . .'

A deep resentment was revealed in those words. He was, I knew, a man of self-contained pride; somehow that pride had been damaged. This it was that had changed him into a stranger; the world of Outlaw Farm, which he had perceived as a home populated by friends, had become hostile.

'Merlin,' I said quietly, 'I do not know what you're talking about.'

'You've known all along that Alice was rich,' he said.

Alice? Rich? What the devil *was* he talking about?

But, wait a minute . . . Alice had come to Outlaw Farm, like the rest of us, without dragging along her history, her antecedents. Quietly she had made a place among us, a valued member of the community.

The girl had always been discreet. All I really know about

Alice, I reflected, is that she loves and understands horses better than anyone I know, she is a good girl, she does her work conscientiously. And every evening at quitting time she walks down the lane and through the hedge into another world where she has never invited any of us. Not even, I suddenly knew, her beloved Merlin. Especially Merlin.

It had been my thought – if I had thought about it at all – that she was ashamed of living in that cluster of low-income houses. Perhaps her family was, to put it mildly, unprepossessing. Whatever the reason, we of Outlaw Farm had respected her reticence. But . . . rich?

'Whatever in the world gave you that idea?' I said.

Surprisingly for Merlin, he turned sullen, hunching his shoulders in an attempt to avoid the question.

'It was Whitey,' he said reluctantly. 'He let me in on the secret. Come sneering at me, one day last week, saying he knew now why I was so hot after Alice. I was hunting a fortune along with a wife.'

'He's putting you on, trying to cause all the trouble he can. You know what Whitey's like.' I paused. 'And you believed him! Merlin, does Alice *act* like she's got money?'

'She's got it,' he said. 'You know that big white house over there, all that bluegrass land that's so perfect for horses, but all they run on it is Kentucky Charolais cattle? That's hers . . . her father's, I mean. One of these days it'll belong to her.'

'Are you *sure*?'

'I'm sure, Miss Maude. She's had it all, private schools, a year's trip to Europe for her graduation present.' His face was miserable. 'I reckon she's been laughing at me all this time. You know, she never once asked me to meet her father, like she ought to have done if she was serious about being engaged.'

'I can't believe it of Alice,' I said, my tone as flat and assertive as his own. 'Not that she's from a wealthy family – I suppose that's a fact if you say so – but that she would do you that way.'

He nodded sharply. 'Never meant any of it. Just another rich girl playing a game, that's all. She knew all along, one of these days she'd get tired of pretending she had to work for a living. One night she'd just walk through that hedge and not come back; and, as far as she was concerned, that would be the end of Merlin Honeycutt, too.' His face tightened. 'It ain't going to happen. Because I've done quit her.'

'Merlin, you're wrong,' I said, wondering why I felt so desperate. But damn it, in a sense, they were *my* kids. In a sense, my responsibility. 'The girl loves you. OK, so may be she *is* rich, maybe she *did* keep it a secret. Only because, I'm sure, she found a more satisfying life at Outlaw Farm than all her riches could provide. A good life . . . and a good man. You said yourself she'd marry you tomorrow.'

'Maybe she would,' he said, serenely unaware of the contradiction. 'But I won't marry her. I couldn't live like that, everybody thinking I was after her money. Sooner or later she'd get to suspecting it herself. Bound to.'

'Don't you feel man enough to marry a rich girl?' I said provocatively. 'Don't you think your breeding is up to hers?'

He told me then, in desperate self-defence, the story of his family (as unrevealed until now as Alice's wealth, which I didn't point out). His father, a Pennsylvania man, had come in late middle age to the Kentucky mountains to marry a mail-order bride. A remarkable person, to hear Merlin tell it; educated, world-travelled, he had brought to the mountains trunks full of books. Hiring a family to work the farm he bought, he occupied himself with reading and meditation, in that early-to-bed community keeping a kerosene lamp burning the night long to annotate the volumes of his library in a miniscule script as clear as copperplate.

'Those books of his, he wrote all over the margins on every page,' Merlin said. 'His thoughts, his ideas, put down so tiny it took a magnifying glass to read.'

'Since he was an educated man, why didn't he send you to college?'

Merlin looked sad. 'When I was a boy, Daddy always talked how he meant for me to go to his old school, Princeton University, how he had the money set aside for the purpose. I was the only boy, you see, and he didn't want me raised ignorant like the people he'd married into.'

He paused, thinking back into the years. 'By the time I got old enough, though, Daddy had gone stone blind. Because, he decided, of all those years sitting up at night reading by the light of a coal-oil lamp. He got so mean and bitter, wouldn't let any of us go to school any more. My sisters didn't care, they were already thinking about getting married anyway, but I would slip off to the schoolhouse. Mama helped all she could, lying for me, anything.' He looked into my eyes. 'I hated him, Miss Maude. Because he had cut me off from the promise he had made when I was just a tad of a boy.' He dropped his gaze to his knotted hands. 'He couldn't help it, I reckon. He died hating everything and everybody because his whole scholarly life had been proved wrong.'

'Why did he come to the mountains in the first place?'

Merlin shook his head. 'Nobody ever knew. He had cut off all that part of his life. Never wrote a letter, never got one. So I don't know anything about his side of the family.' Merlin braced himself. 'But I ain't ashamed of my daddy. He was a fine, smart man, who had read everything and thought about it, he had travelled everywhere there is to travel, and wrote it all down in diary books. I just wish I had that library of his, with all his thinking on the blank pages and in the margins. It would teach me a lot.'

'What happened to the books?'

He was shamefaced. 'Well, you know, Mama couldn't read *or* write – she was just a slip of a girl when they wedded, and she had respect for him, I never heard her call him anything but *Mr Hunnicutt*. After he died, though, she didn't appreciate having those bulky old things stacked all over the house, so she tore out pages to start fires with, or put them in the outhouse, saying they might as well give some value of use.'

'What a shame.'

It was strange to see Merlin look so belligerent. 'Don't think I'm ashamed of Mama's family, either, even if they didn't know enough to hold old books safe. Miss Maude, they were amongst the first families to come into the mountains, long before this country was ever called the United States of America. We've got in our house a quilt box, all hand carved, that, it's told, travelled all the way from England in the olden days.'

Absorbed as I had been in his family history, I brought the conversation back to the present. 'So why are you ashamed to marry Alice?'

'I won't be counted as marrying for money,' he said, his face setting anew into the lines of stubborn pride. 'That's the all of it.'

No point in trying to argue, I realized. I shifted ground. 'Still, no reason to turn down your promotion.'

'I don't want the responsibility.'

'You mean you're quitting life, just like your father,' I said harshly. 'At a considerably younger age, I might add.'

He stood up. 'Miss Maude, thank you, but I reckon it's my business,' he said with dignity, and left my presence.

I sat thoughtful. God, the stubbornness of the human male, once he's picked out a wrong place to stand. Nothing to be done about it, either. No one – not me, not Dancy – could drill some sense through that barrier of pride.

But Alice, now . . . she was a female of the species, wasn't she? If she truly loved the boy . . .

I found Alice in the Filly Barn, brushing one of the yearlings we were grooming for the Summer Sale. Absorbed in the task, she was talking to the filly as she worked, the yearling responding with affectionate shakings of her head.

A pretty girl; so much prettier now that she was solidly into a good love. The long clean blonde hair, the somewhat chunky body in the tight blue jeans and boy's shirt, the sure competence of her hands. A girl, I decided, worth a man's time and attention. But there was trouble in her countenance over a good love turned bad.

'Hello, Princess,' I said.

She forced a grin. 'What's this *Princess* bit, Miss Maude?'

I said dryly, 'I understand you're a secret princess, living and working amongst us peasants in disguise.'

Her face clouded. 'What do you mean?'

Coming into the stall, I sat down comfortably on the feedbox. 'Exactly how much money will you inherit, Alice?'

Surprised by the question, she yet answered to it honestly. 'I don't know exactly . . . several million, I think. But what . . .'

'Alice, you may be an heiress, but you're pointing towards being a damned lonely one,' I said bluntly. 'That is, if you really care about Merlin Honeycutt.'

The curreycomb slipped out of her hand, dropping to the straw-bedded floor. She stood still, her head lowered. 'Oh Lord,' she said hopelessly. 'So he's found out.'

She stood exposed to my gaze. I ought to have seen it; there is an unmistakable patina only old money, the right schools, can give a girl. An accomplished rider, I remembered; that alone should have given her away. Even in a boy's shirt and blue jeans, her habitual costume except when she put on a dress for Merlin, she betrayed a definite aura of class and breeding. Obvious, now that I was truly seeing her.

'Yeah, Merlin's good friend Mr Dahl found out, somehow, and let him know,' I said. 'What was your idea, anyway? You've been living a lie, girl. But I guess you know that.'

She nodded unhappily. 'I ought to have told *you*, at least. But . . . I was afraid you wouldn't hire me.'

'You could operate your own damn breeding farm,' I pointed out. 'At least, once you inherit the money.'

'I've already got a million in my own name,' she confessed, so miserably I almost laughed. 'It came to me out of my mother's trust fund.'

'And you've let me swank my paltry inheritance around here all this time,' I said, intent on making her smile.

She didn't respond. 'But Father won't have a horse on the place. He's *always* hated horses. His mother was a great steeple-chaser, a marvellous horsewoman. She was killed taking a fence when Father was only a boy. He . . . couldn't forget that a horse killed his mother.'

Her eyes were shadowed with memories she was much too young to harbour in actuality; they could only have been dreams of the past learned from old photographs and trophy cups, shared in family stories.

'In her day, Mayfield Manor was one of the Thoroughbred showplaces of Kentucky. My grandmother was into steeple-chasers and hunters, though, not flat racers. She stood two of the greatest sires of jumping horses ever known in the history of the sport. People came from all over the world . . . it wasn't a commercial thing, you understand, I think she would have been ashamed to have made money at her hobby.'

'And when she was killed?' I said softly.

'Father was seventeen. My grandfather had died when he was five, so he knew only his mother. She was a beautiful woman, he's always kept her portrait hanging over the mantel-piece. She must have been a wonderful person, too; you can see in the painting how alive she was. Father saw the horse go down, saw her die . . .

'He insisted on disposing of the entire stable – the executors had to do it, he wasn't of age yet, you understand – she had spent so many years getting established.' She sighed. 'No horse has lived on Mayfield land since.'

God, yes, come to think of it, in my studies I had read some-where about the grand steeplechasers of Mayfield Manor. I had not, of course, connected the name with Alice.

'So . . . how did you manage to ride?'

She made a face. 'Sneaked it. When I went away to school, I made a private bargain with the headmaster that I could ride without my father's knowledge.' She lifted her head proudly. 'I was good, too, won all sorts of cups and ribbons.' She made a short laugh. 'In my senior year, I had to miss the final horse show because Father was there for graduation, and so my school team lost.' The unmerited defeat still rankled.

'How do you get away with working at Outlaw Farm?'

'Father lives most of the time in Palm Springs now. There's only me and our old cook in that big house. She'd never betray me.'

I remained puzzled. 'So what's been your idea? Didn't you realize that Merlin would have to know, sooner or later, that you're not exactly the girl-in-the-cottage?'

'I thought,' she looked wistful, 'if we got married before he knew, no one could accuse him of marrying for money.' She raised her head. 'Least of all himself. And then, with our experience of working with your horses, we could make Mayfield Manor into a breeding farm again.' She looked directly into my face. 'When Father is gone – he has a bad heart and I've . . . long since accepted that the phone call can come any minute . . .' She pulled herself together. 'When the time comes, I planned to ask you to sell me a half share in Outlaw Prince, let him stand at Mayfield Manor. We can work together, Miss Maude, on your breeding nick. Of course, there's War Admiral blood on Outlaw Prince's top line, so it will be necessary to work out a promising cross for the next generation . . .'

Her voice faltered. 'I knew something was wrong when Merlin quit walking with me. He didn't say anything, so I hoped . . . It never occurred to me he knew about the money.'

'If anybody should be a breeder of Thoroughbreds, it's you.' I said. 'Only thing is, you'll have to talk Merlin into it . . . and you know how he is. He's made up his mind it's not right to marry you, under the circumstances, and . . .'

She was woebegone. But, resolutely, she lifted her chin. 'I won't let it make any difference. He doesn't understand that we'd be true partners; he'd bring as much to Mayfield Manor as I.' She sagged. 'But *he* doesn't know it. I guess . . . the money scares him.'

'Money doesn't count to you. Because it's always been there. It counts to Merlin. And, just offhand, I don't know exactly what can be done about it. Though two women ought to be able to put their heads together . . .'

Her body was drooping into despair. 'I love him, Miss Maude. All my plans for Mayfield Manor won't mean a thing unless . . . He must know how I love him. And he loves me. I know he does.'

'You wouldn't want him any other way than how he is, would you?' I said. 'Now Whitey Dahl, he'd be happy to enjoy your riches.'

She flushed. 'I don't . . . want to think about him.'

I stood up; the feed trough was cutting into my butt. 'All right, girl. If a couple of women can't outdo a mere man in a matter of marriage . . .'

'I don't want to . . .'

'You want him any way you can get him, right?' I said sharply. 'So all right, it'll take some connivance, maybe a shifty trick . . . women have been doing it, girl, since time immemorial. That's why it's immemorial: We don't care to remember.' I stopped suddenly. Then I went on. 'Now, you know Merlin, and I know Merlin. An old-fashioned gentleman in the best sense of the word.'

'Yes,' she breathed. 'That's why I love him . . . *one* reason. I've never known anyone who . . .'

'No time for sentimentality. Just think about the man for a minute.' I stopped again. 'You two . . . you've been lovers quite a long time, haven't you? Ever since that thing with Whitey.'

She blushed. 'Miss Maude!'

'Oh, come on now, I wasn't born yesterday. That's the style of young people nowadays, with The Pill and the will and the time and the place. So, just between us girls, you *have* made love.'

She lowered her eyes. 'Yes. Not often, because Merlin says . . .'

'Once is enough,' I said brutally. 'You need to get careless, Alice. You've got to come up pregnant.'

Her face was a puzzle. I rushed on. 'If you really want to marry him, you won't hesitate,' I said. 'After all, you do want his baby, don't you? Well, now's the time. Don't doubt for a minute that Merlin will marry you. His honour as a Kentucky mountain gentleman will be involved.'

'But . . .'

'Go to him right now,' I said steadily, taking the next logical step into feminine ruthlessness. 'Tell him the big lie. Say you've got to talk, whether he likes it or not, because he's made you pregnant.'

'I can't do it,' she whimpered.

'You'll do it,' I said. I chuckled ribaldly. 'But don't forget, girl, once you go walking again in the Kentucky evening, you must proceed to make yourself an honest woman. Can't let him catch you in a lie. He'd resent it the rest of his life.'

'But it's . . . it's not a lie,' she blurted. 'I *am* pregnant.'

I stared. 'What?'

Her face flamed. 'I'm not ashamed of it. I was just getting ready to tell Merlin when he quit me.' Her head hung again. 'If he didn't come back, I meant to have his baby anyway.'

I chortled with sudden glee. 'Then you got no problem, girl.'

She was troubled. 'But . . . is it right to use our baby to make him marry me? Even if it *is* the truth?'

I paused shrewdly. 'Do you have the right to let him make the decision he's making without knowing the whole truth of the situation? Think about that, Alice.'

Humming to myself, I returned to the office. And when, that evening, I watched from the tack-room window as the poor Kentucky mountain boy and the rich Kentucky Bluegrass girl walked down the lane, I congratulated myself, as well as them. Good bloodlines there, on both sides; I'd be interested in seeing the progeny of this begetting.

Dancy Clutterbuck couldn't understand why, as I watched, I kept chuckling so warmheartedly to myself. I didn't tell him. There are *some* things men must never know.

I had rather expected my newly established social life to end with the departure of my aspirant partner and husband. However, Irene Shipwright called a few days after their return from Florida – without Count Gracchi, needless to say – and readily accepted my invitation to dinner. Harris Harris made a fourth; and Tiffany Thomas enlisted a reliably ancient bachelor friend-of-the-family to balance the table. Payson Shipwright took advantage of the occasion to let me know, in his shy manner, that he was pleased to see I had come to my senses about Gracchi. I liked that man, as I also liked Harris Harris.

The next week, I went to the Shipwrights for a large party, Harris calling the day before to say we might well go together, since we were likely to be the only singles. Other invitations followed, scattered during the busy season but accelerating with the social pace as the Select Summer Sale loomed nearer. Harris Harris, on a friendly, impersonal basis, was often my escort; we could talk horses for hours at a stretch, and he was a wonderful companion for a lady permanently retired from the sexual wars . . . with honourable scars to confirm her status as a veteran. Of course I had to realize, with a wry honesty, that without the experience of the banished Count Gracchi I would never have achieved social acceptance.

Harris planted the seed of a larger success the day he came to Outlaw Farm in his official capacity to inspect our nominations for the Sale. He had viewed them during the spring, had even advised me, unofficially, which yearlings were likely to be accepted. So the inspection was strictly *pro forma*; I am sure he had long since made up his mind.

Nevertheless, he carried out the duty with solemnity and attention to detail. Merlin and Alice and Dancy brought them forth one by one, their coats shining, their conformation poses well-schooled. From time to time Harris nodded in appreciation.

'Your Sir Outlaw foals out of the War Admiral mares . . . Maude, they're *all* good-looking individuals. Keep it up and you'll have a valuable sire there. They *look* like runners.'

'Yes,' I said, primly noncommittal. 'Sir Outlaw does breed on, doesn't he?'

Harris laughed. 'Have you considered the possibility of syndicating him? I'll take a couple of shares if you ever do . . . not for my own modest mares, but on speculation.'

'I intend to keep him in private ownership.' I laughed. 'Unless I get in a bind for additional capital.'

Harris looked thoughtful. 'That colt . . . Outlaw Prince . . . any chance of him starting soon?'

I knew the direction of his mind. 'Not before the Summer Sale, I'm afraid.'

'Damned pity.'

'There's nothing wrong with him,' I hastened to assure my friend. 'It's just that it's necessary to give him time to grow.' I paused, thoughtful in my turn. 'It may well be a characteristic of the cross between those particular bloodlines.'

'Which is not so good for the American style of racing,' Harris said nodding in agreement. 'When a man puts a chunk of money into a yearling he's likely to go for the kind which can quickly earn himself out.'

My voice quickened. 'But you know and I know that, often, it's the best ones which come along slowly. There's too much sprint racing of two-year-olds anyway; that's why so many runners break down before they've had a chance to prove themselves.'

He shrugged in an intricate and characteristic gesture. 'That's the game, Maude. Don't get too far out front, or you'll suddenly find there's nobody following with money burning in their pockets.'

'They'll come to recognize my pedigree cross,' I said stoutly. 'Just wait until Outlaw Prince wins a few stakes . . .'

'But he won't help any this year, will he?'

I was deflated. 'No. They all know about him, though. When he takes the track in the morning over at Daingerfield, you can see those Kentucky hardboots take an interest. But . . .'

Harris finished it for me. 'But a Kentucky hardboot won't let himself believe in the grandest colt in the world until he's seen him come first to the wire against the best competition.' He paused. 'Well, you'll receive official notification of your acceptances.'

Emerging from the Great Stone Barn, Harris stopped to gaze up at the sunrise burst of stone on the façade.

'Beautiful place you've got here,' he remarked. 'Shaping up every year, isn't it? Bought it yet, or still leasing?'

'I've made arrangements to exercise the option to purchase,' I said. I chuckled. 'You're going to have to deal with Maude Sage for years to come, Harris.'

I didn't mention that it was all on the line now. I was fully committed, root hog or die. If I came up to the seventh year of operation with a hobby loss, I'd be a Licensed Practical Nurse for the rest of my life. Yet, somehow, making that final decision to buy the land had liberated me; there is something to be said for, just once in your life, going for broke on something you believe in.

'I'd already figured that out, somehow.' He waggled his winged eyebrows, a signal I had come to understand. 'Isn't it time you started thinking about giving a grand Open House for all the folks? So many people know of Outlaw Farm, but have never been here. A day or two before the Summer Sale, say, when everybody who *is* anybody will be in town.'

My breath caught. That old fiasco remained rankling in my soul, cut so deeply permanent I had not let myself think about anything similar, not even after my modest social success under the Shipwright sponsorship.

Of course, Harris – without mentioning it – was aware of that old failure; so, with eyebrows signalling the importance of his message, he was passing on a meaning out of the social consensus of the Kentucky Bluegrass.

'Give you a chance to show your yearlings privately to the people who count,' Harris continued smoothly.

'An interesting idea,' I murmured. 'I'll have to think about it.'

I had made up my mind immediately . . . you don't need to hit Maude Sage between the eyes more than once or twice to get her attention. But, as I worked with Tiffany Thomas in planning the Open House, I kept thinking about both the occasion and its significance; so that, starting from an original inspiration that I simply woke up with one morning in my head, it flowered into a daring concept that, if not as big a failure as the first episode, would be a smashing success. Fifty-fifty, I figured; it all depended on how much residual resentment of Maude-Sage-the-interloper remained. Well, I took a bigger gamble every time I sent a mare to a stallion.

I would do it, for better or for worse. Because . . .

Here's the truth of the matter of Maude. I had arrived at it by stages, hard-fought battles, hurts and losses and defeats. I was far from being the woman who had arrived what seemed a lifetime ago in the yellow Volkswagen with the British racing green stripe. On the other hand, neither was I the Maude Sage that woman had expected to become.

I knew now, deep in the gut where it counts, that it was not a permanence I had achieved, though permanence, stability, had been my inner-directed goal; because the very essence of my new life, purely and simply, was Change.

Change. Continuity through change. The condition of all existence. The biggest mistake the human race makes is the failure to recognize the inevitability of constant change – along with the ensuing failure, out of the conditioned rigidities of old heartbreaks and disappointments, to adapt oneself into a consonant rhythm with the changes of the world. It is not future shock, but the resistance to change, that is the one thing, above all other perils, that is most likely to trigger the final destruction of the race, causing it, with all its glorious history, to vanish with the dinosaurs from this earthly arena.

These new realizations – this philosophy, if you will, though I don't like to use large, open-ended words like that – permeated the days of my life, engendering in my soul an unsuspected strength.

In the revived preoccupation with a plan for an Open House, I had to explore myself in this particular regard also. I had emerged from that original fiasco bruised and sore, content to shield my hurts in the controlled environment of a common endeavour which constituted the commonwealth of Outlaw Farm. A needful mercy; but the need, the time, had changed and now I could open myself – had, indeed, in my infatuation with the charming Count Antonio Gracchi, already started along that uncharted pathway – and Outlaw Farm.

A necessary change also; I had created here a band of outlaws, both horses and people, penetrating as ruthlessly as a Mongol horde into the smug complacencies of the Bluegrass. The duly recognized horse capital of the world, they had resented – and resisted – my barbarian assault, to a certain extent rightfully. For I had been, in my own heedless manner, also smug and complacent.

But any closed system, whether of a nation, a society, or in Thoroughbred bloodlines, vitally needs regular infusions of new blood – even though it resists all such invasions with all the monolithic strength of human resistance to change. Only new blood, new ideas, can generate the hybrid vigour that is, ultimately speaking, an absolute essential for both permanence and change. Any system that has become impervious to change – though imperviousness is a major motivation and goal for any system – is already dead.

What I had failed to recognize until now was that, though the invading barbarians change the establishment, the establishment also changes . . . absorbs . . . adapts . . . the barbarian. In direct proportion to the success of his assault.

At the beginning, I had insisted righteously on being accepted on my own terms. Still true, in a way. I remained, in spite of all, Maude Sage. But there was also an altered truth, in a dimension surprising even to me: I didn't much *care*, any more, whether I was socially acceptable or not. And that, to a considerable extent, is real wealth – and is often the very key to acceptance.

Oh, it was gratifying to mingle pleasantly with these people whose life, like mine, was predicated upon the enormous gamble of breeding Thoroughbreds. In a strictly commercial sense, it was valuable to be counted a social peer, because the horse business has for generations operated on the comfortable basis of intensely personal associations.

I had at times regarded the horse people as mortal enemies, intent upon destroying all that we were endeavouring to build. The Daingerfield Association had seemed their inimical instrument. Closing themselves against the alien, they had held in contempt Maud's overweening ambition; they had laughed at my purchase of an unfashionable stallion from a flamboyant man, who despite his great wealth and influence, was himself something of a despised outsider, valued only to the extent that he could be cozened into spending immense sums on the purchase of Kentucky yearlings.

But I had come to realize that, underlying its idiosyncrasies of idea and conduct, with all its blind clinging to the outrageous notion that the right Thoroughbreds can be bred only by the right people, there remains to the society of the horse people a definite sense of honour. The Daingerfield Association perceives its reason for existence in serving as a bulwark against half-baked ventures fuelled by rash new money. Just as the American Stud Book is a bulwark against contamination of the Thoroughbred bloodlines. Often arbitrary and capricious in its rulings-beyond-appeal, yet, for all its occasional wrongness or blindness, the Association is basically moral in its impulse . . . and deadly long-range, like all self-perpetuating institutions, in the daily application of its principles.

And who – most especially ex-LPN Maude Sage – could say the system was all wrong? I, like the new foals brought to life each spring of every year, had to establish a track record. Sooner or later, because of the honesty underlying the system, like a good stakes winner of whatever bloodlines, I would be accepted for whatever value I had in the world of horses. The Kentucky hardboot, above all else, appreciates, recognizes, a winner.

So I had arrived, perhaps against my own will, at an understanding of the system in its major aspects, good and bad. As I had come to recognize myself, in a very solid sense, as a being who could no longer be shaken fundamentally by social rejection or ordinary ill fortune. Maude Sage also likes a winner.

I had found myself, in that I had found my place.

My place. First of all, the farm in all its permanence of change. The people, I knew, would change as I had changed; there would be comings and goings, as there were inevitably comings and goings of horses. Merlin and Alice would depart, in time, into their joint endeavour of marriage and raising horses. Whitey Dahl would disappear into the world of racing, either to rise to the top in a burst of glory or to sink without a trace into the mediocrity of claiming races at minor tracks. And Dancy Clutterbuck, even after the Italian campaign was over, would probably continue for a while in the only attitude he could find tenable: friendly but remote. And surely – I could read the signs as well as I can read a pedigree – the day would come also for his departure. Whatever the changes, Outlaw Farm would remain Outlaw Farm, as Maude Sage would remain Maude Sage . . . whatever the changes.

Such a simple truth, yet so difficult to realize. But there is no mistaking it when one arrives at a resolution of the classic dilemma.

In this style, therefore, I came to the evening of Open House at Outlaw Farm. The scene was set as before, Japanese lanterns strung glowing from one great oak to another, around tables gleaming with starched linen and polished silver, a bar with two bartenders ready to serve all comers, a great Kentucky burgoo pot bubbling in the background, steaming savoury hints of its tastiness.

Only necessary to add people to taste, and stir. But with a difference, two differences. This time the horse people came, were coming in a steady stream of handsome automobiles up the curving driveway, where Merlin and his assistants parked the cars and directed my guests up the *luminaria*-lit pathway to the mansion grounds. I had specified formal attire, so it was a gathering of dramatic contrasts, the ladies resplendent in the varied hues of evening gowns and jewellery and lovely light suntans, the men handsome and ruddy in white jackets.

The other difference was greater, a shock to my unprepared guests. Price tags were prominently displayed on everything. *Outrageous* prices: four dollars for a shot of Bourbon, ten dollars if one desired a buffet plate, three dollars to fetch a bowl of burgoo. The service, except for bar and burgoo, was provided by the children of the orphanage, flitting their bright young faces among the guests to lead them to seats at the table or directing them towards the liquid refreshment.

These self-possessed children were exuberantly at ease with my guests; more than could be said for the adults, who, not understanding what was expected, milled about indecisively. Flanked on the stone steps by Harris Harris and Reverend Tompkins, I took the microphone of the public address system installed temporarily for a later showing of this year's yearlings. As I spoke, I could hear my voice echoing eerily from the huge oak trees where the speakers were nestled.

'Ladies and gentlemen,' I said, 'welcome to Outlaw Farm. Later on, we plan to show you some grand yearlings, but right now I want you to eat and drink and be merry.' I paused, waiting for their full attention.

'You may be surprised, to say the least, to see prices on all the good food and drink. Well, Outlaw Farm is a commercial operation . . . but we're not quite that mercenary.' (A relieved spatter of applause.) 'Oh, yes, you're expected to pay . . . pay through the nose. But it's all in aid of a good project, a sort of halfway house – we intend to call it Horseway House – which will be established at Outlaw Farm in the near future. Here's Reverend Tompkins, director of the orphanage, to tell you all about it.'

Reverend Tompkins took the mike to launch forthrightly into our plan.

'When our charges reach the age of eighteen, we can no longer care for them at the orphanage. Often, given our limited budget, we must send them into the world ill-prepared to make their own way. Horseway House will provide a transitional period out of institutional care for those boys and girls who have a desire to work with horses. A resident couple, selected from my staff, will take charge of Horseway House, while the people here at Outlaw Farm, led by Mr Dancy Clutterbuck, will provide both daily instruction and daily practical experience.' He turned towards me. 'It is a noble and needful idea, originated by Miss Maude Sage and advocated with such enthusiastic conviction. I could only agree to lend it both my support and my prayers. Miss Sage . . .'

I took the microphone again. Soberly, I said, 'Not such a noble idea, Reverend. Because I know, as all these people know, that a major problem in operating a breeding farm is attracting and retaining competent help. So, ladies and gentlemen, when you pay the price for your food and drink and entertainment tonight – by the way, I forgot to mention that a ticket to remain for the viewing of the Outlaw Farm yearlings is going to cost you twenty-five dollars a couple' – That brought a groan and a laugh! – 'you're not contributing to charity, but to the future efficient operation of your own farms – and to the wonderful world of the horse. Whenever you need a stable hand, once Horseway House gets into operation, all you'll have to do is call Miss Tiffany Thomas and ask her to check her register of available employees. Horseway House will constitute a pool of young, eager, and well-trained workers for all the horse farms of the Kentucky Bluegrass.' I grinned. 'Needless to say, Outlaw Farm will get first shot.'

'Now, I'm sure some of you are walking around without a dime of actual cash money in your pockets.' (Several laughs in rueful recognition of the truth.) 'Well, we happen to believe that the horse people of Kentucky might well nail your hide to the barn door in a horse trade; but, beyond that, you are the souls of honour and rectitude. So we will be delighted to take your markers if you've happened to get caught not holding tonight. Just be sure to write your signature legibly . . . and remember to send us a covering cheque in the morning.'

The burst of applause was so enthusiastic and sustained I knew the venture was a success. It had been risky; I might well have offended them by turning my hospitable gesture into a charitable benefit. But, because they had accepted me, they accepted my idea.

I held up my hand for one further word. 'If you're moved to write down a larger sum than your bill for the evening, that's all right, too. And . . . these bright young people serving you are from the orphanage. You might as well get acquainted; within the near future they could be one of your valued employees, or your manager, or your friend.'

Relinquishing the microphone, I went down into the crowd. As they pressed about, laughing, marvelling over the 'marvellous' idea, I had to tell over and over again the story of its genesis: how the boy named Whitey Dahl, now an apprentice jockey riding at Daingerfield Race Track, had run away from the orphanage to come to Outlaw Farm; how, this spring, after his victorious, swanking, smirking return in tailored clothes and Cadillac convertible to his old stamping grounds, three more boys – too young, however, to be allowed to stay – had run away to Outlaw Farm.

'We really ought to name it the Whitey House, after Dahl,' I said. 'Maybe we will, one day, if he becomes as great a jock as he thinks he is right now.'

There were photographs to be posed for, an interview about the detailed plans for Horseway House with a *Blood-Horse* reporter, good laughter and good talk. Bedazzled by success, I floated in a rosy glow. But the moment of the great evening came when, standing to one side, I watched as Merlin and Alice, wearing the cheerful Outlaw Farm uniform of Kentucky blue trousers and Florida orange shirt, led out our yearlings one by one.

First came Sir Outlaw, himself, stepping with the arrogant pride of a sire, heavier now in retirement, his crest massive, his head high and beautiful. Then Outlaw Prince, belly tight, walking with the nervous, controlled energy of a young horse in training. His appearance elicited a collective gasp of admiration for the length of his stride, the smooth strength of his muscles moving massively, gracefully, under his chestnut-gleaming coat.

Then came the yearlings, Dancy reading over the public-address system their credentials of pedigree. When it was over, I sighed in blissful fulfilment. Outlaw Farm had made its mark in the Kentucky horse world.

Later, as I shook the hands of departing guests, accepting their compliments on the condition and appearance of the yearlings, their congratulations for Horseway House, I felt the greatest happiness I had known. At the very last came Harris Harris, who stood holding my hand for a moment, hunching forward on his crutches to say with a grin, 'Maude, I've never seen a lady kill so many birds with one stone. A whole covey. You're just one surprise after the other.'

I grinned back at him. 'I hoped you'd approve.'

He nodded soberly. 'God knows, the Kentucky horse people have needed for years to do something positive about training stable help. Maybe your Horseway House will show them the direction towards a partial solution. And show these kids a way into the world.' He chuckled. 'At the least, Maude Sage, I've decided the horse business needs you to keep them on their toes.'

'Fine,' I said, laughing. 'So get a good price for the yearlings you'll be selling for me next week.'

I don't know exactly when I realized that our offering of yearlings at the Daingerfield Select Summer Sale would not be the success I had hoped for; had, indeed, believed in so strongly that I had come to count on it.

Nothing wrong with the yearlings – they were in magnificent condition and, because of the previous private showing at what had become the sensational party of the year (you were *nobody* in the Kentucky Bluegrass if you hadn't been at Outlaw Farm's Open House, contributing mightily to the success of the Horseway House for Apprentice Farm Workers), there was a steady traffic of lookers during the Sunday-afternoon showing.

It was simply a matter of timing. Outlaw Prince had not passed a starting gate (Brock Walter and Bob Shirley now hoped to have him ready for the September meeting of Daingerfield Race Track) and so could not stimulate the sale of his younger siblings. Indeed, John Domino, by Sir Outlaw out of the Prince John mare Marry The Man, was our stallion's only starter and winner to date, proving himself a useful runner at moderate distances but not the potential ability to get a classic distance of ground.

The timing was wrong. The luck was bad. Our best yearling, a chestnut colt by Sir Outlaw out of the War Admiral mare Old Blue Eyes – she a stakes producer, out of stakes producer Big Event, the granddam being that great foundation mare La Troienne – had to be withdrawn from the sale at the last minute after having cast himself in the stall during the night following the Sunday showing. No permanent injury – a horse can often rupture himself in his panicky struggles if he gets on his back in the tight confines of a stall – but he was so shaken and cut and bruised, there was no recourse but to bring him home.

We sold on Tuesday afternoon. Our four colts and four fillies realized an average of seventeen thousand five hundred dollars – the high being twenty-seven thousand; the low, nine thousand two hundred.

'Just wait till next year,' Dancy said in consolation.

'It's jam tomorrow, never jam today,' I said, unconsoled.

Dancy tried to argue me out of the mood. 'Not a bad average, Maude. After all, Sir Outlaw's fee is still only five thousand – I think we might well raise it next year if Outlaw Prince shows us something – and the average price realized is more than three times the stud fee. That's good return on your money in anybody's book.'

'All right,' I said. 'It's still not what I hoped for. After all the enthusiasm people showed at the Open House, the hundreds of lookers at the sale . . .' I gave vent to the oppressive knowledge that shadowed forth in the back of my mind. 'It's not enough, Dancy. You know it's not enough to put us on the right side of the ledger.'

'Next year, Maude. Next year, if only Outlaw Prince will come to hand, win us a stakes race or two . . .'

'Next year is the last shot we've got in our locker,' I reminded him.

'But if . . .'

'Next year,' I said. 'And if. Jam tomorrow.'

Dancy smiled. 'I'll bet you a hundred dollars you get a hundred-thousand-dollar yearling at next summer's Select Sale.'

I looked at the man. 'You don't know what you're saying.'

He was suddenly serious. 'Yes. I do know. Just like I can have two dollars on Outlaw Prince's nose when he goes to break his maiden.'

For a moment we were as close – closer – than we had ever been.

'Are you sure?' I asked anxiously. 'I *can't* let you turn into a gambling man again, Dancy. I . . . this farm needs you too badly.'

He chuckled lightheartedly. 'Maude, it's gone out of me. Been gone so long I hadn't even noticed. But it's gone, out: I know it like I know my own name.'

I whooped, suddenly knowing with him that, however mysteriously, the great change had taken place. 'All right. Cover your hundred and raise you a quart of sour mash. To be drunk only in the company of the loser.'

'You've got a bet,' he said, smiling. He regarded me fondly. 'Sorry, but you're gonna lose, Maude.'

'Can't,' I said. 'Anyhow, next year.'

CHAPTER 6

I shall not go deeply into the glory and the agony of Outlaw Prince's racing career. But, because it was important to the fortunes of Outlaw Farm, I must detail it, as briefly as possible.

Outlaw Prince, until September of his two-year-old year, showed us at times a terrific turn of speed; on other days he seemed lethargic. Brock Walter told me that he was developing unevenly, like a boy with growing pains, most of his strength and energy so bound up in the process of growth it was necessary to stop on him every two or three weeks in order to give his body-development enough time to catch up. Alice, still his exercise rider, though Whitey Dahl clamoured daily for the opportunity, had such intimate rapport with the colt she sensed exactly when to rest him, when to ask him for more than he had yet shown.

With the Select Summer Sale past history, I was content to be patient. It had long been my belief that we ask too much, too early, of our Thoroughbreds . . . and maybe other kinds of stars. Explosive speed at short distances over hard tracks is the prime reason so many brilliant juvenile runners fail to live up to their three-year-old promise. Lack of soundness, at best, is a serious problem in the breed.

After resting Outlaw Prince for the first two weeks in September – we brought him home to the peaceful quiet of Outlaw Farm to turn him out – the colt came back into training showing a whole new dimension of maturity. He – not only his body but his mind – had decided it was time to run.

His new confidence was reflected in the excited stir of interest that greeted him the morning he came out for his first gallop. There was about him suddenly the aura of a Big Horse, as the backside calls the top runners. He seemed to know it; stepping out delicately but strongly, he took an active pleasure in the attention given his appearance on the track.

With both Brock Walter and Bob Shirley holding a stopwatch on him, as well as the official clockers, he turned in a sparkling work, going a quarter of a mile handily in twenty-three seconds flat, then galloping out the half. Brock and Bob, heads together over the stopped watches, nodded solemn approval at each other.

Shirley, however, did not reveal his plan until we were in the security of a tack room adjacent to Outlaw Prince's stall.

'A five-furlong maiden, in about a week,' he said. 'He'll win it going away against anything stabled at Daingerfield. I'll work him a slow three quarters, then rest him a day. Two days before the race, I'll break him out of the gate for three eighths of a mile.'

It was not my place, as the mere owner, to offer an opinion. But, with a tightening in my chest, a lift of excitement, I said, 'He's good, isn't he?'

The trainer was scornful of such modest appraisal. 'Miss Maude, I'll tell you right now, before he ever passes an entry box, he's the best colt I've ever trained. He's fast, and when the time comes he'll get a distance of ground, because he can be rated. Take my word.'

I warmed to the man. I had, until now, found Bob Shirley rather unprepossessing in his contradictions. He looked like a cowboy, with lean hips and broad shoulders, wearing always cowboy boots run down at the heels. With a craggy, ugly, weathered face and distance-seeing eyes, one would have expected him to be wisely laconic, slow-talking, a peaceful man sure of himself. Instead, he was voluble in a nervous, high-pitched voice, talking faster than most of his horses could run. I had taken the word of Brock Walter that he was an excellent trainer who hadn't had the opportunities his skill deserved.

The door to the tack room was flung open, to reveal Whitey Dahl.

'What do you want, Whitey?' Brock demanded, annoyed by the interruption.

Whitey, in stained riding breeches and hardboots and a green shirt, the helmet dangling from one hand, looked sweaty and excited.

'I ought to work that colt a couple of times before I ride him in the race,' he said. 'What about tomorrow morning? Got a couple of mounts, but I can scratch one if need be.'

Brock, lips tight, looked to Bob Shirley. Shirley turned to Whitey.

'You're not riding the colt in his maiden, Whitey. Charlie Winter will be up.'

'*Charlie Winter!*' His voice exploded with the name. 'Charlie can't ride a sheep. He's not the boy for a Big Horse.'

'Who told you you were?' Shirley said in a hard voice.

Whitey was breathing fast. 'Listen,' he said, 'you knew all

along I aimed to be Outlaw Prince's regular jockey.'

'A first-starter, he might run greenly,' Brock interjected. 'He'll need an experienced hand on the reins. For God's sake, boy, you're still riding with a bug.'

'He's *my* mount!' Whitey flamed. 'You can't take him away from me.'

'Nobody ever told you he was your horse,' Shirley said. 'You'll take the mounts I give you , . . unless you're willing to tear up the contract.'

Whitey stood glaring, so full of venom it was repellent to gaze into his face. Without another word he flung away, slamming the door.

Brock sighed. 'He'll settle down, Bob. At least, he always has.'

'How's Whitey doing, anyway?' I asked.

'Coming along,' Brock said gloomily. 'If he can only learn a little patience. God knows he works, but . . .'

'But he's not ready for Outlaw Prince?' I asked.

'No way. He's got to show me something beyond skill and determination before I'll trust him with the Big Horse. You know what I mean, Maude, we've talked about it before.' He shook his head, gloomier than ever. 'Sometimes I don't think the boy is capable of any sort of feeling, beyond the greed to win, and keep on winning.'

'So it's *your* decision. Not Mr Shirley's.'

Shirley nodded. 'Brock is only his agent. Since I hold his contract, I'm in a better position to tell Whitey what to do.' He nodded again, decisively. 'Whitey Dahl will ride Outlaw Prince – maybe – when Brock tells me he's ready to ride Outlaw Prince.'

'This Charlie Winter . . .'

'A good boy with a green horse. Steady as a rock, strong hands and a good seat. Nothing to worry about with Charlie Winter up.' His voice brightened. 'He'll win laughing, watch what I tell you.'

That night, as I was finishing dinner, the doorbell rang . . . to my surprise, for I was not expecting a caller. Jan opened the door to admit Whitey Dahl. It was the first time he had been inside the house.

'Why, Whitey!' I said, coming from the dining-room. 'Come on in.'

He stood defiantly in the hallway. He was wearing an outfit I had not seen before, a cream-coloured linen coat, chaste necktie, slacks in a delicate tint of green.

'I've got to talk to you,' he said, so accusingly he must have expected me to instruct Jan to throw him out.

'Come on into the living-room,' I said equably, ignoring his belligerence. 'My, you look prosperous. Must be winning a lot of races.'

'Win my share, and then some,' he said. One nervous hand flinging aside the chitchat, he burst out, 'Miss Maude, you're the owner. You've got to talk to Bob Shirley.'

'Sit down, Whitey,' I said gently but firmly. I took a place on the sofa, while Whitey perched tensely on the hard edge of a chair. 'Whitey, I have nothing to say about who rides Outlaw Prince. As long as I leave him to the training of Mr Shirley, I can't . . .'

'You could if you wanted to. So you've *got* to!'

Firmly I shook my head. 'Sorry, Whitey. You're just wasting your time.' I sat still, regarding the boy. 'Hasn't it occurred to you that maybe Brock and Mr Shirley are right? Maybe you're not ready yet for a Big Horse like Outlaw Prince.'

The sound of his breathing was rapid in the stillness of the room. 'So it's Brock, too,' he said. 'I thought so.' His voice took on a savage note. 'I'm gonna pay that man off if he won't give me running room. All he does is hold me back.'

'Whitey,' I said, 'Brock Walter is the best friend you've got. Whether you know it or not. Without him, you'd still be an exercise boy.'

'Without him, I'd be Outlaw Prince's regular jockey,' he said, the savagery unabated.

I persisted. 'Isn't he getting you outside mounts now? Winners?'

Unrelenting, he said, 'He ain't getting me Outlaw Prince.' He paused, his eyes shifting into cunning. 'Listen, I'm under apprentice contract. I ride your colt, it won't cost you ten per cent of the purse.'

I shook my head. 'I only care about getting a good rider who'll do his best to take care of him, Whitey, win *or* lose. Because he's going to be a good one.'

'Miss Maude, let me have Outlaw Prince and I'll win the Derby for you. I promise, Miss Maude. Even if I . . .'

'Even if you have to kill the colt to do it?' I said softly.

He stared. He didn't know what I was talking about. 'Don't you *want* a Derby winner?' he said incredulously. 'Think about it, me and you having our picture took in the winner's circle.

Think of the purse money. Think of his stud fee as a winner of the Kentucky Derby.'

I stood up. 'Whitey. Think of the colt. That's what I'm doing. That's what Bob Shirley is doing. If you could only learn . . .'

He rose also. He still didn't hear what I was trying to tell him. His voice came on driving, as he drove a mount through the stretch, heedless of everything but winning. 'You just don't *believe* I can do it, do you? That's what's the matter.'

'They tell me you're a good jock,' I said judiciously. 'They tell me you're going places, if you'll only give yourself time. As we had to give Outlaw Prince time. You see it with horses every day, Whitey, you ought to understand it. So why can't you . . .'

'All right,' he said. 'You'd rather not have a winner than give me a chance. All right, if that's how you like it. I'll just show you, that's all.'

I felt a chill. 'What do you mean?'

His breathing was loud again. 'I'll show you, that's all,' he said. 'And Brock. And them. And everybody.'

So violent was his anger, he was sweating through the linen coat. He stalked to the archway, a bravado movement made slightly ridiculous by his small stature.

'Whitey!' I said, my tone giving him pause. I eased my voice, searching for something that would tell him I was his friend. 'Whitey, I've never told you this, but I think you're a marvellous dresser. Where did you acquire such good taste in clothes?'

He shook his head unbelievingly. 'What are you talking about now?'

I smiled. 'Remember the time you were banished to the bus for fighting, the first day the kids came to Outlaw Farm, and how I took you on a tour of the barns myself? We had a good time, didn't we? Then, when you came to us, wanting to learn how to ride . . .'

He was gone, as violently and suddenly as he had arrived. I sighed; no way to touch the boy with sentiment, reminiscence . . . with rational sense. No wonder Brock wouldn't allow him on Outlaw Prince's back. At this rate, he never would. I sighed again, and went to get some coffee.

Though it had not been my intention to get into racing, I must admit I enjoyed – or suffered, it was hard to tell which – a special quality of excitement as I sat in an owners' box at Daingerfield Race Track to watch Outlaw Prince come out for the first time in a post parade. I was dressed for the occasion, on the outside the picture of a Kentucky horsewoman in a cool linen dress, a simple sheath set off by an emerald horseshead brooch with ruby eyes, and emerald rings. On the inside, I was a quivering mass of hot anticipation and cold fear.

I had, of course, watched John Domino and Olden Song run and win last spring, and Olden Song had already won again this fall. But Outlaw Prince was the Big Horse, and everyone at the track knew it.

Strangely enough, I occupied the same box as on that occasion, so long ago, when I had bought Sir Outlaw from John Paul Jones. This time, however, I was alone, because I had reserved the box for the season. I had asked Dancy to join me, but, wishing to remain with the colt until the last minute, he would watch the race down below . . . he was an inveterate railbird, anyway, didn't feel as though he had experienced a horse race if he didn't get dirt thrown in his face.

My desire was exactly opposite; I wanted to see the grand colt for the first time in the post parade. So I didn't go down to the walking ring, but remained in the box, leaving it only to put a hundred dollars on his nose (remembering with pleasure and a residual tremor of apprehension that Dancy had boldly declared his intention of betting a ritual two dollars) as soon as the preceding race was declared official and the mutuel windows had opened for the fifth. Returning to my seat, the tote board showed that Outlaw Prince was already odds-on, a prohibitive favourite. Much of that money, I knew, had been wagered by the backside.

The bugle sounded – and here they came. Suddenly my eyes were wet, so that I saw Outlaw Prince through a shimmering rainbow haze that made him seem as unreal as the moment. Wearing Number One, he led the parade, his ears pricked, as cool as if out for an accustomed morning work. When the applause came, acknowledging both his noble appearance and his status as favourite, he tossed his head, lifting his feet higher as he pranced slightly sideways. He *liked* the applause, recognized the honour.

Charlie Winter sat, knees high, in the saddle, my colours gracing his shoulders: orange jacket with blue sleeves, blue cap with orange visor, large red cross front and back. Orange for Florida, of course, blue for the Kentucky Bluegrass, and I suppose the red cross was in honour of my abandoned nursing career. Alice, on a lead pony, was at Outlaw Prince's head; there had been argument about the advisability of a lead pony, since he had not needed it during morning works. Bob Shirley, remembering too vividly the reputation of his sire, had insisted, however. Alice had rather resented the imputation but, once the decision was made, had demanded the right to ride the lead pony.

The colt, showing no disposition to make trouble, moved sedately, even though – knowing instinctively, with the crowd and the noise and the afternoon time of day, that this time it was for real – he was obviously on the muscle for the race.

So concentrated on my chestnut colt, I didn't see Whitey until the post parade was almost past the stands. Wearing bright-red silks with red polka-dot sleeves, he was mounted on a good-looking bay, smaller than Outlaw Prince but with an equal ease of stride. My stomach clutched. How could Brock and Bob Shirley allow him to take an outside mount in Outlaw Prince's maiden effort? Didn't they *know* . . . ? But I had decided not to share the ugly threat he had made in my living-room.

With dread in my soul, I watched Whitey kick up his mount to range alongside Outlaw Prince. Putting my glasses on the two horses, I could see Whitey's lips moving, read the angry jerk of Charlie Winter's head, the threatening lift of his whip hand. Whitey, laughing, eased his colt into a trot, going out ahead.

Maiden race, five furlongs out of the chute. Which meant the runners had to come explosively out of the gate to race around one turn into the stretch, the equivalent of a ninety-yard dash for humans. No room for error, hesitation, a faltering stride. And, as I glanced again at the tote board, just about everybody believed it a foregone conclusion: Outlaw Prince was such a prohibitive favourite the second betting choice was going off at six to one. Whitey's mount, Number Four, I was happy to see, was rated at twelve to one. Not the longest shot in the race but unlikely to be a factor. He's desperate, that's all, I told myself with some comfort. If he couldn't win with Outlaw Prince, he sought the glory of beating him at his first asking. But the only shot he could get was at long odds.

Daingerfield Race Track doesn't use a track announcer, which I like; one must perforce know the silks in order to follow a race. I had my binoculars on the flag as the horses milled in back of the starting gate. With little delay – unusual for a field of maiden runners – the flag came down and there was a roar from the crowd as the gates clanged open.

Outlaw Prince was centred in my field of vision as he broke cleanly out of the Number One gate. To my relief he had not, in the tenseness of competition, forgotten his training. Others did not fare so well; one horse stumbled, throwing his boy, and another veered wildly to the outside.

Outlaw Prince opened daylight immediately, going flat out as he skimmed along the rail. He had a length, then two lengths, with Charlie Winter hand-riding, his crouching body, bright in my colours, rising and falling with the chestnut colt's easy stride. The roar of the crowd was sustained on a higher pitch as he opened another length on the backstretch, then muted as another runner, breaking from the pack, angled in and began coming to the leader.

My throat locked so tightly I was unable to breathe. The red jacket with red polka-dot sleeves. Whitey, his whip hand rising and falling, was challenging before the turn into the stretch. When they leaned into the turn – only five furlongs, remember, a hard sprint from wire to wire, hardly time to capture the flashing images – Whitey's mount was lapped on Outlaw Prince, Charlie's head half-turning to take note of the threat.

A two-horse race now, everybody else nowhere. They flailed into the stretch, Outlaw Prince still running easily, holding the other colt safe. Charlie had not gone to the whip, only holding it low in his right hand so Outlaw Prince could see the flick of its readiness. As they straightened into the stretch run, it was obvious that, his rider having already asked for and got his drive, the bay colt would not pass the leader. Wire to wire! With Outlaw Prince running so smoothly, in a lengthening stride, his head thrust strongly forward, his hindquarters squatting and digging, he was magnificent, racing towards victory.

Then, with the spectacular win gloriously secure in my heart – Outlaw Prince changed leads. He faltered only for an instant before Charlie set him down into the new stride and went to the whip, getting the immediate response of a blazing surge of speed. But in that fatal second of hesitation and recovery the red polka-dot sleeves had swept past Outlaw Prince to cross the finish line a bare nose in front. In the next stride, Outlaw Prince, running as hard as ever, caught the bay colt.

But too late. I sank into my seat, trembling all over. The spectators, ominously silent as the sweated runners returned, regarded Outlaw Prince, the favourite, with jaundiced eyes. He seemed to know he had been beaten, walking slowly, even sadly, though still with the grace and beauty which was his inheritance from his sire.

Whitey Dahl's winner was the last horse to pass the stands.

Hearing the scattered applause of long-shot betters, he lifted his whip in salute, gazing directly towards my box. For a blinded minute, I hated the little bastard; he had set out to do my colt in and, damn his black heart, he had succeeded. Reaching the winner's circle, he jauntily tossed his whip whirling into the air, slid to the ground, and caught it deftly to tuck into the small of his back.

Charlie Winter, leaving the scales with his saddle and blankets, stalked angrily past Whitey coming to weigh in. My glasses on them, I saw unheard words exchanged, a sudden swivelling of heads in the immediate vicinity; But Charlie, body stiff with anger, went on.

Feeling as body-sore as if I had run the race myself, I stumbled down the stairs to the back of the stands. In the shed-row, I found grim faces surrounding the colt as Alice washed him down with sponge and scraper.

'Did he come back all right?' I asked of everyone in general.

Dancy answered in a subdued voice. 'Sound as a dollar, Maude. Nothing to worry about.'

I looked at Brock Walter. 'Why did you let the boy ride another mount in Outlaw Prince's maiden race?' I demanded. 'You knew how he felt about not getting the colt.'

Brock's face was pinched with misery. 'Miss Maude, he hustled the ride for himself, didn't even tell me about it until this morning. Probably offered to ride for nothing but a quiet bet laid down, just to get the chance to beat the Big Horse.'

'And the little bastard's so goddamn good he did it,' I said bitterly. 'So why didn't you let him wear *my* colours?'

'He's got to learn,' Brock said. Angrily, he added, 'Or is winning all you care about, like him?'

I faltered, turning in self-defence to look at the colt, now being draped in his cooler preparatory to being hot-walked. 'No,' I said slowly. 'No . . .'

Charlie Winter was suddenly among us, wearing street clothes now, walking with quick strides of anger. An older rider, at least thirty, maybe more, with starved lines in his lean face from years of cruel dieting. He showed a hard-lipped rage and a livid bruise high on his forehead.

'The son of a bitch was talking to my colt from the minute he hooked us,' he said. 'Finally made him change leads. *Made* him do it, I tell you, just with the sound of his voice, giving me no chance to claim foul. It happened so quick there wasn't time to do anything.'

'Don't worry about it, Charlie,' Bob Shirley said, anxious to soothe the jockey's rage. 'We win next time out.'

Charlie was unmollified. 'The colt knew his voice, answered to it. Another furlong, I win it.' He looked grimly pleased. 'I let him know my feelings, by God, once he got inside the Jockey Room. I'll be given days for starting the fight, but damn it, it was worth it.'

'Looks like Whitey got in his licks, too,' I said.

The jockey turned on me. 'Yeah. But it didn't take three of us this time to whip his ass, either, lady.'

'Don't talk like that to your owner,' Bob Shirley said. 'Go on now. He's still the Big Horse, and Whitey knows it as well as you do.'

'Sorry, Miss Sage, I just hate to lose it by a lousy trick,' Charlie said contritely. 'Anything over five furlongs, he couldn't of done it to us.'

'I understand, Charlie. I feel the same way, believe me.'

Winter departed; fortunately, for he had scarcely disappeared before Whitey came towards us down the shedrow.

One would have expected Whitey Dahl to be strutting vaingloriously, But, walking with his head down, avoiding our eyes, it would have been easy to believe he had ridden the loser. No one spoke. Wearing well-cut street clothes, he yet cut a sorry figure, his mouth puffed and bruised, scratches on his face, a purpling eye.

His face suddenly working, he cried out into the unfriendly silence, 'I told you! If you'd let me ride him, he'd have broke his maiden. It's worth something to win at first asking.'

His only answer was an ostracizing silence. Unable to face us – for there were tears now, I couldn't believe in tears from Whitey Dahl but there they were, running shamefully down his bruised cheeks – he turned to gaze forlornly at Outlaw Prince.

As though hypnotized, he moved forward, putting out one hand to touch the bright chestnut muzzle. 'I had to make you lose, damn it,' he cried, begging forgiveness now from the colt, not the people. 'I had to. Don't you see that I had to?'

Outlaw Prince, halted by the gesture, blew his nostrils gently in greeting, pushing his nose into the palm of Whitey's hand. With a guttural cry of anguish, Whitey ducked under to throw both arms around the muscled neck. The tired colt didn't break away from the too-sudden move, but accepted the embrace placidly, leaning his head over the boy's shoulder as Whitey clung in desperate affection.

Whitey was crying openly now, his slender body trembling with grief and shame. I looked at his mentor. Walter Brock, in astonishment and incomprehension, was staring at the boy. I shifted my eyes towards the others. They didn't believe what they were seeing, either.

I believed it. Perhaps because I had sensed, from the beginning, that behind the cruel ruthlessness of a harsh shield between Whitey Dahl and the world, his mean soul, like every human soul, harboured a capacity for love.

So it was me, Maude Sage, who moved to touch Whitey gently on the shoulder, tell him, 'It's all right, Whitey. Outlaw Prince has forgiven you. And so can I.'

Refusing to look at me, he buried his face deeper into the warmth of the colt's neck. Outlaw Prince, in response to such demonstrative love, rubbed his chin, head bobbing, against Whitey's shoulder blades.

'If I have anything to say about it, you're his regular rider from now on.' I pressed my hand against his shoulder. 'Do you hear what I'm saying?'

He gave me a ravaged face to look at. 'I'll win for you,' he said fervently. 'I promise, Miss Maude. I *promise*.'

'Win or lose, just bring me back a sound colt every time,' I said. 'Only promise that.'

He nodded vigorously, dashing a shamed hand at the tears wetting his cheeks. 'I wouldn't do anything to hurt him. Why, he's . . . he's a *Big* Horse, Miss Maude. He can win 'em all.'

'All right, Mr Brock?' I said in challenge. 'All right, Mr Shirley?'

A moment of silence, before Brock said quietly, but with a lift of fulfilled realization, 'All right, Miss Maude.'

The rest of the story can be quickly told. Whitey Dahl kept his promise, as did Outlaw Prince; the colt didn't lose again in his two-year-old campaign. Next time out, he won off by seven lengths to break his maiden in spectacular fashion; dropped into an overnight allowance at seven furlongs, he picked up a nice purse. Running in the twenty-five-thousand-dollar-added Breeders' Futurity, the last big race on Daingerfield's fall schedule, he moved into stakes competition, crossing the finish line eased and laughing, Whitey Dahl sitting chilly all the way. Shipping over to Keeneland, he picked up their Breeders' Futurity purse also, holding the good second-place runner safe by a nose, showing he had heart as well as speed.

Outlaw Prince proved himself a solid, mature runner, a kind horse with nothing of his sire's reputed temperament, and when Bob Shirley began to stretch him out he learned quickly to let himself be rated off the pace, saving something for the stretch run, and he experienced no difficulty in going around two turns.

The two-year-old stars of that year were well established by the time Outlaw Prince had come to hand; nevertheless, he made his mark, winning nearly two hundred thousand dollars, and was ranked third on the Experimental Free Handicap at one hundred and twenty-four pounds . . . only two pounds below the leader.

What excited people about Outlaw Prince was his appearance, his style of running. Over sixteen hands now, but so beautifully proportioned he didn't look big . . . until one noted the length of stride. A bright chestnut, he gleamed so richly in the afternoon sunlight he stood out, instantly recognizable, in the post parade. He had his little ways, too, not to mention a sense of humour; at times he would study the crowd as though counting the house, and regular racegoers soon caught on to the fact that, at least once in every post parade, he would take a gander at the flashing lights of the tote board, sending a ripple of affectionate laughter through the audience. It became a standing joke that he wanted to see the closing odds so he'd know how hard he'd have to run.

He made winning look easy, running with such relaxed co-ordination he never seemed to find it necessary to exert the last full ounce of strength and speed; yet, if another runner came to him, looked him in the eye, as they say, it only served to put new vigour into his effort. Really digging in, he had a way of flattening his back that actually lengthened his stride, and he never took the initiative of easing himself up on a long lead, but ran full-tilt until Whitey Dahl told him it was time to quit.

Whitey, for once serene in his bitter soul, practically lived with the colt – insisting on being up for all morning works, and paying him a last-minute visit with a carrot in his pocket before he left the track for the day – even though, with the prestige of being named regular jockey for a Big Horse, Brock Walter could pick and choose his outside mounts.

After a month's turn-out at home, Outlaw Prince was shipped to Florida to be put back into training for the three-year-old campaign. Counted a definite factor as third choice in the winter book for the Kentucky Derby, he arrived in Florida with a fanfare . . . accompanied by considerable trepidation on the part of his 'connections' (the race-track term for the humans involved in the colt's racing career). It is a strange thing – maybe not so strange, considering how hard we try our juvenile runners – that so many brilliant two-year-olds fail to make the transtition into the classic season.

With the new foals coming along, I could not remain with the Big Horse all the time. However, I flew down for his first start as a three-year-old, an overnight allowance designed as a prep for the fifty-thousand-dollar-added Alligator Handicap at one and one-eighth miles. Bob Shirley had decided to pass on anything less than a mile; he wanted to keep on stretching out Outlaw Prince as early as possible. In his view, too many colts come up to the Kentucky Derby without ever having got the distance of ground. In the Alligator, he would be going against older horses but, with his weight allowance as a three-year-old, combined with the weight allowance awarded Whitey's apprentice bug, Shirley felt he had a chance.

For the allowance race, they might as well have handed him the purse money in the starting gate. Outlaw Prince looked as relaxed as if out for a morning work as he fled down the back-stretch, the pack in hot pursuit but falling further behind with every stride. Whitey looked back only once, as he crossed the finish line, then settled to his business to work him on out to the Alligator distance, a mile and an eighth.

Bob Shirley was beaming with voluble satisfaction when I reached the stable area.

'He win it,' he told me.

'Slightly,' I said. 'Looked like ten lengths to me.'

'The Alligator, I mean,' he said. 'He win it.' To a race-track man, a horse always runs in the present tense.

He did, he won it. But it wasn't easy. All along the back-stretch, Outlaw Prince was battling head to head with the great grey gelding which, at five years of age, was carrying top weight and the sentiments of the betting crowd. They raced stride for stride, the gelding saving ground on the rail, Outlaw Prince outside, for so long they looked like a mechanical toy. The palms of my hands were wet and cold as I stood silent, unable to utter an encouraging cry, waiting for the gelding to break my colt's heart. He could not prevail against such competition, older and stronger and a proven winner.

Wild thoughts fled through my mind. Like his sire, he would quit running and start fighting. He would break down. Whitey Dahl, going desperately to the whip, would cause him to lug into the other runner, bringing a disqualification.

None of the crazy things happened. Outlaw Prince, once having hooked the grey gelding, wouldn't give up. They came thundering around the curve into the stretch, running into the solid wall of noise that a race-track crowd makes during the finish of a great race. And at the end, no more than three strides short of the wire, it was the gelding whose courage faltered, allowing Outlaw Prince to put his nose in front to win by a photo. Just incidentally, one of the two colts ranked above him for the Derby was never a threat.

In that moment, as I went down into the winner's circle to collect the Golden Alligator trophy, I loved my great horse more than ever before. Because, no matter what he did or did not do in the future, he had proved today that he had the courage, the endurance, of the truly classic runner. And recognized as such: Outlaw Prince was featured on the covers of both the *Blood-Horse* and the *Thoroughbred Record*, and installed as favourite to win the Kentucky Derby.

Bob Shirley, afraid the race had taken too much out of him, eased off, simply walking the colt for two or three days before asking him to breeze. But Outlaw Prince had come out of the race apparently unscarred by the gruelling duel; he didn't even go off his feed, as so often happens after a hard race.

Shirley was undecided whether to opt for the Widener, for three-year-olds and up, at one and a quarter miles, or save him for the Flamingo, where he would face only his own age group at one and one-eighth miles.

'We'll just have to let the colt tell us,' he said on the phone. 'He'll know when he's ready to run again.'

In the interval, Bob prepared him with another overnight, saying it would be just another work, but he might as well bring home a purse while getting his exercise. I didn't fly down, getting the news of another easy win over the telephone minutes after the race was finished. A new phenomenon had developed, Bob told me; trainers had started avoiding the colt, so there were only five other runners in the allowance, all going for second money.

His last big Florida race before shipping to Kentucky turned out to be the Flamingo Stakes . . . and Outlaw Prince ran third, beaten for the first time since his maiden effort.

I couldn't read, from the stands, what made the difference. He ran well, with as much eagerness as ever, except that when Whitey asked him to take the lead in the stretch he didn't respond. You can't win 'em all, I told myself in attempted consolation as I hurried towards the stable area. But there remained a knot of apprehension in my heart; perhaps we had asked too much of him too soon, perhaps he had already given all that his great heart had to give.

Bob Shirley was enthusiastic again . . . with an anxiousness lurking in his darting eyes. 'I'm satisfied, Miss Maude,' he told me. 'He run good, I tell you, he run good.'

'There's something wrong with the colt,' Whitey said flatly. He was turned half away from us, watching as Outlaw Prince, wearing his cooler, circled steadily, led by the hot-walker. 'Don't ask me what. But he ain't right.'

Bob Shirley turned on him. 'Don't bad-mouth the Big Horse just because he didn't win for you, Whitey,' he said angrily. 'I tell you, I watched every stride. He didn't put a foot wrong once.'

'He's picked up a bug maybe, I don't know what, but something,' Whitey persisted. 'He told me in the post parade he was off today, that's why I didn't ask him but once in the stretch, and then just rode him out. I know the colt better than anybody, because he talks to me.'

In angry disbelief, Bob Shirley motioned for the hot-walker to stop, and stooped to feel the colt's ankles with probing fingers. 'Cool as anybody could ask,' he declared, the anxiousness in his eyes belying his voice.

'What's the plan?' I asked.

'Give him a couple of days, then ship to Daingerfield,' he said. 'The Daingerfield Memorial will be perfect for him . . . just a quarter less than the Derby distance, and at level weights. Might as well have been put in the condition book for him.'

'All right,' I said. 'I'll see you in Kentucky, then. I've got a plane to catch.' I turned to Whitey. 'Don't fret, Whitey. You and Outlaw Prince will wear the roses this year for sure.' I smiled. 'We'll have our picture taken together in the winner's circle . . . he just didn't run his race today.'

The morning Dancy and I drove over to Daingerfield Race Track, Whitey's intuition was proved right. I knew it the moment I laid eyes on the colt; he stood too quietly, in his stall, head low, not even acknowledging my greetings. His coat had lost much of its gleaming lustre. My glance met Dancy's dismayed eyes. I turned to the groom, squatted against the shedrow wall.

'Where's Mr Shirley?'

He shook his head. 'Ain't here yet.'

'I can see that for myself. When do you expect him?'

The groom was intimidated. 'Ought to be here now,' he said defensively. 'Told me when he left last night to have the Big Horse ready to work this morning.'

I turned to Dancy. 'That's not like Bob,' I said. 'What's going on?'

He shook his head. 'Don't ask me, Maude. You know as much as I do.'

'That's a sick colt we're looking at. Get in there, Dancy, and see if you can tell what's wrong.'

Dancy looked doubtful. 'I'd better not, Maude. Not before Bob comes. He's the trainer . . . I'm only the farm manager.'

He wanted to get his hands on the colt; it is the instinct of a horseman to test the legs and ankles of any horse. But I didn't insist that Dancy break protocol by assuming the right to examine the colt.

Brock Walter came, nodding soberly in greeting, and stood with his hands in his pockets, gazing at Outlaw Prince. The colt took a mouthful of hay, chewed dispiritedly, let it drop into the straw bedding.

'How long has he been like this?' I asked.

'Been getting worse ever since the Flamingo,' Brock told me. 'Bob's had a vet with him damn nigh every day, took x-rays and everything, thinking there might be a hairline fracture. The vet couldn't find anything.'

'I've talked to Bob every day. All he's told me, the colt is fine,' I said. 'Do you know where Bob is?'

He shook his head. 'Didn't tell me where he's staying. Ought to be here . . . told Whitey he'd want to work him this morning.'

'In *this* condition?'

Brock nodded. 'His ankles are cool. Been off his feed, but not by that much.'

'But look at him.'

'Yeah,' Brock said gloomily.

Whitey Dahl arrived, outfitted in worn riding gear, a whip stuck into the back of his breeches. Nodding to us, he went immediately to speak to the Big Horse. Outlaw Prince raised his head, whuffling softly in greeting, let his dead droop again.

Whitey turned to Brock. 'Mr Shirley?'

'Not here yet.'

We waited for more than an hour, standing glumly in desultory conversation that avoided the main topic of concern.

Around us the morning routine of the backside went on; horses coming and going from the track, singly or in sets; down the shedrow a stable hand busily mucked out a stall, an exercise boy came whistling along the pathway. A roan colt, as tall as an Irish hunter and wearing a checkered blanket, was being walked around the shedrow, forcing us to shift out of the way every time he came around. Dancy fetched coffee from the track kitchen, bringing the paper cups in the cut-down half of a Pet Milk carton. The beverage tasted bitterly of the plastic lining and, after drinking only half, I dumped the rest and tossed the flimsy cup into a trash bin.

Bob Shirley arrived at last. He wouldn't look us in the eyes, but his voice carried a forced heartiness. 'Good morning, good morning, how's everything this bright morning?' Turning briskly to the groom, 'Tack him up, son, should have got that work into him an hour ago.'

'Is he all right to work?' I asked, forcing the words.

'All right to work?' Bob echoed in an unbelieving tone. 'Of *course* he's all right to work.'

'Might be a bit off,' Dancy remarked carefully.

'That's shipping,' Bob said, the words hurrying after Dancy's implied criticism. 'Shipping by air is always rough on this colt. Get a good work into him, he'll come right in no time.'

I studied Bob Shirley critically. He had always bragged about how well Outlaw Prince shipped. If I had been asked, I would have made affidavit Shirley was suffering from a hangover. His hands were too nervous, his eyes shifty and bloodshot. But of course, I reassured myself, he's as concerned about Outlaw Prince as anybody. After all, he had never trained a prospective Derby starter, much less a favourite.

The groom led Outlaw Prince from the stall, held him while Bob squatted on his heels to feel the ankles. As he went around to the other side, Dancy took the opportunity to make his own examination. He stepped back, nodding silently, letting me know that as far as he could tell nothing was wrong.

'Don't you think it would be a good idea to have Doc Powers take a look?' I ventured. I stopped, for Bob Shirley, directing his eyes past me, was saying with vigorous cheerfulness, 'Well, good morning, good morning, how are you this bright day?'

The new arrival was Walter Paxton, noted columnist for the *Daily Racing Form*; lanky and reportorial, dressed with studied carelessness in a disreputable suit, the tie, as thin as a string, pulled loose from the shirt collar.

'Morning, Bob,' he said. His eyes were on Outlaw Prince. 'Is the Big Horse ready for the Derby, Bob?'

Bob sputtered. 'The Derby? We're not even thinking Derby yet. Win the Daingerfield Memorial first, then we think Derby.'

The *Racing Form* man put his hands into his pockets, standing with slumped shoulders. He glanced at me, at Dancy, at Whitey and Brock, giving us a brief nod. Then his eyes again studied the colt.

'Only a week to bring him into form if you plan to run in the Daingerfield Memorial,' he remarked.

'What are you talking about, bring him into form? He's as sharp as a tack,' Bob said with spurious conviction. 'A touch of shipping fever, that's all we've got here. Going to put a work into him right now.'

'Yeah, that's what I understood.'

Bob clapped his hands nervously. 'All right, let's go, Whitey.'

Whitey put one foot into Shirley's cupped hands and Shirley boosted him into the saddle. Bob himself took the shanks; we followed after the colt in a silent cluster.

So late, the last wisps of mist were curling up from the track, the odours of horse sweat and manure drying into faint memory with the rising of the sun. Most of the horses had already finished training and a gang of harrows, pulled by three bright-red tractors, stood ready to condition the track for the afternoon races. We progressed through a silent regard as the backside people, trainers and rubbers and hot-walkers, idle observers, all, took note of Outlaw Prince's lacklustre appearance. In the next half hour it would be the talk of the track kitchen. We stopped at the horse entrance. Bob Shirley nervously checked the saddle girth as he talked to Whitey.

'Break him at the half-mile pole. I'll be satisfied with forty-eight . . . I just want a smart move to let him know he's still a race horse.' He stepped back as Whitey, with a click of his tongue, a movement of his body, took the colt out on to the track. 'That boy's got a clock in his head,' he said to Paxton. 'Ask him for forty-eight and he'll give it to you, not forty-eight and change. Wish you could say that of all jocks . . . most of 'em, you can't even get out of bed this time of day. I like a boy who'll ride his morning works.'

I watched anxiously as Whitey urged the colt into a job. He seemed to be moving well; indeed, he had picked up interest. When a lone runner came thudding past, the exercise boy setting him down on the rail, he evinced a pleased desire to race with him, so that Whitey had to take a strong hold.

'Yes, sir this colt win the Daingerfield Memorial,' Bob Shirley asserted to all in the vicinity. 'He win so fast the other jocks will think it's a false start.'

Whitey took his time getting around to the half-mile pole, giving the colt ample opportunity to loosen his muscles and set his mind. Both Brock and Shirley had stopwatches in their palms, thumbs at the ready. Up in the stands, two men in plaid coats, the official clockers, one watching through binoculars, stood ready to pick up the start.

I didn't have my binoculars, but I could see that the colt broke smartly, Whitey Dahl laying himself low over the withers as he launched into speed. He came pounding around the curve into the straightaway, clods of track dirt flying, and he seemed to accelerate without urging as he came to the wire. Whitey, standing up in the stirrups after the finish, took a smooth hold to let him gallop out to a stop.

I was heartened by the smart move. There had seemed nothing wrong, his action clean and smooth, his desire to run apparent. Once on the track, he looked to be all the horse he had ever been.

Shirley consulted with Brock, their heads together over the stopwatches. 'Forty-six and change,' Bob announced. 'Faster than I wanted, but it's all right.'

'Thought you said the boy had a clock in his head,' the columnist said.

'He does, he does, the colt was a little rank this morning, just shows he wants to run,' Bob said nervously. 'Rates good, you know, it's just that he hasn't had a really fast work for some days now, and . . . forty-six and change, that's a good move, more than I would have asked for, but if he wants to give it . . .'

Abruptly he stopped talking. I turned to look down the track to where Whitey was bringing Outlaw Prince back.

I saw what Bob Shirley had seen. Outlaw Prince had halted after taking a bad step on his left fore. When he came on again he moved slowly, trying to walk on three legs. He flinched every time the fourth hoof touched the ground.

'Oh boy,' Dancy murmured unhappily.

Whitey let the colt take his time. Once through the gate, he sat in the saddle for a moment, his face grief-stricken, before sliding to the ground. Bob Shirley moved quickly to snap on the lead shank, patting the sweaty neck, talking to the colt in a hospital tone. Silently we followed as Bob led him limping to the shedrow. The track people carefully averted their eyes; knowing that tragedy had struck Outlaw Prince's connections, they were as discreet as if at a funeral.

When we reached the stall, Whitey Dahl, who had not spoken a word since dismounting, had disappeared. Bob, relinquishing the shank to his groom, carefully examined the colt's ankle, seconded by Dancy, then Brock.

'No heat,' Bob said, and the others nodded in confirmation.

Bob shook his head, stooped to test the ankle again, straightened and said to the groom, 'All right, wash him down and cool him out.' Too tense to stand still, he immediately snatched the sponge and scraper from the groom and did the job with his own hands. Then, standing separate from our dispirited group, he watched intently as the hot-walker led the limping colt in the patient circling necessary to cool him out after the brisk run. I wondered, without asking, how the colt could have run so well if his leg had been hurting. No doubt about it; when asked, he gave what he had to give.

Outlaw Prince had made less than a dozen circuits, everyone watching with a gloomy concentration, when Bob said sharply, 'Stop him.'

The hot-walker obeyed. Bob Shirley went down on both knees to examine the hoof with minute care. He looked up with a changed face. 'It's a gravel,' he said. 'Just broke out. See there, along the coronet band, the pus oozing out?'

I looked at Dancy, at Brock. Their faces were showing such distinct relief I couldn't believe it.

'What's a gravel?' I asked Dancy in a half-whisper. 'Does he mean the colt picked up a piece of gravel in his hoof, it's been hurting him all this time?'

'Just an infection, not a foreign object,' Dancy said, explaining carefully in a low tone. 'Gets started between the hard outer shell of the hoof and the soft inner part, keeps spreading, climbing, until it works out at the coronet band.'

He glanced to see if I understood.

'Is that good?' I demanded. 'I mean, Bob acts like somebody just paid him back some money he never expected to see again.'

'At least, knowing the problem, he can begin to do something about it,' Dancy said. 'The infection has broken out, so it should drain rapidly.' He paused. 'You see, it's like having a bruise under a fingernail – the pressure building against the outer shell of the hoof can be dreadfully painful even if there isn't much actual infection present.'

The colt was walking again, putting tentative weight on the left fore now, still limping but not nearly as badly.

Bob turned to Dancy. 'You know the local vets better than I do. Can you get me one?'

'Sure,' Dancy said. 'I'll call Doc Powers.'

'I want somebody who'll live with this colt,' Bob said. He didn't look hung over any more, but ready and willing to take charge.

'Do you still plan to start him in the Daingerfield Memorial?' the *Racing Form* man asked. 'Pretty quick, don't you think?'

'You saw yourself how the gravel broke out, right here while he was being hot-walked,' Bob Shirley said aggressively. 'Best thing could of happened, putting that work into him this morning, maybe wouldn't have found it out for days.' He paused to emphasize a note of prudent caution. 'We'll just see how the Big Horse goes, that's all, wouldn't think of starting him if he's not right. But he'll be in the starting gate, don't you worry.'

'Will you be here tomorrow morning?' Paxton asked. 'Like to take a look at him again, if you don't mind.'

'Sorry, got to fly to New York this afternoon,' Bob said quickly. 'Fellow up there got a couple of nice fillies, anxious for me to take over their training when I ship into Belmont with the Big Horse.'

'Back the next day?'

'Sure. Maybe. Still got some horses in Florida, you know, with my assistant trainer. Got a big race coming up, ought to be there to saddle my winner.'

The *Racing Form* man nodded and, without a further word, walked away, hands snugged into his coat pockets. Bob Shirley gazed after him.

'He can cut this colt down pretty good if he wants to,' he said, worried. 'He saw it all.'

'Is this the time for you to be gone?' I asked.

He glanced at me. 'Miss Maude, I ain't going nowhere. Aim to sleep with this colt. I just don't like to tell those fellows any more than I have to, that's all.' He was still worried. 'Wonder what he'll say about the Big Horse in tomorrow's column?'

Doc Powers arrived. After an examination of the hoof, he started a Tetracycline series, gave Bute for the pain, and put on an Osmo-Pak poultice – a magnesium-sulphate base made up into a gel – and began icing the foot. It was nearly noon now, with much work to be done on the farm, so Dancy and I left before he was through.

The gravel didn't clear up as quickly as Bob Shirley had so optimistically prophesied, though Doc Powers spent twenty-four hours straight with the colt, went home for four hours' sleep then returned for another twenty-four-hour stretch. The *Racing Form* man was discreet, even kind, in his column, only tabbing Outlaw Prince as a doubtful starter for the Memorial and speculating on his chances of using the Steppingstone, only a week before the Derby, as a prep for the big race.

It became obvious to everyone – though Shirley stoutly maintained otherwise to the last moment – that Outlaw Prince must be scratched from the Memorial. Dancy brought me news even more disturbing.

'Bob Shirley cut out the frog of the bad hoof last night.'

The frog is the triangular, horny pad in the sole of a horse's foot that serves as a shock absorber.

'Why would he do that? And, anyway, isn't it the vet's job?'

Dancy shrugged. 'Shirley is the trainer. He decided there must be more than one centre of infection, maybe two or three, you know, and only one has drained. Cutting out the frog, it's pretty drastic, but maybe it'll drain now soon enough to get the colt into the Steppingstone.'

I picked up the telephone to call Doc Powers. Not in his office. I got him at home, rousing him out of a sound sleep. Sounding disgruntled and exhausted, he gave only unsatisfactory answers. No, he hadn't recommended the procedure; Shirley had cut into the frog entirely on his own. Since he was the trainer, he had the right to use his own judgement.

'Most of these trainers, they think they're as good a vet as anybody with a diploma,' he said, with what I diagnosed as a trace of jealousy. 'They do learn a lot from practical experience, you understand; any trainer must know how to keep a horse's legs and ankles in shape . . .'

'Would you have done it yourself?' I asked.

'Miss Maude, I won't go behind your trainer's back and tell you he did the wrong thing,' Doc said carefully. 'We'll just have to see how it works out.'

I avoided talking directly to Bob Shirley about the matter, primarily because the procedure did seem to promise success. Passing on the Daingerfield Memorial gave the hoof time to heal; we were now definitely pointing for the Steppingstone. The colt was eating better, his coat had recovered much of its usual bloom, and he had resumed the amusing mannerisms that showed he was feeling himself again.

Bob Shirley vanned to Churchill Downs a week early to bring the colt along with easy works for the prep race. The Saturday we drove over, the now-familiar queasy anticipation rampant in my stomach, the Kentucky Derby was only a week away. Today the colt would tell us whether we had a chance of running in the big race.

He looked great in the saddling enclosure; I was there, instead of waiting in my box, because I was so anxious to see how he was. Bob, saddling the colt, was his usual nervously exuberant self; and as Outlaw Prince walked in preparation for the post parade he seemed eager to run, looking every inch a winner.

It didn't turn out that way. He broke slow and ran dead last. Showing nothing. It was heartbreaking to see him trailing the pack, when he had always been on the lead, or near it, every time out of the starting gate. To this day, I can't remember which horse won the Steppingstone, because I couldn't take my eyes away from my poor colt running ten lengths behind everybody from wire to wire.

Whitey Dahl dismounted and disappeared, unable to talk to anyone. Bob Shirley, however, remained grimly optimistic.

'Have to lay him up,' he said. 'Take him back to Daingerfield, get him out of all this Derby hullabaloo, and give him some time. There's the Preakness yet, the Belmont, no Triple Crown but he still win . . .'

'Don't you think he ought to come home to Outlaw Farm?' I said slowly.

His eyes, nervous in avoiding me, were as shifty as his unreassuring laugh. 'Sure, if that's how you want to do it. Be better, though, to keep him stabled at the track; I've got other horses to look after, you know . . .'

'But not a Big Horse like this one,' I said.

He was unhappy. 'Never had a Big Horse like this one.' He sighed. 'If he'd of been right, he win the Derby by so many lengths the other jockeys would have believed it was a false start.' It was a line he had been using for some time now. In my opinion, he had worn it out.

'Ship him to Outlaw Farm,' I said. 'We'll have to rethink our programme, Bob, maybe forget the Triple Crown races entirely, save him for the handicaps next year at four. I plan to stand Outlaw Prince at stud, so I don't want to run the risk of breaking him down, maybe having to be destroyed.'

'But think what a Belmont or a Preakness would do for his stud fee,' Bob Shirley said unhappily.

'We'll just wait and see,' I said firmly. 'I don't want to *think* about starting him before he's absolutely sound. Van him to Outlaw Farm . . . I'll have Doc Powers standing by to take charge.'

Dancy blamed himself, afterwards, for not remaining with the colt until he was loaded on the van, then following the van home. Which was silly; no one of us realized how desperate a man can be to saddle a runner in a classic race.

We waited until long after the van should have arrived, Dancy and Doc Powers sharing my increasing bafflement and concern, before phoning Churchill Downs in an attempt to talk to Shirley. He had departed on schedule, but no one knew his whereabouts. I was frantic by the time we found the colt, a full day later – then, only by Dancy tracing down the van driver. Dancy called from Lexington, giving the barn number at Daingerfield Track where the colt had been unloaded, saying he would meet me there. Enlisting Doc Powers by phone, I hastened to the track.

Outlaw Prince was sequestered in the most remote stall of the most distant barn on the backside. He stood with his foot in a bucket of ice, the bloom gone again from his coat, his head hanging. He gazed at me with suffering eyes, so filled with pain and lack of understanding of what was happening to him that I wanted to cry.

'Where's Mr Shirley?' I asked the groom.

'Reckon he must of gone over to the track kitchen to get a *Racing Form.*'

Dancy arrived, followed immediately by Doc Powers. We waited, soon to be joined by Whitey Dahl and Brock Walter.

'I don't know what's going on here,' I declared. 'But I'm not waiting a minute longer, by God, I'm taking Outlaw Prince home. Doc, get in there and take a look at that hoof.'

'We ought to give Bob Shirley a chance to explain . . .'

'A chance, hell!' I said.

'Why, hello, good morning, good morning.'

I turned to face the trainer, hastening hospitably towards us along the shedrow. 'Mr Shirley, I want to know what's going on. I left instructions to ship Outlaw Prince home. Instead, you hid him out from me.'

His eyes shifted away, came back to my face, flitted again. 'Why, Miss Maude, after looking the Big Horse over, I couldn't see any reason why we shouldn't point him for the Belmont. Get the infection out for good, put him back into training, you'll stand in the winner's circle for sure, Miss Maude, because if this colt is right, he win by so many . . .'

'Yeah, I know,' I said, cutting across the flow of excuses. I turned to Doc Powers. 'Get in there and examine him, Doc. I want to know . . .'

'Miss Maude . . .' A strangely apologetic note showed in his voice. 'I decided to bring in my own vet, he's flying up from Florida today. The doc here, he aint' got the experience with horses in training, he's only a farm vet . . .'

'He's *my* vet,' I said flatly. 'I'm asking him to examine the colt.'

Bob Shirley made no further effort towards interference, but stood ostentatiously aside as Doc Powers entered the stall. Speaking to Outlaw Prince, gentling him, he lifted the crippled leg. The examination seemed to take forever. Outlaw Prince stood quietly on three legs until Doc Powers eased the hoof again into the bucket. He came out of the stall.

'Bob. What was the idea?'

Bob's voice sprang forth so loaded with nervous energy it seemed to vibrate in the air. 'Can't run a horse with an infection, Doc, you ought to know that, not even if you load him with Bute, like you can do now in some states. Get all of it out, he'll come sound before you know it, I'm pointing for the Belmont, you understand, don't want to take a chance with the Big Horse, wouldn't think of starting him in the Preakness, that's 'way too soon . . .'

I raised my voice. 'Doc. What did he do to Outlaw Prince?'

Doc Powers' answer was slow, precise. 'He's cut out the entire hoof, leaving only a shell.'

'Cut out all the infection, that's what you mean,' Bob Shirley chattered. 'Pack it solid, be as good as new, he run for years on a hoof like that . . .'

I stared at the man. I didn't believe it. 'That's why you hid him out. So you could do that, Knowing Doc wouldn't stand for it, knowing I wouldn't.'

He was, suddenly, deadly quiet. 'Want a Belmont winner, don't you?'

I was still staring. I knew there was no way – no way at all –

to make him understand. I turned to Dancy. 'Get a van in here.'

'You can't do that!' Shirley was making a last desperate protest. 'He can't be moved. I worked on the foot just last night, he . . .'

Dancy cut in. 'Don't you get the message, Shirley? She wants the Big Horse shipped home.'

I was grateful. Not so much that I needed Dancy's support. But it was good to know that he felt I was doing the right thing.

'Move my Big Horse, I'm not your trainer,' Bob said to me, trying to ignore Dancy. 'I take no responsibility. I warn you of that.'

Dancy would not be ignored. 'I think you quit being Miss Maude's trainer about ten minutes ago,' he said.

Shirley motioned to his groom, saying loudly, 'All right, go on down to the other horses, look after them. This ain't our horse any more.'

The groom moved unhappily. Shirley started to follow. But Whitey Dahl got in his way. He was shaking with something so much more intense than anger that it frightened me. I had a premonition that he was ready to do murder. But his response to the emotion was larger than his habitual physical assault.

His voice trembled, but he spoke with painful clarity. 'Mr Shirley, you might as well tear up my contract. I won't never ride for you no more.'

Shirley felt capable of coping with this challenge. 'Fine,' he snapped. 'I don't want anybody riding for me that thinks he can tell me how to train a horse . . . like everybody else around here.' He paused to give his further words an ominous weight. 'I just want you to know you won't ride for anybody else, either, not after I pass the word.'

'I don't care,' Whitey said, his voice steadying. 'I'd rather quit the track than let a horse killer put me on another horse.'

'He'll ride if I have to take out a trainer's licence myself,' I said coldly. 'Goodbye, Mr Shirley.'

He turned on me, opening his mouth for harsh words. He closed it. Then he said, his words few for once, 'I never had a Belmont winner. Not even a Belmont starter.'

I suppose it was as close to an explanation, if not an apology, as he could come. At the least, he left us in peace with our grand, crippled, misused colt.

Brock Walter's face was a study. 'Miss Maude, I'm sorry,' he said, his voice faltering over the words. 'I recommended him. But . . . he's never been known as a horse killer, he was always . . .'

'You can never tell what a Derby fever, a Belmont fever, can do to a man,' I said.

'But how could he do it to *Outlaw Prince*?' Whitey said in pain.

I looked at the boy. 'Because he doesn't know how to love a grand colt,' I said gently, 'the way you do.'

Outlaw Prince never started again. Indeed, the drastic surgery, performed in haste and almost certainly under unsanitary conditions, nearly killed him; the infection spread into the ankle, requiring further surgery amid all that delicate complex of bones, and it was a full year before we could be sure of saving him for stud duty.

As it is, he walks with a distinct limp on the club of a foot; it breaks my heart to see him when, turned out into his paddock and feeling full of good health and energy, he tries to run in stallion freedom, only to stop very soon because he knows himself so far from the gallant race horse he had once been.

But, standing one year at Outlaw Farm, the next at Mayfield Manor, he covers his mares with all the enthusiasm and dispatch with which he won his races.

The Tuesday-night vendue this time. And this time would tell the tale, which I well knew as I settled early into my seat. Failure – or success – in the breeding of Thoroughbreds, as in most human endeavours, does not arrive with the clap of doom. It is, rather, a slow tide setting fair for you, or against you.

Last year's yearling sale had been indecisive. But now, this year – Outlaw Prince had done us all the good, as far as racing was concerned, that he could do. It was simply a question whether or not his abortive career had made Sir Outlaw's future get desirable enough in the eyes of the yearling buyers to make Outlaw Farm a profitable operation. There was, of course, that business about hobby losses staring us in the face. For, with the purchase of the acreage, all financial resources had been committed.

I was alone because Dancy, as ever, wished to watch along with the other Kentucky hardboots from the area where the horses are led into the sales pavilion. The good scene. The great excitement. Every seat in the pavilion filled, people milling about outside, the rise and fall of the chanting voice in the auction spiel, the ripples of excitement as the prices reached the higher ranges. I watched my first filly go for a nice forty thousand with a degree of equanimity because I knew, as everyone knew, that the grand colt would come up later, by Sir Outlaw out of Old Blue Eyes. (Her last year's yearling, scratched from the Summer Sale, had brought forty-nine thousand at the Fall Sale, so she looked to become a foundation mare for us). Only then would I know if the tide was running for us.

I didn't let myself think about it – too much – beforehand, but absorbed myself in the parade of yearlings, studying my catalogue, assiduously noting down the prices realized. So our prize colt entered the arena almost before I was ready. As I gazed at him, standing with intelligent ears pricked to look out over the audience, he was so much like Outlaw Prince as a yearling my heart ached with reminiscence.

At the least, I won't have to buy back this one and race him, I assured myself silently. No chance in the world of anyone pin-hooking him.

Quickly, it was under way. Harris Harris, gazing benignly down upon the colt from his high stool, said in his richest, most reassuring tones:

'Now, ladies and gentlemen, if you haven't already looked this colt over and made up your mind to own him, you haven't been tending to business. Because what we have here is just about the finest yearling I've seen yet by that great young stallion Sir Outlaw, sire of the grand two-year-old stakes winner Outlaw Prince, now standing beside his daddy at Outlaw Farm. Out of a stakes-producing *and* stakes-winning mare, Old Blue Eyes, carrying in her veins the blood of War Admiral and Blue Larkspur, a pedigree-cross the owner of this colt is bringing back into deserved prominence. The sire is of the Domino line, as you ought to know, so all you've got here is speed on stamina. If you don't want a runner like this one in your racing stable, you haven't been studying your lessons. So I'm not going to start him for less than fifty thousand . . .

'Do I hear fifty, fifty, fifty, no I won't take thirty-five, Little John, gotta have a fifty, fifty, thank you sir, got a fifty, now let's go, boys, let's sell a grand colt here, he can't do nothing but win . . .'

God, the wonderful moment of it! I listened to Harris Harris's voice – my good friend now, a wonderful man. So many of the people in this sales pavilion were friends now, I belonged to Kentucky and to the horse people as I had never truly dreamed I could belong. And so I listened to the rising chant as if it were a song, a family song . . .

'Sebenty, sebenty, gimme five, five, gotta fi', gimme eighty, eighty, you're out, Big Al, Whistler's got it in the back, eighty, eighty, gotta ninety, HEY! new bidder there boys, get with it now, ninety, ninety, who'll gi' me fi', fi', fi', gotta two, ninety-two, don't quit now you just got stretched, gimme fi', fi', all right, take a three, three, three, still needa five.'

The bidding was spirited, Harris's magic voice lifting them, inspiring them, orchestrating the auction into a quick beat of pride and competition, the price faltering at ninety-five thousand, then sweeping upwards so quickly I caught my breath, feeling faint at the speed with which it went over one hundred thousand.

I had won. Outlaw Farm, and all that it meant, would continue.

Harris's voice soared with the magnificent news. 'Gotta hundred thousand, let's go to work boys, let's get the price this yearling deserves. Gimme one, one, gimme one, gotta one, you're out, Whistler, are you all done back there? Hunnert'n'-one, gotta one, needa two, gimme two, are you all done? Gotta two, I'm gonna sell this colt now, gotta two, gimme three, three, three . . .'

Harris Harris was getting ready to close.

'Gotta two, gimme three, everybody all done? . . . I'm gonna sell him!' The arm lifting the gavel. But there remained a last spurt of competition. 'Gotta three, gimme four, four, four, wanta four, gotta four, gi' me fi', fi', one hundred and five, gotta five, gimme six, gotta have a six, gonna sell him now, six, six, six, gotta five and wanta six . . .' The gavel came down with a crack as Harris Harris announced, 'One hundred thousand and five hundred dollars . . . sold to Mr John Paul Jones.'

Limp with the exhaustion of excitement and fulfilment, at least I had the strength to walk down the aisle to congratulate the buyer.

'Mr Jones. I thought you had given up purchasing yearlings.'

He gazed at me blandly. 'I have, Miss Sage. Never ignore the advice of my doctors. Pay them too much.'

'I hope he'll be a greater runner for you than his sire ever was,' I said sincerely.

'We don't know about that, though, do we?'

I laughed. 'I guess not. But that's the fun of the game.'

A convulsion of the massive face, resolving into a wink. The man intended to be humorous. 'Of course you stand ready to buy him back for a million?'

'Miss Sage . . . a picture of you and Mr Jones, looking at the sales receipt?'

A photographer. I glanced at John Paul Jones. 'That depends on Mr Jones, I guess.'

He grunted. 'Spend that much money, guess I've got a right to have my picture took.'

We posed, smiling, and I returned to my seat through a flurry of congratulations. Harris was continuing with the sale, of course, but I decided to escape immediately. I wanted to savour the triumph in private. Great moments demand privacy, always.

But the best of all came later. Home at Outlaw Farm, I got out of the car to be greeted by the entire staff, including the night watchman and the kids from Horseway House, for the news had already reached them. They crowded about, laughing, talking, cheering when I announced there would be a bonus for everybody in their next paycheque.

After their reluctant dispersal at my plea of emotional exhaustion, I said to Dancy, 'A little nightcap, a little sour mash, to celebrate?'

'Let me look at that sick foal, first.'

'All right. I won't wait on you, though. I need a drink!'

The Great Stone Barn was alive with the night sounds of horses as I settled into the rocking chair. Here in the heart of my domain, I tasted the Bourbon appreciatively, reliving all over again, even more emotionally now that I could play it in slow motion through my mind, the moment of triumph. A hundred-thousand-dollar yearling . . . fewer than three hundred Thoroughbreds had ever reached that figure at public auction. Outlaw Farm had achieved the status of the elect.

So absorbed, I looked up only after Dancy, standing in the doorway, made a sound to let me know he had returned. 'The colic medicine is working.'

I grinned. 'Seem to remember we had a bet going. Got your hundred dollars right here,' I motioned with my hand. 'And a quart.'

He grinned, holding out his hand ostentatiously to receive

the money. 'I'm getting used to collecting winnings, with all my two-dollar bets on Outlaw Prince.'

Motioning for him to sit down, I poured fresh drinks and we toasted Old Blue Eyes' yearling with due ceremony. Then we toasted each other, we toasted the wonderful world of Kentucky horses where such marvellous things could happen.

'You've done it, Maude,' Dancy said at the end. With a wry smile, he confessed, 'Had my doubts from time to time. But *you* never did, did you?'

'Plenty, at the beginning,' I confessed. 'And growing new doubts all along the way. I shudder at the ignorance with which I started. Knowing what I know now, I wouldn't have the nerve.'

Dancy nodded. 'But you have done it. You've made the Domino blood, the War Admiral blood, fashionable once again. The breeding nick is working, so you'll produce the runners. All you have to do is keep on turning out well-conditioned yearlings. One of these years, maybe sooner than you think, an Outlaw Farm yearling will set a new Summer Sale record.'

'I don't want only to go with what we've started, though,' I protested. 'There's a whole world of horses, Dancy, we haven't even touched yet. Our produce would do well, don't you think, in the European style of racing? I want to see our bloodlines return to the source of all Thoroughbred pedigrees: Epsom Downs and the French classics.' I hesitated against the rush of euphoria, remembering that Count Gracchi had planted that seed in my mind. I experienced a wave of sadness at the realization. Resolutely I pushed on.

'Has any American breeder ever shipped a consignment of yearlings to Tattersall's auction in England?'

'I don't know,' Dancy said. He looked at me oddly. 'Are you thinking of selling there, when you can walk them over to Daingerfield . . .'

'We just might do it next year. I could fly over to London this fall, get to know the people . . . after all, Thoroughbred breeding is international. We ought to contribute to it.'

'No reason not to, if that's what you want,' Dancy said cautiously. 'Calls for a lot of thought, though. After all, the buyers will come to Kentucky. One of yours sold to Countess Margit Batthyany tonight, remember?'

'Listen, what is this? I keep talking about *we*, and you keep changing it to *you*. We're in this together, aren't we?'

Inexplicably, his eyes avoided mine. 'Well, Maude, I've been thinking. You've accomplished what you set out to accomplish . . . in style, I might add.'

'I couldn't have done it without you,' I said, speaking it plainly and simply because I meant it so truly.

'That's what I've been thinking about,' Dancy said. 'It's time you found out that you don't depend on me all that much any more.'

A shocked silence. Finally I found words to fill it.

'What are you talking about?'

Dancy smiled. A very soft, very gentle, smile. 'Maude, you've moved so far out ahead of me already, I can't even hold your coat while you do the fighting. Sure, in the beginning, you relied on me. But not for a long time, not since . . .' He hesitated, then said it. 'Not since Count Gracchi, in fact. It's time you recognized it.'

'You're trying to tell me something I don't want to hear,' I said slowly.

He took a deep breath. 'I'm leaving, Maude. For your sake, more than mine. Now's the time to do it, when you've reached the peak you started climbing so long ago,' He smiled. 'Of course, you've got a whole new mountain range in view, haven't you, Tattersalls and all that.'

'Dancy, don't think for a minute I won't need you for that, too.'

He moved his shoulders. 'Sure. To manage the farm, do the routine maintenance, hold things together when your attention is elsewhere.'

'Is that so bad?'

'No,' he said readily. 'It's a fine job. But . . .' His voice changed, revealing a tinge of sadness. 'Maude, we had so much more, in the beginning and for a long time. And don't think I don't know it was the best thing that ever happened to me when you hired old D. Clutterbuck. Somehow it has burned out the gambling fever – exactly how I don't know – just knowing, I guess, that you not only depended on me, you *counted* on me to live straight.'

I sat very still, listening not so much to Dancy as to Maude Sage. A truth was whispering inside me. I had to know what it was saying.

Dancy filled his glass again, drank deeply, motioned the bottle towards my glass. I nodded and he poured, adding more ice from the bucket. I was still yearning towards the tiny voice pushing its message against the resistance of my conscious understanding.

'Dancy,' I said. 'Look at me!'

He looked at me. I looked at him. His eyes wavered.

'Dancy,' I said again. '*Look at me*.'

It required all his strength, all his regard, to keep his eyes steady. Even so, his face flushed, lips tightening almost as though in anger. But it was not anger.

Damn, I said silently. I'll be damned.

The voice didn't have to whisper the rest of the message. I had known for a long time – perhaps, even, before the time of Tony Gracchi – about myself, though I had never, strictly speaking, admitted it into my understanding. But I had not realized that Dancy felt it also.

'You'd leave Outlaw Farm, then,' I said accusingly, gesturing broadly, forgetting the glass in my hand. 'Those foals our brood-mares dropped this spring, you can live the kind of life where you'd never know what prices they'll bring, what kind of runners they'll turn out to be.'

'Yes, Maude,' he said gravely. 'I reckon so.'

My hand was wet and warm with the spilled whisky. 'You'd leave *me*.'

'Yes. Because I have to. For . . . for personal reasons.'

So he had heard the whisper of a voice, too. But it had not told him all the truth there was to be told.

I looked at him. While he looked at me. I lifted the glass and swallowed the last drop. I stood up, to look down at him, still seated.

'The hell you are,' I said.

He knew the meaning of the words. Carefully, he said, 'What about your society friends?'

'If they can put up with Maude Sage, they can learn to put up with Mr Dancy Clutterbuck. They ought to know a gentleman when they see one,' I said. I looked at the man, reading him whole. I walked to the doorway. 'Give me ten minutes. Then come on.'

A look of resolution took command of his dear face. 'I won't do it . . . unless you'll agree to marry me.'

I grinned. 'Just try to get out of it, Dancy. All right?'

He wavered. 'There are people up there. Tiffany Thomas, Jan and Eva.'

'To hell with the people,' I said. 'It's the first doorway at the head of the stairs on the second floor.'

I didn't wait for an answer. I knew the answer. I knew love. So, without a trace of impatience in my impatient soul, I walked slowly, thoughtfully, through the Kentucky darkness. No time for impatience. Only for completion, in the ampleness of time.

Ampleness? I had told him ten minutes. It couldn't have been more than eight before he stood in the doorway.

'What are you laughing about?' he said.

'Laughing?' I said. 'Am I laughing?'

'Yes,' he said.

'I guess it's just the idea of being known as Maude Clutterbuck for the rest of my life,' I said.

He came to me, as I rose to meet him. And he was laughing, too.

The phone rang.

'Oh, hell!' I said.

'Let it go,' Dancy said with urgency.

It can't be done on a horse farm. He knew it as well as I.

The night watchman. 'Miss Maude, there's another sick foal, and I can't locate Mr Dancy anywhere. Got pretty bad colic.'

I made a face at Dancy. 'All right, be right there. I'll see if I can find the man.'

We went to see about the sick foal. It didn't matter. We had all the time in the world.

THE END

May 20, 1974 – January 7, 1976
Elmendorf Farm, Lexington, Kentucky
Shandygaff, Guntersville Lake, Alabama
Finisterre, Casey Key, Florida

BLUEGRASS Book One
by Borden Deal

'In order that my faithful companion and nurse may have the opportunity to become the person she was meant to be, I hereby bequeath to her the sum of six million, two hundred and sixty-three thousand, four hundred and twenty-two dollars and thirty cents.'

All her life Maude has dreamed of horses, has studied form and placed her paper bets. Now she can fulfil her ambition of owning a breeding stable in Kentucky's bluegrass country. It proves to be the biggest gamble in her life. She has no experience, she is a complete stranger to the notoriously exclusive and cruel Kentucky society, and she is a woman. But she knows she can make it.

NEW ENGLISH LIBRARY

THE RICH AND THE RIGHTEOUS

by Helen Van Slyke

Joseph Haylow, the dynamic, well-meaning founder of a billion-dollar empire, faces his testimonial retirement dinner with trepidation. Unwilling to retire from the company that is his creation, he must name his successor, a decision still unresolved as the dinner begins. Haylow's world, faith and family are examined as, in his last year of office, he learns the truth about those who surround him – the weak, the ruthless, the loving and the fallible.

NEW ENGLISH LIBRARY

THE BEST PLACE TO BE

by Helen Van Slyke

Sheila Callahan had everything she wanted – comfort, security and a marriage that had lasted for twenty-seven years. Then, one summer afternoon in a Cleveland suburb, everything changed. Suddenly all she has left of her husband is the memory of his overpowering and free-spending ways – she is on her own. But can she face the problems of self-reliance or will the pressures of her family drag her down? Is it too late to start again – and does she have it in her to do it?

NEW ENGLISH LIBRARY